DESIRE

BOOKS BY AMANDA QUICK

DECEPTION
DANGEROUS
RAVISHED
RECKLESS
RENDEZVOUS
SCANDAL
SEDUCTION
SURRENDER

DESIRE

Amanda Quick

BANTAM BOOKS

NEW YORK   TORONTO   LONDON   SYDNEY   AUCKLAND

DESIRE

ISBN 0-553-56153-7

Bantam Books are published by Bantam Books, a division of Bantam Doubleday Dell Publishing Group, Inc. Its trademark, consisting of the words "Bantam Books" and the portrayal of a rooster, is Registered in U.S. Patent and Trademark Office and in other countries. Marca Registrada. Bantam Books, 1540 Broadway, New York, New York 10036.

PRINTED IN THE UNITED STATES OF AMERICA

For Stella Cameron—
another one of the
sisters whom I never
had.

DESIRE

PROLOGUE

"It is extremely unlikely that the lady of Desire is still a virgin," Thurston of Landry said. "But under the circumstances, I'm certain you'll find yourself able to overlook that aspect of the situation."

Gareth looked at his father impassively. His reaction to the news that his future bride had already dishonored herself with another man was virtually undetectable, a mere tightening of his fingers around his wine cup.

As a bastard son who'd been obliged to make his way in the world with his sword, he'd had years of experience concealing his emotions. In truth, he had become so skilled at the business that most people concluded that he possessed no strong feeling of any kind.

"You say she is an heiress?" Gareth forced himself to concentrate on the most important element of the matter. "She holds an estate?"

"Aye."

"In that case, she'll do as a wife." Gareth hid his intense satisfaction. His father was right. As long as the lady was not pregnant with another man's babe, Gareth was prepared to overlook the issue of his bride's honor or lack of same for the sake of gaining lands of his own.

Lands of his own. The words shimmered with promise.

A place where he belonged; a place where he was not just the bastard son whose presence must be tolerated; a place where he was welcomed and needed not merely because his skill with a sword made him temporarily useful. He wanted to live in a place where he had a right to sit in front of his own hearth.

Gareth was thirty-one years old and he knew that he might never again be granted this opportunity. He was a man who had long since learned to seize whatever chance fate brought his way. It was a philosophy which had served him well in the past.

"She is now sole mistress of the Isle of Desire." Thurston sipped wine from his finely crafted silver cup and gazed thoughtfully into the fire. "Her father, Sir Humphrey, favored travel and intellectual pursuits over working the land. Unfortunately, word has reached me that he died several months ago while on a journey in Spain. Murdered by bandits."

"There are no male heirs?"

"Nay. Two years ago, Humphrey's only son, Edmund, broke his fool neck in a tournament. Clare, the daughter, is the only one left. She inherits the manor."

"And as Sir Humphrey's liege lord, you have wardship of his daughter. She will marry at your command."

Thurston's mouth twitched. "That remains to be seen."

Gareth realized that his father was barely restraining a grin. The knowledge made him uneasy.

As a man whose own natural temperament had always been of a profoundly serious and deeply restrained nature, Gareth was not much given to mirth. He rarely responded with even mild amusement to the jests and japes that made others laugh aloud.

His unsmiling countenance nicely complemented his reputation as a ruthless man who could be exceedingly dangerous to cross, but it was not deliberate. He had no particular objection to smiles and laughter; he simply was not often inclined to indulge in either.

Now he waited warily to learn what it was that Thurston found so amusing in what should have been a straightforward matter of business.

He studied his father's lean, elegant profile in the light of the flames on the hearth. Thurston was in his mid-fifties. His thick, dark hair was streaked with silver, but he still captured the attention of every female who came within his sphere.

It was not only the power Thurston wielded as one of Henry II's favored barons that made him an object of interest to the female of the species, Gareth knew. It was also Thurston's handsome face and form that made him attractive to women.

Thurston's skill at seduction, employed quite freely in his younger days both before and after his arranged marriage, had been legendary. Gareth's mother, the youngest daughter of a noble family in the south, had been one of his many conquests. As far as Gareth knew, he was his father's only adult illegitimate offspring. If there had been others over the years, none had survived infancy.

To Thurston's credit and his wife's thinly disguised displeasure, he had done his duty by his bastard son. He had acknowledged Gareth from the start.

Gareth had been raised by his mother until the age of eight. During those years Thurston had been a frequent visitor to the quiet manor house where Gareth and his mother had gone to live. But when Gareth had turned eight, the age when the sons of nobles went into training for knighthood, his mother had announced that she intended to take the veil.

There had been a fierce argument. Gareth would never forget his father's rage. But his mother had been adamant and in the end she had won. Thurston had even provided the magnificent dowry that had made the convent more than happy to accept Gareth's mother as a novitiate.

Thurston had taken his bastard son home to Beckworth Castle. He had seen to Gareth's education as a knight with the same care and diligence that he had applied to the rearing of his legitimate sons and his heir, Simon.

Thurston's wife, Lady Lorice, beautiful, cold, and proud, had had no option but to tolerate the situation. Perhaps not unnaturally, however, she had not gone out of her way to make young Gareth welcome in the household.

Deeply aware of his status as an outsider, missing the studious, contemplative atmosphere of his mother's household, Gareth had poured all his energies into his training with lance and sword. He had practiced endlessly, seeking an elusive satisfaction in a quest for perfection.

When he was not honing his fighting skills, he had sought out the solitude of the library of the local Benedictine monastery. There he had read anything and everything that Brother Andrew, the librarian, had given him.

By the time he was seventeen, Gareth had studied a wide variety of subjects. He had delved into treatises on mathematics and optics that had been translated from the Greek and Arabic by Gerard of Cremona. He had pondered Aristotle's theories of the four elements: earth, water, air, and fire. He was fascinated by Plato's writings on astronomy, light, and matter.

Gareth's interests in scholarly subjects had never proven to be of much practical use, but his skills as a knight and as a commander of men had enabled him to carve out a lucrative career for himself.

Many a powerful lord, including his own father, had considerable use for a man who knew how to hunt the thieves and marauding, renegade knights who were a constant threat to their remote estates and manors.

The business of snaring outlaws paid well and Gareth was adept at it. He had never been particularly enamored of the profession, but he was a man of means, thanks to his talent with a sword. He could not, however, satisfy his smoldering desire for lands of his own. Only his liege lord, his father, could grant him the manor that would make him a landed knight.

Four days ago Gareth had received Thurston's summons to Beckworth Castle. Tonight he had learned that his greatest wish was about to be fulfilled. It only required that he accept a lady with a blemished reputation as his wife.

It was a small price to pay for gaining the one thing he craved most in the world. Gareth was accustomed to paying for what he wanted.

"How old is the lady of Desire?" he asked.

"Let me think. Clare would be three and twenty now, I believe," Thurston said.

Gareth frowned. "And still unwed?"

"I am told that she has no great wish to be wed," Thurston said. "Some women do not, you know. Your own mother, for example."

"I doubt that my mother had much choice in the matter after I was conceived," Gareth said in a carefully neutral tone. This was old and all too familiar ground. He knew well how to conceal his bitterness. "She was fortunate to find a nunnery that would take her."

"On that score you are wrong." Thurston rested his elbows on the carved wooden arms of his chair and laced his long fingers beneath his chin. "With the dowry that I provided, you may be assured that your mother had her choice of convents. Indeed, the most important houses competed for her." His mouth curved wryly. "Little did any of them realize, of course, that whichever house took her in would soon find itself under her command."

Gareth shrugged. He saw his mother infrequently, but he corresponded with her regularly and he knew that Thurston was correct. His mother was a brilliant, formidable woman. Every bit as brilliant and as formidable as his father, in fact.

Gareth focused his attention on the matter at hand. "Is Lady Clare ill-formed in some fashion?"

"Not to my knowledge. I have not seen her since she was a child, but as I recall, she was a well-made girl. She showed no promise of being a great beauty, but I noticed naught that would be deemed ugly or misshapen in her appearance." Thurston cocked one brow. "Are her looks a matter of great concern?"

"Nay." Gareth gazed into the fire. "Only her lands are of concern to me."

"I thought as much."

"I was merely seeking reasons to understand why she has never wed."

Thurston moved one hand in a dismissing gesture. The exquisite crimson and gold embroidery on the sleeve of his tunic gleamed in the firelight. "As I said, some women have no great desire for the marriage bed, for one reason or another. From all accounts, Lady Clare is apparently one such female. She has agreed to wed now only because she knows she must."

"For the sake of her holdings?"

"Aye. The Isle of Desire is a plump bird, ripe for the plucking. It needs protection. She writes that there have been problems already with her neighbor, Nicholas of Seabern, as well as with a band of brigands who are harassing her shipments of goods to London."

"So she is in need of a husband who can defend her manor and you, sir, wish to be certain that Desire continues to be profitable for you."

"Aye. The isle itself is not large. The lands produce a certain amount of wool and the crops are reliable. But that is not the true source of the manor's wealth." Thurston picked up a small, delicately embroidered bag that lay on a nearby table. "This is what provides the income from Desire." He tossed the small bag to Gareth.

Gareth caught the little sack easily. The scent of flowers and herbs wafted from it. He held the bag to his nose and inhaled the lush, rich, strikingly complex fragrance. It was a heady aroma that elicited a strangely sensual hunger somewhere inside him. He took another sniff. "Perfumes?"

"Aye. 'Tis an isle of flowers and herbs. And the products it sends to market are perfumes and creams of every description."

Gareth looked at the fragrant little bag in his hand. "So I am to become a gardener?"

Thurston smiled. "It will be something of a change for the Hellhound of Wyckmere."

"Aye, that it will. I have little knowledge of gardening, but I expect that I shall soon learn whatever is necessary."

"You have always been quick in that regard, no matter what the subject."

Gareth ignored the comment. "So the lady of Desire is willing to wed a man to protect her vast flower garden. And I want lands of my own. It would seem that she and I can strike a fair bargain."

"Mayhap."

Gareth narrowed his eyes. "Is there some doubt?"

The smile that had been hovering around Thurston's mouth turned into a brief, laughing grin. "I fear there is some competition for the position."

"What competition?"

"Nicholas of Seabern, Clare's nearest neighbor, is also one of my vassals. He's had his eye on Desire for some time. In fact, he is the chief reason why I suspect that the lady is no longer a virgin."

"He seduced her?"

"From what I can gather, my sources tell me Nicholas virtually kidnapped her last month and held her at Seabern Keep for some four days."

"And then tried to force her to accept him as a husband?"

"Aye. The lady, however, has refused."

Gareth raised an eyebrow at that news. He was not surprised at the tale. Kidnapping unwed heiresses was a common enough sport. But he was startled to learn that the lady had not been immediately wed after the incident. Few women would have had the temerity to refuse marriage after having lost their virginity and their reputation to an encroaching lord. "A most unusual female."

"Aye. It seems Lady Clare has some very particular requirements regarding the man who will be her lord." Thurston grinned again. "She has sent me a *recipe* for a husband, in fact. She wishes to select one who meets her exacting specifications, you see."

"Hell's teeth. A recipe?" Gareth muttered. "What nonsense is this? I knew there was something you were keeping from me."

"She has written her requirements out in great detail. Here, see for yourself." Thurston picked up a folded sheet of parchment that was lying on a nearby table. He handed it to Gareth.

Gareth glanced at the broken seal and saw that it was in the shape of a rose.

He read swiftly through the greeting and opening paragraph of the beautifully scripted letter. He slowed down when he reached the portion which detailed the lady's requirements in a husband.

> *I have given your wishes and the needs of my people much thought, my lord. I regretfully accept the necessity of a marriage. To that end, I have considered the matter with extreme care. Desire is a very remote place, as you well know. I know of no eligible men in the vicinity except my neighbor, Sir Nicholas, who is unacceptable.*
>
> *I therefore respectfully request that you send me a selection of at least three or four suitors. I shall choose a husband from among them. To assist you in the task of selecting the candidates for the position, I have prepared a recipe which specifies the qualifications I require.*
>
> *You, my lord, obviously have an interest in these lands. I understand that you wish them to be protected, as do I. From your point of view, therefore, the future lord of Desire must be a*

trustworthy knight who can command a small but effective company of fighting men. I will remind you that he must bring such a company with him, as there are no trained men-at-arms here on the isle.

In addition to that obvious requirement, which I know that you will see to, I have three more requirements of my own. I wish to specify them in great detail so that you will have no trouble comprehending them.

First, as regards his physical qualities, the future lord of Desire must be a man of moderate proportions and stature. It has been my observation that extremely large men prefer to rely on brute strength to achieve their ends rather than upon their wits and learning. I do not care for men who try to overwhelm one with their physical prowess. Therefore, please keep size in mind when you make your selections for me.

Second, my future lord must be a man of cheerful countenance and well-mannered, pleasing disposition. I am certain you will understand when I tell you that I have no wish to be bound to a man who is melancholic or given to fits of temper and foul moods. I wish my husband to have the gift of laughter, a man who will be able to take pleasure in the humble forms of entertainment which we enjoy here on the isle.

Third, it is absolutely essential that my husband be a learned man, one who is capable of reading and who enjoys intellectual discourse. I will wish to engage in much conversation with him, especially during the cold winter months when we shall both be obliged to spend a great deal of time together indoors.

I trust my three requirements are quite plain and that my recipe is clear. There should be no problem in selecting several candidates from among your acquaintances.

Please send these suitors to me at your earliest convenience. I will make my choice as quickly as possible and inform you of my decision.

Written at the manor of Desire, the seventh of April.

Gareth refolded the letter, aware of the unholy amusement in his father's eyes. "I wonder how she set about creating her recipe for a perfect lord and husband."

Thurston chuckled. "I suspect she took the basic elements from some minstrel's romantic ballad. You know the sort. They generally feature a chivalrous hero who slays evil magicians for sport and vows undying love to his lady."

"A lady who usually belongs to another man," Gareth muttered. "The hero's liege lord, for example. Aye, I know the sort of song you mean. I do not care for such, myself."

"The ladies love them."

Gareth shrugged. "How many candidates will you send, my lord?"

"I am a great believer in indulging females up to a point. I shall allow Lady Clare to make her choice from between two suitors."

Gareth's brow rose. "Not three or four?"

"Nay. In my experience one only asks for trouble when one grants a woman too many choices."

"Two suitors, then. Myself and one other."

"Aye."

"Who shall I be competing against?"

Thurston grinned. "Sir Nicholas of Seabern. Good luck to you, son. The lady's requirements are simple, are they not? Her recipe specifies a man who is of moderate size, much given to laughter, and able to read."

Gareth handed the letter back to his father. "She is fortunate, is she not? I meet one of her requirements. I can read."

1

Clare was in the convent gardens with Margaret, the Prioress of Saint Hermione, when word reached her that the first of the suitors was on the Isle of Desire.

"A grand company of men has arrived, Lady Clare. They are coming toward the village even now," William called.

Clare paused in the middle of a detailed discussion of the best method for extracting oil of roses. "I beg your pardon, madam," she said to Prioress Margaret.

"Of course." Margaret was a stoutly built woman of middle years. The wimple of her black Benedictine habit framed sharp eyes and gently rounded features. "This is an important event."

Clare turned to see young William hopping about in great excitement near the convent gatehouse. He waved his bag of gingered currants at her.

A plump, brown-haired, dark-eyed lad of ten, he was a good-natured combination of lively curiosity and unquenchable enthusiasm. He and his mother, Lady Joanna, had come to live on the Isle of Desire three years earlier.

Clare was very fond of both of them. As her own family had dwindled down to nothing, leaving her alone in the world, she had grown very close to William and Joanna.

"Who is here, William?" Clare braced herself for the answer. Every inhabitant on Desire, with the exception of herself, had been eagerly anticipating this day for weeks. She was the only one who was not looking forward to the selection of a new lord for Desire.

At least she was to have a choice of husbands, she reminded herself. That was more than many women in her position got.

"'Tis the first of the suitors you said Lord Thurston would send." William stuffed a handful of gingered currants into his mouth. "They say he appears to be a most powerful knight, Lady Clare. He brings a fine, great host of men-at-arms. I heard John Blacksmith say that it took half the boats in Seabern to get all the men and horses and baggage from the mainland to our island."

A curious flutter of uneasiness made Clare catch her breath. She had promised herself that when the time came, she would be calm and businesslike about the matter. But now that the moment was upon her, she was suddenly vastly more anxious than she had thought to be.

"A great host?" Clare frowned.

"Aye." William's face glowed. "The sunlight on their helms is so bright, it hurts your eyes." He gulped down two more fistfuls of the currants. "And the horses are huge. There is one in particular, John says, a great gray stallion with hooves that will shake the very earth when he goes past."

"But I did not request a great number of knights and men-at-arms," Clare said. "Desire requires only a small company of men to protect our shipments. What on earth am I to do with a large number of warriors underfoot? And all their horses, too. Men and horses eat a great deal of food, you know."

"Do not fret, Clare." Margaret smiled. "Young William's notion of a vast host of fighting men is likely very different from our own. Keep in mind that the only company of armed men that he has ever seen is Sir Nicholas's small household force at Seabern."

"I trust that you are right, madam." Clare lifted the fragrant pomander that hung from a chain on her girdle and inhaled the soothing blend of roses and herbs. The scent comforted her, as it always did. "Nevertheless, it will be a great nuisance having to feed and house so many men and horses. By Saint Hermione's ear, I do not like the notion of having to entertain all of these people. And this is only the first of the candidates."

"Calm yourself, Clare," Margaret said. "Mayhap the crowd that has disembarked down at the harbor is composed of more than one suitor. The three or four you ordered may have arrived all at the same time. That would explain why there are so many men and horses."

Clare cheered at the notion. "Aye, that must be it." She dropped the small pomander so that it dangled once more amid the folds of her gown. "All my suitors have arrived together. If they have each brought their own entourages, that would explain the large number of men and horses."

"Aye."

Another thought along the same lines struck Clare, one which immediately wiped away her momentary relief. "I do hope they will not stay long. It will cost a fortune to feed them all."

"You can afford it, Clare."

"That's not the point. At least, not entirely."

Margaret's eyes twinkled. "Once you have made your selection from among the candidates, the others, including their men and retainers, will take their leave."

"By Hermione's sainted toe, I shall choose quickly, then, so that we do not waste any more food and hay on this lot than is absolutely necessary."

"A wise plan." Margaret eyed her closely. "Are you so very anxious, my child?"

"No, no, of course not," Clare lied. "Merely eager to get the matter concluded. There is work to be done. I cannot afford to waste a great deal of time on this business of selecting a husband. I trust Lord Thurston has only sent me candidates who meet all of my requirements."

"I'm sure he has," Margaret murmured. "You were most specific in your letter."

"Aye." Clare had spent hours formulating her recipe for a new lord of Desire.

Those hours had been spent after she had wasted even more time concocting dozens of clever reasons why she did not need a husband. To that end, she had called upon all the skills of rhetoric, logic, and debate that Margaret had taught her. She had been well aware that if she was to avoid the inevitable, she would need to give Lord Thurston a truly brilliant excuse for refusing marriage.

Clare had tried out each finely reasoned argument first on Joanna and then on Prioress Margaret before committing it to parchment. Sympathetic to the cause, both of the women had considered the string of carefully crafted excuses one after the other, offering criticism and advice.

In the months since her father's death, Clare had been developing what she was certain was an absolutely unassailable, logically graceful argument against the necessity of marriage based on the naturally secure position of the Isle of Desire when disaster had struck.

Her neighbor on the mainland, Sir Nicholas of Seabern, had wrecked the endeavor by kidnapping her while she was on a short visit to Seabern.

Furious with Nicholas because he had ruined everything by providing clear evidence of her personal vulnerability, Clare had proceeded to make life at Seabern Keep a living hell for him. By the end of her enforced stay, Nicholas confessed himself glad to see the last of her.

But it was too late.

Coming as it did on top of the increased predations of the robbers who infested the region, the kidnapping was the last stone in the sack. Clare knew that it was only a matter of time before Lord Thurston heard the rumors. He would conclude that she was incapable of protecting Desire and he would act at once to see to the matter himself.

Outraged and frustrated by events as she was, Clare had to admit she could not entirely blame Thurston for taking such a course of action. In his position, she would have done the same. The portion of the revenues to which he was entitled as Desire's liege lord were too plump and healthy to be put at risk.

And Clare could not risk the lives of the men from the village who accompanied the shipments of perfume. Sooner or later, the robbers were going to kill someone when they attacked.

In truth, she had no choice and she knew it. She had a duty and an obligation to the people of Desire. Her mother, who had died when Clare was twelve, had taught her from the cradle that the wishes of the lady of the manor came second to the needs of her people and the lands that sustained them.

Clare knew full well that although she possessed the skills to keep Desire a fat and profitable estate, she was no trained warrior.

There were no household knights, nor even any men-at-arms left on Desire. The few who had once lived in the hall had dispersed over the years. Some had accompanied her brother Edmund to the tournaments and had not returned to the isle after he had been killed. Desire, after all, was not a very exciting place. It did not suit young knights and squires who were eager for glory and the profits to be made competing in the endless round of tournaments or by going on Crusade.

The last two men-at-arms who had lived on Desire had journeyed to Spain with Clare's father, Sir Humphrey. They had sent word back to her of her father's death, but they themselves had not returned. With their lord dead, they had been freed of their vows of fealty. They had found new masters in the south.

Clare did not have the least notion of how to go about obtaining a reliable troop of armed men, let alone how to train them and control them.

The first letter of warning from Thurston had arrived six weeks ago. It had been politely worded, full of gracious condolences on the death of Sir

Humphrey. But there had been no mistaking the implications of the veiled comments concerning the defense of Desire. The second letter had made it clear that Clare must wed.

Clare, much to her annoyance, had reached the same decision.

Knowing that marriage was inevitable, Clare had done what she always did when it came to matters of duty. She had set about fulfilling her responsibilities.

In typical fashion, however, she had taken charge of the situation in her own way.

If she was to be saddled with the encumbrance of a husband, she had told Joanna and Margaret, she was determined to have some say about the man she would wed.

"They are coming closer, Lady Clare," William yelled now from the gatehouse.

Clare brushed the fine dark earth of the convent garden from her hands. "I pray that you will excuse me, madam. I must get back to the hall so that I can change my clothing before my guests arrive. These fancy knights from the south will no doubt expect to be received with a certain amount of ceremony."

"As well they should," Margaret said. "I know you are not looking forward to this marriage with any enthusiasm. But be of good cheer, my child. Remember, there will most likely be three, possibly even four candidates. You will have a goodly choice."

Clare slid her old friend and teacher a quick, searching glance. She lowered her voice so that neither William nor the porteress at the nearby gatehouse could overhear. "And if I do not care for any of the three or four suitors Lord Thurston has sent?"

"Why, then, we shall have to ask ourselves if you are merely being extremely selective, mayhap even too particular about the choice of a lord for Desire, or if you are seeking excuses not to go through with the thing."

Clare made a face and then gave Margaret a rueful grin. "You are always so practical and straightforward, madam. You have a way of going to the heart of the matter."

"It has been my experience that a woman who is practical and honest in her reasoning, especially when she is arguing with herself, generally accomplishes more than one who is not."

"Aye, so you have always taught me, madam." Clare straightened her shoulders. "I shall continue to bear your words of wisdom in mind."

"Your mother would have been proud of you, my child."

Clare noticed that Margaret did not mention her father. There was no need. They were both well aware that Sir Humphrey had never been interested in the management of his lands. He had left such mundane matters to his wife and later his daughter, while he himself had pursued his scholarly studies and experiments.

A loud shout went up from the street on the other side of the convent wall. Voices rose in wonder and excitement as the villagers gathered to see the new arrivals.

William shoved his packet of gingered currants into the pouch that hung from his belt and hastened over to a low bench that stood against the wall.

Too late Clare realized what he had in mind. "William, don't you dare climb up on top of that wall. You know what your mother would say."

"Don't worry, I won't fall. I just want to see the knights and their huge horses." William got up on top of the bench and started to hoist his pudgy frame atop the stone wall.

Clare groaned and exchanged a resigned glance with Margaret. There was no doubt but that William's overprotective mother would have had a fit if she were present. Joanna was convinced that William was delicate and must not be allowed to take any risks.

"Lady Joanna's not here," Margaret said dryly, as if Clare had spoken aloud. "So I suggest you ignore the matter."

"If William falls, Joanna will never forgive me."

"One of these days she'll have to stop coddling the lad." Margaret shrugged philosophically. "If she does not cease hovering over him like a mother hen with her chick, he's going to turn into a fearful, anxious, extremely fat young man."

"I know, but one cannot entirely blame Joanna for wanting to protect William," Clare said quietly. "She's lost everyone else. She cannot bear the risk of losing her son, too."

"I can see them." William swung one leg over the top of the wall. "They're already in the street." He shaded his eyes against the spring sunlight. "The giant gray horse is in front of the rest. I vow, the knight who rides the beast is almost as big as his horse."

Clare frowned. "I requested candidates of moderate size and stature."

"He is wearing a shiny helm and a mail hauberk," William exclaimed. "And he carries a silvery shield that glitters like a great mirror in the sun."

"A great mirror?" Intrigued, Clare hurried forward along the garden path to see the newcomers for herself.

"It is very strange, my lady. Everything about the knight is silver or gray—even his clothing and his horse's trappings are gray. It is as though he and his stallion were fashioned entirely of silver and smoke."

"Silver and smoke?" Clare looked up at William. "Your imagination is running off with your wits."

"'Tis true, I swear it." William sounded genuinely awed by the sight he was witnessing.

Clare's curiosity grew swiftly. "Just how big is this smoke and silver knight?"

"He is very, very big," William reported from his perch. "And the knight who rides behind him is almost as large."

"That will not do at all." Clare went to the gate and peered out into the street. Her view was blocked by the throng of excited villagers.

Word of the newcomers' arrival had spread quickly. Virtually everyone had turned out to witness the grand spectacle of a troop of mounted knights on Desire. John Blacksmith, Robert Cooper, Alice the brewer, and three muscular farmers stood in Clare's way. All of them were taller than she was.

"Do not alarm yourself about the matter of this gray knight's size." Margaret came up to stand beside Clare. Her eyes gleamed with amusement. "Once again, we must allow for young William's somewhat limited experience of the world. Any knight astride a horse would appear huge to him. It's all that armor that makes them seem so large."

"Yes, I know. Still, I would like very much to see this gray knight for myself." Clare measured the height from the bench to the top of the wall with her eyes. "William, prepare to give me a hand."

William tore his gaze away from the sights long enough to glance down at her. "Do you wish to sit up here on the wall with me, Lady Clare?"

"Aye. If I remain down here, I shall be the last person on the isle to see the invasion." Clare lifted the skirts of her long-waisted overtunic and stepped up onto the bench.

Margaret gave a small snort of disapproval. "Really, Clare, this is extremely unseemly. Only think how embarrassed you will be if one of your suitors sees you comporting yourself like a village hoyden up there on the wall. He might chance to recognize you later at your hall."

"No one will notice me sitting up here. From the sound of it, our visitors are far too occupied with putting on a fine show for the village. I mean to see the performance for myself."

Clare grasped the edge of the wall, found a chink in the stones with the toe of her soft leather boot, and struggled to pull herself up beside William.

"Have a care, my lady." William leaned down to catch hold of her arm.

"Do not concern yourself," Clare panted as she swung first one leg and then the other over the broad stone wall. "I may be a spinster of three and twenty, but I can still climb walls." She grinned at William as she righted herself and adjusted her skirts. "There, you see? I did it. Now, then, where is this knight made of silver and smoke?"

"He's at the top of the street." William pointed toward the harbor. "Listen to the thunder of the horses' hooves. 'Tis as if a great, howling tempest were blowing in off the sea."

"They are certainly making sufficient noise to wake the dead." Clare pushed back the hood of her mantle and turned to look toward the top of the narrow street.

The rumble and thunder of hooves was closer now. The villagers grew quiet in anticipation.

And then Clare saw the knight and the stallion fashioned of silver and smoke. She caught her breath, suddenly comprehending William's awe.

Man and horse alike appeared to be composed of all the elements of a magnificent storm: wind, rain, and lightning made solid flesh. It needed only a single glance to know that this bleak, gray fury, once roused, would be capable of destroying anything that lay in its path.

For a moment the sight of the silver-and-smoke knight left Clare as speechless as it had the villagers in the street below. A desperate sinking sensation seized her stomach as she realized that she was undoubtedly looking at one of her suitors.

Too big, she thought. *Much too large. And too dangerous. Definitely the wrong man.*

The gray knight rode at the head of a company of seven men. The group was made up of knights, men-at-arms, and one or two servants. Clare gazed curiously at the warriors who rode behind the great gray war machine. She had seen very few fighting men in her time, but she knew enough to be aware that most of them favored strong, brilliant hues in their attire.

These men all followed the fashion of their leader. They were dressed in somber shades of gray and brown and black, which somehow made them seem all the more lethal.

The new arrivals were very close now. They filled the narrow street. Banners snapped in the breeze. Clare could hear the squeak and glide of steel on leather. Harness and armor moved together in well-oiled rhythms.

The heavily shod horses came forward like the huge engines of battle that they were. They moved at a slow, relentless pace that underscored their power and made certain that all those present had ample opportunity to view the spectacle.

Clare stared at the strange sight with the same degree of amazement as everyone else. She was vaguely aware of low-voiced whispers rising and falling across the crowd in a wave that had its starting point at the small stone cell that housed the village recluse.

Fascinated by the mounted men in the street, Clare ignored the low murmurs at first. But as the whispers grew in volume, they finally drew her attention.

"What are they saying, William?"

"I don't know. Something about a hound, I think."

Clare glanced over her shoulder toward the cell, which was built into the convent wall. Beatrice the recluse lived there, having chosen to become an anchorite nearly ten years earlier. According to the dictates of the religious path she followed, she never emerged from her cell.

As a professional recluse, Beatrice was supposed to dedicate herself entirely to prayer and meditation, but the truth was, she devoted herself to village gossip. She was never short of that commodity because during the day nearly everyone passed by her window. Many stopped to talk or seek advice. Whenever someone paused to visit, Beatrice dealt with that individual the way a milkmaid dealt with a cow. She drained her visitor for every tidbit of information.

Beatrice also performed the offices of her calling, which included offering advice to all who came to her window, with great zeal. Not infrequently she offered advice even though none had been requested. She favored predictions of dark foreboding and was quick to warn against impending doom and disaster.

Occasionally she was right.

"What are they saying?" Margaret called up to Clare.

"I'm not certain yet." Clare strained to hear the rising tide of whispers. "William says it's something about a hound. I think the recluse started the talk."

"Then we had best disregard it," Margaret said.

"Listen," William interrupted. "You can make out the words now."

The crest of the whispers raced forward, riding the sea of villagers.

". . . *hellhound.*"

"*They say he be a hellhound from someplace in the south. I did not catch the name . . .*"

"*The Hellhound of Wyckmere?*"

"*Aye, that's it, Wyckmere. He is known as the Hellhound of Wyckmere. 'Tis said he carries a great sword named the Window of Hell.*"

"*Why do they call it that?*"

"*Because it is likely the last view a man has before he dies beneath the blade.*"

William's eyes widened. He shivered with the thrill of the whispered words and promptly reached into his belt pouch for another handful of gingered fruit. "Did you hear that, Lady Clare?" he asked around a mouthful of currants. "The Hellhound of Wyckmere."

"Aye." Clare noticed that several people in the crowd crossed themselves as the news reached them, but the glitter of awestruck excitement did not fade from their expressions. If anything, she realized with dismay, the villagers appeared more enthralled than ever by the oncoming knights.

When all was said and done, Clare thought, her people were an ambitious lot. They were no doubt envisioning the prestige that would devolve upon them if they were to gain a lord who wore the trappings of a fearsome reputation.

A reputation was well and good, Clare reflected, unless one was obliged to marry it.

"The Hellhound of Wyckmere," William breathed with a reverence that by rights ought to have been reserved for a prayer or a holy vision. "He must be a very great knight, indeed."

"What I would like to know," Clare said, "is where are the others?"

"What others?"

Clare scowled at the approaching riders. "There are supposed to be at least three other knights from which I shall choose a husband. These men all appear to ride beneath one man's banner."

"Aye, well, this Hellhound of Wyckmere is nearly as large as three men put together," William said with great satisfaction. "We don't need any others."

Clare narrowed her eyes. The Hellhound was not *that* big, she thought, but he was certainly formidable-looking. He was not at all of the moderate proportions she had requested.

The gray knight and his entourage were almost in front of her now. Whatever else could be said, the new arrivals were providing a wondrous entertainment for all present. It would be interesting to see if the other suitors could improve upon this display of steel and power.

She was so caught up in the unusual sights and sounds of the event that she barely noticed another ripple of whispers as it washed through the crowd. She thought she heard her own name spoken, but she paid no attention. As the lady of Desire, she was accustomed to having her people discuss her. It was the way of things.

Margaret peered up at her. "Clare, you had best return immediately to your hall. If you stay up here on the wall, you will not be able to get back in time to receive this grand knight in a proper manner."

" 'Tis too late now, madam." Clare raised her voice to be heard over the din of voices and thudding hooves. "I shall have to wait until they have gone past before I can make my way through the street. I am trapped here until the crowd has dispersed. Joanna and the servants will see to the business of greeting our visitors."

"What are you saying?" Margaret chided. "Joanna and the servants can hardly provide the sort of welcome the future lord of Desire will be expecting."

Clare turned her head and grinned down at Margaret. "Ah, but we do not know if this gray knight will be the future lord of Desire, do we? In fact, I think it highly unlikely. From what I can see, he is not at all the right size."

"Size, my child, is the least of it," Margaret muttered.

The thunder of hooves and the rattle of harness ceased abruptly. An astonished gasp from William and the sudden hush that had fallen over the throng brought Clare's head back around very swiftly.

She was astonished to see that the troop of mounted men, which had been making slow, stately progress through the center of the village, had came to a complete halt right in the middle of the street.

Directly in front of where she sat on the wall.

Clare swallowed uneasily when she realized that the gray knight was looking straight at her. Her first instinct was to slide back over the edge of the wall and drop discreetly out of sight into the garden.

But it was too late to flee. She would have to brave it out.

Clare was suddenly acutely conscious of her dirt-stained gown and windblown hair. Her palms grew moist as she gripped the edge of the sun-warmed stone wall.

Surely he wasn't looking at her.

He could not be looking at her.

There was no reason she should have caught the attention of the gray knight. She was just a woman sitting on a wall watching the spectacle along with the rest of the villagers.

But he *was* looking at her.

An odd stillness settled over the scene as the silver-and-smoke knight gazed thoughtfully at Clare for an endless moment. It seemed to her that even the very breeze had ceased. The leaves of the trees in the convent garden hung motionless. Not a sound could be heard, not even the snap of a banner.

Clare looked into shadowed, unreadable eyes framed by a steel helm, and prayed that the Hellhound of Wyckmere would take her for one of the villagers.

At some unseen command, the great dappled gray stallion started toward the convent wall. Those who stood in the beast's way instantly melted aside to clear a path. Everyone's eyes went straight to Clare.

"He's coming over here, my lady," William squeaked. "Mayhap he recognizes you."

"But we have never met." Clare's fingers tightened on the stone. "He cannot know who I am."

William opened his mouth to say something else but closed it abruptly again when the massive war-horse halted directly in front of Clare. The gray knight's gaze was level with her own.

Clare looked deeply into brilliant, unsmiling eyes that were the color of smoky rock crystal. She saw the cool, calculating intelligence that blazed in the depths of the crystal and knew in that moment that the gray knight was aware of her identity.

Clare held her breath, trying frantically to think of a clever way to deal with the situation. She had never faced such an awkward moment in her life.

"I seek the lady of Desire," the knight said.

A curious tremor flashed through Clare at the sound of his voice. She did not know why she reacted so strangely to it, because it certainly suited him. It was low and dark and vibrant with controlled power.

She clutched at the stone in order to keep her fingers from trembling. Then she raised her chin and straightened her shoulders. She was mistress of this manor and she intended to conduct herself in a manner that befitted that title, even if she was facing the most formidable-looking man she had ever met in her life.

"I am she whom you seek, sir. Who are you?"

"I am Gareth of Wyckmere."

Clare remembered the whispers. *The Hellhound of Wyckmere.* "I have heard that you are called by another name."

"I am called by many other names, but I do not answer to all of them."

There was a clear warning in the words. Clare heard it and decided to fall back upon the safety of good manners. She inclined her head in a civil fashion.

"I bid you welcome to Desire, Sir Gareth. Allow me to thank you on behalf of the entire village for the fine entertainment you have provided for us this day. We are rarely fortunate enough to be allowed to view such grand spectacles here in our small village."

"I am pleased that you are satisfied with what has transpired thus far, my lady. I trust you will be equally pleased with the remainder of the performance." Gareth released the reins, raised his mailed hands, and removed his helm.

He did not glance over his shoulder nor give any signal that Clare could see. He merely held the gleaming helm out to the side. Another knight rode forward at once, took the steel helm from Gareth's hand, and retreated back to join the other warriors.

Clare studied Gareth with a curiosity she could not completely conceal, even for the sake of good manners. This was one of the men who had been sent to vie for her hand, after all. She was surprised to discover that something deep within her was oddly satisfied by the look of him.

He was definitely too large, but somehow that glaring fault did not seem quite as alarming now as it had when she had composed her recipe for a husband. The reason was obvious. In spite of his size and obvious physical power, something told her that this was not a man who would rely on brute strength alone to obtain his ends.

Gareth of Wyckmere was obviously a trained knight, well versed in the bloody arts of war, but he was no thick-skulled fool. Clare could see that much in his face.

The sunlight gleamed on his heavy, shoulder-length mane of near-black hair. There was that about his fierce, stony features which reminded Clare of the great cliffs that protected her beloved isle. In spite of the intelligence that gleamed in his eyes, she sensed that he could be implacable and unyielding.

This was a man who had fought for everything he wanted in life.

He watched Clare as she examined him. He did not appear to object to her scrutiny. He simply sat waiting calmly and patiently for judgment in a manner which suggested that the verdict did not concern him. It struck her then that he had his own ends and he intended to achieve them regardless of her decisions and conclusions.

That realization worried Clare. The Hellhound of Wyckmere would not be easily denied once he had determined upon a goal.

But then, she could be just as determined in the pursuit of her own goals, Clare reminded herself. For all intents and purposes she had been in command of this isle and everything on it since the age of twelve.

"Well, my lady?" Gareth said. "Are you satisfied with your future lord?"

Her future lord? Clare blinked in amazement. She did not know whether to laugh or scold him for his breathtaking arrogance. She settled on a polite but distinctly cold smile.

"I cannot say," Clare murmured. "I have not yet met the other candidates for the position."

"You are mistaken, madam. There are only two, myself and Sir Nicholas of Seabern."

Clare's lips parted in shock. "But that's not possible. I requested a selection of at least three or four knights."

"We do not always get what we request in this life, do we?"

"But you do not meet any of my requirements, sir," Clare sputtered. "I mean no offense, but you are not precisely the right size. And you appear to be very much a man of war, not a man of peace." She glowered at him. "Furthermore, I do not gain the impression that you are of a cheerful temperament."

"My size I can do nothing about. And 'tis true that I have been well trained in the art of war, but I swear to you that I seek a quiet, peaceful life. As for my temperament, who is to say? A man can change, can he not?"

"I'm not at all certain of that," Clare said warily.

"I can read."

"Well, that is something, I suppose. Nevertheless—"

"My lady, it has been my experience that we all must learn to make do with what is granted to us."

"No one knows that better than I," Clare said icily. "Sir, I shall be blunt. You have come a long way and given us a fine show. I do not wish to disappoint you, but in all fairness, I fear I must tell you that you are very unlikely to qualify for the position of lord of Desire. Mayhap it would be best if you and your men left on the same boats that brought you here."

"Nay, lady. I have waited too long and come too far. I am here to claim my future. I have no intention of leaving."

"But I must insist—"

There was a soft, deadly sigh of sound. Gareth's sword appeared in his hand as if by magic. The swift, terrifying movement brought a collective gasp from the crowd. Clare halted in the middle of her sentence. Her eyes widened.

Sunlight danced and flashed on steel as Gareth held the blade aloft.

Once again everything and everyone seemed to freeze into utter stillness.

It was young William who managed to shatter the spell.

"You must not hurt my lady," he yelled at Gareth. "I will not let you hurt her."

The crowd was as stunned by William's boldness as it was at the sight of the drawn blade.

"Hush, William," Clare whispered.

Gareth looked at William. "You are very brave, boy. There are those who flee in fear when they gaze at the Window of Hell."

It was clear that William was frightened, but he wore an expression of stubborn determination. He glared at Gareth. "Do not hurt her."

"I will not hurt her," Gareth said. "Indeed, as her future lord, I am well pleased to see that she has had such a bold protector to watch over her until my arrival. I am in your debt, lad."

William's expression became one of uncertainty.

Gareth reversed the sword with another lightning-swift movement. He extended the blade, hilt first, toward Clare in an unmistakable gesture of homage and respect. He waited, along with everyone else, for her to take hold of the weapon.

A murmur of astonishment and approval swept through the crowd. Clare heard it. She sensed William's barely contained excitement. The expectant tension in the atmosphere was overwhelming.

To refuse the sword would be a move fraught with risk. There was no telling how Gareth would react or what his mounted warriors might do to retaliate. They could destroy the entire village in a matter of minutes.

To accept the blade, however, was to give Gareth and everyone else cause to believe that his suit would be favorably received.

It was a trap. A rather neat one, Clare had to admit, but definitely a trap. It was a snare with only two exits, both of which were dangerous. And it had been very deliberately set. But then, she had known from the first that this was a man who used his wits as well as his strength to gain his ends.

Clare looked down at the hilt of the polished length of steel. She saw that the pommel was set with a large chunk of rock crystal. The cloudy gray stone appeared to be filled with silvery smoke from unseen fires. Suddenly Clare knew whence the blade had taken its name. It did not require much imagination to envision the crystal in the pommel as a window into hell.

Clare met Gareth's steady gaze and saw that the smoky crystal was a fine match for his eyes.

Knowing that there was no way out of the trap, Clare chose one of the only two options available. Slowly she reached out and grasped the hilt of the sword. The weapon was so heavy that she had to use both hands to hold it.

A great cry of jubilation went up from the crowd. William grinned. Cheers filled the air. Armor clashed and rang as the mounted knights and men-at-arms brandished their lances and struck their shields.

Clare looked at Gareth and felt as if she had just stepped off one of the high cliffs of Desire.

Gareth reached out with his huge, mail-covered hands, caught her up, and swept her off the wall. The world spun around Clare. She very nearly dropped the big sword.

An instant later she found herself settled safely across the saddle in front of the Hellhound. She was steadied by a mail-clad arm the size of a tree. She looked up and saw the satisfaction blazing in Gareth's eyes.

Clare wondered why she felt as if she were still falling.

Gareth raised one hand to summon a knight. A hard-faced warrior rode forward.

"Aye, Sir Gareth?"

"Ulrich." Gareth pitched his voice so that his man could hear it above the thundering cheers of the crowd. "Escort my lady's noble protector in a manner which befits his excellent service."

"Aye." Ulrich eased his mount closer to the wall and held out his arms to seize William by the waist. He lifted the lad off the wall and settled him onto his saddle bow.

Clare saw William's eyes grow huge as he was carried off through the crowd astride the massive war-horse. She realized with wry chagrin that Gareth had just gained a loyal follower for life.

Clare listened to the exultant shouts of her people as the Hellhound of Wyckmere walked his gray stallion through the crowded street. She glanced back over her shoulder and saw Margaret standing in the gatehouse entryway.

The prioress waved cheerfully.

Clare clutched the Window of Hell and considered carefully the excellently set snare in which she had been caught.

2

"Presenting the Window of Hell to the lady was a pretty gesture." Ulrich grinned as he watched Gareth soap himself in the large bathing tub. "Quite unlike you, if I may say so."

"You think me incapable of pretty gestures?" Gareth shoved his wet hair out of his eyes and looked at his trusted friend.

Ulrich lounged on a cushioned window seat. The sunlight shone on his totally bald head. A seasoned knight some six years older than Gareth, Ulrich was a heavily muscled man of surprisingly handsome countenance.

Lord Thurston had hired Ulrich to be Gareth's mentor when Gareth had turned sixteen. The older man was both a thoughtful tactician and a skilled warrior. He had been present the day Gareth had won his spurs and the knighthood that went with them. The event had followed a violent encounter with a band of renegade knights who had been terrifying villagers on some of Thurston's lands.

Ulrich and Gareth had been together since that day. Their association was founded on friendship and anchored by trust and mutual respect. Gareth had learned a great deal from Ulrich in the beginning and he still listened to the other man's advice. But somewhere along the way their relationship had gradually shifted from mentor and student to that of professionals who dealt with each other as equals.

It was Gareth who now gave the commands, however.

It was Gareth who had gathered a tightly knit, well-disciplined band of men around him and shaped them into a formidable weapon whose services went for a very high price.

It was Gareth who had selected potential employers and decided how and when to sell the services of his men.

He had assumed the role of leader not because of his connection to Thurston of Landry, but simply because it seemed natural for all concerned. For Gareth, the will to command was inherent, as unquestioned an impulse as breathing.

Ulrich had no great interest in the position of leader. His was an independent nature. He swore fealty to those of his own choosing and the lord to whom he gave his loyalty could be assured of unswerving service. Four years earlier Ulrich had sworn fealty to the Hellhound of Wyckmere.

Ulrich knew Gareth better than anyone, including Thurston. He was well aware that Gareth had never before offered the Window of Hell to man or woman, lord or lady, master or mistress.

"I will admit that you have a way with grand and impressive gestures." Ulrich stroked his jaw thoughtfully. "With you, such gestures always conceal clever traps. But this was an unusual move, even for you."

"It was an unusual situation."

"Still, it was merely another snare, was it not? You left the lady little alternative but to accept the Window of Hell."

Gareth shrugged.

"It would have been awkward if she had turned the blade on you and tried to run it through your gut."

"She was hardly likely to do that. The greater risk was that she would refuse to accept it." Gareth held the scented soap to his nose and sniffed cautiously. "Does it seem to you that everything here on Desire smells of flowers?"

"The whole damned isle smells like a garden. I vow, even the village ditch is perfumed."

"It appeared that it was linked to the sea through a channel of some sort." Gareth frowned thoughtfully. "The refuse is no doubt washed out with the tide. The garderobes here in the hall empty into a similar sort of system. Very interesting."

"I have never understood your curiosity about clever devices." Ulrich drew in a long breath, inhaling the scent of spring that poured through the open window behind him. "Tell me, what would you have done if the lady had refused the blade?"

"It no longer matters, does it? She did take the blade."

"And sealed her fate, is that what you believe? I would not be too certain of that, my friend. I have a feeling that the lady of Desire is a resourceful female. From what you have told me, 'tis she who has kept this manor so fat and profitable."

"Aye. Her mother taught her the secrets of perfume making. Her brother apparently spent all his time riding from one tournament to another until he finally got himself killed. Her father was a scholar who had no interest in managing his lands. He preferred to spend his time in Spain translating Arab treatises."

Ulrich smiled slightly. "What a pity you never made his acquaintance. The two of you would have had much to discuss."

"Aye." Gareth felt a sudden surge of satisfaction. Once wed, he would retire from hunting outlaws and return to his first love—hunting the treasures buried in books and manuscripts, such as those Clare's father had collected. Water cascaded off his big frame as he stood and reached for a drying cloth. "Hell's teeth. I smell like a budding rose."

Ulrich grinned. "Mayhap your new lady will appreciate the scent. Tell me, how did you guess that the wench on the convent wall was in truth the mistress of Desire?"

Gareth made a small, dismissing movement with one hand while he dried his hair with the cloth. "'Twas obvious she was the right age. And she was better dressed than any of the villagers."

"Aye. Nevertheless—"

"She bore herself with an air of confidence and authority. I knew that she must be either an inhabitant of the convent who had not yet taken the veil, or the lady of the manor. I gambled on the latter."

Gareth recalled his first view of Clare. From his position astride his stallion, he had noticed her as she clambered up to sit atop the stone wall. She had been a lithe, graceful figure dressed in a green gown and saffron mantle. The neck, hem, and sleeves of her tunic had been embroidered in yellow and orange, as had the wide girdle. The latter had rested low on her hips, emphasizing a narrow waist and the womanly flare of her thighs.

To Gareth, the woman on the wall had been the embodiment of spring itself, as fresh and vivid as the fields of roses and lavender which carpeted the isle.

Her long, dark brown hair, loosely secured by a narrow circlet and a tiny scrap of fine linen, had gleamed with a rich luster in the sun. But it was her face which had caught and held his attention. Her striking, fine-boned features had been as alight with unabashed curiosity and excitement as the face of the lad who sat beside her. A gracious but unmistakable pride glowed in her expression, the look of a woman accustomed to command.

Her huge green eyes, however, had held a deep wariness. His own falcon-sharp gaze, schooled by years spent hunting outlaws to note the smallest of details, had not missed that look of caution. It had, in fact, provided him with the final clue to her true identity.

The well-dressed lady on the wall had a very personal interest in the knights who were invading her domain.

Gareth knew that he had taken a calculated risk when he had decided to ride over to the wall to confront her. He had been a little concerned that she would slip back into the convent garden. But she had done no such thing. As he suspected, she possessed far too much feminine arrogance to retreat.

He had noticed the dirt on her gown as he rode toward her, and told himself it was a good omen. The lady of Desire was not above getting her hands dirty.

Gareth shook off the memories. He tossed aside the herb-scented linen drying cloth and reached for a fresh gray tunic.

As he dressed, he glanced at one of the large tapestries that warmed the stone walls of the chamber. Flowers and herbs, the source of Desire's profits, appeared to be a common theme everywhere on the isle, he noted. Even the beautifully woven hangings depicted garden scenes.

This was a land of scented blooms and lush greenery. Who would have guessed that the Hellhound of Wyckmere would come to such a pretty, sweet-smelling place to claim his own hearth? Gareth thought.

But he was well satisfied with the Isle of Desire. He sensed that it held that which he sought.

He fastened his long leather belt around his hips and then he padded barefooted past one of the narrow windows cut into the stone wall. The warm, perfumed breeze made him think of Clare's hair.

Gareth had been obliged to inhale the scent of her dark tresses as he had carried her before him through the village and along the road to the hall.

The smell of flowers had blended with but had not disguised the sweet, intriguing scent that was hers and hers alone. The fragrance had captivated Gareth. She smelled like no other woman he had ever known.

The subtle, heady perfume combined with the feel of her softly rounded hips pressed against his leg had done something to Gareth's insides. A deep, powerful hunger had stirred to life within him.

His brows drew together and his jaw tightened as he recalled the raw force of that hunger. He would have to make certain it stayed within bounds. He had not survived this long by allowing his emotions to rule him.

Ulrich caught his eye at that moment. "So you knew the lady of Desire on sight?" He shook his bare, gleaming skull with wry admiration. "I congratulate you, Gareth. As usual, you were quick to add the facts together and determine the correct sum."

"It was not very difficult." Gareth sat down on a stool to pull on soft leather boots. "Enough of that discussion. I'm interested to hear whatever you learned about the kidnapping incident."

"There is not much to tell. As you know, I downed a few mugs of ale with the crowd at the local tavern in Seabern last night. The most interesting thing I learned is that all parties concerned, including Sir Nicholas, his entire household, and the lady herself, insist that there was no kidnapping."

Gareth shrugged. "Only to be expected. A lady's reputation is involved."

"Aye. The tale is that she made an unexpected visit to Sir Nicholas which lasted four days."

"After which he offered marriage?"

"Aye. The lady refused." Ulrich chuckled. "You must admit that took courage under the circumstances."

"That it did. Most women would have yielded to the inevitable." Satisfaction flowed through Gareth. His future bride was not one to collapse in the face of blatant intimidation. He approved of that sort of courage.

Up to a point.

"By way of excuse she told him that her guardian, Thurston of Landry, had agreed to allow her to choose her own husband."

"That must have been when she decided to write to my father and request a selection of candidates for the position."

"No doubt."

"It also explains why my father instructed me to waste no time claiming my bride." Gareth reflected on that briefly. "He suspects that Nicholas will soon make another attempt to get his hands on Desire."

"A second kidnapping might not be so easy to brush aside." Ulrich paused briefly. "As a matter of curiosity, what do you intend to do about Nicholas?"

"Nothing for now. I do not expect that Clare will willingly charge him with kidnapping or rape, even though she is now safe."

"She has her reputation to consider. As do you, Gareth. The lady will not thank you for dragging her honor through the mud."

"Nay. And I have other concerns at the moment. I will deal with Nicholas later."

Nicholas of Seabern would pay for what he had done, but that payment would be made at a place and hour of Gareth's choosing. The Hellhound of Wyckmere sometimes took his time when it came to exacting revenge, but sooner or later, he always claimed it.

He had his own reputation to consider.

Ulrich got to his feet, turned toward the window, and braced his hands on the ledge. He looked out over the fields of flowers that lay beyond the old wooden curtain wall that surrounded the hall. He drew a deep breath of the fresh, flowery air.

"'Tis a most unusual land you have come to claim," Ulrich said. "And a most unusual lady. To say nothing of the rest of the household."

"Aye. What is the boy to Lady Clare?"

"William?" Ulrich smiled. "A spirited lad, is he not? He could do with some exercise, though. He has a fondness for sweet cakes and puddings."

"Aye."

"He and his mother, the Lady Joanna, both live here at the hall. Lady Joanna is a widow."

Gareth glanced at Ulrich. "The boy is all Lady Joanna has left?"

"It seems her husband sold everything he owned, including his lands in the north, to raise money for his adventures in the Holy Land. He managed to get himself killed there. Joanna and William were left penniless."

"So Lady Joanna came to Desire seeking a place for herself and her son in this hall?"

"Aye." Ulrich's expression turned speculative. "I have the impression that your lady is very softhearted about such matters."

"Is that so?"

"Joanna and her son are not the only ones to whom she has given a home. Her elderly marshal, who should have been replaced years ago, by the looks of him, and her old nurse still live here, too. Apparently they had nowhere else to go."

"Any other strays about?"

Ulrich frowned slightly. "William said that a couple of months ago a young minstrel showed up on the hall doorstep. Clare took him in, too. He will no doubt entertain us this evening. William told me that Clare is very fond of love songs."

Gareth reflected on Clare's recipe for a husband. "I feared as much."

"The minstrel's name is Dallan. William informs me that the troubadour is devoted to his new lady."

"'Tis the way of troubadours," Gareth muttered. "They are a great nuisance with their silly songs of seduction and cuckoldry."

"The ladies love such ballads."

"There will be no songs of that sort sung here," Gareth said quietly. "See that Dallan the troubadour is instructed in that regard."

"Aye, sir." Ulrich's teeth flashed in a grin before he turned back to the window.

Gareth ignored his companion's ill-concealed mirth. As usual, he did not pretend to comprehend what Ulrich found so vastly entertaining. The important thing was that Gareth knew his orders would be carried out.

Satisfied that he was once again clean and clothed in fresh garments, Gareth strode toward the door of the chamber. "I believe it is time for me to present myself again to my future wife. She and I have much to discuss."

"You will find her in her garden."

Gareth looked back over his shoulder. "How do you know that?"

"Because I can see her from here." Ulrich gazed down through the open window. A smile still hovered about his thin lips. "She is addressing her loyal household. I'll wager that she is giving them instructions for the defense of the hall."

"What in the name of the devil are you talking about? This hall is not under attack."

"That, my friend, is clearly a matter of opinion. It seems to me that your lady is preparing to withstand a siege."

"From me?"

"Aye."

Gareth shrugged. "Then she is wasting her time. The battle is over and won."

"I'm not at all certain of that." Ulrich started to grin. The grin became a chuckle and the chuckle exploded into laughter.

Gareth made no attempt to reason out what it was that Ulrich found amusing. More important matters awaited him.

"All of the men and horses are properly settled?" Clare frowned intently as she paced the garden in front of her assembled household.

Her makeshift family, composed of people who had no other home, sat on the stone bench beneath the apple tree or stood nearby.

William, his face still aglow from his first ride astride a real war-horse, was positioned on the bench between his mother, Joanna, and Dallan, the thin, anxious young troubadour.

Eadgar, the elderly marshal of the hall, stood at the end of the bench, his expression one of great uneasiness. He had good reason to be alarmed. As marshal, he was charged with the day-to-day tasks of running the household. He was the one who had to make certain that the kitchens were supplied with the vast quantities of food required to feed the new arrivals. It was also his responsibility to ensure that the servants saw to such matters as preparing baths, mending clothes, and cleaning the garderobes.

It was all a great nuisance, Clare thought.

She was concerned about Eadgar's ability to cope with the crowd. Although loyal and hardworking, he was nearly seventy and the years had taken their toll on his joints and his hearing.

When Eadgar did not respond to her question, Clare sighed and repeated it in a louder voice. "I said, are all the men and their horses settled, Eadgar?"

"Oh, aye, my lady. Certainly. Indeed." Eadgar straightened his stooped shoulders and made an obvious effort to appear in control of the situation.

"I am amazed that you found room for so many. I trust I shall not find any of these great oafs sleeping on the stairs or in my solar?"

"Nay, my lady," Eadgar assured her earnestly. "There were chambers enough for his lordship and some of the others on the upper floors. The rest will sleep on pallets in the main hall or in the stables. Rest assured all will be carried out properly."

"Calm yourself, Clare." Joanna looked up from her needlework and smiled. "All is under control."

Joanna was five years older than Clare. She was a pretty woman with golden blond hair, soft blue eyes, and gentle features.

Married at the age of fifteen to a man who had been thirty years her senior, Joanna had soon found herself widowed and penniless with a small son.

Desperate, she had arrived on Clare's doorstep three years earlier to claim a very distant relationship based on the fact that her mother and Clare's had once been close friends. Clare had taken Joanna and William into the household.

Joanna had immediately begun to contribute to the income of Desire by virtue of her brilliant needlework.

Clare had been quick to see the possibilities inherent in Joanna's talent. The revenues from the sale of Clare's dried flower and herb concoctions had increased markedly due to the fact that many were now sold in exquisitely embroidered pouches and bags of Joanna's design.

The demand had grown so great that Joanna had instructed several of the village women in the art of embroidery. Some of the nuns of Saint Hermione's also worked under her supervision to create elegantly made pouches for some of Clare's fragrance blends.

"Eadgar, inform cook that she must resist the temptation to dye all of the food blue or crimson or yellow tonight." Clare stalked along the graveled path, her hands clasped behind her back. "You know how much she likes to color the food for special occasions."

"Aye, madam. She says it impresses guests."

"I see no need to go out of our way to impress Sir Gareth and his men," Clare muttered. "And personally, I do not much care for blue or crimson food."

"Yellow is a nice color, though," Joanna mused. "When Abbess Helen visited last fall, she was much struck by being served a banquet done entirely in yellow."

"It is one thing to entertain an abbess. Quite another to be bothered with a bunch of very large knights and their men-at-arms. By Hermione's sainted sandal, I'll not waste the vast quantity of saffron it would take to dye everything on the table yellow tonight. Saffron is very costly."

"You can afford it, Clare," Joanna murmured.

"That is beside the point."

Eadgar cleared his throat. "I shall speak to cook."

Clare continued to pace. The walled garden was usually a source of pleasure and serenity for her. The flower and herb beds had been carefully planted so as to achieve a complex and tantalizing mixture of scents.

Normally a stroll along the paths was a walk through an invisible world of enthralling, compelling fragrance. Clare's finely honed sense of smell delighted in the experience.

At the moment, however, all she could think about was the very unflowerlike, very unsettling, very masculine odor of Sir Gareth, the Hellhound of Wyckmere.

Beneath the earthy smells of sweat, leather, horse, wool, steel, and road dust that had cloaked Gareth, had lain another scent, his own. During the ride from the village to the hall, Clare had been enveloped in that essence and she knew she would never forget it.

In some mysterious fashion that she could not explain, Gareth had smelled *right*.

Her nose twitched in memory. There had certainly been nothing sweet-smelling about him, but her reaction had reminded Clare of the feeling she got when she had achieved the right blend of herbs, spices, and flowers for a new perfume recipe. There was a sense of completion, a sense of certainty.

The realization sent a shiver through her. Even Raymond de Coleville, the man she had once loved, had not smelled so *right*.

"Was the Window of Hell fearfully heavy?" William asked eagerly. "I could see that the Hellhound let you to carry it all the way to the gates of the hall. Sir Ulrich said that was most amazing."

"Did he, indeed?" Clare said.

"Sir Ulrich said that the Hellhound has never offered his sword to anyone else in the whole world," William continued, "let alone allowed anyone to carry it in a procession in front of a whole village."

"He did not allow me to carry it," Clare grumbled. "He more or less forced me to do so. He refused to take it from my hands until we reached the hall. I could hardly drop such a valuable blade into the dirt."

Joanna quirked a brow but did not raise her eyes from her needlework. "Why do you think he simply did not resheath it?"

"He claimed he could not get the thing back into its scabbard with me seated in front of him. And he refused to put me down from the beast. He said it would not be *chivalrous*. Hah. What arrogrance to discourse on the finer points of courtesy when he was, for all intents and purposes, holding me captive."

Joanna pursed her lips. "I have the distinct impression that his lordship does not lack boldness of any kind."

"Sir Ulrich says that the Hellhound is a very great knight who has destroyed scores of robbers and murderers in the south," William said. "Sir Ulrich says he showed you great honor by allowing you to carry the Window of Hell."

"It was an honor I could have done without," Clare said.

She knew full well why Gareth had politely refused to take back his sword until they had arrived at the very steps of her hall. He had wanted to make certain that everyone along the way, from shepherd to laundress, witnessed the spectacle of the lady of Desire clutching the Hellhound's great sword.

No, the Hellhound had shown her no great honor, she thought. It had all been a very calculated gesture on his part.

"If you ask me, I do not believe he showed you any great honor, my lady," Dallan declared with passionate intensity. "On the contrary. He mocked you."

Clare glanced at her new minstrel. He was a gaunt young man of barely sixteen years who was easily startled by unexpected sounds or a raised voice. If one chanced to come upon him unawares, he jumped or froze in the manner of a panic-stricken hare.

The only time he seemed to find any inner calm was when he sang his ballads.

His thin features had begun to fill out slightly since he had arrived on Desire. But Clare could still see too many traces of the anxious, hunted look that had been in his eyes that first day when he had appeared at the hall.

Dallan had told her that he was seeking a position as a minstrel in the household. Clare had taken one look at him and had known that whatever lay in the young man's past was not pleasant. She had taken him in on the spot.

Clare scowled as she considered Dallan's impassioned remark. "I do not think he was mocking me, precisely."

"Well, I do," Dallan muttered. "He is likely a cruel and murderous man. They do not call him the Hellhound of Wyckmere for naught."

Clare whirled around, exasperated. "We must not read too much into a silly nickname."

"I don't think it's silly," William said with great relish. "Sir Ulrich says he got that name because of all the outlaws he's killed."

Clare groaned. "I'm sure his exploits have been greatly exaggerated."

"Do not alarm yourself, Clare," Joanna said. "I comprehend how uneasy you are at the prospect of this marriage. But I feel certain that Lord Thurston would not have sent you a candidate who did not meet the majority of your requirements."

"I'm beginning to wonder about that," Clare said.

She halted her pacing abruptly as a very large shadow fell across the graveled path directly in front of her.

As if conjured up by a sorcerer, Gareth appeared. He had come soundlessly around the corner of the high hedge, giving no warning of his presence until he was directly in front of her.

She glowered at him. It did not seem right that such a large man could move so quietly. "By Saint Hermione's little finger, sir, you gave me a start. You might have said something before you popped out from behind the bushes in such a sudden manner."

"My apologies. I give you fair greeting, my lady," Gareth said calmly. "I was told I would find you here in your garden." He glanced at the small group still gathered beneath the apple tree. "I have already made the acquaintance of young William. Will you introduce me to the lady seated beside him and to the other members of your household?"

"Of course," Clare said stiffly. She rattled off the introductions.

Joanna studied Gareth with assessing interest. "Welcome to Desire, my lord."

"Thank you, madam." Gareth inclined his head. "It is good to know that I am welcomed here by some. Rest assured that I shall endeavor to meet as many of my lady's requirements as possible."

Clare flushed and motioned quickly to a reluctant-looking Dallan.

"Welcome to Desire, sir," Dallan muttered. He looked mutinous but he wisely kept a civil tongue.

Gareth raised one brow. "Thank you, master minstrel. I shall look forward to hearing your songs. I should tell you now that I have very specific preferences in music."

"Have you, sir?" Dallan asked, tight-lipped.

"Aye. I do not care for songs about ladies who are seduced by knights other than their wedded lords."

Dallan bristled. "Lady Clare delights in songs that tell of the love affairs of ladies and their devoted knights, sir. She finds them very exciting."

"Does she, indeed?" Gareth arched a brow.

Clare felt herself grow warm. She knew that she was turning a bright shade of pink. "I am told that such ballads are very popular at the finest courts throughout Christendom."

"Personally, I have seldom found it either necessary or convenient to follow the latest fashion," Gareth said. He gave the small crowd a cool, deliberate look. "I trust you will all excuse your lady and me. We wish to converse in private."

"Of course." Joanna rose to her feet. Then she smiled at Gareth. "We shall see you at supper. Come along, William."

William hopped off the bench. He grinned at Gareth. "Is the Window of Hell very heavy, Sir Gareth?"

"Aye."

"Do you think that I could lift it if I tried?"

Joanna frowned at him. "Certainly not, William. Do not even suggest such a thing. Swords are very dangerous and extremely heavy. You are much too delicate for such weapons."

William looked crestfallen.

Gareth looked down at him. "I do not doubt that you could lift a sword, William."

William beamed.

"Why don't you ask Sir Ulrich if you can examine his sword?" Gareth suggested. "It is just as heavy as the Window of Hell."

"Is it?" William looked intrigued by that information. "I shall go and ask him at once."

Joanna looked horrified. "I do not think that is at all wise."

"You may be at ease, Lady Joanna," Gareth said. "Sir Ulrich has had a great deal of experience with such matters. He will not allow William to hurt himself."

"Are you quite certain it is safe?"

"Aye. Now, if you do not mind, madam, I would like to speak with Lady Clare."

Joanna hesitated, obviously torn. Then good manners took over. "Forgive me, sir. I did not wish to be rude." She hurried off after her son.

Clare bit back her annoyance. Now was probably not the best moment to inform Gareth that Joanna did not want William encouraged in his growing enthusiasm for all things pertaining to knighthood. She tapped her toe impatiently as the others took their leave.

Dallan lingered a moment, giving Clare an urgent, searching glance. He looked frightened but determined.

Clare frowned and quickly shook her head once in a small negative gesture. The last thing she wanted was for Dallan to attempt to be her champion in this awkward situation. The young troubadour stood no chance against the Hellhound of Wyckmere.

When they were alone in the garden, Clare turned to face Gareth. He no longer stank of sweat and steel, but the rose-scented soap he had recently used did not disguise that other essence, the one that smelled so right to her.

She could not help but notice that even though he had discarded hauberk and helm, he did not appear any smaller than he had earlier.

Clare was forced to acknowledge that it was not his physical size, intimidating as that was, which made him seem so large and so very formidable. It was something else, something that had to do with the aura of self-mastery and clear-minded intelligence that radiated from him.

This man would make a very dangerous adversary, Clare thought. Or a very strong, very loyal friend.

But what kind of lover would such a man prove to be?

The question, unbidden and deeply unsettling, had a shattering effect on her.

To cover her strange reaction, Clare sat down quickly on the stone bench. "I trust my servants have made you comfortable, sir."

"Very comfortable." Gareth sniffed a couple of times, as if testing the air. "I seem to smell of roses at the moment, but I expect the odor will soon fade."

Clare set her teeth. She could not tell if he was complaining, jesting, or merely remarking upon the fragrance. "The rose-perfumed soaps are among our most profitable wares, sir. The recipe is my own invention. We sell great quantities to the London merchants who come to the spring fair in Seabern."

He inclined his head. "That knowledge will greatly increase my appreciation of my bath."

"No doubt." She mentally braced herself. "There was something you wished to discuss with me, sir?"

"Aye. Our marriage."

Clare flinched, but she did not fall off the bench. Under the circumstances, she considered that a great accomplishment. "You are very direct about matters, sir."

He looked mildly surprised. "I see no point in being otherwise."

"Nor do I. Very well, sir, let me be blunt. In spite of your efforts to establish yourself in everyone's eyes as the sole suitor for my hand, I must tell you again that your expectations are unrealistic."

"Nay, madam," Gareth said very quietly. " 'Tis your expectations that are unrealistic. I read the letter you sent to Lord Thurston. It is obvious you hope to marry a phantom, a man who does not exist. I fear you must settle for something less than perfection."

She lifted her chin. "You think that no man can be found who suits my requirements?"

"I believe that we are both old enough and wise enough to know that marriage is a practical matter. It has nothing to do with the passions that the troubadours make so much of in their foolish ballads."

Clare clasped her hands together very tightly. "Kindly do not condescend to lecture me on the subject of marriage, sir. I am only too well aware that in my case it is a matter of duty, not desire. But in truth, when I composed my recipe for a husband, I did not believe that I was asking for so very much."

"Mayhap you will discover enough good points in me to satisfy you, madam."

Clare blinked. "Do you actually believe that?"

"I would ask you to examine closely what I have to offer. I think that I can meet a goodly portion of your requirements."

She surveyed him from head to toe. "You most definitely do not meet my requirements in the matter of size."

"Concerning my size, as I said earlier, there is little I can do about it, but I assure you I do not generally rely upon it to obtain my ends."

Clare gave a ladylike snort of disbelief.

"'Tis true. I prefer to use my wits rather than muscle whenever possible."

"Sir, I shall be frank. I want a man of peace for this isle. Desire has never known violence. I intend to keep things that way. I do not want a husband who thrives on the sport of war."

He looked down at her with an expression of surprise. "I have no love of violence or war."

Clare raised her brows. "Are you going to tell me that you have no interest in either? You, who carry a sword with a terrible name? You, who wear a reputation as a destroyer of murderers and thieves?"

"I did not say I had no interest in such matters. I have, after all, used a warrior's skills to make my way in the world. They are the tools of my trade, that's all."

"A fine point, sir."

"But a valid one. I have grown weary of violence, madam. I seek a quiet, peaceful life."

Clare did not bother to hide her skepticism. "An interesting statement, given your choice of career."

"I did not have much choice in the matter of my career," Gareth said. "Did you?"

"Nay, but that is—"

"Let us go on to your second requirement. You wrote that you desire a man of cheerful countenance and even temperament."

She stared at him, astonished. "You consider yourself a man of cheerful countenance?"

"Nay, I admit that I have been told my countenance is somewhat less than cheerful. But I am most definitely a man of even temperament."

"I do not believe that for a moment, sir."

"I promise you, it is the truth. You may inquire of anyone who knows me. Ask Sir Ulrich. He has been my companion for years. He will tell you that I am the most even-tempered of men. I am not given to fits of rage or foul temper."

Or to mirth and laughter, either, Clare thought as she met his smoky crystal eyes. "Very well, I shall grant that you may be even-tempered in a certain sense, although that was not quite what I had in mind."

"You see? We are making progress here." Gareth reached up to grasp a limb of the apple tree. "Now, then, to continue. Regarding your last requirement, I remind you yet again that I can read."

Clare cast about frantically for a fresh tactic. "Enough, sir. I grant that you meet a small number of my requirements if one interprets them very broadly. But what about your own? Surely there are some specific things you seek in a wife."

"My requirements?" Gareth looked taken back by the question. "My requirements in a wife are simple, madam. I believe that you will satisfy them."

"Because I hold lands and the recipes of a plump perfume business? Think twice before you decide that is sufficient to satisfy you, sir. We live a simple life here on Desire. Quite boring in most respects. You are a man who is no doubt accustomed to the grand entertainments provided in the households of great lords."

"I can do without such entertainments, my lady. They hold no appeal for me."

"You have obviously lived an adventurous, exciting life," Clare persisted. "Will you find contentment in the business of growing flowers and making perfumes?"

"Aye, madam, I will," Gareth said with soft satisfaction.

"'Tis hardly a career suited to a knight of your reputation, sir."

"Rest assured that here on Desire I expect to find the things that are most important to me."

Clare lost patience with his reasonableness. "And just what are those things, sir?"

"Lands, a hall of my own, and a woman who can give me a family." Gareth reached down and pulled her to her feet as effortlessly as though she were fashioned of thistledown. "You can provide me with all of those things, lady. That makes you very valuable to me. Do not imagine that I will not protect you well. And do not think that I will let you slip out of my grasp."

"But—"

Gareth brought his mouth down on hers, silencing her protest.

3

Gareth had not intended to kiss her. It was no doubt too soon. But she looked so tantalizing sitting there in the shade of an overhanging branch that for once he did not stop to contemplate all the possible consequences of his actions.

So he did something he rarely allowed himself to do. He surrendered to impulse. And to the new hunger that had arisen deep within himself.

She would soon be his wife. His desire to learn the taste of her had been clawing silently at his insides since the moment he had plucked her off the convent wall. He was suddenly desperate to know if there was any hope of finding some warmth waiting for him in his marriage bed.

Likely he was a fool to seek the answer to such a question. Marriage was a matter of duty for Clare. She had approached the business in the same manner in which she no doubt concocted her perfumes; she had created an ideal recipe and then attempted to find all the various ingredients combined in one man.

She was bound to be disappointed that her alchemic brew had failed, and bold enough to make that disappointment plain.

Logic told Gareth that in spite of her intriguing title, he could not expect much in the way of passion from the lady of Desire. Nevertheless, some deeply buried part of him yearned to find a welcome here on this flowered isle.

The long years that he and Clare would spend together stretched out ahead for both of them. Gareth hoped those years would not be spent in a cold bed.

She seemed startled but not frightened by his kiss. Gareth was relieved. At least her experience with Nicholas of Seabern had not left her fearful or repulsed by passion.

Mayhap she had been seduced rather than raped by Nicholas.

Mayhap she even had some affection for her neighbor. It was possible that she had enjoyed her four days with Nicholas but had not wanted to marry him for some reason that had nothing to do with passion.

That last thought did not please Gareth.

Clare stood stiffly in his arms at first, her back rigid, her mouth tightly sealed. A strange sense of despair welled up within him. He wondered if the aura of spring that radiated from the lady was a false one. If she had ice in her veins, he was doomed to a wintry bed.

It should not matter, but it did.

By the devil, it mattered.

And then Clare trembled slightly. She made a tiny little sound and her lips softened beneath his own. Gareth discovered what his senses had suspected from the first. Kissing Clare was like kissing the petals of a flower. She tasted fresh and sweet.

There was nectar buried deep within the petals. Gareth found it and drank deeply. His tongue touched her own. She started but did not pull away. Instead she leaned closer, apparently as curious as he to learn what their future held.

Her fingertips glided along the back of his neck beneath his hair. She sighed softly into his mouth. It was a breathless little sigh of budding passion.

Gareth's entire body reacted as though he had downed a potent elixir.

A surging rush of desire swept through him. His hands shook a bit as he tightened his hold on her. Her mouth was soft, ripe, and very inviting.

Gareth had promised himself only the briefest of sips, but the potion in the heart of the blossom proved too intoxicating. The urge to down it all overwhelmed his senses and threatened to destroy his self-mastery.

He cupped her face in his hands and drew his thumbs along the line of her firm little jaw. She was as finely made as the exquisite tapestries that hung on the walls of her hall.

He let his hands skim the curves of her body. The promise of vibrant life was waiting for him here in the gentle curves of Clare's breasts and in the flare of her hips. An aching need twisted his gut. He flexed his fingers around her waist.

Clare's hands shifted to settle like butterflies on his shoulders. She touched the tip of her tongue very tentatively to his lower lip. Gareth could feel her breasts, round and full as summer fruit, pressing against his chest.

"You will give me fine, strong sons," he said against her mouth.

She drew back with a small frown. "And mayhap a daughter or two." There was a crisp edge on her words that told him he had somehow managed to offend her.

"Aye." He stroked her spine with the sort of soothing movement he would have used on his proud, temperamental war-horse. "'Twould suit me well to have a clutch of daughters as well made and as intelligent as their mother."

She looked up at him with perceptive, searching eyes as though trying to peer into his very soul. "I cannot guarantee that you will have children of me, sir, let alone that they will be sons. No woman can make such promises."

"The only guarantee I seek and will most certainly have from you, madam, is a vow that any babes you do give me will be of my blood."

Her gem-green eyes widened, first in shock and then in anger. She took a swift step back, wrenching herself out of his grasp.

"How dare you even imply that I would deceive you in such a fashion," she shot out fiercely.

He studied her, trying to read the truth in her eyes. But he could see only the blazing feminine outrage. He had blundered badly. That much was clear. On the other hand, he thought, mayhap it was time for plain speaking.

"I demand an oath of fealty from the men who serve me and I will ask no less from my wife. I mean to have such matters understood between us."

"I am not one of your liege men, sir. I consider that I have been gravely insulted."

"Insulted? Because I seek to ensure that my wife will be loyal?"

"Aye. You have no right to question my honor. I demand an apology."

"An apology?" Gareth eyed her thoughtfully. "Pray, which of your devoted admirers will you ask to avenge this grave insult if I do not apologize? Young William? Your new minstrel? Or mayhap your marshal, who looks as though he would have trouble lifting a tankard of ale, let alone a sword."

"I do not appreciate your poor jest, sir."

"I never speak in jest."

"I beg leave to doubt that. I think you enjoy a very dangerous notion of amusement. I do not care for it."

Gareth grew bored with the silly game. He had made his point. Clare had been warned. He made it a practice to give only one warning. "Enough of this nonsense. We have other matters to discuss."

"You are correct in that, sir. I shall not forget your insult, but we most certainly do have other matters to discuss." A speculative gleam appeared in Clare's gaze. "I have been considering this situation and have come to some conclusions."

"Have you?"

"Aye. I believe Thurston of Landry is a kind, compassionate lord."

"What in the name of the devil gave you that impression?"

Clare ignored the interruption. "I cannot imagine that he would insist that I marry a knight who is so unchivalrous as to actually question my honor before the wedding."

"Lady Clare—"

"Obviously Lord Thurston did not fully comprehend your true nature before he selected you as one of my suitors. He will be shocked, *shocked*, to learn that he made a grave mistake."

Gareth knew by the expression in her eyes that she was seriously contemplating the possibility of sidestepping the marriage on such flimsy grounds. The lady would have made an excellent lawyer. He felt an odd tugging sensation around the edge of his mouth. One corner even started to curve upward into what might very well prove to be a smile. He restrained himself with an effort.

"If you think to delay this enterprise by writing to Thurston to complain of my unchivalrous behavior, I'd advise you not to waste your time. Or Thurston's. He will not thank you for it." Gareth paused to add weight to his next words. "Nor will I."

"So." Clare nodded once, very briskly, as if some inner suspicion had just been confirmed. "Now we have threats from our unchivalrous knight. This business grows darker by the moment." She swung about and began to tread deliberately along the garden path. "The better acquainted you and I become, sir, the more I fear that you simply will not do as a husband."

"How strange." Gareth clasped his hands behind his back and fell into step beside her. He was beginning to enjoy himself. "I have had just the opposite experience. The deeper our acquaintanceship grows, the more certain I am that you will make me a most satisfactory wife."

"Highly doubtful, sir." Clare pursed her lips with an air of regret. "Highly doubtful. In any case, I must write to Lord Thurston to clarify some aspects of this situation before we proceed further."

"Which aspects do you refer to, lady?"

"To began with, I am concerned that thus far you are the only suitor to arrive on Desire."

"I told you, your choice is limited to Nicholas of Seabern or myself. There are no other suitors."

She scowled. "There must have been other suitable candidates for the position. Likely you are merely the first to arrive on the isle. The others might be journeying here even as we speak."

"Mayhap I overtook the other candidates en route and persuaded them that their cause was hopeless."

"Aye." Her brows snapped together. "There is that possibility."

"Or, having failed to persuade them to abandon their quest, mayhap I simply dispatched them," Gareth added helpfully.

"That is not at all amusing, sir."

"This has gone far enough." Gareth reached inside his outer tunic and withdrew a folded parchment leaf. "You had best read this letter from Thurston of Landry before you proceed with your schemes, my lady."

Clare regarded the letter warily before she took it from his hand. She studied the seal intently and then slowly broke it. Her mouth tightened as she read.

Gareth examined the neatly framed flower beds and the carefully trimmed borders of the garden as he waited for Clare to read through the letter. He was familiar with the contents of Thurston's missive. His father had dictated the letter in Gareth's presence. It would be interesting to see how Clare reacted when she had finished reading.

He did not have long to wait. Clare was obviously very skilled at reading. Just as he was.

"I find this very difficult to believe," Clare muttered as she hurriedly perused the first paragraph. "Lord Thurston claims that you are the best candidate he could find. He says that you are the only one who was even remotely comparable to Lord Nicholas."

"I told you as much."

"I would not boast of it, if I were you. Nicholas is hardly a model of gracious chivalry."

"I have heard that he is skilled with a sword and that he is loyal to his liege lord," Gareth said softly. "Those are Thurston's primary concerns."

"It is easy for Lord Thurston to be satisfied with such simple qualifications. He is not obliged to marry the future lord of Desire."

"I'll concede that much."

Clare frowned as she returned her attention to the letter. "Surely there must have been others who . . . By Hermione's elbow, sir, this is impossible." Clare looked up, clearly dumbfounded. "Lord Thurston claims that you are his eldest son."

"Aye."

"That cannot be true. Never expect me to believe that Thurston of Landry would want his heir to wed someone like me."

Gareth slanted her a sidelong glance. "What is wrong with you?"

"Nothing, of course. But Thurston's heir will be expected to make a fine match with a truly great heiress, the daughter of a family which enjoys influence with King Henry. A grand lady whose dowry will include much wealth and vast estates. I have only one small manor and it is already bound to Lord Thurston."

"You do not understand."

"I most certainly do understand." Clare's voice rang with fresh outrage. "You, sir, are attempting to deceive me."

The accusation annoyed him. "No, madam, I am not trying to cheat you."

"Do not think you can trick me so easily. If you were truly the baron's heir, he would not settle this tiny little manor on you."

"Madam—"

"And why would you wish to live here in this remote place when, as Thurston's son and heir, you could have your choice of many fine holdings and great castles?"

"'Tis true that I am Thurston of Landry's eldest son," Gareth said through set teeth. "But I am not his heir."

"How can that be?"

"I'm his natural son, not his legitimate heir." Gareth looked at her, curious to see how she would react when she learned the full truth. "To be blunt, madam, I am Thurston's bastard."

Clare was speechless for a moment. "Oh."

He saw that she was surprised, but he could not tell if she was shocked or angered or horrified to discover that she would soon be wed to a bastard. "Now mayhap you understand."

"Aye, sir, I do. Under the circumstances, Desire is no doubt as much as you can expect to receive by way of an inheritance, is it not?"

He did not like the hint of sympathy in her voice. "'Tis enough. More than I expected."

Clare glowered at him and then bent her head over the letter. "This is too much. Your father states that I am to marry at once and that he hopes I will choose you, but if not, he will accept Nicholas of Seabern as the new lord of Desire."

"I told you that Thurston is most anxious to see the matter settled," Gareth said neutrally. "He was much alarmed to discover that this manor had been without a lord for some time."

"Ah—"

"For some reason, he did not learn of your father's death until very recently. Apparently your letter notifying him of the sad event was delayed for a few months."

"Well, as to that, aye, there was some small delay." Clare cleared her throat discreetly. "I was numbed with grief for a time, of course."

"Of course."

"And then, when I eventually recovered, I discovered that there were a great many business matters that needed to be settled."

"Naturally."

"And then, the first thing I knew, it was winter," Clare continued blithely. "I reasoned that the roads would be impassable, what with the snow and ice. I decided it would be best to wait until early spring to send a message to Thurston."

Gareth almost smiled. "And while you waited for the roads to clear, you sought to discover a way to avoid marriage."

Clare gave him a disgruntled look. "It was worth a try."

He shrugged. "But the effort failed. So now we must go forward along a new path."

"We?"

"Aye. There is no reason the marriage cannot be celebrated on the morrow, is there?"

"Impossible." Desperation flashed in Clare's eyes. "Absolutely impossible. It simply cannot be done."

"It most certainly can be done, and well you know it. All that is required is that a priest be summoned—"

"We do not have a priest here on Desire," Clare said swiftly.

"I'm sure that one can be found in Seabern. We shall make our vows in front of witnesses, and that is that."

"But there is so much more to the matter," Clare protested. "A suitable celebration must be arranged. My marshal already has his hands full organizing the household to accommodate all of your men. He will need weeks to arrange a wedding banquet and a proper feast for the villagers."

"I am certain all can be arranged very quickly once you have made your selection. A day or two at most," Gareth conceded.

"You speak as one who has never had to organize such an event," she informed him with lofty disdain. "Great quantities of bread must be baked. Fish must be caught. Chickens plucked. Sauces prepared. Casks of wine and ale will have to be purchased. It will be necessary to send someone to Seabern to obtain some of the supplies."

Gareth came to a halt and confronted her. "Lady, I have organized entire battles with less notice. But I am willing to be patient."

"How patient?"

"Now we are to bargain on that point? I begin to comprehend that I am to marry a woman with a head for business. Very well, my terms are simple. I shall allow you a day to make your decision and to prepare."

"One day?"

"Aye. An entire day. All of tomorrow, in fact. I am feeling in an indulgent mood."

"You call that indulgent?"

"I do. We shall be married the day after tomorrow even if we are obliged to serve naught but bad ale and stale bread at the banquet. Do you comprehend me?"

"Sir, I am not one of your knights to be ordered about in such an overbearing manner."

"And I am not one of your household servants or a fawning young minstrel devoted to serving your every whim," Gareth said calmly. "Unless you have decided that you wish to wed Nicholas of Seabern—"

"I most certainly will not marry that obnoxious oaf."

"Then I will soon be your lord and the lord of this manor. 'Tis best that you remember that when you think to gainsay me."

"What I choose to remember is that I am the lady of Desire and I will expect to be treated with the respect that is my due."

Gareth took a single step forward. He was pleased when Clare stood her ground, but he was careful not to show his satisfaction. He was, after all, well skilled in the arts of combat. He knew better than most that it was extremely unwise to show weakness of any kind.

"Be assured that you have my respect, madam. But you cannot avoid the facts. Lord Thurston has commanded you to wed as soon as possible."

Clare tapped Thurston's letter against her palm and regarded Gareth with narrowed eyes. "Are you quite certain that you did not overtake my other suitors on the road, do something dreadful to them, and then write this letter yourself?"

"That is Thurston of Landry's seal. Surely you recognize it."

"Seals may be stolen or duplicated and used for fraudulent purposes." Clare brightened. "Aye. I should have thought of that immediately. 'Tis quite likely that this seal is false. I shall have to write to Lord Thurston to ascertain if he actually wrote this particular letter."

Gareth regarded her with dawning amazement. Clare certainly did not surrender easily, not even to the inevitable. "Madam—"

" 'Twill no doubt take several days, mayhap weeks, to receive an answer from your father. 'Tis unfortunate, of course, but we shall have to postpone the selection of a husband until he sends a message to me verifying that this letter is genuine."

"Hell's teeth."

Her eyes shone with a mock innocence that did not completely veil the underlying shrewdness. "Only think of the complications that would ensue if I were to act in haste."

Gareth caught her chin on the edge of his hand and leaned very close to brush his mouth lightly across hers.

"Give it up, lady," he said softly. "The letter is genuine. Your lord, my father, wants you safely wed as soon as possible. There is no way out of this snare. Go and see to the preparations for our marriage banquet because, unless you wish to marry Nicholas of Seabern—"

"I most definitely do not wish to wed him."

"Then come the day after tomorrow, you will be my wife."

Clare watched him in silence for a few taut seconds. A sudden crackling sound made Gareth glance down. He saw that she had crushed Thurston's letter in her hand.

Without a word, Clare whirled around and walked away from him. She did not glance back as she stalked out of the garden.

Gareth did not move until she had gone. Then he turned slowly to contemplate the well-ordered garden for a long while before he went to find Ulrich.

Clare sought the refuge of her study chamber. It was a place where she could usually find as much satisfaction as she could in her garden or in the workrooms where she concocted her perfumes and potions.

The walls of the sunny chamber were covered with beautifully worked tapestries featuring garden scenes. The air was scented by urns full of flowers that had been crushed and dried and then painstakingly mixed to yield complex fragrances.

The braziers in the corners, which provided heat on cold days, burned scented coals that delighted Clare's sensitive nose.

In the days following the death of her brother, Edmund, and again, after receiving the news of her father's death in Spain, Clare had found solace and comfort in this chamber.

A few months ago, seeking a way to take her mind off her myriad problems, she had begun a book-writing project. She determined to write down many of her intricate perfume recipes.

The task gave her a great deal of satisfaction.

Today, however, there was no escape to be found from the troubles which beset her.

She sat for a while with pen and parchment in front of her and tried to concentrate on the book of recipes, but it was no use.

After three botched attempts, she gave up the effort and tossed aside the quill. She gazed moodily out the window and thought about the feel of Gareth's mouth on hers.

His kiss had shaken her more than she wished to admit. It had been nothing like the wet, obnoxious kisses Nicholas had forced on her last month when he had carried her off to Seabern Keep.

She had disliked everything about Nicholas's embrace. When he had crushed her against his great, oversized body, she had been repelled, not only by the bulge of his aroused manhood, but by the very smell of him.

Part of the problem, of course, was the undeniable fact that Nicholas was not overly fond of bathing. But it was not just the odor of sweat and dirt that had repulsed her; it was the personal, utterly unique scent of the man, himself. Clare knew she would never learn to ignore it, let alone accept it in the same bed with her.

She touched her lips with her fingertips and inhaled deeply, seeking a trace of Gareth's scent.

"Clare?" Joanna frowned from the doorway. "Are you all right?"

"What? Oh, aye, I'm fine, Joanna." Clare smiled reassuringly. "I was just contemplating something."

"Sir Gareth, by any chance?"

"What else?" Clare waved Joanna to a stool near the window. "Did you know that he is Lord Thurston's son?"

"Aye. I heard the news just now downstairs in the hall." Joanna studied her with a perceptive look. "He is Thurston's bastard, to be precise."

"But still a son." Clare fiddled with the quill. "Some would say I have been honored."

"Some would say that Lord Thurston places great value on this manor," Joanna said dryly. " 'Tis obvious he wishes to be certain that he can depend upon the loyalty of its new lord. What better way to make sure of that than by seeing you wed to a man who is tied to him by blood?"

"True enough." Clare glanced at the letter that lay on her desk. "He claims he could not find any suitors who came close to meeting my requirements except Sir Nicholas and Sir Gareth."

"Indeed?"

"Personally, I am beginning to doubt that he tried very hard."

"Men tend to be very practical about such matters," Joanna murmured. "At least he has given you a choice."

" 'Tis not much of a choice, if you ask me."

Joanna clucked unsympathetically. " 'Tis more of a choice than I had."

Clare winced. She knew very well that at fifteen, Joanna had had no say whatsoever in the selection of a husband. "Were you very unhappy in your marriage, Joanna?"

"Lord Thomas was no better and no worse than most men," Joanna said philosophically. "He was never deliberately cruel to me or to William."

"That is something, I suppose."

"'Tis a great deal," Joanna retorted.

"Did you ever grow to love him?"

Joanna sighed. "Nay. I respected him as a wife should respect her husband, but I could not love him."

Clare tapped the quill gently on the desk. "Abbess Helen wrote in her last letter that a good man will cause his wife to fall in love with him after the marriage."

"I mean no offense, Clare, but what would Abbess Helen know of marriage?"

"Aye, you have a point." Clare glanced at the bookshelves which contained her precious books and treatises.

Two of the volumes had belonged to her mother. Some of the others Clare had obtained in her endless quest for information concerning the making of perfumes. The remainder had belonged to her father. He had returned from each journey with new ones, some of which he donated to the convent library in the village. The last, a book that he had scripted himself and was almost indecipherable, had been shipped to her shortly before his death.

One of the large, heavy volumes, a work devoted to herb lore, had been written by Abbess Helen of Ainsley. Clare had purchased a fair copy from a monastery in the south.

Clare had studied every word of Abbess Helen's treatise. She had been so impressed by Helen's book that she had boldly undertaken to write a letter to the abbess. To her astonishment the abbess had penned a response.

The correspondence between the two women, nourished by their mutual interest in flowers and herbs, had flourished during the past year. Last fall Clare had been delighted and deeply honored when Abbess Helen had journeyed to Desire for a short visit.

The Abbess had stayed at the hall, rather than at Saint Hermione's, and she and Clare had stayed up very late every night. They had talked for hours, discussing every conceivable subject.

But Joanna was right. As intelligent and learned as Abbess Helen undeniably was, she had never been a wife. She could not know much about the intimate side of marriage.

Clare studied the tip of her quill while she tried to find a tactful way to ask her next question. "Did you ever develop any feelings of, uh, warmth for Sir Thomas, Joanna?"

Joanna snorted. "Few women find passion in the marriage bed, Clare. Nor should they seek it. 'Tis a frivolous thing, passion. A woman marries for other, far more important reasons."

"Aye, I'm only too well aware of that." But still, she had hoped to find some warm feelings in her marriage bed, Clare thought wistfully. And with Gareth's kiss still burning her lips, she sensed she might find such feelings with him.

How could that be? she wondered. Other than the ability to read, which Gareth claimed to possess, he did not appear to be made up of any of the ingredients she had specified in her recipe for a husband.

She could not begin to comprehend why she had responded so unquestioningly to his embrace.

"I shall be honest with you," Joanna said. "Thomas was thirty years older than me and he had little patience with a new bride. Our wedding night was unpleasant but bearable, as it is for most women. One gets past it and it is done. After that, I grew accustomed to the business and so will you."

Clare groaned. "I know you are trying to encourage me, Joanna, but you are not succeeding."

"It is not like you to complain about your responsibilities, Clare."

"I do not complain without reason. Sir Gareth has virtually ordered the wedding to take place the day after tomorrow. Thurston's letter gives him the authority to insist."

"What did you expect?" Joanna sighed. " 'Tis no surprise, I suppose."

"Nay." Clare got to her feet and went to stand at the window. "I wish I had more time. It is the one thing I crave most at the moment. I would pay dearly for it."

"Do you think that time would make much difference? Sir Nicholas grows more encroaching by the day. You have lost the last two shipments of perfumes to thieves. You have said yourself that Desire needs a lord who can protect it."

"Aye. But I need a husband whom I can tolerate in my bed and at my table for the rest of my life." A strange panic welled up inside Clare. *The rest of her life.*

"What makes you think it will be impossible for you to tolerate Sir Gareth?"

"That's the problem," Clare whispered. "I simply do not know yet whether he and I can come to some sort of accommodation. I have only just met the man. All I have learned about him thus far is that he meets only one of my requirements. Apparently he can read."

"That is something."

"I need more time, Joanna."

"What will that buy? You have known from the first that you were unlikely to contract a marriage that was also a love match. Few women in your position enjoy that opportunity."

"Aye, but I had hoped for a marriage that would be based on friendship and the pleasures of shared interests." Clare chewed reflectively on her lower lip. "Perhaps that was too much to ask. Nevertheless, if I just had a bit more time, I believe I could . . ."

"Could what?" Joanna eyed her uneasily. "I do not like that expression on your face, Clare. You are scheming again, are you not? You are concocting plans in the same manner with which you create new perfumes. Do not trouble yourself with the effort. In this instance I fear there is no time for such alchemic cleverness."

"Mayhap, but it occurs to me that I might be able to delay events if I could convince Sir Gareth that he must allow himself some time."

Joanna looked astonished. "Time for what?"

"Time to discover whether or not he will be truly content to settle down here as lord of Desire." Clare recalled Gareth's cautiously neutral attitude toward the rose-scented soap he had used in his bath. "I do not believe he has given much thought to what it will mean to become the lord of an isle of flowers."

"You are hoping that a man who has made his living fighting murderers and outlaws may conclude that becoming a gardener is a somewhat dull prospect?"

"It is a possibility."

Joanna shook her head. "I doubt it. At the moment, I suspect that all Sir Gareth can think about is the prospect of becoming lord of his own rich lands."

"But what if I could convince him that he himself needs time for some calm reflection?" Clare swung around, suddenly enthusiastic about her new notion. "He is an intelligent man, the sort who thinks carefully and plans well before he acts."

"You are certain of this?"

"Oh, yes, absolutely." Clare did not pause to consider how she could be so sure of her analysis. "If I can convince him that he should consider long and well on the matter of this marriage, I shall be able to secure the time I want."

"How will you use that time?"

"First, to become better acquainted with him," Clare said. " 'Twill be useful if we do go forward with the marriage. I would at least know more about my husband before I am obliged to share a bedchamber with him. Second, if I discover that I simply cannot bear the thought of tying myself to Sir Gareth for life, my scheme will provide me with an opportunity to discover a way out of the dilemma."

"It will not work, Clare. From what I can learn, the Hellhound is eager to be wed. He wants to claim his bride and his new lands immediately."

"But mayhap I can persuade him to hold off for a while."

"How will you do that?"

"By telling him that I will not search for any other candidates for the position of lord of Desire while he himself is considering the post."

"You do not know much about men, Clare. Trust me, your scheme is hopeless."

"You cannot know that," Clare insisted. "At the moment, a goodly portion of the Hellhound's eagerness for this match is based on his belief that I am uneasy about the poor selections that have been offered to me. But if he can be convinced that I will not attempt to find another to replace him until he has contemplated the matter further, he might be willing to postpone the wedding."

"Highly unlikely."

"Why must you take such a gloomy view, Joanna?" Clare broke off at the sound of hoofbeats in the distance. She went back to the window.

"What is it?" Joanna asked.

"A small party of men is approaching from the village." Clare peered at the cloud of dust in the distance. She spotted a familiar yellow banner. "Oh, no."

"Clare?"

"By the hem of Saint Hermione's gown, I have never known a man to show poorer timing. What an idiot he is."

"Who?"

"Sir Nicholas."

"Oh, no, surely not." Joanna rose from the stool and hurried to the window. Her mouth tightened at the sight of the party of mounted men. "I vow, this could prove to be somewhat awkward."

"That is putting it mildly."

"Do you think that Sir Gareth knows anything about the kidnapping?"

"How could he?" Clare frowned. "We hushed the matter up quite thoroughly. I made it clear to everyone that I had been a willing visitor to Seabern Keep. And I did not mention the incident in my letter to Lord Thurston. Sir Gareth cannot be aware of it."

"I hope you're right," Joanna said grimly. "Because if the Hellhound of Wyckmere is given cause to believe that his bride has been ravished by another man, I fear there will be the devil himself to pay."

A sudden thought struck Clare. "Do you think that he would withdraw his suit if he were to learn that I had been kidnapped?"

Joanna looked alarmed. "Now, Clare—"

"Mayhap a previously ravished bride would not be to Sir Gareth's taste. He is a very proud man for one who was born a bastard." Clare paused. "Or mayhap because of that fact."

Joanna scowled. "Do not even contemplate such a notion. There is no telling what would happen were Sir Gareth to suspect the worst, and I, for one, do not want to find out."

"Hmmm," Clare said. She turned toward the door.

"What are you going to do?" Joanna called after her.

"I am going to welcome our visitors, of course. What else?"

"Clare, I beg of you, promise me that you will not do anything rash."

"I vow, you are beginning to sound just like Beatrice the recluse with all your warnings and dire prophecies." Clare gave her a quick, reassuring smile. "Do not fret. I shall consider carefully before I move the next piece in this game of chess."

She hurried out the door and along the corridor to the stone steps in the corner tower. She flew down them to the great room of the hall, where confusion and alarm seemed to reign.

Eadgar came up to her, his face creased in lines of grave anxiety. "'Tis Sir Nicholas and several of his household knights, my lady. They are already in the courtyard. What am I to do with them?"

"We shall first determine why they have come from Seabern without any notice. Then we shall invite them to sup with us and stay the night."

"The night?" Eadgar looked almost faint at the thought. "But we have a house full of guests. There is no room for any more."

"I am certain we can find space for a few more pallets here in the hall."

Clare crossed the hall and went outside to stand on the steps. The courtyard was even busier than the hall. Grooms ran from the stables to take the horses as the newcomers dismounted. Several of Gareth's men appeared. Their eyes were watchful and they held their hands close to the hilts of their swords.

A large, familiar figure flung his helm to his squire and climbed down from his horse.

"Greetings, my lady." Nicholas's voice boomed across the courtyard.

Clare groaned.

Sandy-haired and blue-eyed, Nicholas of Seabern was not an unhandsome man. Clare thought his features rather coarse, but she knew that some woman found his thick neck, bulging chest, and sturdy thighs appealing. She had once overheard a giggling maid confide to a friend that Nicholas's male member was as well muscled as the rest of him.

Clare had no desire to discover the truth of that statement.

"Welcome, Sir Nicholas," she said coolly. "We were not expecting you."

"Word has reached me that the chase is on." Nicholas smacked his hand into his palm with great relish. "I've always enjoyed the sport to be had from a rousing hunt."

"What hunt?" Clare glared at him. "What are you talking about, sir?"

"I hear that you have finally been cornered and forced to choose a husband. Past time, if you ask me."

"No one did."

"What's more, I have it on good authority that a suitor for your hand has arrived on Desire." Nicholas chuckled. "I could scarcely let a stranger have the field to himself."

"This is not a hunt, sir, and I am not a helpless hart to be run to earth and captured. I have a choice in the matter."

Nicholas chuckled. "And have you made your choice, madam?"

"Nay, I have not."

"Excellent. Then it is not too late. I shall join the chase."

"I fear the lady jests." Gareth materialized behind Clare. He stood with arrogant ease on the top step, one big hand resting lightly on the hilt of the Window of Hell. "The hunt is over."

"Who are you?" Nicholas demanded.

"Gareth of Wyckmere."

"The one they call the Hellhound." Nicholas grinned. "I have heard of you, sir."

"Have you?"

"Aye, you've got a reputation that would do credit to the devil. So you're here to woo the lady, eh?"

"She finds it amusing to pretend that she has not yet selected a husband. Who can blame her for attempting to prolong the entertaining game of courtship? But in truth the matter has been decided. I am the only suitor who meets any of her requirements."

"Not necessarily," Clare muttered. She was annoyed by the way the two men towered over her. Between the two of them they managed to block out the spring sunshine. She found herself standing in the shade.

Nicholas's eyes narrowed as he took Gareth's measure. "I know well that Lady Clare has certain very specific requirements in a husband. I would not want to see her settle for less than she deserves."

"You need not concern yourself with the matter," Gareth said.

"But I must." Nicholas switched his attention back to Clare. "We have been friends and neighbors for years, is that not right, madam?"

"We have certainly been neighbors for years," Clare said.

"Aye, and because of that close relationship, I feel it is my duty to be certain that any husband of your choosing knows exactly what he is getting in the bargain." Nicholas smirked. "A man should not be surprised on his wedding night."

A deep sense of alarm unfurled within Clare. She sniffed delicately and smelled the heavy, dangerous tension in the air between Gareth and Nicholas.

There had never been violence of any kind on her fair isle. She would not allow it to flare up now.

In that moment Clare knew that she would have to abandon her half-formed plan to turn the situation to her own advantage. She was suddenly faced with another, more pressing problem.

She had to find a way to keep Gareth and Nicholas from each other's throats.

Supper proved to be the perilous performance Clare had feared. Seated at the head table between Gareth and Nicholas, she felt as though she were the acrobat she had seen at last year's harvest fair. Surely the effort of balancing oneself on a taut rope strung between two poles could be no more difficult than attempting to maintain peace in a chamber full of quarrelsome knights.

Not that there had been any open conflict as yet. But Clare could feel the anticipation growing in the hall. It was a direct reflection of the hostility that emanated from the two men seated at the head table.

In an effort to lessen the opportunity for small provocations between Gareth's and Nicholas's men, Clare had seen to it that they were seated on the opposite sides of the long trestle tables. She hoped that the short distance that separated the warriors would prove a useful barrier in the event hostilities broke out.

Violence, if it erupted, would start at the head table, she reminded herself. As long as she controlled Gareth and Nicholas, she would control the entire hall.

It was a daunting task.

"Nay, not more vegetables?" Nicholas looked askance at the array of new dishes that had been set down amid the primroses scattered atop the table. "I vow, you eat more greenery here on Desire than do the hares and deer in my forest."

"We are very fond of fresh vegetables, my lord," Clare said with a determinedly cheerful smile. "Mayhap you would prefer the oysters? The cook does them with almonds and ginger. I'm sure you will enjoy them."

Nicholas lowered his lashes and looked at her with a slumberous gaze. The expression was no doubt intended to stir fires in her loins, but in reality it made him appear as though he were about to fall asleep at the table. "I will enjoy them all the more if you offer them to me with your own tender fingers, my lady."

Clare gritted her teeth around a frozen smile. It was common enough to offer a special guest a particularly tasty morsel, but she had no intention of honoring Nicholas in that fashion. In the first place, she did not think of him as a special guest. He was, in actual fact, a great nuisance. Clare's second consideration was not knowing how Gareth would react if he believed she was favoring Nicholas.

This was what came of trying to select a husband. Life had once been so peaceful and uncomplicated here on Desire, Clare thought.

"I do not believe I care for any oysters myself, sir," Clare said. "But please take as many as you like. And don't forget the pottage. Cook seasons it with fennel and coriander. It's delicious."

"Aye." Nicholas scooped up a handful of oysters and stuffed them into his mouth. "You always set an excellent table, my lady," he said around the oysters. "And your presence is the tastiest dish of all."

"Thank you." Clare gave him a repressive look, silently beseeching him to behave. If Nicholas read the plea in her eyes, he gave no indication.

Nicholas was rapidly becoming oblivious to a great many things, she reflected. He got that way after a few tankards of ale.

"But as lovely as you are tonight seated here in your own hall," Nicholas continued in a drawling, provocative tone, "I believe I prefer the memory of how you looked when you were seated beside me in Seabern Keep less than a month ago." He paused to swallow more oysters in a single gulp. "I thought at the time that you looked as though you belonged there."

Clare felt Gareth stir silently in the chair to her left. She panicked for a second. Her spoon clattered loudly against the edge of a bowl. "'Twas a pleasant visit, sir and you were a gracious host. But here is where I belong."

"And here is where you will stay," Gareth said very gently.

Clare glanced at him uneasily from the corner of her eye. She did not like the lethal softness of his tone. It seemed to her that the more Nicholas taunted and provoked, the softer and more polite Gareth's responses became.

Clare was growing increasingly alarmed by Gareth's chilling politeness. She wondered if she was the only one in the hall who realized just how dangerous it was. It seemed to her that everyone present ought to be able to see the obvious threat.

Nicholas, thickheaded fool that he was, apparently did not. In fact, Clare thought, Gareth's soft speech seemed to be emboldening him.

It dawned on Clare that Gareth was deliberately baiting Nicholas.

Gareth caught Clare's eye as he used his knife to slice a wedge of mixed-meat tart. He did not quite smile—the man never smiled—but there was that in his expression which suggested this was as close to being amused as he could get.

The Hellhound of Wyckmere was enjoying himself.

Clare wanted to dump the contents of the pottage bowl over his head.

"Mayhap we would all enjoy some music," Clare said firmly. She looked at Dallan, who was sulking at the end of one of the long tables. "Will you give us a cheerful song, Dallan?"

Dallan leaped to his feet and swept her a deep bow. "As my lady commands."

He picked up his harp and began to play a familiar melody. Clare relaxed as she recognized one of her favorite songs. Dallan had composed it for her shortly after his arrival on Desire. It was called "The Key."

> *My lady's smile doth shine as bright*
>
> *as moon and stars on a summer's night.*
>
> *Her eyes are emeralds, soft and green,*
>
> *Her face is as pure as a clear, fresh stream.*
>
> *Tonight I shall take the key,*
>
> *The key that she has given to me.*

"Aye, aye, the key." Nicholas banged his tankard on the table. "Take the key." He belched.

Clare shuddered.

"Aye, the key." One of Nicholas's burly men, already drunker than his master, rapped his knife against his tankard. "And what will ye do with the key, lad?"

More tankards clashed as the rest of the men from Seabern called encouragement to Dallan. Clare saw Nicholas start to grin. He downed another swallow of ale and then reached for his goblet of wine.

'Tis the key to her chamber that she has given me.

She will welcome me there most graciously.

"Graciously, graciously," one of the men chorused with a hoot of laughter.

'Tis unfair that her lord keeps such a treasure hidden.

I shall risk my life to climb through her window this night.

I shall part her bed curtains and behold the fair sight.

Nicholas slammed the table with his fist, rattling cups and dishes. "Aye, lad, on to the lady's bed. 'Tis worth the risk." He leered at Clare.

Clare looked helplessly at Joanna, who in turn glanced uneasily at Ulrich. Ulrich gazed impassively at Gareth, as if waiting for a signal.

Her thighs are alabaster columns, round and smooth.

When I lay between them I shall see

The golden door that awaits my key.

"Aye, aye, the key." Nicholas roared.

Out of the corner of her eye Clare saw Gareth pick up one of the delicate yellow primroses that decorated her table. The blossom looked small and extremely fragile in his large hand. Slowly he began to stroke the petals.

Clare held her breath.

Another shout went up from the men seated below the head table. Clare pulled her fascinated gaze away from the sight of the primrose cradled in Gareth's hand.

She tried to signal Dallan to stop singing, but he pretended not to notice her attempt to gain his attention. He strummed his harp with grim defiance.

Nicholas sprawled in his chair. "You appear bored, Hellhound. What's the matter? Don't you care for the minstrel's song?"

"Nay." Gareth continued to stroke the petals of the primrose, apparently intrigued by their delicacy.

Clare shot to her feet. She fixed Dallan with a pointed look. "Master minstrel, I would prefer another song, if you do not mind. Mayhap the lovely one you wrote about the flowers of spring."

"But 'The Key' is one of your favorites, my lady," Dallan protested.

"Aye, but tonight I would like to hear another of my favorites."

For an instant she thought Dallan was going to refuse. But he finally nodded brusquely and began to pluck a different tune, one that featured flowers.

Clare sighed with relief, sat down, and quickly signaled Eadgar to send out more food and ale.

The marshal moved with astonishing alacrity for a man afflicted with stiff joints. It was clear that he, too, had sensed impending doom and was eager to do his part to avoid it.

Joanna visibly relaxed. Clare saw her smile weakly at Ulrich, who gallantly offered her a morsel from his plate. To Clare's amazement, Joanna blushed prettily and took the proferred bite.

Nicholas's mouth turned down in a sullen fashion, rather like that of a boy bent on mischief who has seen his teasing game halted before the jest has been played.

Gareth set the primrose aside and calmly picked up his wine goblet as though nothing out of the ordinary had occurred. "I am well pleased with your minstrel's new song, madam."

"I am very glad to learn that, sir." Clare gave him an irritated smile. Her manners were wearing thin. She was thoroughly annoyed with Gareth, just as she was with Nicholas, and she did not particularly care if he knew it. "I certainly would not want any of the guests in my household to have cause to be displeased with the entertainment."

Nicholas slammed his goblet down on the table. "Well, I do not much care for the new song. All that nonsense about spring flowers is dull and boring."

"Do you find it so?" Gareth glanced at him very casually. "Mayhap you lack the wit to enjoy the more refined aspects of the verses."

Nicholas glowered at him. "Are you saying I lack wit?"

"Aye. 'Twas no doubt one of the reasons Lady Clare sought other suitors. She has stated quite clearly that she desires a husband who is both clever and well educated."

Nicholas flushed with fury. A reckless glitter lit his eyes. "I'll wager Lady Clare prefers the other song. Is that not right, madam?"

Clare tried to think of an excuse to end the evening and send everyone off to bed. She wished someone would do her a favor and raise the alarm for fire or siege.

"I take pleasure in all types of music." Desperately she sought a distraction. "Would you please pass me the bowl of figs, Sir Nicholas?"

"Certainly." Nicholas smiled slowly. "Allow me to choose a fig for you." Instead of handing her the bowl, he reached into it with his short, broad fingers and plucked out one of the figs. He dipped the dried fruit into a dish of cinnamon and honey and held the morsel to Clare's lips.

She stared at the dirt under Nicholas's nails and tried to think. She was intensely aware of Gareth watching the small scene, a deceptively neutral expression in his eyes.

The whole situation was getting ridiculous, she thought angrily. This was her hall and she was in command here. She refused to surrender it to either of these large, overbearing males.

She smiled coolly at Nicholas and removed the fig from his hand. She set the dried fruit down on her plate without taking a single bite.

"I have changed my mind. I believe I have eaten enough this evening," she said.

"You disappoint me, lady," Nicholas said. "Why, when you stayed with me at Seabern last month, your appetite was much keener." He paused to leer. "And not just for figs."

Clare experienced a distinct chill. "I do not recall."

"Ah, but I do," Nicholas said. "How could I forget those enticing meals we shared? I confess that my fondest memories are of how very pleased you were when I satisfied your extremely delightful appetites. I trust you have not forgotten your sweet satisfaction?"

"You tease me, Sir Nicholas," Clare said. Foreboding, dark and disquieting, stole over her. She was rapidly losing all hope of staving off disaster. "I would have you cease at once. I do not find it amusing."

"Nay?" Nicholas watched her, but it was obvious his real attention was on Gareth. He was weighing each goading word he spoke, pushing a little harder, searching for the point where blood could be drawn. "I am devastated to learn that, madam. I certainly found you to be most entertaining. Indeed, I eagerly await your return to Seabern so that we may again satisfy our appetites together."

The implication of Nicholas's words were clear to all who heard them. Joanna toyed nervously with her spoon. Ulrich gazed at Gareth in stone-cold silence.

Gareth helped himself to a fig. He said nothing.

"I wish to discuss something else." Clare realized her voice was starting to rise.

"But I prefer to reminisce about the meals we have shared." Nicholas took back the honeyed fig Clare had placed on her plate. He sucked on it and then made loud smacking noises. "They were so very pleasurable."

Gareth lounged in his chair. "Lady Clare has requested that the topic of conversation be changed. She does not find it amusing. Nor do I."

Nicholas chuckled. "Do you think I care whether or not you find it amusing?"

"'Tis the lady's wishes that concern me. They should be a matter of some concern to you, too."

Clare's heart sank. The situation was worsening rapidly. Mayhap if she could get both men sufficiently drunk, they would both fall into stupors. "Would either of you care for more wine?"

Nicholas ignored her. He kept his narrowed gaze on Gareth. "Do you believe that you can please the lady better than I, Hellhound?"

"Aye."

"'Tis highly doubtful, if you ask me. Why would she give the key to her chamber to a bastard after she has known the touch of a well-born knight?"

A shocked silence fell like molten lead on the hall. Clare saw Joanna's eyes widen in horror at the insult. Ulrich sat grim-faced beside her.

Dallan fumbled with the strings of his harp. He ceased playing and jumped to his feet. He glanced wildly around the hall, as though seeking a place to hide.

Eadgar paused in the doorway, a fresh flask of wine in his hand, and gazed helplessly at Clare.

Clare found her voice. "That is quite enough, Sir Nicholas. I believe you are drunk."

"Not too drunk to know what he's doing," Gareth said softly.

"Agreed." Nicholas's eyes glittered. "But what of you, Hellhound? Do you still have your wits about you?"

"Aye. I keep them about me at all times. You would do well to remember that."

"Lady Clare appears to have a problem deciding which of us will make her the better husband." Nicholas's booming voice rang through the silent hall. "I propose that we resolve the matter for her. Here and now."

"How?" Gareth asked gently. "Shall we play a game of chess for the hand of the lady of Desire? Very well, I suppose that is a reasonable enough solution."

Clare was so outraged she momentarily forgot about the impending disaster. "A game of chess? For my hand? How dare you, sir?"

Nicholas smiled malevolently. "Aye, how dare you, Hellhound? Most unchivalrous."

"I suppose there is no possibility of a fair match," Gareth conceded. "Chess is a game that requires wit and intelligence from both players. Sir Nicholas would be at a great disadvantage."

"By the devil, this is not a matter of wits," Nicholas snarled. "You insult the lady by suggesting we play a game of chess for her hand."

Clare closed her eyes briefly and sent up a frantic prayer to Saint Hermione.

"What game do you suggest that we play?" Gareth asked.

"Trial by combat. Here and now."

"Agreed." Gareth appeared no more concerned about that suggestion than he had about the first one. "You may choose the weapons."

Clare leaped to her feet again. "*I have had enough of this idiocy.*"

Everyone stared at her.

She planted both hands flat on the table to keep them from shaking and swept the hall with furious eyes. "Hear me, all you who eat and drink at my board tonight. Know that I have had my fill of this foolish business of selecting a husband. Thurston of Landry has promised me that I can make my own choice. I will do so now and put an end to the matter."

A rustle and murmur of interest went through the hall. Men whispered to their neighbors, eager to place hasty wagers on the outcome of this new turn of events.

"My bold and noble suitors wish to play *games*," Clare said with scathing emphasis. "Very well, a game it shall be. But I shall choose the sport and I shall be the only player."

Gareth's smoky crystalline eyes never left Clare's face.

Nicholas smirked.

"It seems that I must choose between Sir Gareth of Wyckmere and Sir Nicholas of Seabern." Clare gestured toward each man in turn. "Was ever a woman so fortunate in her suitors?"

There were roars of approval from the crowd in the hall. No one seemed to notice the sarcasm in Clare's voice.

She snatched up one of the yellow primroses and held the bloom aloft in front of her so that all could see it. "I shall pluck the petals from this flower. As I do so, I will call out, by turns, the names of each of these fine, chivalrous knights who would be lord of Desire. By my oath, I will wed the man whose name I call out last."

Nicholas's smile vanished. "God's eyes, Clare, you cannot mean to make such an important choice in such a haphazard manner."

She glared at him. "'Tis no more haphazard and a good deal less bloody than the trial by combat which you proposed, Sir Nicholas."

"Hellfire," Gareth muttered. "Do you know what you're doing, lady?"

"Aye." Clare did not give anyone else time to interfere. She plucked the first petal from the primrose. "Sir Gareth."

A stir of excitement went through the crowd. More wagers were placed.

Gareth's gaze shifted to the primrose. He studied it intently for a few seconds and then he sat back in his chair with an expression of quiet satisfaction.

"Sir Nicholas." Clare tore off another petal and let it flutter to the table.

Nicholas scowled at the flower. "This is an idiotic way to select a husband."

"When one has been given a choice between idiots, one uses an idiotic method of selection." Clare smiled sweetly and ripped off another petal. "Sir Gareth."

There were only two petals left on the primrose. Clare plucked the next to the last one. "Sir Nicholas."

Hisses of dismay mingled with shouts of triumph as the crowd realized who the winner would be.

Clare held up the primrose to display the single remaining petal. She tore it ruthlessly from the stalk. "Sir Gareth of Wyckmere."

A thundering din arose from the hall as the diners pounded their tankards on the tables.

Nicholas's face contorted with fury. "Damn it to the pit, woman, what do you think you're doing?"

"Choosing the new lord of this manor." Clare swung around with a flourish and handed Gareth the denuded primrose. "Welcome, my lord. I trust you will be content with what you have gained."

Gareth took the naked stalk and rose to his feet with fluid grace. "Aye, my lady." His eyes gleamed. "I am well content."

"God's blood," Nicholas surged to his feet. "I am far from satisfied. You cannot choose a husband in this fashion."

"'Tis done. I have made my selection, as I was commanded to do by Thurston of Landry." Clare stepped back from the table. "And now you must excuse me. I am going to my bedchamber. I find myself much wearied by the excitement."

"God's blood," shouted Nicholas. "I'll not stand for this."

"You, sir, have nothing more to say about the matter." Clare raised her chin. "As it is too late for you to return to Seabern, you are welcome to stay the night. Arrangements have been made."

She picked up her skirts and started around the table. Joanna rose quickly to join her.

Clare was aware of everyone watching her as she crossed the room to the tower stairs. She paused on the first step and looked back toward the head table, where Nicholas and Gareth sat.

"Before I take my leave, sirs, I have one more thing to say." She met Gareth's eyes. "Know this, my future lord. There has never been violence here on this isle. I will not tolerate any tonight. Is that understood?"

"Aye, my lady," Gareth said softly.

"If blood is shed in this hall before morning," Clare continued through set teeth, "I vow, I will take the veil rather than wed you or any other man."

More whispers of wonder and speculation washed over the crowd. Nicholas looked suddenly sly.

Clare glanced disdainfully at Nicholas and then she returned her attention to Gareth. "And lest both of you decide that you would be better off without me to contend with, remember that if I enter a nunnery, I will not go empty-handed. I shall take all the secrets of my perfume recipes with me. They will be my dowry to the convent."

Another hushed silence fell on the hall as the impact of that statement made itself felt. There was not a soul on the isle who was not aware that the revenues from Desire were based on Clare's perfume recipes. Without them the fields of flowers and herbs were useless.

Satisfied that she had made her point, Clare smiled grimly at Gareth. "Your first task, Sir Gareth, is to keep the peace in this hall. If you would enjoy future profits from my perfumes, you must accomplish the business without drawing blood. I bid you good night."

She picked up an oil lamp that was burning on a nearby table, whirled about, and rushed up the narrow, twisting stairs. Joanna followed at her heels.

"Dear heaven, how could you make your choice in such a whimsical manner?" Joanna gasped as she flew up the steps in Clare's wake. "What if the winner had been Sir Nicholas? You despise him after what happened last month. You said yourself that you would rather marry almost any man than him."

"There was no way that Sir Nicholas could have been the winner. I knew who would be the new lord of Desire before I pulled the first petal off the flower." Clare reached the upper floor and stalked down the corridor to her bedchamber. "There are only five petals on a primrose, after all."

"But how did you know which name would be called out last?" Joanna's brow cleared. "Oh, I see. You had counted the petals and reasoned it out before you started."

"Aye." Clare opened the heavy wooden door of her chamber. She went inside, set the lamp down on a table, and walked to the window. She took a deep, calming breath of the perfumed darkness. "I knew the answer. Indeed, I knew it hours ago."

Joanna watched her closely. "Then why did you stage the fine performance with the primrose?"

Clare tapped one finger against the windowsill. "I was furious with both men but most especially with Sir Gareth. Nicholas is, to be blunt, simply Nicholas. He hasn't the wit to be anything other than obnoxious."

"And Sir Gareth?"

Clare's mouth tightened. "Sir Gareth most certainly possesses a high degree of intelligence and common sense. It angered me that he was willing to resort to intimidation and violence to gain his ends."

Joanna frowned. "Do you think that was what he was doing?"

"Aye. Did you not see the way he toyed with the flower while Dallan played 'The Key'?"

" 'Twas merely a flower, Clare. What made you deem the gesture intimidating?"

"I cannot explain it. 'Twas something about the manner in which he stroked the petals that alarmed me." Clare gazed out at the moonlit sea. "He was telling me quite clearly that he could be gentle or he could be dangerous. He wanted me to know that the choice was mine."

Joanna stared at her. "Do you really believe that was his intent?"

"I believe that he has created a very nasty reputation for himself and is not above using it on occasion. He is a practical man, no doubt given to expediency. If he is to be the lord of this manor, he must learn that we do things differently here. I want no violence on Desire."

"He is a man who is very familiar with violence, Clare. 'Tis likely natural for him to use violent methods when he deems it necessary."

"Aye, he will use them if need be." Clare hesitated. "But I do not believe that he takes pleasure in violence. At least, he has assured me that he does not. That is his saving grace. If we get through this night without a brawl downstairs, I shall have cause to hope that I have made the right choice."

Two hours later Ulrich heaved a sigh of relief and grinned at Gareth. "My congratulations on your successful completion of your first task as lord of this manor."

"Thank you."

"I confess I was not certain we would get through the evening without a bit of bloodshed. But as always, you proved as swift with your wits as you are with the Window of Hell."

" 'Twas not difficult to persuade Nicholas and his men to drink themselves into oblivion. They were already halfway there when my lady quit the hall." Gareth prowled his chamber with a restlessness that was unusual for him. "You have assigned the guards?"

"Aye. If any of Nicholas's men awake before dawn, he will be given another cup of wine."

"And Nicholas?"

"Fast asleep as a newborn babe, thanks to his efforts to defeat you in the contest to see who could down the most wine." Ulrich chuckled. "Speaking of that bloodless tournament you staged with your rival, I have a question."

"Aye?"

"What did you do with all the wine that you were supposedly downing?"

"I poured it into the rushes beneath the table whenever Nicholas turned his head."

"I thought as much." Ulrich's mouth turned down wryly. "The hall will not be a pretty sight tomorrow morning when Lady Clare's guests awake with splitting headaches and heaving stomachs, but there will be no bloodshed tonight."

"And that is the important thing." Gareth felt the odd tugging sensation around the corners of his mouth. He almost smiled. "My lady's wishes will be carried out insofar as possible until she is safely wed to me. I would not want her to think that she made the wrong choice."

"You are surprisingly pleased with yourself for a man whose destiny was recently linked to the fragile petals of a flower and a woman's whim."

"It is not the first time that my future has been decided by fortune and fate. I doubt it will be the last."

"I thought you would be as enraged as Nicholas was when you saw the method Lady Clare intended to use to make her choice."

Gareth halted in front of the window. He braced a hand against the stone sill. "I knew I would win the contest as soon as she plucked the first petal and called my name. More to the point, so did she. Given her knowledge of flowers, 'tis certain that she knew the answer before she began."

Ulrich frowned. "How do you know that?"

Gareth remembered the primrose he had examined while Dallan defiantly played the bawdy ballad. "There are only five petals on yellow primroses. Or at least there were only five on the flowers that were scattered about on the table tonight."

"Ah." Ulrich smiled. "I take your meaning. Given the uneven number of petals, it was inevitable that whichever name Lady Clare started with, that name would be the one she called out last."

"Aye."

"Why do you think she went to the trouble of acting out the small play? Why not merely announce that you were her choice and be done with it?"

Gareth gave in to the smile that hovered at the edge of his mouth. "She finds me arrogant. I believe that she was attempting to teach me a lesson."

"*A lesson?*"

"She wanted me to think that as far as she was concerned, there was little difference between Sir Nicholas and myself. It was her way of letting me know that I have yet to prove to her that I am the better choice."

Ulrich eyed Gareth's curved mouth with great caution. "You are amused by this?"

Gareth considered the matter more closely. "I believe I am."

Ulrich swore. "I can count on the fingers of one hand the number of times I have seen you amused."

"You exaggerate."

"Nay, my memory is clear because on each occasion you came within a hair's breadth of getting us both killed."

C lare held her tiny scented pomander to her nose as she gingerly made her way through the ruin of her main hall the next morning.

Even the fragrant herbs that had been scattered amid the rushes could not disguise the odor of brimming chamber pots, spilled wine, and stale bodies.

It would take hours to get the hall cleaned. Fresh rushes would have to be put down before the chamber was habitable. Clare wrinkled her nose in dismay. The servants could not even begin the task of sweeping out the hall until the sleeping men, who were sprawled everywhere, were removed.

She picked her way among the pallets, ignoring the snores of her guests, and managed to reach the front steps without getting ill. The young guard who stood there nodded respectfully.

"Good morning, my lady."

"Good morning." Clare dropped the pomander to let it dangle from her girdle. "You're one of Sir Gareth's men, aren't you?"

"Aye, my lady. My name is Ranulf."

"How is it that you look clear-eyed this morning, Ranulf? The others appear to be sleeping so soundly that it will likely take the crack of doom to awaken them."

Ranulf smiled. "The men who are still asleep in the hall are all in Sir Nicholas's employ. You may be certain that those of us who follow Sir Gareth are awake and at our assigned tasks. Most are in the stables at the moment."

"What makes Sir Gareth's men immune to the effects of too much wine and ale?"

Ranulf chuckled. "The Hellhound forbids any man in his service to drink so deeply that he cannot rise betimes in the morning and perform his duties."

Clare approved of the rule, but Ranulf's words aroused a sudden new concern. "Sir Gareth is a harsh master?"

Ranulf stared at her in astonishment. "Nay, madam. He is a most just and honorable knight. I meant only that he does not tolerate disobedience or laziness from those who serve him. He says such things can get others killed."

Clare relaxed slightly. The guard appeared sincere. "I could not tolerate a harsh master for this manor, no matter how intelligent he happened to be," she said under her breath. Better a fool such as Nicholas than a clever but vicious man.

"I pray your pardon, my lady?"

"Nothing." She smiled at Ranulf. "I trust there were no serious problems last night?"

Ranulf blinked. He seemed momentarily dazzled by her smile. He blushed furiously. "Nay, my lady."

"No one was hurt?"

"I belive Sir Ulrich may have used a tankard on one or two thick skulls when the wine failed to take effect, but no one was seriously injured. Sir Gareth gave strict instructions that there was to be no bloodshed." Ranulf shrugged. "So none was shed."

Clare was pleased that Gareth had harkened to her orders. It boded well for the future. "Am I right to conclude that Sir Gareth deliberately got Nicholas and his men drunk?"

"Aye, my lady. He said it was the easiest way to deal with the matter."

"Very clever." Clare smiled more broadly. Her smile turned into a chuckle as she recalled the very similar tactics she had used to deal with Nicholas during the precarious nights at Seabern. "Sir Gareth appears to be every bit as shrewd as I believed him to be."

Ranulf grinned proudly. " 'Twas merely a hall full of feasting men, my lady. Hardly a difficult battle for the Hellhound of Wyckmere. You should have seen him deal with the pack of murderous robbers who were laying waste to Galtonsea last fall. Now, there was a sight to behold. Sir Gareth had us set a trap and when the cutthroats fell into it we—"

"I'm sure it was all very exciting," Clare interrupted quickly. The last thing she wanted to hear about this morning was Gareth's more bloodthirsty skills. She wanted to suppress the realization that she was to marry a man who had, until recently, made his living in a violent manner.

Dallan emerged from the kitchens on the other side of the courtyard. He was munching on a large wedge of freshly baked bread.

"My lady," he called when he caught sight of Clare. He shoved the last of his bread into his mouth and hurried toward her."I bid you good day."

"Good day to you, Dallan. I pray you will not choke on your morning meal."

"Nay, my lady." Dallan swallowed hastily and wiped his mouth on the sleeve of his tunic. "I trust that you slept well last night?"

"Aye, thank you."

"'Tis a wonder." Dallan frowned darkly. "I thank the saints that you were not kept from your rest by the dreadful events which took place in your hall after you left."

Clare raised her brows. "I did not think that anything dreadful occurred. The hall is in an unpleasant condition this morning, but that is only to be expected with so many guests scattered about."

Dallan's thin face assumed a grave expression. "'Twas a scene that would have shocked and horrified a lady as refined and gracious as yourself. Aye, it was a sight that could have come straight from the depths of hell."

Clare frowned. "Come, now, it cannot have been that bad."

"You were not there, madam, saints be praised." Dallan straightened his thin shoulders. His eyes flashed with indignation. "Need I remind you that the awful events of last night were presided over by the Hellhound himself?"

"What's this, minstrel?" Gareth asked casually as he walked out onto the steps to stand behind Clare. "Carrying tales so early in the day? One would think that you could find more useful employment to occupy your time."

Dallan started and took a step back. His fingers twitched in agitation. Then he recovered himself, scowled resentfully, and turned to Clare. "I pray you will excuse me, my lady."

"Yes, of course," Clare murmured.

She watched Dallan hasten away and mentally composed herself to face the man who would soon be her husband.

Her husband. The thought made her feel light-headed.

"Good day to you, madam," Gareth said.

"Good day, sir." Clare fixed a smile in place and turned to greet him. Although she thought that she had prepared herself, she realized she was nonetheless a little breathless.

After her conversation with young Ranulf, it did not surprise her that Gareth's eyes showed no trace of an evening spent drinking Nicholas into the rushes. She suspected most of the Hellhound's wine had, in fact, gone under the table along with Nicholas and his men. That was certainly where hers had gone during that first, dangerous evening when she had found herself a virtual prisoner in Seabern Keep.

She had escaped Nicholas that night after encouraging him to drink his fill. Then she had rushed upstairs to a tower chamber and locked herself inside.

Clare had spent the next three days there, ignoring Nicholas's rage, his threats, and the pounding on the door. She had managed to free herself one afternoon when, frustrated by his failure to convince Clare that she must wed him, Nicholas had gone hunting.

It occurred to Clare now that if her captor had been the Hellhound, she likely would not have escaped.

Gareth looked even larger this morning than she had remembered. The strong, sleek power that he exuded was as much a part of him as his intelligence and his determination. Clare had a fleeting wish that her father and brother had lived to meet him.

But, she reminded herself, if her father and brother had still been alive, she would likely never have met Gareth of Wyckmere herself, let alone contracted a marriage to him. She would never have sought him out as a husband and Gareth would not have been interested in her because she would not have been an heiress.

Life played odd tricks on a woman.

Gareth had on a gray tunic over his undertunic, which was the color of charcoal. Although he wore no armor this morning, the Window of Hell was at his side, secure in its scabbard. The crystal pommel mirrored its master's eyes. Clare got the impression that the sword was as much a part of Gareth's daily attire as his boots and tunic.

His gaze was thoughtful as he watched Dallan scurry away. "Your minstrel and I are going to have to have a long talk."

"Dallan means no harm, sir. He is merely concerned on my behalf." Clare frowned. "I trust you will not make a practice of frightening the members of my household?"

"It won't hurt your pet poet to learn a few manners. He is not merely protective of you, madam. I believe he is jealous."

"*Jealous.*" Clare's mouth fell open in disbelief.

"Aye. 'Tis not difficult to comprehend."

Clare blushed. "Thank you, sir, but in truth I have had little experience with jealous men."

"'Tis not an uncommon malady. Many men fall victim to the fever when they are Dallan's age."

"The fever?"

"Love sickness. The symptoms are easily recognized. When the disease strikes, young males become overly earnest and passionate, determined to worship the very hem of their beloved's gown."

"I see."

"Dallan has obviously devoted himself to your service with the whole of his pure young heart and he does not wish to share your attentions."

"Are you certain? I hadn't realized his feelings were of such an intense nature."

Gareth shrugged. "As I said, 'tis a common enough problem in boys his age. 'Tis nothing he will not outgrow."

Clare crossed her arms beneath her breasts. "Tell me, sir, were you ever prey to the sort of fever you describe?"

"There was a brief time in my life during which I succumbed to the hellfires of unrequited passion. But that was long ago." Gareth's eyes gleamed. "I decided there was no profit in it and soon wearied of the pangs. I have no talent for worshiping a lady from afar."

"A pity." Clare did not want to admit it to herself, but the truth was that Gareth's easy dismissal of gallant love and pure passion was disheartening. She must remember that this marriage was as much a matter of business for him as it was for her.

"I trust you do not expect me to fall ill with love sickness at my age," Gareth said softly.

Clare looked into his crystal eyes and realized with a sense of startled wonder that he was once again amused. The knowledge did much to lift her flagging spirits. Gareth was a man of well-concealed emotions, but at least he possessed some. Yesterday she had not been entirely certain of that.

She reminded herself that she had never expected to gain a passionate lover in this marriage. All she could hope for was a husband who would make an intelligent friend and companion.

She needed time.

She cleared her throat and decided to seize the opportunity. "Although you speak in jest, Sir Gareth, I would—"

"Never, madam."

She blinked in confusion. "I pray your pardon?"

"I merely said that I never speak in jest."

She brushed that aside. "Nonsense, of course you do. However, your last comment raises a rather delicate issue, one that I wish to address before our marriage takes place."

"Later, if you do not object. There are one or two matters I must deal with before Nicholas and his men awake." Gareth glanced across the courtyard and raised a hand to catch Ulrich's attention.

"But Sir Gareth, the matter I wish to speak to you about is quite important."

"So is sweeping out the refuse from your hall."

Clare was distracted by that remark. "Well, that is certainly true. Do you propose to take charge of the task?"

"How could I do anything less? I am the one who caused the mess."

She swallowed a smile. "Aye, so you are. But under the circumstances, I am prepared to overlook the matter."

"You are indeed a most gracious and generous lady."

"I am pleased that you think as much." She frowned thoughtfully. "I suppose our discussion can wait. Mayhap you will be free sometime this afternoon?"

"I am always available to you, madam."

"Except when you are in the process of cleaning out a hall?"

"Aye."

A groom chose that moment to lead one of the massive war-horses across the courtyard. The animal's steel-shod feet rang on the stones. The horse and groom were followed by a clattering cart full of hay.

A pained groan sounded from just inside the hall.

"In the name of the devil and all his minions, what is all that damnable noise?" Nicholas lurched into view from the shadowed doorway behind Gareth. He absently scratched the stubble on his cheeks as he peered, bleary-eyed, into the courtyard. "Oh, it's you, Clare."

Clare tried to ignore the stench that emanated from him. "Good day to you, sir."

"Is it? I hadn't noticed."

She scowled. "You appear ill."

"I am." Nicholas winced. "My head feels as if some fool used it for quintain practice."

"Do not expect sympathy from me," Clare said. "After your extremely annoying behavior last night, you do not deserve any pity."

Nicholas gave Gareth a beseeching look. "You have won the lady's hand. She's all yours with my blessing. The least you can do is protect me from the sharp edge of her tongue."

Gareth glanced at Clare. "Lady Clare was just about to take a brisk walk along the cliffs."

"I was?" Clare gazed at him in astonishment.

"I think it would be for the best," Gareth said. "By the time you return, your hall will be swept clean."

Clare hesitated. "Mayhap a walk is not such a bad notion. I often take one in the mornings. As it happens, I have an errand in the village." She brightened. "I'll just run upstairs and fetch an item that I promised to take to Beatrice the recluse. I pray you will both excuse me, sirs."

"Aye," Nicholas muttered. "You're excused. Good riddance."

Clare glowered at him as she went past. "Really, Sir Nicholas, you should be ashamed of yourself for the way you acted last night."

"I pray you will read me no lectures," Nicholas said. "This sore skull of mine is punishment enough for any offense I may have committed last night. You are welcome to your Hellhound if he is, indeed, your choice."

"He is no longer the Hellhound of Wyckmere," Clare said forcefully. "On the morrow he will become Gareth, lord of Desire, and I would have you show him proper respect."

Gareth raised one brow and watched Clare with mild curiosity, as if she were an odd and unfamiliar creature.

Nicholas cradled his head between his hands. "I will call him by any name you wish, if you will cease screeching, lady."

"I am not screeching." Clare stepped around him and went toward the tower stairs.

"'Tis a matter of opinion."

Clare ignored him. But halfway up the curving staircase, she realized that she had forgotten to inquire as to whether or not Nicholas intended to stay for the wedding. If he and his men were going to spend another night under her roof, she would have to alert poor Eadgar.

Lifting the skirts of her gown, she hurried back down the stone steps. She evaded a snoring man who had slid halfway off his pallet into the stinking rushes, and crossed the shadowed hall to the main entrance.

Gareth and Nicholas still stood talking quietly in the doorway. Neither man noticed her as she came to a halt at the sound of her own name.

"Nay, by all that's holy, I have no desire to stay another day to see lady Clare wed," Nicholas said. "She's yours and I wish you joy of her."

"That is generous of you under the circumstances," Gareth said.

"'Tis true that she brings a fine, fat manor as her dowry. I felt obliged to try to get my hands on it, but to be honest, I'm not sorry I lost to you. The man who takes Clare as wife will pay a high price. You'll discover that soon enough."

"'Tis no concern of yours," Gareth said.

"Aye, and I confess that this morning I am eternally grateful for that." Nicholas rubbed his temples. "God save me from clever women."

"Rest assured that you have been saved from this particular woman."

"The difficulty is that she's had the running of this manor ever since she was a young girl," Nicholas complained. "She's grown far too accustomed to command. I warn you, Hellhound, she'll not tolerate any man's hand on the reins."

"Mayhap that will depend upon the man who lays hold of those reins."

"Nay, you do not know what you're getting into." Nicholas heaved a heartfelt sigh. "I concocted a shrewd plan for managing her, you know."

"Did you?"

"Aye, and being the generous man that I am, I'll give you the advice I had intended to take myself."

"What's that?"

"Once you've got her well and truly wed, bed her day and night until you've planted your seed. When you're certain that she is with child, you can leave the isle."

"Leave?" Gareth sounded curious.

"Why not? Let her stay here to see to the running of Desire. 'Tis what she's good at. You can spend most of the year somewhere out of range of her tongue."

There was a short pause.

"That was your brilliant scheme for dealing with Lady Clare?" Gareth finally inquired. "Get her with child and then leave the isle?"

"Aye, and it would have worked, too. If you've got half the wit they say you have, Hellhound, you'll heed my advice."

Nicholas's words hurt. Clare tried to ignore the pain and embarrassment they caused, but it was impossible. She took a step closer to the entrance.

"You are even more of a fool than I believed you to be, Nicholas," Gareth said quietly.

Clare brightened a little. It was nice to be defended by her future lord.

"Bah. We'll see how much of a fool I am after you've had a chance to get better acquainted with Clare," Nicholas grumbled. "Do not expect me to offer you shelter at Seabern whenever you've had enough of the little harpy's tongue."

"Seabern Keep is the last place I will go to seek refuge from my wife."

"You may suit yourself." Nicholas started to turn back into the hall. "If you have no objection, I'll rouse my men and we'll be on our way. I wish to God I did not have to face that boat trip back to Seabern."

"There is just one more thing before you leave."

"Aye?" Nicholas paused. "And what would that be?"

"It has to do with that visit that Clare made to Seabern Keep a month ago."

"What about it?"

"I am well aware of the true circumstances of her stay there. I know that you held her against her will."

" 'Twas merely a friendly visit. Ask the lady yourself."

"It was kidnapping, so far as I'm concerned. And make no mistake, Nicholas, there will be a reckoning."

Clare froze.

"God's eyes, man." Nicholas sounded genuinely taken aback. "You don't mean to say that you intend to challenge me because of that visit?"

"Not today. Clare does not want any violence on Desire and I am of a mind to indulge her for the present. But there will come a time and a place when you and I will settle the matter."

"But nothing happened," Nicholas exploded. "I never touched the lady."

"That was not the impression you gave last night."

"I gave out that impression because I hoped you might decide to quit the field if you believed it to be the truth. I knew it was my only chance. I was drunk at the time, if you will recall. 'Twas the wisdom of the wine."

"You cannot expect me to believe that you kidnapped Clare, kept her for four days at Seabern, and did not touch her."

"You don't know much about Clare yet, do you?" Nicholas retorted. "Devil take it, why am I standing here arguing with you? You'll learn the truth tomorrow night when you claim your bride."

"Aye," Gareth said. "I will." The tone of his voice made it clear that he did not expect to find that his bride was a virgin.

Clare was speechless. Nicholas's earlier words had hurt, but Gareth's calm assumption that she had been dishonored enraged her. He had not even had the grace to ask her for the truth. He had simply accepted the gossip of others as the final verdict.

Her cheeks burned and her stomach clenched. She had never expected much from Nicholas, but she had begun to believe that Gareth was a man of reason and some courtesy. Obviously she had been mistaken.

Clare stalked out of the shadowed hall and onto the sunlit steps.

Gareth glanced at her. "I thought you were fetching something from your chamber."

"I overheard every word." Clare ignored Nicholas and fixed Gareth with a steely gaze. "Sir Nicholas speaks the truth when he says that he did not dishonor me while I was at Seabern."

"Does he?"

"Aye, he does," Clare said very loudly.

Nicholas winced. "Pray, madam, have some consideration for my poor head."

Clare spun around to confront him. "By Saint Hermione's little finger, will you cease prattling on about your aching skull, sir? I do not care if your head falls off your shoulders and rolls down the road."

Nicholas cringed and made for the door. "I shall leave you two to continue this delightful conversation without me. I am going home to Seabern.

When I arrive there, I shall go straight to the chapel and thank the saints for sparing me from this match."

"Aye, you do that, Sir Nicholas." Clare was more incensed than ever by his cowardly departure. "Would that I could also be spared. I am very well aware that it was only my lands and perfume recipes that attracted the attention of two such noble and chivalrous knights as yourself and Sir Gareth."

Nicholas groaned and clapped his hands over his ears.

"Lady Clare," Gareth said gently, "mayhap it would be best if we conducted this discussion in a more private place."

She turned on him. "I care not who hears me. Everyone on this isle knows I spent four days at Seabern Keep. 'Tis no great secret."

Gareth's gaze was contemplative. "Aye, madam."

"I do not expect passion and devotion from you sir, but I do expect that you will believe me when I give you my oath. And I swear to you now that Sir Nicholas did not share my bed while I was at Seabern."

"Your virginity or lack of it has no bearing on our marriage," Gareth said soothingly. "I knew about your stay at Seabern before I came to this manor."

"And you suspected the worst, did you not?"

"'Tis only logical to assume that Nicholas took you while you were at his keep in an effort to force you to marry him."

"Why? Because you would have done so, had you been in his position?"

"Calm yourself," Gareth said. "You are growing agitated."

"Am I? How unfortunate." Clare wanted to scream with frustration. "You have my most solemn vow of honor, sir, that I have never lain with Nicholas of Seabern."

"There is no need to proclaim your virtue to the world." Gareth cast a meaningful glance around the bustling courtyard. "I shall have proof of your words tomorrow night, will I not?"

"Nay, you will not," Clare said through her teeth.

A shocked silence settled on everyone in the immediate vicinity. The groom who had been leading the war-horse across the courtyard jerked the lead and caused the big stallion to rear.

Gareth studied Clare with unreadable eyes. "What does that mean, madam?"

"It means, sir, that I have absolutely no intention of giving you proof of anything, least of all of my virtue." Clare's hands clenched at her sides. "And that, sir, brings me to the subject I told you I wished to discuss with you this afternoon. We may as well have the conversation here and now."

"Nay, madam, we will not have it here and now." Gareth eyed her with cool challenge. "Unless you mean to put on a performance for everyone present?"

"Why not? I confess that I did not originally intend to discuss this in front of the entire household." She gave him a frozen smile. "I thought to show some respect for your pride, you see."

"My pride?"

"Aye." Clare's smile vanished. "But as you do not appear to have any qualms about discussing my virtue with another man right here on the front steps of my own hall, why should I concern myself with your honor?"

"Lady, I think this has gone far enough."

"I have not yet begun, sir. Hear me well, Sir Gareth, you who would become the lord of Desire. Hear me and know that I mean every word of what I say. We shall wed tomorrow, as you demand and as my guardian insists."

"Aye, madam, we will."

"But we will not consummate this marriage of ours until I am satisfied that you will make me a suitable husband," Clare finished triumphantly. "You, sir, will have to prove yourself worthy of my regard and wifely respect before I will share the marriage bed with you."

The crowd of onlookers who had gathered to enjoy the quarrel stared in openmouthed astonishment. Ulrich's face twisted. He shook his gleaming head.

Out of the corner of her eye Clare saw Dallan's sulky, resentful expression turn to something approaching sullen satisfaction.

A murmur of eager whispers swept through Gareth's men. Clare knew they were once again placing wagers.

Nicholas started to laugh. "By the devil, 'tis worth everything, even this aching skull of mine, to see this fine play today. I believe I shall stay for the wedding, after all."

"I think not," Gareth said. "Gather your men and prepare to depart. You have caused sufficient trouble. Give me any more grief this morning and I will likely give you a close look into the Window of Hell."

Nicholas held up his hands, palms out, in a placating gesture. "Fear not, Hellhound. My men and I are already on our way back to Seabern. I am in no condition to fight you today. Mayhap some other time." He grinned slyly. "I believe you have another battle to wage first, oh great lord of Desire."

"Begone, before I change my mind about seeking vengeance today."

"One more thing before I take my leave," Nicholas said. "If you would know how difficult the coming battle is going to be, ask your lady where she got her recipe for a husband."

"I have given you fair warning, Nicholas." Gareth rested his hand on the hilt of his sword. "I only provide one warning."

"Ask her about Raymond de Coleville. He is the bold knight who gave her the inspiration for her recipe. None of us mere mortals can hope to match him, not even you, Hellhound. The man could not only read, he could write poetry."

Nicholas was laughing so hard now that he could hardly catch his breath. Several of his men staggered to their feet behind him. They started to grin.

"If you discover that your lady is no virgin," Nicholas managed, "do not look to me for an explanation. Seek out Raymond de Coleville."

A disquieting shiver went through Clare. She met Gareth's eyes and wondered belatedly if she should have held her tongue until she had regained control of her temper.

But it was too late to retract her rash proclamation. And she was not one to back down.

"It would seem that the battle I am to wage will be even more of a challenge than I had first anticipated," Gareth said.

It was not his soft words which worried Clare.

It was his smile.

6

"Sir Ulrich says that Sir Gareth is at his most dangerous when he smiles." The brisk morning breeze off the sea ruffled Joanna's mantle. She anchored the hood in place over her neatly braided hair and looked at Clare with troubled eyes. "He says that the Hellhound is seldom amused and on those odd occasions when he does appear to find mirth in a situation, no one else ever comprehends the jest."

"There's no denying that Sir Gareth enjoys a somewhat misguided notion of amusement," Clare muttered. She had pushed back the hood of her orange mantle, allowing her loosely bound hair to play with the crisp, snapping wind.

"Sir Ulrich claims that something dreadful frequently occurs after the Hellhound smiles."

"Now, that is utter nonsense. Sir Ulrich sounds a bit like Beatrice, always predicting doom and gloom." Clare adjusted the weight of the small pouch that was suspended from her orange and yellow girdle. She had a pot of a specially scented herbal skin cream stashed inside.

"Sir Ulrich is Sir Gareth's closest companion. He tells me he has served him for many years. But Ulrich says that even he treads cautiously whenever the Hellhound shows signs of being amused."

Clare glanced impatiently at Joanna. Her friend looked subdued and distinctly uneasy, not at all her normal, serene self. It was unsettling and at this particular moment in her life Clare did not want to become any more unsettled than she already was. She had to keep a clear head and a logical outlook on matters.

And she must remember her duties and responsibilities to the manor.

The walk along the cliffs into the village should have been a splendid way to steady her churning thoughts. Although it had been Gareth's suggestion this morning, in reality it was Clare's custom to take an early walk each day. She just did not care to be *commanded* to take a stroll, she thought, irritated by the memory of how Gareth had virtually ordered her out of her own hall.

It was obvious that Gareth was accustomed to command.

So was she.

That could be a problem.

"It seems to me," Clare said, "that you and Sir Ulrich have had some rather intimate conversations regarding Gareth."

Joanna turned an astonishing shade of pink. "Sir Ulrich is a most courteous knight. William is quite fond of him."

"I noticed."

Joanna frowned. "This morning William was still talking about his ride on Ulrich's war-horse yesterday. I do hope my son does not become too interested in war-horses and armor and such."

Clare gazed out over the sunlit sea. William's increasing fascination with knighthood was worrisome for Joanna. "I understand your fears. But it will be difficult to keep a boy of William's nature away from Gareth's men-at-arms."

"Mayhap it would help if I saw to it that William spent more time on his studies."

"Aye. Mayhap." But Clare privately doubted if any distraction, least of all an educational one, could deflect the boy's interest in the rough-and-tumble world of men-at-arms.

She understood Joanna's concerns better than most because she had lost her only brother to the lure of the tournament circuit. But Clare also knew that Joanna's overprotective attitude toward William was probably not the best method for dealing with a young boy.

Clare took a deep breath, reveling as always in the fresh, scented air. She loved the purple-pink sea lavender that carpeted the clifftops.

She looked out across the narrow channel that separated Desire from the mainland. The dark tower of Seabern Keep rose behind the small village on the shore. The sight sent a shudder of disgust through her.

"I confess that I have some serious doubts about Sir Gareth's suitability as a husband," she said. "But I suppose things could have been worse. I might have been forced to put up with Sir Nicholas."

Joanna slanted her a strange look. "At least we know you could have managed him, Clare."

"Sir Gareth will prove manageable," Clare said optimistically.

"Do not be too certain of that." Joanna eyed her closely. "Do you really mean to keep him out of your bed until he has proven himself to be a suitable husband?"

"I told you, I want some time to get to know him. I would have some degree of mutual understanding between myself and my husband before I join him in the marriage bed. 'Tis little enough to ask."

"Sir Ulrich says it will never work. He says you should never have challenged the Hellhound the way you did. I am inclined to agree with him."

Clare's mouth firmed. "Sir Gareth should never have challenged my honor."

"Come, now, it was logical for him to assume that you are no longer a virgin. Thurston of Landry obviously told him of the rumors about the kidnapping and of how you had stayed four days at Seabern."

"I do not care what gossip Thurston gave Gareth. The Hellhound should have asked me for the truth of the matter. He should not have made assumptions. And he had no business vowing revenge on poor Nicholas."

Joanna's smile was wry. "So it's poor Nicholas now, is it? That is not how you referred to him last month after you escaped from Seabern Keep."

"He is a nuisance and I am grateful that I will not have to wed him. Nevertheless, I confess I felt a little sorry for him this morning."

"I would not waste any sympathy on Nicholas, if I were you," Joanna said. "Save such feelings for yourself. You are the one who has challenged the Hellhound."

"Do you really believe that I made a mistake this morning when I told Gareth that he would not be welcome in my bed?"

"Aye. A very serious mistake. One for which I can only pray that you will not have to pay too dearly."

Clare mulled that over as she and Joanna left the cliff path and walked into the village. The narrow street was already bustling with morning activity.

There was no one seeking advice from the recluse when Clare and Joanna arrived at the anchor-hold. Clare knocked on the stone that surrounded one of the cell's two windows.

"We bid you good morning, Beatrice," she called. "Do we disturb you at your prayers?"

"Aye, but no matter. I have been waiting for you, lady." There was a rustling sound inside the cell. A moment later Beatrice, dressed in a pristinely draped wimple and a dark gown, appeared at the window.

She was a large woman in her fifties who wore a perpetual expression of doom and foreboding. She had retired to the life of a recluse ten years earlier after being widowed, having gone through the long process of seeking and gaining permission from a bishop to become enclosed. She seemed quite content with her choice of careers.

The second window of the two-room cell looked toward the church. It was designed so that Beatrice could follow the services and contemplate the inspirational view when she was at her prayers.

But everyone in the village knew that she spent most of her time at the other window, the one where Clare and Joanna stood. That was the window where gossip flowed like a river.

"Good day, Beatrice," Joanna said.

"Nay," Beatrice said grimly, " 'tis not a good day. And the morrow will bring worse. Mark my words, Clare of Desire, your wedding day will be heralded by icy gray smoke from the very fires of hell."

"I doubt that, Beatrice." Clare studied the cloudless sky. "The weather has been quite clear and warm lately. I have not heard anyone say that a storm is on the horizon. Come, I am to be wed. The least you can do is wish me well."

" 'Twould be a waste of time to do so," Beatrice grumbled. "Hear me, my lady, violent death shall descend upon this fair isle after the Hellhound claims his bride."

Joanna clucked disapprovingly. "Beatrice, you cannot possibly know that."

"Ah, but I do know it. I have seen the sign."

Clare frowned. "What sign?"

Beatrice leaned closer and lowered her voice. "The ghost of Brother Bartholomew walks these grounds again."

Joanna gasped. "Beatrice, that is ridiculous."

"Aye," Clare agreed crisply. "Surely you do not believe in ghosts, Beatrice."

"I believe in what I know," Beatrice insisted. "And I have seen the specter."

"Impossible," Clare said.

"You doubt me at your peril, lady. It has long been known that whenever Brother Bartholomew appears within the walls of this convent, someone dies a violent death soon thereafter."

Clare sighed. "Beatrice, the legend of Brother Bartholomew and Sister

Maud is naught but an old tale that is told to children. 'Tis used to frighten them into minding their elders, nothing more."

"But I saw the ghost myself, I tell you."

"When was that?"

"Shortly after midnight last night." Beatrice made the sign of the cross. "There was enough moonlight to see that he wore a black cowl. The hood was drawn up over his head to conceal his unfleshed skull. He stood in front of the gatehouse and when Sister Maud did not appear to join him, he went straight through the gates to seek her out."

"The gates are locked at night," Clare said patiently, "and Sister Maud has been dead for more than fifty years, God rest her soul."

"The gates opened for the ghost," Beatrice declared. "No doubt he used the black arts to unlock them. I saw him enter the grounds and go through the garden. Then he disappeared."

"You must have been asleep and dreaming, Beatrice," Clare said. "Do not concern yourself. Brother Bartholomew would not dare enter the grounds of this convent. He knows very well that he would have to face Prioress Margaret. She'll not tolerate any trouble from a mere ghost."

"You jest, lady of Desire, but you shall know the truth soon enough," Beatrice said. "Your marriage to the Hellhound of Wyckmere has roused the ghost of Brother Bartholomew, I tell you. Death will soon follow in his wake, as it always does."

"Mayhap I should come back here tonight and have a long chat with Brother Bartholomew," Clare said.

"Similar to the conversation you had this morning with Sir Gareth?" Joanna arched her brows. "Would you put this ghost in his place, just as you did your future lord?"

Clare grimaced. "I vow, we did very well here for years without being obliged to put up with all these difficult men traipsing about the manor. Now we seem to be dealing with one annoying male after another."

Beatrice shook her head dolefully. "Woe unto all of us, lady. The Hellhound has summoned the demons of the Pit. Brother Bartholomew is merely the first."

"I am certain that Sir Gareth would not summon any demon that he could not control." Clare reached into the sack suspended from her girdle. "Before I forget, here is your cream, Beatrice."

"Hush, not so loud, lady." Beatrice poked her head through the window. She glanced anxiously up and down the street, apparently to reassure herself that no one else stood nearby. Then she snatched the pot of scented cream from Clare's fingers and whisked it out of sight.

"No one would ever accuse you of succumbing to worldly temptations merely because you use my cream on your skin," Clare said. "Half the women in the village use it or one of my other potions."

"Bah, people will say anything and think worse." Beatrice stashed the pot in a cupboard and came back to the window.

"Oh, there's Sister Anne." Joanna lifted a hand to catch the attention of one of the nuns who had just emerged from the gatehouse. "Pray excuse me for a moment, Clare. I wish to have a word with her about a new embroidery design."

"Of course." Clare watched as Joanna hastened off to chat with Sister Anne.

Beatrice waited until Joanna was out of earshot. "Psst, Lady Clare."

"Aye?" Clare turned back to her with a smile.

"Before you go to your doom on the morrow, I would give you a small gift and some advice."

"I'm going to my wedding, not my doom, Beatrice."

"For a woman, there is often little to choose between the two. But that is neither here nor there at the moment. Your fate was sealed on the day your father died. There is nothing that can be done about it." Beatrice thrust a small object through the window. "Now, then, take this vial of chicken blood."

"Chicken blood." Clare stared at the vial in astonishment. "What am I supposed to do with this?"

"Keep it hidden near the bed on your wedding night," Beatrice whispered. "After the Hellhound has fallen asleep, unseal the vial and pour the chicken blood on the sheets."

"But why in Saint Hermione's name would I want . . . Oh." Clare felt herself turn a dull red. "Obviously my future husband is not the only one who fears that I am no longer virgin."

"As to that, 'tis neither here nor there as far as I am concerned. But men take a different view." Beatrice peered intently at her. "Why take chances? I say. This way honor will be satisfied all around and the Hellhound will not be angered."

"But I—" Clare broke off at the sound of hooves thudding on the road behind her.

She turned to see Gareth riding toward the anchor-hold. He was mounted on a sturdy-looking gelding, not his war-horse. He had Clare's small white palfrey in tow.

"Saint Hermione protect us," Beatrice whispered. " 'Tis the Hellhound himself. Quick, hide the vial." Beatrice reached through the open window to drop the small container of chicken blood into the sack that hung from Clare's girdle.

"Beatrice—"

"Now, then, you must heed my words, lady, if you would live through your wedding night."

"Live through my wedding night." Shocked, Clare spun back to face the recluse. "By Saint Hermione's nose, this is too much nonsense to tolerate, even from you."

"I fear for your very life, madam. I have heard that you swore to deny your husband his rights in the marriage bed."

"Gossip travels quickly. I spoke those words less than an hour ago. Do you imply that Sir Gareth might murder me if I refuse to share his bed?"

"He is the Hellhound of Wyckmere." Beatrice grabbed her wrist to hold her attention. "He is dangerous, Lady Clare. You must not risk his wrath by denying him his husbandly rights. *Do not defy him on your wedding night.*"

"But Beatrice—" Out of the corner of her eye, Clare saw Gareth draw his horse to a halt. He dismounted leisurely.

"If you defy him, he will draw his sword." Beatrice's eyes were grim. "I have seen it in a vision. Blood will flow in the bedchamber. I fear it will be your blood, my lady. My advice is to do your duty as a wife and then use the chicken blood."

Gareth walked toward the window where Clare stood. "May I join this conversation?"

"It would be of little interest to you, sir." Clare summoned a determined smile. "Beatrice was giving me advice on marriage."

"If I were you, I would not pay any heed to advice on marriage that comes from the lips of a recluse. She is bound to have a very limited view of the estate."

"Beatrice was merely trying to be helpful, sir."

"For all the good it will do," Beatrice muttered. "'Tis pointless giving advice to young brides these days. They never listen."

"'Tis just as well in this case." Gareth did not take his eyes off Clare. "I prefer to be the one who instructs my bride."

Fresh alarm etched Beatrice's expression. "I pray you, Hellhound, show some mercy to your lady on your wedding night. She has had no mother to guide her, and her father, God rest his soul, did not protect her as he should have done. Whatever has happened to her, bear in mind that it was not her fault."

"Beatrice, please," Clare hissed, exasperated. "That is quite enough advice for one day."

"Blood and death," Beatrice whispered as she retired deep into the shadows of her anchor-hold. "Blood will flow and violent death will come. I have seen the ghost."

Gareth looked at Clare with deep interest. "This grows more interesting by the moment. Is my latest rival a ghost?"

Clare glared at him. "Don't be ridiculous. Beatrice has a very lively imagination. What are you doing here, sir? I thought you were overseeing the departure of Nicholas and his men."

"Ulrich will attend to that. I came to find you."

"Why?"

"I wish to ask you to give me a tour of the manor."

"Oh." Clare could think of no immediate excuse to refuse. It was an eminently reasonable request. "But I should return to the hall as soon as possible. There is much to be done before tomorrow."

"Ulrich and your marshal have everything well in hand at the hall, and your friend Joanna is busy, I see," Gareth said. "Come." He took Clare by the arm and guided her toward the white palfrey. "I am eager to acquaint myself with Desire."

The ride to the top of the hill overlooking the village took fifteen minutes. It was accomplished in silence. Clare stole several sidelong glances at Gareth's calm, expressionless face in an effort to determine his mood and finally concluded that he was not angry.

She did not know whether to be irritated or impressed. She had never met a man possessed of such seemingly inexhaustible self-mastery.

"Tell me how you go about concocting your perfumes and potions." Gareth drew his gelding to a halt and looked out over the fields of spring flowers.

"Are you certain you wish to hear all the details, sir? Mayhap you will find them boring."

Gareth surveyed the brilliant patchwork of flowers and herbs that flowed across the gentle hills and valleys of Desire. There was cool possessiveness and keen interest in his gaze. "How could I be bored with even the smallest of details? I am responsible for the safety and protection of this isle. I must learn all that I can about it."

Clare stroked the palfrey's neck. "Very well. But please let me know if you grow weary. I have been told that I tend to wax overly enthusiastic about my subject."

She began to talk, slowly at first, unsure of just how much he really wanted to learn. Heretofore the only man who had ever taken a genuine interest in her work had been Raymond de Coleville.

She soon realized that Gareth was anything but bored by the topic. His intelligent questions soon caused her to forget all of the nonsense Beatrice had been spouting about ghosts and drawn swords.

"The flowers and herbs are then collected and either dried or infused in oil, according to the recipe," she concluded a long while later. "It takes great quantities of petals to create the basic scented oils."

"The oils are the basis of the various perfumes and soaps you create?"

Clare nodded. "They are combined with a variety of ingredients such as beeswax and honey to create different potions and creams. But I also employ dried flowers and herbs in several preparations."

"A fascinating business."

Clare smiled shyly. "I am writing a book of recipes which will include instructions for the making of many of the perfumes which have proven most profitable for Desire."

"You are a woman of many talents." Gareth's gaze grew serious. "I am a most fortunate man."

Some of Clare's enthusiasm faded. It was replaced by caution. "I am pleased that you think so."

"Tell me, Clare, do you do everything according to a recipe?"

Clare drummed her fingers on the pommel of her saddle. "You refer to Sir Nicholas's idiotic remark about my recipe for a husband, do you not?"

"I was well aware that you had created a recipe for a husband. I did not know that you had based your list of ingredients on a living, breathing man. I believe Nicholas said that his name was Raymond de Coleville."

Clare hesitated. "Do you know him, sir?"

"Nay. But naturally, I am interested to learn more of this pattern of perfect chivalry and knighthood."

"He's not exactly perfect."

"How does he fall short?"

"He's married."

"Ah." Gareth fell silent for a moment. "When did you last see him?"

"It has been nearly a year since he was last here." Clare gazed out across the water toward the mainland. "He came to see me one last time to tell me that his father had contracted a marriage for him."

"I see."

"He told me that he was to wed a great heiress, one who could bring him many manors and lands in Normandy. I could offer nothing to a husband but a remote isle filled with flowers."

"And that was not enough for Raymond de Coleville?"

Clare glanced at Gareth in astonishment. "How could it possibly compare to what a great heiress could bring him? You yourself would not be here on Desire now if you had been in a position to contract a better match."

"And you would not have contracted any match at all if you had had a choice. Is that correct?"

"Aye."

"Unless, of course, you could have married Raymond de Coleville."

Clare did not like the edge she heard in Gareth's voice. She decided it was time to change the subject. "'Twill soon be time for the spring fair in Seabern. That is where we sell many of our potions and perfumes. Rich merchants journey all the way from London and York to buy them. Would you care to learn about that aspect of the business?"

"Later. At the moment, I wish to learn how you met de Coleville."

Clare sighed. "He was a friend of my father's, a fellow scholar. They met two years ago when my father traveled to Paris to attend the lectures on Arab treatises that are given there."

"Raymond de Coleville was also studying in Paris?"

"Aye. Although trained as a knight, Raymond is, in truth, a very learned man."

"Astounding."

"He is far more interested in books and treatises than in tournaments and warfare."

"Is he?"

"Like you, he was gracious enough to show a great curiosity about my potions and perfumes. Indeed, he and I often conversed on the subject for hours."

"Did you?" Gareth asked softly.

"Of course his interest in the subject was purely intellectual, while yours is based on more practical reasons."

"You think my interest is merely mercenary in nature?"

Clare flushed. "I meant no insult, sir. 'Tis only natural that your curiosity stems from the fact that my perfumes will be the source of your future income."

"I do not come to you a poor man, Clare. Landless, aye. But not poor. Hunting outlaws for rich lords pays well."

Things were getting more uncomfortable by the minute. Clare sought for a way out of the quagmire. "If I offended you, I beg pardon."

Gareth's expression grew thoughtful. "A ghost, a neighboring lord, an obnoxious young troubadour, and now a man from your past who serves as the measure by which you judge all other men. Is there no end to the list of rivals I must defeat, madam?"

Clare had the uneasy impression that Gareth was once again amusing himself at her expense. "I do not know what you mean, sir. 'Tis obvious that you need defeat no other man for my hand. The matter of our marriage is settled, is it not?"

"Nay, not entirely. There is something else that must be discussed."

"What is that?"

"Our wedding night."

"Oh, that." Clare straightened in the saddle. "Aye, now that you mention it, mayhap we should clarify the details."

"Mayhap."

She took a deep breath. "I regret that the matter came out in such an awkward fashion this morning."

"Awkward? I would term it something more than awkward."

"Very well, embarrassing." Clare scowled. "I assure you that I had intended to deal with it far more privately."

"You issued a challenge this morning, madam. And you did so in front of your entire household and the lord of a neighboring manor. By now everyone on Desire is aware that you intend to deny me my rights as a husband."

Clare cleared her throat and prepared to stand her ground. "As I said, I did not intend to make such a public spectacle of the thing. It was your fault, sir."

"My fault?"

"Aye. The threats you made to Nicholas were insulting to my honor."

"So you lost your temper and said things in front of the world that you had originally intended to say when the two of us were alone."

Clare exhaled deeply. "I regret to say that I do not have as much control over my temper as you appear to have over yours, Sir Gareth."

"Mayhap you merely lack practice."

She met his eyes. "How is it that you have learned to hold your emotions on such a tight rein?"

"I am a bastard, remember?"

"I do not understand. What does that have to do with your skill at self-mastery?"

"An illegitimate son learns early in life that he will be offered only the leavings. And he soon discovers that he will have to do battle in order to hold on to those things to which he does succeed in laying claim. Strong emotions are dangerous for bastards."

"But why? Surely you must feel such emotions even more keenly than most simply because you are forced to struggle harder to get what you want."

Gareth gave her an odd look. "You are a perceptive woman. But as it happens, reason, logic, and determination are the weapons that have served me best, lady, not wild, uncontrollable passions."

Clare searched his face and saw that he meant every word of that statement. "I understand. The nature of your temperament is your own business, sir. However, I trust you will comprehend that my temperament is somewhat different from yours."

"Aye." Gareth smiled one of his exceedingly rare smiles. "Yours no doubt causes you a great deal more trouble than mine causes me."

Clare abandoned that argument. She had a more important one to pursue. "Sir, I shall be blunt. 'Tis not merely the offense you gave my honor this morning that I wish to discuss."

"I was preparing to defend your honor this morning, not offend it."

"Well, I was offended," she snapped. "But putting that aside, I must tell you that I wish to become better acquainted with you before we consummate our marriage."

"We are as well acquainted as most husbands and wives are before marriage."

"That may well be, but it is not saying much. I want us to learn more about each other. I want time for us to become friends, sir."

"You were friends with Raymond de Coleville, were you not?"

"Aye, but that has nothing to do with this." Clare grew more annoyed. The man was as slippery as a trout. "Let us return to the matter at hand. I am sorry if I embarrassed you, but I meant what I said this morning. I wish to wait before we consummate our marriage. Do you comprehend me?"

Gareth studied her in silence for a long moment. Then he turned his head and gazed out over the fields of spring flowers. "I comprehend your wishes, my lady. And I respect those wishes."

"Excellent." Clare felt relief well up inside her. She gave him a warm smile. "Then there is no need to continue with this discussion."

"But I wonder if you have considered the problems you created this morning with your failure to control your temper and your tongue."

Clare's relief vanished. "What problems?"

"Your people will not accept me as their new lord until you do. The challenge you issued this morning will likely make things very difficult for me to assume my duties as the lord of Desire."

"Nay, that is not true, sir."

"I can enforce my authority through the usual methods," Gareth agreed. "After all, the men that I brought with me are loyal only to me and they are well trained. Furthermore, they are the only armed men on the isle. They should have no great trouble making certain that my commands are carried out. But I doubt that you would care for the means by which they will do so."

For an instant Clare was so shocked at the unsubtle threat that she couldn't speak. Then fury swamped her. "Sir, I assure you that there is no need to employ armed men in order to establish your authority here on Desire. Nor will I allow such a thing. This is a peaceful land and I intend for it to stay that way."

Gareth's eyes were the color of silver and smoke. "Logic and reason would seem to dictate that the peacefulness of a manor must begin in the household of its lord and lady. Do you agree?"

"Aye, but—"

"If you would have your people trust me and honor me as their lord, then they must see that I enjoy your respect."

Clare saw the trap yawning wide before her. She hated to admit it, but she was very much afraid that Gareth was right. The peace and contentment of her people were her most important consideration.

Once again, as the lady of Desire, she had no choice but to do her duty.

"You have caught me in one of your clever snares, have you not, sir?"

"Nay," Gareth said gently. "I merely offer you a carefully reasoned argument to explain my view of the problem. I know that you, being an exceedingly intelligent woman, will see the inescapable conclusion."

Clare gave a small, unladylike snort of sheer disgust. "And to think that I yearned for a husband who relied on his wits rather than his muscle. Something tells me that Sir Nicholas would have been easier to manage."

Gareth gave her a quizzical look. "Did you want a man you could manage easily? That requirement was not mentioned in your recipe, as I recall."

Clare glowered at him. "Do not jest with me, sir."

"I told you, I never jest."

"But you do, and in a most irritating fashion. However, that is neither here nor there at the moment. I concede that you have won your point." She paused, thinking quickly. "It would probably be best if we gave the appearance of sharing the marriage bed."

It was Gareth's turn to grow wary. "The appearance?"

"Aye." Clare began to smile, well satisfied with her own logic. "I see no reason why we cannot share a bedchamber."

"I am pleased that you agree with my conclusion."

"But," Clare finished triumphantly, "I see absolutely no need for us to actually share a bed."

"Hell's teeth, madam, you reason like a man of law."

Clare gave him her brightest, most dulcetly innocent smile. "As far as everyone else is concerned, we two shall retire to the same chamber every night, just as would any married lord and lady. But what goes on inside that chamber is no one else's concern but our own."

"As to that," Gareth began ominously. "I do not believe—"

Clare seized the initiative. "No one else need know that we wish to become better acquainted before we consummate the marriage. It will be our private business."

"It will?"

"Aye. This way we shall both gain our objectives, sir. As far as my people will know, you will enjoy my wifely respect. I, in turn, shall have the time I want to grow better acquainted with you."

Gareth contemplated her with an expression of grudging admiration. "It occurs to me that Nicholas of Seabern does not know how truly fortunate he is to have escaped marriage to you. You would have made a minced-meat tart of him, my lady."

The silvery fog that shrouded Desire on the morning of Clare's wedding was seen as an ill omen by virtually everyone on the isle. The murmurs of concern began among the small group of female servants who helped Clare bathe and dress.

"The recluse said this day would be dimmed by cold smoke from the fires of hell," one of the women muttered. "She was right."

"'Tis merely a bit of fog," Clare said. "It will be gone by midmorning." She stood patiently while her best gown, a vibrant blue-green in hue, was slipped over her head. The long, deep sleeves of the dress were turned back to reveal the brilliant yellow lining. The neck and hem were embroidered in yellow and white silk thread.

"I trust my lady is correct." Eunice had been a serving maid in the household since the days of Clare's infancy. She did not hesitate to voice her opinion. She adjusted a silver circlet around Clare's hair, anchoring the delicate gold net in place.

"All will be well, Eunice."

"Do not be so certain, my lady. Everyone knows how ye threatened to deny the Hellhound his rights in the bedchamber. I warrant he'll not tolerate such defiance. I fear for yer very life."

"If you are referring to our small argument yesterday morning, calm yourself," Clare said airily. "My threat was spoken in the heat of anger. I intend to accept Sir Gareth as my husband just as I have accepted him as lord of this manor. I have already told him as much."

"Saints be praised." Eunice sighed with relief. "Everyone on the isle will be well pleased to learn that, madam. 'Tis for the best, y'll see."

"That's what Sir Gareth says," Clare said dryly.

"Now, then." Eunice cleared her throat. She glanced quickly to the left and then to the right, apparently assuring herself that the other servants were busy delving into the carved chest on the far side of the chamber. She leaned close and lowered her voice to a whisper. "Just in case there is a bit of a problem tonight, I want ye to take this."

Clare glanced down at the tiny, cloth-wrapped object Eunice thrust into her hand. "What is it?"

"Hush, not so loud. 'Tis a small vial of chicken blood."

"Oh, no, not you, too, Eunice."

"There, now, not another word, madam. 'Tis neither here nor there, as far as I'm concerned. What's done is done, and it weren't yer fault, whether the man was Sir Nicholas or that grand knight ye lost yer heart to last year."

"But Eunice—"

"The thing is, men as proud as the Hellhound tend to get fair exercised about this sort of thing. A man such as he will want to be assured that his lady's honor is as unstained as his own."

"An interesting thought." Clare grinned. "Mayhap I should make a speech at the feast to assure everyone that I shall go to my marriage bed at least as virginal as my husband."

"'Tis nay a matter for jest," Eunice grumbled. "Just promise me y'll keep the chicken blood close to hand tonight. Sprinkle a bit on the sheets afore morning and all will be well."

"I must remember to ask Sir Gareth how he intends to prove his virginity to me."

Unfortunately, the gray mist did not evaporate by the time the wedding ceremony took place. Clare felt the chill through her wool cloak as she rode her palfrey slowly through the crowded street.

She head the murmurs on all sides and knew that Beatrice's prediction of disaster had spread far and wide. Every villager, every farmer, every member of the convent had heard it.

"Smoke from the fires that burn in hell. . . ."

"They say the mist is the color of the crystal stone in the Window of Hell."

"The same color as the Hellhound's eyes. 'Tis an ill omen."

"Our lady should never have defied him." Alice the brewer crossed herself as Clare rode past. *"I pray he will not murder her in her bed tonight."*

Clare ignored the comments. She kept her eyes on the church door, where Gareth waited for her. He had ridden to the church ahead of her, accompanied by all of his men in a grand procession that had impressed the villagers.

He was good at that sort of thing, she reflected. He knew how to make his presence felt. Gareth could alarm or intimidate or amaze at will. He was adept at the extravagant, very calculated gesture when it suited him.

In spite of the chill in the air, Clare's palms grew damp on the palfrey's reins. She met Gareth's solemn, watchful gaze and prayed that she had done the right thing when she had chosen him as lord of Desire. Her future and the future of her people hung in the balance.

Gareth did not take his eyes off her as she rode forward to meet him. When she brought the palfrey to a halt, he dismounted and walked toward her.

His massive hands were strong and sure around her waist as he lifted Clare down from the saddle. Without a word he led her to the church door, where the priest waited.

Clare took a deep breath and prepared to say the vows that would forever link her fortunes and the fortunes of Desire with those of the Hellhound.

An hour later, in front of the large crowd that had assembled in the great hall, Ulrich opened a massive chest. He lifted out the contents with an air of solemn ceremony. A shimmering rainbow of silks spilled from his hands.

The throng gasped appreciatively.

"My lord's gifts to his esteemed bride," Ulrich announced in ringing tones.

One by one he held aloft long, lustrous lengths of rich fabric from the East. Bolts of crimson silk shot through with gold and silver threads were unwrapped and displayed. Lengths of green silk as dark in hue as precious emeralds appeared. Yellows and oranges the shade of brilliant sunsets streamed forth from the chest. The variety and colors of the exquisite materials seemed unending.

The villagers roundly cheered their approval as they inspected the Hellhound's costly bride gifts.

Everyone was duly impressed. The oohs and aahs cascaded through the hall. Neighbor murmured to neighbor in tones of deep satisfaction. It was clear to one and all that their lady had chosen a wealthy lord.

And apparently a generous one.

The silks were followed by casks of valuable spices. Saffron, cloves, nutmeg, cinnamon, ginger, cumin, and pepper were presented. Again the crowd roared its appreciation of the respect their new lord was showing to their beloved lady.

Clare listened to the comments of her people. They were well pleased. The villagers knew that their lord's wealth reflected directly on the entire Isle of Desire. The inhabitants would be bathed in the glow of his prestige and power.

On a more practical level, Gareth's personal wealth was insurance that people would continue to prosper under his governance.

"A bastard born, yet he has won great riches for himself by his own hand," John Blacksmith said to a farmer. "'Tis a good sign."

"Aye." The farmer bobbed his head sagely. "He'll take good care of these lands. Lady Clare chose well."

John chuckled. "'Tis not clear who did the choosing. If you ask me, Lord Gareth took a hand in making her decision for her."

Clare wrinkled her nose, but she gave no other indication that she had overheard the remark. She was not entirely certain she could refute it.

When Gareth's gifts to his bride had all been properly displayed and suitably admired, yet another chest was brought forward. New murmurs of excitement rippled through the crowd. When the second chest was opened, a great pile of coins was revealed.

The cries of wonder turned to whoops of delight when it became clear that the coins were to be handed out to the villagers.

"Your husband, it would seem, does not come to this marriage a pauper," Prioress Margaret observed quietly. She stood next to Clare and watched as Gareth's men handed out a coin to everyone in the manor.

"Aye, he brings the wealth he earned as the Hellhound of Wyckmere," Clare said. "And he does not mind displaying it, does he?"

"A great lord must display his wealth and power. How else will people know of it?"

Clare sighed. "He had money enough before he married me. But he did not have lands."

"Now he has those, too." Margaret looked at her. "Are you content with this marriage, my daughter?"

"'Tis done," Clare said quietly. "There is no point in debating the matter now."

"'Tis not quite done. There is still the business of your wedding night."

"As to that, I assure you I have everything in hand."

Margaret cleared her throat. "There is gossip that you lost your temper with your new lord yesterday morn and threatened to deny him his husbandly privileges tonight."

"'Twas a foolish challenge," Clare said distantly. "He made me very angry and I made certain statements which I have since withdrawn."

"I am pleased to hear that. You are a woman of strong passions. You do not always govern your emotions as well as you govern your lands. Now that you are a married woman, you must exert more control over yourself."

"Aye, my lady." She could do without an admonishing speech on the importance of self-mastery today, Clare thought glumly. She had enough weighing on her mind as it was.

"You must guard your temper whenever you are in your husband's presence," Margaret continued. "'Tis obvious that Sir Gareth is not a man who will tolerate defiance in his wife."

"I have already heard this lecture. Why is it that everyone else seems to think she knows more about managing Lord Gareth than I do?"

"Mayhap because the rest of us are older and wiser. Heed me, my child. If you would manage your lord, you must do so with a gentle tongue and a woman's clever ways."

"Very well, madam. I shall heed your advice. You need not alarm yourself about my safety tonight. When the time comes, I shall welcome my lord into my bedchamber."

Margaret smiled complacently. "Marriage is difficult enough without starting it off by offending your lord on your wedding night. And since we are speaking of making a good beginning, I may as well give you this now before I forget."

Clare glanced down as Margaret removed a small, carefully wrapped bundle from a pouch that hung from the girdle of her habit. "A gift, madam? How kind of you. What is it?"

"A small vial of chicken blood."

Clare choked back laughter. "I vow, I am going to be awash in the stuff."

"What do you mean?"

"You are not the first one to give me such a thoughtful gift." Clare stuffed the small packet into the little woven pouch on her own girdle. "I thank you, madam. I shall add it to my collection."

"Keep one of the vials close by tonight. Sprinkle a bit on the sheets before your lord awakes and all will be well."

"What would you say, madam, if I were to tell you that such a precaution is unnecessary?"

"As to that, I make no comment," Margaret said briskly. "You are a woman, not a young girl. You have carried out a woman's duties and responsibilities here on this manor since you were twelve years old. I am well aware of your feelings for Raymond de Coleville and as far as I am concerned, whatever transpired between the two of you is your affair."

"Thank you," Clare said. "But in truth, Raymond was a most chivalrous knight. He and I—"

Margaret held up a hand to stop the tale. "As I said, the matter of your virginity is your business and yours alone. But husbands, especially knights as proud as Sir Gareth, seldom see such matters in that light."

"I disagree. I think they are quite capable of overlooking such small details when a woman's dowry is sufficiently large."

"Heed me well, my daughter. Men, even the more intelligent among them, as I believe Lord Gareth to be, are fundamentally simple creatures."

"So?"

"So, as long as they believe honor is satisfied, they are inclined to be generous and chivalrous, especially to a new bride. I would have you give your husband the gift that will content him most on his wedding night so that you, in turn, will find contentment in your marriage on the morrow."

Clare patted the new vial of blood that was safely stored in her girdle purse. "I must remember to say a prayer for all those noble chickens that have died for my honor this day."

"You'll be eating some of them at the banquet."

The feasting began shortly before noon and carried on without pause throughout the afternoon and long into the night. Everyone on the isle was invited, from the poorest laborer to the plumpest farmer. Even the nuns of Saint Hermione's partook of the extravagant array of food and ale along with everyone else.

Although she had given orders to spare no expense, Clare was impressed, in spite of herself, with what Eadgar and the household servants had accomplished in such a short period of time. Elaborate preserves of turnips and carrots flavored with mustard seed were sent to the tables. Stuffed ducks, fragrant pottages, broiled fish, and honeyed chicken and pork tarts were carried to the hall in a constant stream from the kitchens.

The celebration took on the boisterous mood of a fair. Children played games in the courtyard. Men told ribald jokes. Dallan entertained everyone with his tabor, flute, and harp. William helped himself to a bite from every serving plate in sight.

The ominous fog which gripped the isle was forgotten as the river of ale and wine took effect. The main hall was crammed with people who drank toast after toast to the bride and groom at the head table.

Out in the courtyard tables had been set up to feed those who could not be squeezed inside the hall. Braziers warded off the chill in the air.

As the night deepened, the fire in the central hall threw a warm, golden glow over the raucous scene. Although she was seated next to him, the noise and merriment made it nearly impossible for Clare to engage in conversation with her new husband. She was, however, intensely aware of his gaze sliding intimately over her from time to time.

The water clock at the far end of the hall had just marked the hour before midnight when Joanna caught Clare's eye. It was time to go upstairs to the bridal chamber.

For no apparent reason, Clare's fingers suddenly trembled as she gripped her goblet. She put her unfinished wine down very slowly and looked at Gareth.

He leaned toward her so that she would be able to hear him. "I comprehend that it is time for my bride to leave the hall?"

"Aye, so it would seem." Clare did not care for the inexplicable attack of unease that had just assailed her. There was nothing to fear tonight, she reminded herself, no reason to shiver in anticipation or dread. Nothing at all was going to happen. She had made her position clear to Gareth yesterday. He had not argued or raised an objection.

They had an understanding. They would become friends before they became lovers.

Lovers. The word sang in Clare's head. She recalled the one kiss Gareth had given her and grew warm all over.

Gareth rose to his feet. The laughter and the loud conversation ceased abruptly. A hush claimed the crowd as all eyes turned toward the head table.

Clare knew that everyone in the hall was waiting to see what would happen next. It was time for her to carry out her end of the bargain that she had struck with Gareth. She must go to the bridal chamber with the air of a willing, welcoming bride.

Gareth lifted his silver goblet and looked down at Clare. His gaze was brilliant and intent. Clare swallowed. Her smile felt shaky.

Friends first. Then lovers.

She could trust the Hellhound, she told herself. He would keep his end of the bargain.

"I drink a toast to my fair and lovely bride," Gareth said into the taut silence. He took a deep sip from the goblet.

Cheers rang through the hall. The boisterous crowd pounded tankards on the tables.

Gareth set his goblet down and drew the Window of Hell from its scabbard. The steel flashed in the firelight as he held the blade aloft just as he had the day of his arrival. A murmur of excitement rippled through the hall.

"I am a fortunate man, for I have wed a most gracious lady." Gareth's voice carried to the farthest corner of the large chamber.

A shout of agreement went up from the audience. Clare smiled wryly. The Hellhound really was very good at making the grand gesture.

"Hear me, good people of Desire," Gareth said. "Listen well, for I would have all those present here tonight witness that I give this sword, which had never been stained with dishonor, once more into the hands of my lady. This I do as a symbol of regard for her. She is now my wife. She holds my honor in her hands even as she holds my sword."

"*Aye, aye.*"

Another round of enthusiastic shouts and yells echoed from the stone walls, the revelers slamming tankards and knife butts against the tables.

Gareth reversed the blade and presented the sword, hilt first, to Clare. "Know that I am well pleased in my wife."

The thundering yells of approval made it impossible for Clare to say a word. She did not know if she would have been able to speak had the hall been empty.

For some reason, Gareth's extravagantly chivalrous gesture, though she knew it to be carefully calculated for the effect it would have on the crowd, brought tears to her eyes.

She took the heavy, crystal-pommeled sword from his hand and rose to her feet.

Once more the hall fell silent in anticipation. Clare drew a deep breath and prepared to make a formal gesture of her own.

She nodded at William, who immediately came forward down the aisle between a row of trestle tables. He carried a large bunch of dried flowers and herbs.

"My lord," Clare said, "in exchange for the honor and strength that you bring to us this day, I give into your safekeeping the source of the prosperity of our fair isle."

William went down on one knee and handed the fragrant sheaf of dried lavender, rosemary, roses, and mugwort to Clare. She took it from his hand and gave the ribbon-tied bundle to Gareth.

Gareth looked down at the sheaf of flowers and herbs that were symbolic of the perfumed isle. When he raised his eyes, Clare was stunned by the fierceness of his gaze.

"I will guard this isle, its people, and its lady with more care than I would use to guard my own life," Gareth said so that all could hear.

Clare saw the unwavering promise in his strong face. She knew that he meant every word. Their personal relationship was far from settled, but she could be certain that her isle was in good hands.

She smiled tremulously. "I have chosen well."

"I would have you believe so."

Clare could hardly breathe. For a moment it was as if she and Gareth were alone in the hall. She could feel the unbreakable, invisible cords that now bound them together.

Friends first, Clare reminded herself. It was far too soon for her and Gareth to become lovers.

Much too soon.

They barely knew each other.

Joanna rose from her place at the table and hurried toward Clare. The movement freed Clare of the spell that had settled on her. It was time to leave the hall.

Aware of the growing curiosity and expectation of the throng, Clare gripped the heavy sword and looked at Gareth.

"I go now to prepare to welcome my husband to the bridal chamber," Clare said very distinctly.

The crowd cheered and tankards were raised.

Gareth raised his goblet once more. "I pray you will not delay a moment longer, my lady. As a gardener, you know well that some herbs are most potent when they are shriveled and dried. There are others, however, which are best used when the stalk is strong and fully erect. 'Tis the latter variety that I shall bring to you tonight."

Laughter shook the hall.

Clare's eyes widened as the meaning of his words sank home. "For a man who claims that he does not jest, my lord, you have an unusual turn of phrase," she muttered.

"Aye, well, a wedding is an unusual event, madam."

Joanna seized her arm. "Come. We must hurry." She tugged impatiently.

Clare sent Gareth a speaking look as she was led away.

"Have a care with my sword," Gareth called after her. "It is the only one I have."

More shouts of laughter rang through the chamber.

"I vow, I shall find some good use for it." Clare clutched the blade hilt very tightly as Joanna drew her toward the staircase. "'Twill make an excellent stake from which to string pea vines in my garden."

Shouts of encouragement accompanied Clare and Joanna as they picked up their skirts and hurried toward the tower stairs.

"Take this," Joanna whispered to Clare as they went down the hall. "Hide it about your person. Do not let Lord Gareth or anyone else see it."

Clare's fingers closed around yet another small object. "Let me hazard a guess. Chicken blood?"

"Aye. Sprinkle some on the sheets before morning and all will be well."

Several other women appeared in the hall. Giggling and laughing, they all crowded into the bedchamber to prepare the bride.

Within a few minutes Clare's gown had been stripped from her. A beautifully embroidered night robe of fine soft linen was dropped over her head and she was tucked into the sweet-smelling bed.

"There, now, ye look lovely," Eunice said as she ran a comb through Clare's unbound hair. She leaned close and lowered her voice. "Don't be forgetting the chicken blood."

"Believe me, I am unlikely to forget it."

Joanna went to the door and put her ear to the wood. "I can hear Lord Gareth and his men on the stairs."

"Grooms is always an impatient lot." Agnes elbowed her way to the side of the bed. "As yer old nurse, 'tis my right to say good night to the maid I helped raise. On the morrow, I'll greet the woman who rises from this bed."

"Hurry," Joanna said. "They're almost here."

Masculine voices and roars of mirth could be heard echoing down the corridor. The serving girls quickly poured wine into two goblets that stood on a table near the fire. Eunice dabbed a tear from her eye and smiled benignly.

Everyone's attention was on the door, waiting for it to open. Agnes leaned over the bed.

"Here, now, take this, m'lady." She pressed a small object into Clare's hand.

With a sense of resignation, Clare glanced down at yet another small vial. "Thank you, Agnes. You cannot know how much your thoughtfulness means to me."

"Hush." Agnes cast a quick look about to make certain no one had overheard. "Be sure to dab a few drops on the sheets ere morning and all will be well."

"But, Agnes—"

"'Tis just a useful precaution." Agnes fussed with the bedding. "When you've lived as long as I have, ye learn it pays to help nature along now and again. Especially when a man's honor is involved."

The door crashed open before Clare could argue.

Ulrich and the other men thrust Gareth into the chamber. The serving maids shrieked.

"Here's your new lord, my lady." Ulrich swept a deep, mocking bow toward Clare. When he raised his head, he wore a distinctly lecherous grin.

"He has come here tonight to practice with his sword. I trust you'll see to it that he gets a good deal of exercise with it. We would not want the Hellhound of Wyckmere to grow soft."

The men succumbed once more to uproarious laughter. Joanna and the other women shooed them back out of the chamber.

It took a minute or two to clear the room, but at last the door was firmly closed.

Clare and Gareth were alone at last.

Clare held the white linen sheets very tightly to her breast as she met Gareth's eyes.

He looked at her as she lay back against the scented linen pillows. The air of possessiveness in his eyes stole Clare's voice.

Gareth finally broke the short, taut silence. He glanced around the chamber with an inquiring expression. "My sword?"

"Over there." Clare moistened her lips with the tip of her tongue. "On the window seat."

"Ah, yes. Safe and sound." Gareth did not go to the window seat to collect his blade.

Instead, he crossed the chamber to where a small table stood in front of the fire. He picked up the goblets full of wine and turned toward the bed.

Clare realized that she was clutching the sheets with such force that her knuckles were white. She made herself unclench her fingers one by one and then searched frantically for something appropriately casual to say.

This was not a real wedding night, after all.

"Well, I'm certainly glad that business is over and done." Clare shoved aside the bedding and fairly leaped out of the massive, four-posted bed.

Gareth watched impassively as she grabbed a chamber robe and flung it quickly around her shoulders. Holding the garment closed at her throat with one hand, she summoned up what she hoped was a comradely smile. "I suppose weddings are always troublesome affairs, are they not, my lord?"

"I wouldn't know." Gareth watched her intently as he offered her one of the goblets. "I have never been married before."

Clare blushed. "No, of course not. I did not mean to imply that you had." She snatched the wine from his hand and took a healthy swallow. She'd had almost nothing to eat or drink all day. For some reason she'd been too tense to partake of the feast. "I vow, I do not understand why I am feeling so odd tonight. I wonder if I am ill."

"Mayhap you are feeling some of the same things that I am feeling tonight." Gareth took a sip of his own wine. Then he removed Clare's goblet from her fingers. He set both small vessels down on the table.

"My lord?" Clare realized that her voice had risen to a small squeak. "Are you feeling unsettled, also?"

"Aye."

"Mayhap we both could use a draught of camomile and mint tea," she suggested helpfully. "'Tis excellent for an uneasy stomach. I shall summon one of the servants."

"Nay, I know of a far better cure."

Gareth pulled her gently but relentlessly into his arms. When she stood shivering against him, still clutching the chamber robe as if it were a talisman, he claimed her mouth with his own.

Gareth felt Clare's undisguised shiver of surprise; a flash of confusion washed through her, causing her to tremble in his arms. He kept his mouth pressed against hers, willing her to respond the way she had the last time he kissed her.

He knew she wanted him. He had sensed the passion in her that first afternoon. All he had to do was get past the logical defenses she had erected.

Relief soared in him when he heard her tiny, half-strangled gasp of excitement.

She would be a true wife to him. The bastard of Wyckmere had got himself a bride.

And a future.

Her mouth was hesitant at first and then her lips softened deliciously beneath his own. Gareth knew for certain that he had guessed correctly. He had not misread the feminine curiosity in her eyes, nor had he misjudged the significance of her trembling fingers.

The good fortune that had kept him alive during his years as a hunter of outlaws had followed him into his new life as a farmer of flowers. He had gained far more from this match than he had dared to hope.

Clare made a small sound of anticipation. Her fingers clutched at his shoulders. Gareth groaned. He had been enduring the torments of a half-aroused body all day. Now he was fully erect, eager for what awaited him. The time had come to claim his wife.

Gareth felt Clare shudder and press herself against him. An urge to laugh nearly overwhelmed him. He fought it back. This was not the time to succumb to mirth. Still, he reveled in the moment. It was obvious that all Clare's foolish talk of waiting until their acquaintanceship had deepened into friendship was simply that: foolish.

Clare was as eager to taste the pleasure of the marriage bed as he was.

Gareth was relieved and exultant. Now another battle lay ahead of him. But he was accustomed to fighting for what he wanted. And he most definitely wanted Clare.

He recognized that Clare's disgust for Nicholas of Seabern was genuine. He still was not certain what to believe about her past experience of lovemaking. But Clare's sweetly eager mouth told him that whatever had happened between her and Nicholas, it had not given her a distaste for the business.

Mayhap it was Raymond de Coleville who had taught her how much mutual pleasure a man and a woman could find together.

Whichever man had been responsible, Gareth was not particularly grateful to him.

"My lord." Clare's voice was a breathless sigh against Gareth's lips. She was warm and soft against his chest. Her arms wound slowly around his neck. "No doubt we should not kiss in this manner yet, but I vow, I cannot seem to stop."

Her confession sent Gareth's blood pounding through his veins. The heavy beat was a distant echo of his war-horse's hoofbeats. His whole body reacted violently to the promise of Clare's gentle surrender.

The lady was ready and willing, not an anxious, innocent maid who had to be led slowly into bed.

"Be assured that I have no intention of halting these kisses yet." Gareth stroked the edge of her mouth with the pads of his thumbs. Her lips trembled and parted. Her cheeks, flushed and glowing, were warm to the touch. Her eyes were fathomless emeralds that held the secrets of a woman's passion waiting to be unleashed.

If it wasn't Nicholas who had taught Clare the arts of love, Gareth thought, then it had most likely been Raymond de Coleville, her much-vaunted pattern of chivalry. *Damn his soul.*

Which one had it been? he wondered.

Or had she taken two lovers?

In that moment Gareth could cheerfully have given each of his unknown rivals a view of the Window of Hell.

Having made the acquaintance of Nicholas, Gareth concluded that it was the mysterious Raymond de Coleville who worried him the most.

Yet another challenge for the Hellhound of Wyckmere to conquer, he told himself. He had never been one to back down from a challenge.

He deepened the kiss, knowing that he had no right to resent the fact that Clare had lain in the arms of another man. He was no virgin, either, Gareth thought. And he was a bastard into the bargain: no great prize for any lady of her station.

Clare was a healthy young woman of three and twenty years who had been on her own and burdened with the responsibilities of managing the manor for much of her life.

She was also a very curious and obviously intelligent woman who had never planned to wed. Such a woman would not have been averse to tasting the forbidden fruit when the opportunity presented itself in the guise of a handsome young knight.

Gareth knew he was swiftly driving himself mad. It struck him that he had never before known the knife-sharp pangs of raw jealousy.

Jealousy?

The realization brought him back to his senses.

He tore his mouth from Clare's and framed her face between his hands. Her eyes were luminous and full of wonder as she looked up at him.

"What's done is done," Gareth muttered.

"I do not understand, my lord."

"It matters not. From this night forward, you are mine. You are my lady wife, the future mother of my children. I vow, I will make you forget Nicholas and Raymond de Coleville and any other man who has come before me."

Her brows drew together in a quizzical expression. "But why would I wish to forget Nicholas and Raymond? One is a neighbor and the other was a friend."

"Enough. Do not speak of either of them again tonight." Gareth ensured her silence with another kiss.

She mumbled something unintelligible which sounded very much like a protest, or at the very least an attempt to start a spirited argument. Gareth did not want to listen. He eased her lips apart and sank his tongue into her mouth.

Clare made another odd, somewhat strangled sound. Then she tightened her arms around his neck and touched her tongue to his.

Gareth sucked in a savage breath, swept her up into his arms, and tumbled her onto the bed. The hunger to be inside her nearly consumed him.

He lowered himself heavily down onto the white linen sheets and reached for Clare.

"*My lord.*"

"Hush." He flung one leg over her thighs. Conscious of his great weight and her much smaller size, he braced himself on his arms as he leaned over her. "We will discuss the matter later. Right now I only want to kiss you."

"Oh." The frowning uncertainty vanished from her eyes. She touched his cheek with her fingertip. "Well, I suppose there is no great harm in mere kissing, is there?"

"None. And even if there were, I doubt the knowing would stop me tonight."

He gazed, enthralled, at the sight of her dark hair flowing across the herb-laced pillows. Slowly he fisted one hand in it and looped the silken skein around his fingers. He brought the stuff to his nose and inhaled deeply. "You smell of flowers, just like everything else on the isle."

"I expect that you'll grow accustomed to it, my lord."

"Aye." He bent his head to nibble at the elegant line of her throat. "I expect I will."

He eased aside the edge of her chamber robe and listened with deep pleasure to her quickly indrawn breath. He moved his mouth downward to the swell of her breast, which was partially revealed by her white linen night robe.

"My lord—"

"My name is Gareth." She was so amazingly soft. Her skin was finer than the costly silks he had given her as a wedding gift.

"Gareth." She sounded breathless. "You said you only wished to kiss me."

"Aye. Everywhere." The pure, perfect curve of her small breast was the most alluring sight Gareth had ever seen in his life. He ached to see the nipple that was still concealed beneath the daintily embroidered neckline of her gown. The outline of the small, ripe bud was plain. He stroked one finger across it, delighting in its shape.

"*Gareth.*" Clare froze at the caress. She stared up at him, wide-eyed. Her hands gripped his shoulders as if she would push him away. "Sir, I do not think this is a sound notion. You said there was no harm in kisses and I agreed. But this is too much."

"You want kisses, my lady?" He deftly unfastened the laces at the front of the robe. "Kisses you shall have. A hundred of them. A thousand."

"*Gareth.*" She batted ineffectually at his big hands. "I do not think—"

"Aye, madam. Do not try to think. Not tonight. The devil knows well that I certainly cannot."

Her rosy nipples looked even more enticing than he had imagined, and his imagination was very powerful. The crowns that graced Clare's breasts were puckered and firm and full of promise. Gareth put his mouth to one and sucked it gently between his teeth.

Clare's reaction was a small shriek. Her fingers dug into his shoulders. "By Saint Hermion's elbow, my lord. You call this kissing?"

"Aye. Although 'tis more like drinking nectar made of honey and almonds."

"Are you—" Clare seemed to have difficulty getting the words out. She clutched at him. "Are you speaking the truth, sir?"

"The absolute truth."

Gareth wondered if Raymond de Coleville had not bothered to sample Clare's breasts when he'd helped himself to the other delectable dishes she'd offered. It occurred to him then that his rivals had no doubt been obliged to work in haste when they had gone about the business of seducing Clare.

Nicholas had been bent on forcing a marriage.

Raymond's undertaking had been a more perilous affair. He had no doubt been well aware at the time that he had no intention of offering marriage. Mayhap the need for secrecy and haste had made him careless and clumsy.

Gareth kissed the valley between Clare's breasts and decided there was a great advantage to being a husband. A man had all the time in the world to seduce his wife in the privacy of the marriage bed.

Gareth trained his kisses lower, easing apart the night robe as he traveled slowly toward his goal. The scent of Clare's womanly arousal, far more intoxicating than the rose and lavender of her perfume, drew him now. She was responding to him and the knowledge sent another wave of desire crashing through him.

"Sir. My lord. *Gareth.*" Clare squeezed her eyes shut and arched up off the bed. "You must not kiss me anymore. I fear my senses are as scattered as bees in the wind."

"As are mine." Gareth raised his head to look down into her flushed face. He watched her closely as he slid his hand beneath the hem of her shift.

Her eyes flew open. She shook her head once in a gesture that could have meant anything. "Please."

"Aye. I shall do my best to please you. You will forget both of them long before dawn." He leaned down and took her mouth as he moved his hand along the inside of her thigh.

"Forget who? I . . . oh, Gareth, I do not think this is wise. I am concerned for you, my lord."

He had no notion of what she was talking about and was not inclined to ask. Gareth had other things on his mind at the moment. His hand closed over the warm, damp flesh between her thighs.

Clare went rigid beneath his touch. She shut her eyes again and appeared to stop breathing for a few tense seconds. Her short nails were clenched so deeply into his shoulders he knew he would find marks there in the morning. The thought pleased him.

Gareth probed gently, slowly, tenderly. He parted soft, honeyed flesh as if he were parting the leaves of a lush and fragile flower until he discovered the hidden treasure he sought. Clare moaned when he stroked the gem with fingers that had been moistened in her own dew.

He went to work with great care, circling, teasing, tugging, and pressing.

Clare was obviously incapable of further protest. Gareth knew that she was now helplessly lost in the pleasure he gave her. She shivered and twisted and clung. The realization that she was responding to his touch with such passion gave him more satisfaction than anything he had ever known.

She was so caught up in the sensual spell he had woven that she did not even notice when he lowered his head once more to kiss the taut little bud that he had coaxed into full arousal.

He knew the precise instant when she did become aware of what was happening to her.

She convulsed as though she had been struck by lightning.

Gareth vowed that he could see the sparks.

Her lips parted on a high, shocked screech of amazement. The cry of feminine discovery and boundless wonder was choked off almost as soon as it had begun, but it verified what Gareth had begun to suspect. Whatever Clare had experienced at the hands of her previous lovers, she had not learned the pleasures of her own release.

Her response was more than he had dared hope to inspire. She trembled in the throes of it. And so did Gareth. She lifted herself, opened herself, offered herself to him. She was a mystical, magical creature who enthralled his senses. He was literally fascinated by her swiftly approaching release.

She shivered like a blossom in the wind.

Gareth very nearly spilled his seed as the hot satisfaction roared through him. By tomorrow morning, both Nicholas and Raymond de Coleville would be distant dull memories for Clare.

"Gareth, *Gareth*." Clare gulped air. "What have you done to me? *What have you done?*"

"Nothing that cannot be repeated many, many times before dawn."

He waited until she went limp. When the last tiny shiver had ended, Gareth eased himself up the length of Clare's boneless body until he was once more braced on his elbows.

He looked down into her stunned face.

He smiled.

She stared up at him, apparently silenced at last by the enormity of what she had experienced. The play of emotions in her eyes was entrancing.

Confusion, wonder, amazed delight, curiosity, and feminine speculation all blended together to render her mute.

It was the first time that Gareth had ever seen her bereft of speech.

His smile turned into a knowing grin.

Gareth would have laughed in that moment if he had not been so uncomfortable. He was as hard and unyielding as the steel of the Window of Hell, but he was not nearly so cold as his blade. Just the opposite, Gareth thought. He was on fire and there was only one way to quench the flames that burned in his loins this night.

He sat up with his back to Clare and began to strip off his clothing. He was ruefully aware that his hands were shaking with the force of his need as he unbuckled his belt. He tossed the heavy leather strap aside.

"Did you . . . did you feel the same things I felt?" Clare asked. She sounded weak and breathless.

"Not yet. On my oath, it was a near thing, but I managed to keep from disgracing myself on your fine white sheets. Be assured that I have saved myself for you, madam."

Gareth pulled off his outer tunic and hurled it in the same general direction as his belt.

"You mean that you have not yet experienced these strange feelings?"

He hooked one ankle over his knee and jerked off a leather boot. "Have no fear, madam, you'll be well aware of my release when I sheath myself in your silken scabbard." His mouth quirked upward at one corner again. "Unless, of course, you're too preoccupied with your own pleasure at that particular moment to notice."

Clare sat up abruptly. "By Hermione's sainted slipper, this marriage business is far more confusing than I had thought it would be."

"We shall reason it out together."

"But this is impossible."

"Hell's teeth." Gareth's hand stilled on his other boot. He turned his head to stare at Clare. "What are you talking about?"

"I had no notion that you would be able to make me feel such powerful emotions." Clare pushed her hair out of her eyes and gazed at him anxiously. "Or that you would be faced with such temptation yourself, my lord."

"Clare, I don't know what kind of lovers Nicholas and de Coleville were, but I can promise you that I—"

"Raymond de Coleville was never my lover." Clare clutched at the edges of her unlaced robe and scrambled to her knees amid the rumpled sheets. Her eyes flashed. "Nor was Nicholas of Seabern, although no one seems to believe me. I vow, I have had my fill of everyone assuming that I am no virgin."

Gareth reached out to touch her hand. "Calm yourself, Clare. There is no need to protest your innocence to me. It doesn't matter."

"You're right." She scowled. "You will not hear any more argument on the subject from me, my lord."

"So be it. I am pleased to learn that."

"In truth, the status of my virginity is neither here nor there."

"Aye. What's done is done."

"And when all is said and done," she said a little too sweetly, "I have no doubt but that I come to this bed at least as pure and untouched as yourself."

Gareth grimaced. "No doubt."

"Surely no man can ask more than that of a bride."

Gareth was stunned to feel the sudden heat in his face. Belatedly he wondered if she was teasing him. He glared at her. "Mayhap we should change the subject, madam."

"Aye, you are right, sir." Her expression softened. She put out a hand and lightly touched his arm. "In all fairness, our mutual virginity, or lack of it, is not the problem at the moment, is it?"

"Nay." Gareth was unable to think of anything else to say. He did not want to talk about anything at all. He simply wanted to make love to his wife. Was that too much to ask? he wondered glumly.

"The important thing," Clare continued crisply, "is that I have just learned how powerful physical desire truly is when it is wielded by a man of your nature, sir."

Gareth eyed her cautiously. "My nature?"

"'Tis obvious you are a man of great passions."

"'Tis obvious you are a woman who incites great passions, madam."

"I am well aware that I have a responsibility in this matter," she assured him.

"Excellent. We have that much established, then." He dropped his second boot on the floor and rose to remove his undertunic.

Clare frowned in thought. "'Tis plain that we must take care to control this extremely volatile force before it assumes complete command of you, my lord."

Gareth had his tunic half over his head. He stopped, hesitated for the count of three, and slowly released his grip on the garment. The gray gown fell back down over his body.

"What did you say?" he asked very softly.

Her expression of grave concern deepened. "I said that we must exercise extreme caution if we are to protect you, my lord."

"Protect me from what?" he roared, now out of patience.

Her eyes widened, but she appeared startled rather than afraid. "You're shouting."

"Nay, madam," he said through his teeth. "Not yet. But soon, mayhap. Very soon."

She sighed. " 'Tis simply more evidence, of course."

"Evidence of what?"

"The strength of your passions." She smiled with gentle understanding. " 'Tis clear that because of your warm nature, you are on the verge of forgetting our understanding."

"I am?"

"Aye. As your wife and for the sake of our growing friendship, I must help you resist this great temptation. After all, your honor is at stake."

Gareth wondered if he had lost count of how many cups of wine he had downed during the long banquet. He never allowed himself to get drunk. Indeed, he did not feel drunk, he thought, but his wits were beginning to reel.

"Are you trying to tell me that making love to you tonight will somehow put my honor in jeopardy?" he asked very carefully.

"I know how much it would distress you to awake in the morning knowing that you had allowed passion to seize you in its clutches and caused you to forget our understanding."

"By the fires of hell, madam, I do not believe what I am hearing. Forget that damned understanding. We did not have one."

She stared at him. "But we did, sir. We agreed that we would become friends before we consummated this marriage."

"No, we did not agree to that." He spaced each word out with great care. "You announced your foolish intention. But you never asked for my agreement. And by the devil, I never gave it."

"Surely you can see that if we succumb to passion tonight it will ruin our chances of creating a marriage based on friendship and trust."

Gareth grabbed at the reins of his temper and held on to them with all of his strength. "This is the most crazed thing I have ever heard."

"You did not say that yesterday."

"Rest assured I was thinking it."

She looked stricken. "Do you not want trust and friendship to grow between us?"

"They will both come with time." He groped for a way to turn her logic in a new direction. "Do you trust me, Clare?"

"Aye." She sighed. "But you do not trust me."

"That is not true."

"You think that I have allowed other men to make love to me, even though I have told you that I have never lain with any other man."

"I have also told you that your virginity or lack of it does not matter to me. I am not concerned with the past. Only the future."

"I'm sure that is very gallant of you, sir, but we cannot have a satisfactory future together unless that future be built upon a foundation of trust." She fixed him with an unhappy gaze. "And you do not trust me. Admit it. You think I have lied to you."

"Devil take it, madam, your virginity is your own business."

"I appreciate your enlightened attitude on the subject. But that is not really the issue, is it?"

He speared his fingers through his hair. "I feel as though I am sinking into a marsh."

"Sir, I am convinced that we must both learn to trust each other if we are to be mutually content in our marriage."

He saw the pride and the hurt in her eyes and in that moment he suddenly knew that she was telling him the truth. No other man had touched her. He had been a fool to believe otherwise. Clare would never lie to him about such a thing.

Clare was too proud, too spirited, too bold to lie about anything.

Satisfaction rushed through him. He had no right to be so fortunate, he told himself, but he was not one to protest against the happy fate that had given him an untouched wife.

He smiled slowly. "I believe you when you say that no other man has made love to you."

She gazed at him, uncertain and wary. "'Tis the passion talking now, my lord. The lure of it is making you say what you think I want to hear."

He shook his head, still smiling. He recalled her untutored response to his intimate kisses. "Nay. I want you very much, but I am not such a weakling that I am a complete slave to passion. It does not have the power to make me lie. I believe you when you tell me that you are untouched, Clare."

Clare twisted her hands in her lap. "I wish I could be certain of that."

"You can be certain of it. You must learn to trust me as much as I trust you."

"Aye." She looked doubtful.

"You do trust me, do you not?"

"I think so."

"You *think* so?" He was suddenly incensed. "Clare a moment ago you said you did trust me."

"It is all too confusing to sort out tonight, my lord." She smiled apologetically. "I feel it would be best if we carried out my original plan."

"Original plan?"

"Aye. We will not consummate this marriage until we both feel confident that we enjoy each other's full and unwavering trust."

Gareth closed his eyes briefly. "God give me strength, madam."

"I'm sure he will, Gareth." Clare gave him a winning smile. "And in the meantime there is a pallet under the bed for you to use tonight."

He watched, dumbfounded, as she scurried to the edge of the bed, leaned down, and scrabbled around to pull out a sleeping pallet. "What in hell's name do you think you're doing?"

She looked up through the long swath of hair that was falling forward over her face. "Getting the pallet out for you."

He set his jaw. "I will sleep in the damned bed with you, wife."

She blinked and sat up slowly. "You're angry."

"Angry? Why should I be angry?" Gareth asked very softly. He swung around and strode over to the window seat.

"Gareth?"

He grasped the Window of Hell and stalked back to the bed.

"My lord." Clare stared at the sword in his hand. Her hand went to her throat.

Gareth raised the sword on high and then slammed the flat of the blade down onto the bed. Directly in the middle.

Clare gave a visible start. Then she turned her head warily to gaze down at the blade. It gleamed in the firelight, effectively dividing the massive bed into two portions.

"If this is how you wish to begin our married life," Gareth said through his teeth, "so be it. The Window of Hell shall share this bed with us tonight. It will protect you from my touch."

"I really do not think it's necessary to put your sword between us," Clare whispered.

"Have no fear, madam, you will sleep safe enough on your side of the bed. I shall occupy the other half."

"But the pallet—"

"I am not sleeping on the damned pallet. I have a right to my half of our bed, madam."

"I suppose that I could take the pallet."

"Nay. You will share the bed with me, lady. You desire proof of my self-mastery? Very well, you shall have it. Kindly let me know in the morning if you feel you can trust me."

Clare bit her lip but said nothing.

Gareth ignored her as he jerked off the remainder of his clothing and tossed it aside. He heard her small, choked exclamation when she caught sight of his still-aroused body. He pretended to ignore it, but he knew that if he had not already decided that she was innocent, her stunned gaze would have told him the truth.

He was going to pay a high price for his bad judgment and worse management of the situation. And he had no one but himself to blame.

Gareth crossed the chamber in three strides to tend to the fire. Then he went back across the room and yanked the bed curtains closed. He slid into bed beside Clare.

The Window of Hell lay between them, a steel barrier to passion.

It was very dark. The curtains blocked the glow of the dying embers. Gareth folded his arms behind his head and gazed up into the shadows. His loins ached. He was furious with himself.

It was going to be a very long night.

"Gareth?" Clare's voice was very soft and tinged with anxiety.

"Aye?"

"It just occurred to me that a portion of Beatrice's prediction came true."

"What prediction?"

"She said that you would draw your sword in the bridal chamber. And you did."

"Considering my luck of late, 'tis a wonder I did not trip on it and accidentally slit my own throat."

9

Clare awoke shortly before dawn, awash with regret.

She realized that she was alone in the big bed. She could not escape the overwhelming conviction that she had blundered very badly during the night.

She wondered if she had destroyed whatever chance she'd had for a warm and loving friendship with her husband.

Loving.

That was what she wanted, Clare realized. She wanted to love and be loved. She had convinced herself that a solidly built friendship might lead to real love between herself and her husband, but last night she had ruined everything.

Gareth was not going to be feeling at all friendly toward her this morning.

She had made a mistake; she knew that now. But it was too late. She had angered him and in the process no doubt retreated several steps back from the kind of relationship she sought to forge.

Her stubborn pride and her arrogant faith in her own intelligence had gotten her into this mess. This was what came of not following the sound advice of those older and wiser than herself, she thought sadly. Everyone from Beatrice to her old nurse, Agnes, had advised her to fulfill her responsibilities as a wife on her wedding night.

Now she had to start over from the beginning. She must undo the damage she had done and try to rebuild what she had willfully torn asunder last night.

A small, rustling sound from the other side of the bed curtain made Clare freeze.

"Gareth?"

" 'Tis too early to rise on the morning after a wedding. Go back to sleep, Clare."

She listened to him move about and wondered if he was getting dressed. Through the crack in the curtain she caught a brief glimpse of his nude body as he went past the bed. The sight sent a delicious chill through her. Memories flooded back, causing her to grow warm.

She had thought she wanted a slender, lean man, one built like a cat, not a great war-horse. But last night, after she had gotten over the shock of seeing Gareth's unclad body, she had soon changed her mind. She had discovered that she was not nearly as opposed to the notion of a very large husband as she had once believed herself to be.

A bit worried, mayhap, by the size of certain *parts* of him, but definitely not put off entirely by the overall notion.

Size, Clare decided, was only a problem in a man if his brain was quite small. When a man was blessed with intelligence and self-mastery, as Gareth clearly was, his physical size did not matter much at all.

Yet another lesson learned the hard way.

Clare remembered the shattering sensations Gareth had produced in her with his kisses and the touch of his fingers. He was no oafish, heavy-handed boor such as Nicholas of Seabern. He was a man who was willing to be patient with a woman.

And while it was true that Gareth had not vowed undying love nor composed poetry for her as Raymond once had, he was at least honest. He had not deliberately misled her the way Raymond had.

There was a soft thud on the other side of the curtain. Clare stirred and pushed back the covers so that she could sit up against the pillows. She could not hide here all day.

She put out a hand and gingerly explored the tumbled bedding. The Window of Hell was gone. It was no doubt safely stowed back in its scabbard.

Clare winced at the memory of how Gareth has used his sword to divide the bed. From now on, whenever she saw the blade, as she most certainly would every day of her life, she would recall her foolishness on her wedding night.

Some men, she knew, would have lost their tempers in a situation such as she had created last night. Some men would have turned violent.

Not Gareth. It was true that he had been furious, but he had been in full control of his anger.

She had married a man whose skill at self-mastery matched his physical power.

Clare drew a deep breath. She had to face him sometime and apologize. Best to get the thing over and done. It had never been her way to put off a duty or an obligation.

"My lord, I would like to say how much I regret what happened last night."

"So do I."

She wished she could see his face. His tone was so cool and dry that it was impossible to tell what he was thinking. She plunged ahead with her apology. "I am well aware that I did not fulfill my duties as a wife. I had my reasons, as I explained to you, but this morning I have concluded that mayhap I did not proceed in a reasonable and logical fashion."

"In other words, you have decided that the pleasures of physical passion are more interesting than the intellectual joys of trust and friendship?"

"Oh, no, I do not mean that at all," she said quickly. "I still want our marriage to be founded on trust and friendship. 'Tis just that this morning I am not certain that I went about securing those things in the right way last night."

Gareth yanked the curtain aside without any warning. He stood looking down at her with a speculative gleam in his eyes. Clare noticed that he had on his undertunic, but he was still barefoot. His fingers were closed around a small object which she could not make out.

"Are you telling me that sometime during the night you developed some trust in your new husband?" he asked rather casually.

She hesitated, aware that he was deliberately taunting her. The knowledge hurt. She composed herself in quiet dignity. "I would have us start anew, my lord. I am prepared to be a proper wife to you and consummate this marriage."

"That doesn't answer my question."

"I trust you in many ways, Gareth." She waved her hand in an earnest fashion to indicate the chamber and everything that lay beyond. "I trust you to protect this manor. I trust you to fulfill your responsibilities to my people. I believe that you will be a wise and generous lord."

"Is that all?"

She gave him a hopeful smile. "It seems to me that is a great deal to start out with, sir."

"Aye. But I would have more, madam." He studied her face. "I see you have been doing some thinking on the subject of our marriage."

"I spent hours thinking about it last night," she assured him.

"I, too, spent a good portion of the night contemplating our future together. I also came to a decision and your apology this morning does not alter that decision."

She watched him warily. "What decision did you reach?"

"The sword stays between us at night until you are certain that you trust me in all ways, most especially as a husband."

"I do trust you."

"No, madam, you do not. Last night you made it plain that you believed I was incapable of controlling my passions."

Clare's cheeks burned. "You proved me wrong, sir."

"Did I?"

"Aye. I apologize for that stupidity. I believed you to be so carried away by desire that you could not recall our understanding. I know now that you are very much in control of yourself and your passions and that you are very unlikely to be swayed by them."

"At this rate, your manner of reasoning will have us both twisted into knots. We will talk about it some other time. As you are wide awake, you may as well rise and get dressed."

"Gareth, I think we should discuss this further."

"Nay, I am in no mood to continue this idiotic conversation this morning."

"You are still deeply offended by my actions last night, are you not?"

He motioned her to quit the bed. "Rise, madam. As I said, we will discuss this later."

Still she hesitated. A startling thought struck her. "Gareth, were you more than offended last night? Were you hurt because you believed that I was rejecting you after you had given me so much pleasure?"

"Will you kindly get out of this damned bed before I remove you from it myself?"

Clare gazed at him in confusion. "Why must I rush from the bed?"

Gareth's mouth thinned with the expression of a man who is very much put upon but doing his best to be patient. "I thought we might take an early morning stroll together along the cliffs."

Clare brightened immediately. "That would be wonderful. I do love an early morning walk."

"Dress warmly," he muttered. "The fog has lifted, but there is a chill in the air."

"Aye, I will."

Clare scrambled quickly out of bed. She threw Gareth a tremulous smile and then hurried toward the wardrobe chamber which adjoined the main bedchamber.

The room was empty at this early hour, save for the usual chests of clothing and the baskets of needles and thread the maids kept there. Clare sent up a small prayer of thanks that it was still too early for any of the servants to be at their work.

She had opened one of the chests and was reaching for a warm gown when she had a sudden inspiration. Clutching the garment in front of her, she padded quickly back into the bedchamber.

"Gareth, mayhap you would like to ride out rather than walk? I very much enjoyed our . . . By Saint Hermione's eyes." She broke off in outraged shock. *What are you doing?*

Gareth had one knee on the bed. He was in the process of emptying the contents of a small vial onto the sheets. He looked up. Something he saw in her expression must have alerted him. "Now, Clare, I am doing this for your sake."

"My sake?" She pointed a finger that shook with the force of her fury. "That's chicken blood in that vial, is it not?"

"Clare, listen to me."

"You are putting chicken blood on the sheets."

"Aye. I have heard that it's a common substitute for . . . ah, well, you know."

She folded her arms beneath her breasts and slitted her eyes. "I know very well what it's used for, my lord."

"Clare, the servants who come to change the sheets will be looking for evidence of our wedding night. Gossip about the blood on the linen or the lack of it will be all over the isle by this afternoon. You know that as well as I do."

"So you are going to see to it that your honor as a man remains untarnished, is that it?"

"Hell's teeth. 'Tis your honor that I am concerned with, madam. I would not have everyone speculating on why there is no stain on the wedding sheets."

"Hah! I do not believe that for a moment. 'Tis your pride that concerns you. You cannot bear to have the world think that you got saddled with a bride who had given herself to another before the wedding, can you?"

"You believe that 'tis my pride that's involved here?" he demanded incredulously.

"Aye, that is precisely what I believe."

Clare stormed across the chamber, bent down, and dragged a small chest out from under the bed. It was the chest in which she had concealed all of the vials of chicken blood that she had been given on her wedding day.

Gareth scowled as he watched her jerk open the lid of the chest. "What are you doing?"

"You want blood on the sheets?" She straightened, her hands full of the vials. "You'll get blood on the sheets, my lord. Indeed, I shall see to it that you get all the blood any man could possibly want."

He eyed her warily as she stalked toward the bed. "Ah, Clare, mayhap your temper is running off with your wits."

"Oh, no, my lord, I assure you that I am thinking quite clearly at the moment." She gave him a honey-and-steel smile and then clambered up to stand in the middle of the big bed. "In fact, I venture to say that my wits have never been sharper or more clear than they are right now."

He looked at the collection of vials she was juggling. "Then why do I have the suspicion that we are both going to regret what you are about to do next?"

"I cannot imagine, my lord." Clare unstoppered the first vial and held it aloft. "Behold, sir, you are not the only person to doubt my word of honor."

"I do not doubt your word of honor, Clare. I am merely trying to protect you from gossip."

"Bah. You didn't mean a thing you said last night about trusting me. You will be pleased to know that you are in excellent company. Herewith, the chicken blood that was graciously supplied to me by Beatrice the recluse."

Clare turned the open vial upside down and dumped the contents onto the sheets. The old chicken blood, thick and clotted after being stored in the vial for nearly two days, made a nasty reddish brown puddle in the center of the white linen. It completely obliterated the few discreet drops of red that Gareth had sprinkled about.

Gareth looked at the unsightly blob and then regarded Clare with an expression of polite curiosity. "Are you finished?"

"Not at all. We are just beginning, my lord." Clare selected another vial and held it aloft for Gareth's inspection. "Here we have the chicken blood that was so kindly bestowed upon me by Prioress Margaret. I'm sure it was from a very pure chicken. A virgin chicken, mayhap."

Clare turned the second vial upside down with a flourish. The dark red blood spilled onto the sheets, adding to the gruesome stain.

Gareth folded his arms and propped one shoulder against the bedpost.

"From my good friend, Joanna." Clare emptied another vial.

"From my loyal servant, Eunice." She smiled grimly as she unsealed the next container. More blood splashed onto the linen.

"And last, but by no means least, the contribution made to the cause by my old nurse, Agnes."

Clare's outrage was still in full sail as she triumphantly turned the last vial upside down and dumped the blood onto the sheets. She gave Gareth a look of defiant triumph. "Is that a sufficient quantity of blood to satisfy your honor, my lord?"

Gareth studied the large and quite horrifying pool of thick blood which soaked the bed linen. "I am not certain what you hoped to accomplish, madam, but one thing is clear. No one who views these sheets will believe for one moment that I made love to a virgin last night."

"And just what will they think, sir?"

"That I sacrificed one."

"Oh, my God." Clare stared at the awful mess she had created. Reality came back with the force of a thunderbolt. She stood, stricken, in the middle of the bed and raised her eyes helplessly to meet Gareth's gaze.

He smiled slowly.

"By Saint Hermione's maidenhead," Clare whispered. "What have I done?"

Gareth's crystal gray eyes gleamed with gathering mirth.

"This is not at all amusing, Hellhound. This is a disaster. How will I ever explain this vast amount of blood?"

Gareth's smile curved into a grin.

"Gareth, so help me. I'm warning you—"

He began to chuckle.

Outraged all over again, Clare picked up one of the herb-scented pillows and hurled it at him. It struck Gareth squarely on the chest. Clare picked up a second pillow.

Gareth's chuckle became a roar of magnificent, full-throated, laughter. It was a huge sound that originated deep in his chest and poured forth with the unfettered exuberance of a waterfall.

Clare clutched the pillow to her breast and stared at him. She realized it was the first time she had heard him laugh.

The glorious sound boomed off the stone walls and echoed around the chamber. Gareth unfolded his arms, took a grip on the bedpost with one hand, and doubled over with laughter.

Clare tilted her head to one side and watched in growing wonder. "Gareth? Are you all right?"

His mirth increased. His broad shoulders shook with it.

Clare wrinkled her nose. "It isn't all that funny, sir."

Another gale of laughter swept over him.

"Hush." Clare glanced nervously toward the door. "Someone will hear you, my lord."

Gareth braced his forearm against the bedpost, leaned against it, and howled.

Clare started to smile in spite of herself. The sight of Gareth convulsed with laughter was oddly gratifying, for some strange reason.

"I'm glad you find this a cause for such grand mirth, my lord," she said. "I doubt that any of those brave chickens that died for my honor were nearly so amused as yourself."

"Nay." Gareth raised his head to look at her. He tried and failed to swallow another shout of laughter. "I doubt that they were. Mayhap if they could have seen you now, as I do, caught in such an interesting dilemma, they would have felt better about the matter. By my oath, madam, those poor chickens have surely had their revenge."

Clare groaned. "What am I going to do? This is a terrible situation. Everyone will gossip about it. I cannot possibly explain it. What will people think?"

"That the lady of Desire has some very exotic tastes in bed."

Clare beetled her brows at him. "I would like to remind you, my lord, that you are as involved in this as I am."

"Aye."

"Mayhap everyone will think that you did something quite dreadful to me last night. They will likely blame you for this."

"I doubt it. I suspect that whoever changes these sheets will recognize such vast quantities of chicken blood when she sees it."

Clare groaned. "Everyone will conclude that I botched the business of creating an illusion of virginity, will they not?"

"Aye, madam. Very likely. In this sort of thing, as in so many things in life, discretion and restraint are the keys one must use if one wishes to succeed."

Clare collapsed into a sitting position at the foot of the bed. She folded her legs under her, propped her elbow on one knee, and rested her chin in her hand. Glumly she studied the mess on the bed.

"I am going to look like a perfect fool, aren't I?" Clare said.

Gareth's laughter faded into a grin. His eyes remained quite brilliant, however. "Aye, madam. This business will likely prove a stimulating topic of conversation for our people for the next several months. Mayhap for the next several years."

"By Saint Hermione's—"

Gareth held up a hand. "Not her maidenhead, I pray you. Anything but that."

"By her sainted brow." Clare sighed. "This is the most humiliating moment of my entire life."

"Nay, madam. I expect that will occur when you are obliged to face a hall full of people today at dinner."

Clare flinched at the thought. "What are we going to do?"

Gareth arched one brow. "We?"

"'Tis your fault, sir," she muttered. "All of it. If you hadn't made me lose my temper, this would never have happened."

"Mayhap," Gareth said with surprising gentleness, "this is where I should begin to demonstrate to you my many virtues as a husband."

Clare raised her chin from her palm. "What do you mean? What are you going to do?"

"Create another kind of illusion." Gareth walked through the passage-way that led into the wardrobe. "Excuse me. I shall return in a moment."

"What are you doing in there?" Clare called.

"Patience, madam, patience. Ah, here we go. This cloth will do nicely."

Clare watched anxiously as Gareth reappeared from the other chamber. He had a large rag in one hand. He crossed the room to the bed.

"First, I will blot up the excess chicken blood." He went to work with the old rag.

"But that won't get rid of the huge stain," Clare pointed out.

"Nay." Gareth finished his task and wadded the soaked rag into a small ball. "But at least the mark that is left on the sheets will no longer be readily identifiable as the remains of several dead chickens. Now it is simply a reddish stain that could have been made by human blood."

"Do you think so?" Clare was skeptical. "I had thought that there would be only a small stain. This is monstrous."

"Aye, so it is." Gareth opened a chest that contained his personal possessions, pulled our a canvas sack, and dropped the wet rag inside. "We shall get rid of this evidence when we take our morning walk along the cliffs."

"That is an excellent plan." Clare cheered momentarily and then sank back into the depths of uneasiness. "What do you propose to do about this massive stain on the sheets?"

"It will most certainly cause comment." Gareth rummaged around inside the chest. "Unless we provide a suitable explanation for it, people will likely conclude now that I was brutal and clumsy with you."

"I would not have them believe that, my lord. It would not be fair."

"Thank you. I appreciate your wifely concern for my good name."

"Never mind that. How do you propose to deal with this problem?"

Gareth straightened from the chest. He held up a small, extremely wicked-looking dagger. "I propose to provide another explanation for the amount of blood that it obviously took to stain your wedding sheets, my lady."

Clare gazed at the dagger in horror. She recalled Beatrice's prediction. *Blood will flow.* "I don't understand."

"You soon will." Gareth went to the hearth, crouched down, and stoked the flames of the night's fire. "I once read a treatise written by an Arab physician. He claimed that a blade should be thoroughly heated in fire before it is used to perform any sort of surgical operation."

"*Gareth*." Clare sprang to her feet in alarm. "Nay, you must not."

"Calm yourself, madam. This won't hurt you a bit."

"I will not allow you to do such a thing." Clare flew across the room to stop him.

She was too late. In the blink of an eye, Gareth removed the dagger from the flames and drew the point swiftly and neatly across his upper arm.

Clare's hand went to her mouth as she watched blood well gently along the shallow cut. "By Saint Hermione's teeth."

Gareth glanced up from his handiwork. "You need not look so horrified, Clare. 'Tis a very minor scrape. I have had much worse, I promise you."

"Oh, Gareth."

"I would appreciate it if you went into the wardrobe and fetched a clean square of linen that I may use as a bandage."

"Oh, Gareth."

"A large square," Gareth added. "I want this bandage to be quite obvious to all and sundry."

"Oh, Gareth."

"Would you hurry, please, before I get blood on something other than the sheets?"

Clare broke free of the paralysis that gripped her. She swung around and raced madly into the wardrobe. She found what she wanted in a chest and dashed back into the bedchamber.

She grabbed a pot of herbal healing salve from a shelf and hastened over to where Gareth waited on the bed.

"How could you do this?" she wailed as she wiped the blood from his arm. "What will you tell people?"

Gareth shrugged. "That I had a small accident with my dagger."

She looked at him askance. "Do you expect people to believe that?"

"They will if we both tell the same tale." Gareth eyed her meaningfully. "I must have your word that you will not try to embroider the story or alter it in any fashion. Above all, you must not be overcome with a fit of honesty and confess the truth. Let me handle everything. Is that understood?"

She heard the soft but inflexible note of command in his voice and reacted to it unthinkingly. "Aye, my lord."

"Excellent."

"This is terrible," she whispered, hovering over his wound. "You should never have done such a thing for my sake."

"'Tis nothing."

"Nay, 'tis too much, sir." Clare smeared the herbal salve on the shallow slice. "I vow, 'tis the most noble, the most gallant, the most gloriously chivalrous action that anyone has ever performed for me."

128   AMANDA QUICK

Gareth's mouth quirked as he watched her work on his arm. "As your lord and husband, I am only too glad to be of service to my lady."

"You are too generous, sir." Clare carefully wrapped the length of clean linen around his wound. "I shall be forever in your debt. How can I repay you for this gracious gesture?"

"I'm certain I'll think of something," Gareth said.

10

Ulrich studied the white linen bandage plainly revealed by the tied-back sleeve of Gareth's gray tunic. "Dangerous things, daggers."

"Aye." Gareth flattened his hands on the table and leaned forward to study the sketch of the Isle of Desire that was spread out in front of him. "You have done excellent work on this drawing, Ulrich."

"Thank you, my lord." Ulrich's mouth kicked up at the corner. "'Twas done rather hastily from notes I made during the past three days. I shall improve upon it as I grow more familiar with the isle."

"I am pleased. This map will prove useful as we plan the isle's defense."

"Judging by the gossip which had swirled through this hall all morning, it might be wise if you prepared a defense against your bride."

Gareth looked up from the parchment map. "'Twas an accident, Ulrich."

"Aye. Whatever you say."

"I was entertaining my wife by demonstrating some tricks with my dagger. The damn thing slipped."

"Tricks with your dagger." Ulrich looked thoughtful. "In the marriage bed."

"Aye."

"Accidents will happen."

"Aye."

"Is dagger juggling in bed a local custom here on Desire, sir?" Ulrich asked politely.

" 'Tis the custom of a man who has had one too many cups of wine."

"I have never known you to drink a quantity of wine sufficient to make you careless with your dagger."

"You have never known me to get myself wed, either."

"Aye, that is true."

"There is a first time for all things, Ulrich."

"That would, mayhap, explain the laughter that is said to have been heard coming from the bridal chamber very early this morning."

"Laughter?" Gareth gave his friend a quizzical glance.

"A man's laughter. Or so gossip has it. Great peals of it, apparently. Loud enough to be heard by a pair of maids in the hall outside your bedchamber."

Gareth shrugged. "Household servants are inclined to gossip." He went back to the map.

"You would know nothing of any laughter, naturally," Ulrich said.

"Nay."

"Never having been known to laugh at anything in your entire life."

Gareth ignored that. "For the most part, Desire appears to be naturally fortified by its high cliffs."

"Aye."

"The only obvious place to bring a boat ashore is the village harbor."

"Aye. But I noticed a couple of tiny coves here along the side of the isle that looks out across the channel toward Seabern." Ulrich indicated the points with his forefinger.

"Could a boat be landed in either place?"

Ulrich glanced at the sketch. "A small fishing boat, mayhap. But the climb up to the top of the cliffs would not be easy. One definitely could not bring a party of mounted men ashore at either of those two locations. There is no cause for concern there."

" 'Tis often the small things that cause a man to trip and fall."

Ulrich's eyes gleamed with amusement. "Small things such as daggers?"

"Aye. Are there any other interesting features of the isle?"

"Young William is very observant. He tells me that there are some caves in the cliffs near one of the small coves."

Gareth frowned. "Could men or arms be hidden in them?"

"Nay. At least not for more than a few hours. William says that at high tides the caves are filled with seawater."

"Very well." Gareth pondered the sketch. "Let us turn to the matter of this hall. The old wooden curtain wall is weak and sagging in many places. It must be replaced."

"Surely there is no great rush. Desire has never suffered an invasion and is not likely to do so anytime soon."

"I prefer to take every precaution."

"Aye, you always do. Except in bed, apparently."

Gareth frowned. "I want the old wall replaced with one constructed of stone."

"We will need to hire stonemasons in order to do that. I doubt that Desire has any available."

"We can hire them from Seabern. Send a man there as soon as possible to see to the matter."

"Aye, my lord."

Gareth took one last look at the map. "A natural fortress. 'Tis a good land we have come to, Ulrich." He rolled up the parchment. "A fine land."

"They say that there was a very large bloodstain on the bridal sheets this morning," Ulrich murmured. "Far more blood than anyone would expect to discover after the normal activities of a wedding night."

"My dagger wound caused the greater portion of it. Damned thing bled like a slaughtered chicken."

Ulrich grinned. "Gareth, you and I have been as close as two brothers for more than ten years. Surely you can tell me the truth."

"About what?"

"About your little accident with the dagger. What really happened? Is it true that your bride took offense at your lovemaking and that she attempted to fend you off with your own blade?"

Gareth scowled. "Is that what the gossips are saying?"

"'Tis one of the rumors going around." Ulrich raised his brows. "There are others, but none that are nearly so amusing. Mayhap if I knew the truth, I could squelch some of the gossip."

Gareth met his friend's glinting gaze very steadily. "I told you the truth. It was an accident."

"God's eyes, man, this is your old comrade-in-arms, remember? I know how you handle weapons. Do not expect me to believe that you accidentally sliced your arm with your own dagger while acting the juggler in bed."

"As you said, accidents will happen." Gareth paused. "Especially in the marriage bed."

Ulrich swore again, under his breath. "Very well. If that is the way you would have it, so be it."

A knock on the door interrupted Gareth before he could respond.

"Enter," he called.

The heavy wooden door swung slowly inward to reveal the anxious but determined faces of William and Dallan.

"Good day to you, my lord," William said. He had a small chunk of meat pie in one hand.

"Good day." Gareth glanced at the meat pie.

William hastily concealed the pie behind his back and glanced uneasily at Dallan. It was clear he was waiting for either guidance or reinforcement from his older companion.

Dallan swallowed visibly. There were beads of perspiration on his brow. His fingers clenched and unclenched in the folds of his tunic. "We came to speak with you, my lord." He looked pointedly at Ulrich. "We wish to be private."

Gareth studied Dallan. The minstrel was plainly terrified, but apparently he was not about to flee from the confrontation. In Gareth's experience there was only one thing that could fortify a young man's frail courage to such a degree: a woman.

"I comprehend that this conversation would concern Lady Clare, then?" he asked softly.

Dallan blinked several times very rapidly. "Aye, my lord, it would."

William stared, round-eyed, up at Gareth. "Is it true that she cut your arm with a dagger last night because you tried to hurt her, sir?"

Gareth tapped the rolled-up parchment lightly against his thigh. "Is that what she told you?"

"Nay, sir," William began eagerly. "She says—"

"My lady says it was an accident," Dallan broke in angrily. "She claims that you were entertaining her with a clever juggling feat and that the dagger slipped and cut your arm. But I do not believe it."

"What do you think happened?"

"I think you attacked her and she was forced to defend herself. She has told us many times that she does not care for large, arrogant, overbearing knights. She says they are oafish and ill-mannered and they do not have the souls of poets."

Ulrich coughed a little behind one hand.

Gareth kept his gaze on Dallan. "You doubt your lady's explanation of my injury?"

Dallan's hands knotted into fists. His sullen, resentful eyes mirrored his fear, but he did not back down. "I believe that she is afraid to alarm us with the truth, my lord. 'Tis just like her to try to protect William and me."

"From what?" Gareth asked.

"From you," William said helpfully. "Dallan says that we are risking our very lives by coming here to talk to you like this. He says you'll likely be violently angry but that we have to do it in order to protect Lady Clare."

Gareth put the parchment map down. Then he leaned back against the table, folded his arms, and considered the matter in silence for a moment. No one moved. The chamber grew very quiet.

"I am not angry," he said finally.

William heaved a loud sigh and then grinned. "I did not think that you would be." He promptly brought the meat pie out from behind his back and took a large bite. "I told Dallan that you likely had not hurt Clare last night."

"I appreciate your confidence in me," Gareth said. "What makes you so certain that I did not do your lady any great harm?"

William chewed. "Nothing seems amiss with her. She's in her usual good spirits. She is even now in her workrooms as she always is in the afternoons."

"Excellent reasoning, William," Ulrich said approvingly.

William preened. "Lady Clare says I am very intelligent."

"You are correct," Gareth said. "I did not harm your lady last night." He looked at Dallan. "But apparently our minstrel does not agree. What do you propose to do, Dallan? Challenge me to trial by combat?"

William looked thunderstruck. "Combat?" he squeaked.

"Why not?" Gareth watched Dallan's face. "'Tis the usual way such matters are settled when a lady's honor is at stake. Do you favor swords or daggers, Dallan?"

Dallan looked as though he were about to become ill. "My lord, I . . . That is, my lady would never allow me to fight you."

"There's no need to consult Clare on this," Gareth said. "'Tis a matter for men, is it not?"

"Ah, well—"

"I myself would prefer swords." Gareth glanced ruefully down at the linen bandage on his arm. "As you can see, I lack skill with the dagger. I have been known to have accidents."

Dallan paled. "You mock me, my lord."

"Do I?"

"I can hardly challenge you," Dallan sputtered. "You would kill me in an instant."

"Your point is well taken," Gareth said. "You are no doubt more clumsy with a sword than I am with a dagger. Mayhap we should remedy that fault."

Dallan's expression was that of the hare which sees the hawk swooping down on him. "What are you talking about?"

"I did not bring a large company of men with me to defend this isle,"

Gareth said. "Not everyone who served me wished to abandon the lucrative business of hunting outlaws in favor of becoming a gardener. Even my squire, Bradford, chose not to accompany me here to Desire."

"I expect hunting outlaws is very exciting," William said wistfully.

"Nay, 'tis a business like any other, although I'll admit it is more precarious than some careers," Gareth said. "And I cannot deny that it pays well, if one is proficient. But then, so does the business of making perfumes."

"Aye." William looked doubtful about equating the two endeavors.

"'Tis not the financial aspects of Desire which concern me, however," Gareth continued. "That is Lady Clare's business. My task is to see to the safety of these lands and the people who live here. A sound defense requires that every man in this household be well trained in the use of arms."

"Lady Clare says that knights and men-at-arms are a great nuisance to have about underfoot," William said.

"Aye." Dallan sounded a bit bolder now. "Lady Clare doesn't care for men who make their living with their swords. She says her brother, Edmund, died because of his foolish love of tourneying. She says such pursuits are silly and that the sort of men who pursue them are altogether lacking in wits."

Ulrich gave Dallan and William a cool, knowing smile. "Your lady may not be overly fond of fighting men, but she was quick enough to choose a husband she believed to be capable of defending her lands and her people."

"She had no choice," Dallan muttered.

Gareth slanted Ulrich a wry glance. It was the truth and they both knew it. But for some reason, this morning, Gareth discovered that he did not particularly like hearing it voiced aloud.

"Whatever the reasons," Ulrich said, "it would seem that even Lady Clare has some use for a man who can use a sword."

William took another bite of pie. "My mother says that Lady Clare always puts her duty to her people ahead of all else."

"'Tis a great pity that Lady Clare must sacrifice herself for the rest of us," Dallan said defiantly. "'Tis not right."

"Enough," Gareth said quietly. "What's done is done. It only remains for me to earn my keep. And I intend to do just that."

Dallan scowled warily. "What do you mean?"

"As I said, the defense of these lands requires that every able-bodied man in the household be properly trained."

William munched his pie. "There aren't any able-bodied men in this household other than yourself and your men-at-arms, my lord."

"You look fit enough, William," Gareth said. "And you are, what? Ten years old?"

"Aye."

"Then 'tis past time you began a knight's training. When I was your age, I was already practicing regularly with lance and sword."

"Me? A knight?" William sucked in air and promptly choked on a mouthful of meat pie. "Nay, my lord. 'Tis not possible." He succumbed to a fit of coughing.

Ulrich strolled across the room and slapped William between the shoulder blades. "The first thing a future knight must learn is how to eat without strangling himself."

William's eyes watered. He sputtered, recovered, and managed to swallow the pie. He drew in several gasping breaths. "Lady Clare and my mother will never allow me to train to be a knight."

"Why not?" Gareth asked.

"I'm delicate."

Dallan glowered at Gareth. "That's right. They'll never allow young William to practice such skills."

"Lady Clare and Lady Joanna need not concern themselves with William's training. Such matters are my responsibility." Gareth eyed Dallan. "What about you, minstrel? How far did your training progress?"

"Huh?"

"Did you learn any useful skills before you took up the harp and began composing irritating ballads about young knights who cuckold their lords?"

Dallan looked seriously alarmed. "My former master was a scholar."

"A scholar?"

"Aye." Dallan's eyes shifted uneasily as though he were searching for a place to hide. "He raised me to assist him with his studies."

"Was he a trained knight?" Gareth asked.

"Aye, a very great knight. He even went on Crusade. But he said there was no point teaching me knightly skills." Dallan's lips trembled. "He said I was a clumsy weakling who could not be taught such things."

"You were raised in a scholar's household?"

"Aye." Dallan wiped his sweating brow on the back of his sleeve.

"Your father sent you to live in this scholar's hall?" Gareth probed.

"My father does not even know that I exist." Dallan jerked his arm back down to his side. "I don't know his name. I am a bastard, sir."

Gareth met Dallan's fierce, anguished gaze and knew the depths of the younger man's fear as well as his rage. "It would seem that you and I have something in common, minstrel."

Dallan clearly did not want to hear that. "At least you know your father's name. Thurston of Landry is a great lord. I know nothing of the man who sired me except that he was a knight on his way to a tourney. He found my mother alone in a field. He raped her and left her pregnant with me. He went on his way and never came back for either of us."

"You are not the only product of such an unpleasant union," Gareth said. "You must find your own way in the world. At least you will have the satisfaction of knowing that everything you achieve will be won by your own hand. You may well discover that it is useful for a bastard to be able to handle a sword."

"I intend to make my living as a minstrel, or mayhap as a scholar," Dallan retorted. "I do not wish to make a career of splitting skulls or fighting other men's battles."

Gareth caught Ulrich's eye. "It would seem that my lady's poor opinion of fighting men has infected the entire household."

Ulrich's smile came and went. "Aye."

"We must see if we can change her mind."

"I'm sure you will find a way to prove yourself useful," Ulrich said. "You always do."

Gareth returned his attention to Dallan. "Was your mother the one who arranged for you to be fostered in the house of this scholar you mentioned?"

Dallan shook his head. The hunted look reappeared in his eyes. "My mother loved me. She would never have sent me away. But she died when I was eight. Soon afterward my aunt sold me to my master. I mean, my *former* master."

Gareth frowned. "She sold you to him?"

"Aye." Dallan's mouth tightened. "He gave her several gold coins in exchange for me. He wanted a healthy, intelligent lad, he said. One who could be trained to be his assistant."

"This scholar . . ." Gareth said slowly, "he was a harsh master?"

Dallan flinched as if he had been struck by a whip. "He does not—I mean, he *did* not tolerate any mistakes."

"Are you here on Desire because you have run away from his household?" Gareth asked quietly.

"*Nay.*" Dallan looked terrified now. "Nay, I did not run away. I always obeyed my lord's commands." There was a glazed expression in his eyes. "Always. But he was never satisfied. *Never.* I could not please him, although I tried my best. No matter what I did, *I could not please him.*"

William touched Dallan's arm in an awkward gesture. "Remember what Lady Clare said, Dallan."

"Aye." Dallan drew several deep breaths. His eyes refocused.

"What did Lady Clare say?" Gareth asked.

Dallan scowled. The fear in his eyes was gone. " 'Tis not important."

"She said Dallan was to remember that he was safe now," William explained. "When Dallan first came here, he could not sleep at all at night and he was very anxious."

"That is not true," Dallan hissed.

"Aye, 'tis true." William turned back to Gareth. "Poor Dallan was always jumping at the smallest sounds. I came around the corner once and surprised him in the hall outside Clare's study and he nearly fainted. Is that not so, Dallan?"

"Say no more." Dallan whirled furiously on William. "That is enough. My health is no concern of Lord Gareth's."

"But it is my concern," Gareth said. "As is the state of the health of every man under my command. Only men in good health can carry out their duties properly."

"My health is excellent." Dallan raised his chin in open defiance. "And I am not under your command."

"Aye, but you are, as is William." Gareth straightened away from the table. "The first thing we must do is see to your training. Ulrich, take both of these future knights downstairs to the courtyard and get them started in their careers. William and Dallan are to begin practicing with arms immediately."

"Aye, my lord," Ulrich said. He grinned at William. "Are you ready, lad?"

William looked dazzled. "I am to learn how to use a sword?"

"That you are." Ulrich strode across the room and ruffled William's hair. "And how to care for armor and a good war-horse and how to defend your hall. Do you think you will enjoy learning all that?"

"Aye." William looked up at him with glowing eyes. "I shall enjoy that very much."

"Come along, then." Ulrich glanced at Dallan. "You, too, minstrel."

"Nay, you cannot force us to learn such things." Dallan turned a desperate gaze on Gareth. "Lady Clare will never permit it."

Some of the enthusiasm faded from William's eyes. "He's right, my lord. Lady Clare will never allow us to begin a knight's training."

"Lady Clare wanted a husband who could see to the defense of her isle," Gareth said. "She has got one who can do that. I trust that she has sense enough to allow me to get on with the task."

"Clare, are you truly all right?" Joanna looked up from the bunch of lavender and mint that she was binding with a cord.

"Of course I'm all right." Clare stood on tiptoe to hang another fresh bouquet upside down from the overhead drying rack.

The long shed where she and Joanna were working was one of a series of workrooms built against the curtain wall. It was filled with bunches of flowers and herbs in various stages of preparation. Many, such as the lavender and mint, were being allowed to dry. When the process was complete, they would be carefully composed into perfumes according to Clare's recipes.

Some of the complex mixtures made from dried flowers and herbs would be used to fill sweet bags for linen chests. Others would go into small, lidded pots designed to add a pleasant fragrance to chambers. Still others would be combined with oil and honey to create lush perfumes, lotions, and balms.

Clare loved the drying shed. She often walked through it as she did through her garden, delighting in one scent after another. She liked to close her eyes in the midst of the fragrant blossoms and create perfumes in her mind the way Dallan created ballads.

There was a very large bin at the far end of the shed where the dried blossoms and leaves were combined in huge batches. There they were mixed according to Clare's specifications.

Today the bin was heaped full of dried petals from early roses, mugwort, lavender, mint, and rosemary. Clare was still fussing with the concoction, deliberating whether to add cinnamon oil or oil of cloves to fix the scent.

Once she had made her decision, the dried materials would be stuffed into hundreds of small, exquisitely embroidered bags. The sweet bags would be taken to the spring fair in Seabern in a few days, along with the new batch of soaps that was being readied. There they would be sold to eager merchants.

"I have been concerned about you," Joanna said.

"Why?" Clare slung another bunch of lavender onto a drying rack hook.

"There has been gossip all morning in the hall. By now it has no doubt reached the village."

"I am well aware that everyone is overly curious to know the details of my wedding night," Clare muttered, "but I have no intention of discussing it. Some matters are private between husband and wife."

"Clare, you must know that it is not normal for a husband to appear wearing a large white bandage the morning after his wedding." Joanna threw her an exasperated glance. "What really happened last night?"

"'Twas an accident."

"Did you actually use the Hellhound's dagger in an attempt to defend yourself from his embrace?"

"Nay, I most certainly did not. Is that what the gossips are saying?" Clare demanded.

"Aye." Joanna sighed. "I knew you were not looking forward to the duties of a wife, but I did not believe you would do something so outrageous as to stab your husband on your wedding night. How did you dare?"

"I didn't."

"Lord Gareth must have been furious with you." Joanna shuddered.

"'Tis a wonder he did not beat you." She frowned in sudden alarm. "Or did he?"

"Do not be ridiculous, Joanna. Do I appear to have been beaten?"

"Nay."

"Do you think that I would tolerate such treatment?"

"Nay, but he is a very large man, Clare. Much bigger than you."

"Do not forget that I have successfully defended myself against large men in the past."

"Aye, but Lord Gareth is not a fool like Sir Nicholas."

"A fact for which I am extremely grateful." Clare glanced over her shoulder. "Joanna, I did not use my husband's dagger against him last night. There was no need. Sir Gareth behaved himself in a most chivalrous fashion."

Clare felt herself grow warm at the memory of how Gareth had cut his own arm in order to protect her from humiliation and gossip. No man had ever done anything so chivalrous for her, not even Raymond de Coleville.

It was unfair that Gareth had become the object of so much sly speculation and rumor today. After his noble actions, he deserved better. Unfortunately, there was no way to explain that to Joanna.

"A juggling accident," Joanna murmured.

"Aye."

"Forgive me, but that is difficult to believe, Clare."

"Ask Lord Gareth yourself, if you do not believe me."

"You know very well that I could never do such a thing. If I did, he would no doubt merely confirm your version of the tale, just as you are confirming his. For some reason the two of you appear to be as one on this matter."

Joanna was right, Clare thought. More right than Clare had even realized until this moment. Somehow, whether he had intended to do so or not, Gareth had succeeded in binding Clare to him in a wholly unexpected fashion.

Together they shared a secret. A most intimate secret. A secret that, in its own way, was as intimate as the manner in which Gareth had touched her last night.

Clare stilled, one hand frozen around a bundle of lavender and roses. She gazed unseeing at the rows of flowers and herbs hung from the ceiling.

It occurred to her that Gareth had no doubt known exactly what he was doing when he had slashed his arm for her. He had likely foreseen everything, including the way in which it would affect her feelings toward him.

He was very good at making carefully calculated gestures, Clare reminded herself. But even allowing for that, this particular gesture had been undeniably gallant. Moreover, it was a gesture that he could not have planned, she thought. Gareth had had no way of knowing about the vials of chicken blood she had been given on her wedding day. He'd come to the bridal bed equipped with his own supply.

Another calculated gesture. And one that had most definitely been well planned.

Whose honor had he really been concerned with last night? Clare wondered. Hers or his own? She still knew very little about the Hellhound.

"By Saint Hermione's nose," she muttered. It was all dangerously confusing.

Joanna glanced out the open door of the drying shed. "Oh, there is William. Heading for the stables, I believe. I vow, he is spending far too much time with Lord Gareth's men, Clare. It worries me."

"I know, Joanna, but I do not think there is any great harm in it."

"Dallan is with him. I wonder what they are about?"

"I have no notion."

"*Dear God.*" Joanna tossed aside the lavender and leaped to her feet.

"Joanna, what's wrong?"

"Ranulf and Sir Ulrich have given both William and Dallan shields." Joanna stood in the doorway, her hand at her throat. "And wooden swords. Clare, I believe that they are going to give them instruction in swordplay."

"Calm yourself, Joanna. Ulrich and Ranulf are likely just showing them some of the equipment. You know William is very curious about such matters."

"Well, your minstrel is not, but he's out there, too."

"Really?" Clare brushed her hands and walked toward the door of the shed. She peered out into the sunlit yard.

There was no doubt about what was happening. William and Dallan stood awkwardly clutching wooden shields and swords. William looked excited. Dallan looked angry and resentful.

Clare saw Gareth stroll out of the hall onto the steps to watch the lesson.

Ranulf raised his shield and spoke to William, who eagerly hefted his wooden blade and delivered a fierce blow to Ranulf's shield.

Joanna shrieked. She spun about and gave Clare a stricken look. "'Tis obvious Lord Gareth has ordered William and Dallan to be trained with arms. You must stop this at once, Clare, I beg of you."

"I do not think it will do any great harm, Joanna."

"My son is much too delicate for such training. You must stop this at once."

"Uh—"

"Clare, do something. You are the lady of this hall. Tell them to cease this dangerous nonsense."

Clare glanced at Gareth. She had an unpleasant suspicion that the whole situation was out of her hands.

It was that realization which abruptly strengthened her resolve. She was mistress of Desire, she reminded herself. She gave the commands here.

"I shall speak to Ranulf and Sir Ulrich at once." Clare picked up the skirts of her gown and strode purposefully out into the courtyard.

11

"Lady Clare, I would speak with you," Gareth said as Clare strode swiftly past the hall steps.

His voice was pitched low, meant for her ears alone, but it carried the weight of command.

Clare pretended that she had not heard him. She did not dare turn her head to glance at him. It would be easier to ignore Gareth if she did not appear to notice him standing there on the steps.

"Pray, madam, a word with you." There was a slight but very distinct edge in Gareth's voice this time.

Clare's fingers tightened in the folds of her skirt, but she resisted the almost overpowering inclination to obey the soft summons.

"Hell's teeth. I knew you were going to make this difficult." Gareth started down the steps.

Clare ignored him. This was her hall and she was in charge. She had no intention of allowing Gareth to take control. At that moment, however, she comprehended precisely how he had become successful as a leader of men. There was an inborn authority in his voice that would give anyone pause.

Anyone, that is, save another who was also accustomed to command.

Clare reminded herself that she, too, could invest her words with a certain air of authority when the occasion demanded. She had been doing so since the age of twelve.

"Ulrich." Clare smiled coolly as Ulrich turned his head. "What is going on here?"

"Sword practice, my lady. Lord Gareth has ordered William and Dallan to begin training with arms." Ulrich's gaze went from Clare's face to a point just behind her.

Clare knew that Gareth was striding across the courtyard toward where she stood.

Dallan and William looked at her, then at Gareth. They were not the only ones who stopped what they were doing to see what was going to happen.

Disappointment clouded William's expression. "Ah, Lady Clare, please say that I may continue. I shall be most careful. I vow that I will not get hurt."

Dallan's eyes gleamed with vengeful satisfaction. He shot a sly, triumphant glance at Gareth, who had nearly reached Clare. "I knew you would not allow us to be forced to learn such dangerous skills, my lady. You have always said that only thick-skulled lackwits devote their energies to fighting and tourneying."

"Why was I not consulted on this matter?" Clare came to a halt in front of Ulrich and fixed him with a warning glare. Gareth was no more than a few paces away now. She had to act swiftly or the initiative would be taken from her.

Ulrich glanced over the top of her head and met Gareth's eyes. "I assumed that my lord was in command of such things."

"Lord Gareth may do as he pleases with you and the rest of his men. William and Dallan, however, are members of my household and their welfare is my affair."

"Aye, madam," Ulrich murmured. There was a gleam of unholy amusement in his eyes.

"You must save us, my lady," Dallan wailed piteously.

"Please let us practice, Lady Clare," William urged. "I want to learn how to use a sword so that I can help defend this hall. Lord Gareth says he needs more trained men."

"Aye." Gareth reached Clare's side. "One can never have too many well-trained men."

He reached out and caught hold of Clare's arm in what no doubt appeared to onlookers to be a husbandly gesture of affection. Clare, however, was acutely aware of the inflexibility of his fingers. He was not hurting her, but his grasp was unshakable.

"Dallan and William are not under your command, sir," she said.

"I believe there is some misunderstanding here." Gareth's eyes were polite but unyielding. " 'Tis nothing that cannot be cleared up immediately. If you will come with me, madam, I shall explain everything to your satisfaction."

Clare frowned. "I doubt that. My lord, I have not given my permission for William and Dallan to train with weapons."

"Nay, but I have given mine, so all is well."

Clare opened her mouth in astonishment. "You have no right—"

"As to my rights, I believe it would be best if we discussed those in private." Gareth looked at Ulrich. "Continue with the sword practice while I explain matters to my lady wife."

"Aye, my lord." Gareth turned to William and Dallan. "Let's get back to the business at hand, lads. We have a great deal of work ahead of us if we are to make useful knights out of you."

"Lady Clare," Dallan yelped like an abandoned puppy. "Aren't you going to save us?"

Gareth's hand tightened around Clare's arm before she could reply. "Get on with your training, minstrel. Who knows? If you work very hard, you may soon learn how to save yourself when you get into unpleasant situations. You will no longer need to hide behind a woman's skirts."

Dallan turned a dull shade of red. His eyes glittered with helpless rage.

Gareth paid no attention. He led Clare back across the courtyard toward the drying shed.

"*Gareth,* how could you do such a thing?" Clare snapped furiously.

" 'Tis the truth. The boy must become a man. The sooner the better, in his case."

"Why do you say that?"

"Young Dallan tells me that he is a bastard. I suspect that he recently fled the household where he was raised. He is alone in the world, more so than he yet realizes. And he is of an anxious nature."

"Aye, but—"

"If he is going to survive, he must learn how to take care of himself. From what I have heard of his wretched poetry, he cannot depend upon his skill with a harp to make his way in the world."

Clare heard the grim conviction in Gareth's voice. It effectively forestalled the remainder of her angry tirade. "You know whereof you speak, do you not, my lord?"

"Aye. 'Tis true that unlike young Dallan, I had the advantage of being raised in my father's household. But I am still a bastard, for all of that, and nothing can change the fact. A man born into this world without a name must make his own."

The chill in his words told Clare a great deal. Gareth may indeed have been raised in his father's house, but he had never felt welcome there.

At least she had always had Desire, she thought. Even through the worst of times she had always had a home. She had had a place where people wanted her and needed her, a place where she knew she belonged.

She resisted an odd, almost overpowering urge to touch Gareth's fierce jaw and tell him that he now had a home, too. She knew he would not welcome the sympathy.

"I appreciate your concern for my minstrel, but Dallan is safe enough here on Desire," she said briskly.

"Is he?"

"Of course he is. And so is William. There has never been any violence on this isle. No one has ever had to defend the hall or the village. The only reason we need a company of armed men at all is to protect the shipments we send elsewhere."

Gareth's mouth tightened. "I am well aware that you view my role here as a very limited one. But as it is my task to protect this isle, you must allow me to make the decisions that deal with such matters."

Clare slanted him an uncertain glance. She wondered if she had somehow offended him. "Surely you do not need William's or Dallan's assistance for the defense of Desire."

"As to that, who can say? I believe in being prepared for all eventualities."

"Aye, but—"

"Come, Clare. Be reasonable. Young William needs exercise. He is in immediate danger of either being smothered to death by his well-meaning mother or of turning into a stuffed pork pie."

Clare knew he was right, but she could hardly admit it. To do so would be to abandon her present battle. "I do not dispute that William needs more physical activity," she managed austerely. "However—"

"He also craves a man's guidance. So does Dallan."

That was too much. "I am aware that young William has become Sir Ulrich's shadow of late, but Dallan has been quite content in this household."

"Too much so." Gareth looked thoughtful. "I believe your minstrel clings to your skirts and starts at every small sound because he has been badly frightened by his previous master. To combat that fear, he must gain confidence in his own ability to defend himself."

Clare gave Gareth a disgruntled look. He had assessed the situation accurately, confirming some of her own conclusions.

But there was another, much more significant issue involved here, Clare knew. It had to do with the question of who gave the orders on the manor.

"I will not deny that William and Dallan could do with a man's guidance," Clare said cautiously. "And I agree that exercise is of great benefit in restoring balance to the body's humors. But there is no need for either boy to undergo the dangerous and rigorous training of a knight in order to accomplish that."

"They will be safe enough under Ulrich's supervision."

"Joanna will fret."

"She will soon adjust to the situation. That is not the real issue here, is it?"

"Nay." Clare came to a halt and swung around to confront him. "Let us be clear on something here, my lord. I will make the decisions that affect the members of this household."

Gareth's gaze was as fathomless as the crystal in his sword. "I comprehend that you have had the sole responsibility for this household and this manor for a long time, Clare."

"Aye." She eyed him with frosty challenge.

"You are obviously accustomed to bearing the burden alone."

"Precisely."

"But you are no longer alone."

"There is no need to remind me of that fact," she retorted. "I am only too well aware of it."

Gareth's brows rose. "You were the one who wrote to Thurston of Landry to request a husband who could provide protection for your manor."

"What of it? I had little choice in the matter."

"My point is that you have got what you asked for, madam."

"Not quite."

"Aye, that is true enough, is it not? You have made it plain that I do not meet all the requirements of your damned recipe."

Clare badly wished she had not let her tongue run away with her. "I did not mean that the way it sounded, sir."

"Aye, you did mean it. But it matters not. Few of us get exactly what we want." Gareth rested his hand on the hilt of his sword. "We must all make the most of whatever the winds of fortune blow our way."

Likely she was not the sort of wife he had dreamed of marrying, Clare thought. "My lord, I am trying to make another point entirely here."

"As am I, madam. To be blunt, I may not be what you ordered, but I am the only husband you have got. Allow me to perform my tasks without interference."

"What has training Dallan or William got to do with the defense of this manor?"

"*Clare,*" Joanna called.

Clare glanced toward the workrooms. Joanna left the doorway of the drying shed and hurried across the courtyard.

"You must stop them," Joanna said urgently. "William is still playing with that dangerous sword."

"I will deal with this," Gareth said quietly.

"She is my friend," Clare said. "I shall deal with it."

"As your husband and as the lord of this manor, I must ask that you stand with me on this, madam." Gareth's gaze was suddenly very cold and very unyielding. "I warn you, for the sake of all concerned, do not gainsay me in front of Joanna."

"By Saint Hermione's hair, this is too much."

"If you and I do not appear united in our decisions, we will cause confusion and discontent among our people. Do you want that?"

Our people.

The words brought Clare up short. She had to accept that the people of Desire were linked to Gareth now. She knew he was right when he insisted that as lord and lady of the manor, the two of them must stand together.

"You have caught me in yet another of your crafty snares, my lord," she muttered a few seconds before Joanna reached them. "Beware. One day I shall have my revenge."

"You have already had your revenge. And a most telling vengeance it is. I am a husband who has not yet had a wedding night."

She threw him a quelling glance as Joanna fluttered anxiously to a halt in front of them.

"Clare, why did you not instruct Ulrich to cease the training?" Joanna asked. "William could be hurt at any moment. Just look at the way he is swinging that great wooden sword about."

Clare steeled herself. "Lord Gareth feels that such training will be good for both William and Dallan. My lord and I have discussed the matter and I have concluded that he is right. I agree with his decision."

"You agree with him?" Joanna's eyes widened in shock.

Clare did not dare look at Gareth. If he smiled in triumph at that moment, she was not at all certain that she would be able to keep from throttling him.

"Rest assured that I have given my approval for William and Dallan to be taught knightly skills," Clare said. "As a form of healthful exercise," she added quickly.

"But you have never approved of such activities, not even for the sake of health," Joanna said. "After Edmund was killed, you told me that you never wanted to hear the sound of a lance striking a quintain again as long as you lived."

Clare winced. "I was distraught at the time."

"The grief my lady wife must have experienced at the time of her brother's death no doubt prevented her taking an objective view of the benefits of exercise," Gareth said easily.

Joanna looked uncertain. "She was much saddened and prone to melancholy at the time. Nevertheless, I heard her say very distinctly that training a man to be a knight was a great piece of idiocy."

Clare saw the gleam in Gareth's eye. She flushed.

"At the time, my wife was not aware of the many healthful advantages of training and exercise for young men," Gareth said. "I have explained those benefits to her, however, and she is eager for William and Dallan to receive them."

"What benefits?" Joanna gave him a beseeching look. "William could be seriously injured."

"He could be hurt climbing an apple tree or falling down a staircase, but 'tis not likely," Gareth said with surprising gentleness. "Your son is safer under Sir Ulrich's eye than he is in his own bed."

"William has a most delicate constitution," Joanna insisted. "Such training and exercise will exhaust him."

"A regimen of properly supervised exercise will strengthen his constitution and align his humors," Gareth said. "I have seen many examples of frail young boys who have greatly improved their health through regular, vigorous activity."

"I am not at all certain of this." Joanna looked at Clare, seeking support.

Clare managed what she hoped was an encouraging smile. "We must trust that my husband and Sir Ulrich know what they are about, Joanna. They have both had a great deal of experience in such matters."

"Their experience is in hunting outlaws, not in educating young boys," Joanna said desperately.

"Nay," Gareth said. "I have been training the men who serve under my command for years. So has Ulrich. We know what we are doing."

Joanna looked from Gareth to Clare and back. Some of her visible agitation subsided. She did not appear completely satisfied, but it was clear she realized she was facing a united lord and lady. In an odd way, it seemed to give her some further reassurance.

"Well, if you are certain William will not be hurt, I suppose it will be all right to try an exercise program."

"Why don't you discuss the particulars of William's training at supper with Sir Ulrich?" Clare suggested to Joanna. "I believe that he will answer all of your questions."

Joanna brightened. "Aye, I will do that. Sir Ulrich is a very kind and courteous knight. And very knowledgeable."

"He will be an excellent example for young William and for Dallan." Gareth's eyes gleamed. "He is not one of your typical thick-skulled, ill-mannered, foul-tempered knights."

Clare rolled her eyes heavenward and called on Saint Hermione for strength.

"Aye, mayhap Sir Ulrich will, indeed, be a good influence on William." Joanna inclined her head politely to Gareth. "Pray, excuse me, my lord. I believe I shall go and observe the training."

"Do it from a distance," Gareth advised. "Otherwise you will divert your son's attention and he will lose much of the benefit."

"Aye."

Clare watched Joanna walk toward the hall steps to join a handful of other people who had gathered to observe the training practice.

"Well done, madam," Gareth muttered. "I know that was not easy for you. But in truth 'tis time she stopped coddling the lad. She cannot protect him forever."

Clare narrowed her eyes against the bright sunlight and turned to face Gareth. "You have had your way in this, my lord. I trust you are satisfied. Next time, you will consult me before you make any decisions which affect those in my charge, is that quite clear?"

"You and I must share the responsibilities for the decisions that affect the people of this manor now, Clare."

"All the more reason for you to discuss things with me first before you make sweeping decisions."

Gareth took her arm again and started toward the drying shed. "I think it would be best if we finished this conversation in private. I have been the subject of enough speculation and gossip today."

Clare's gaze went to the linen bandage on his arm. Guilt shot through her. "I am aware of that, my lord, and I cannot tell you how much I regret it."

"Try."

"I beg your pardon?"

"I said, try to tell me how much regret my act of personal sacrifice has caused you." Gareth urged her through the door into the fragrant, shadowed interior of the shed.

"Are you teasing me, my lord?" she demanded suspiciously.

"Nay, madam." Gareth stopped just inside the shed and surveyed the long rows of flowers that hung from the drying racks. "So this is where you produce the wealth of Desire."

Clare frowned. "This is one of my workrooms, yes."

"I would see the rest of your facilities." Gareth started slowly down an aisle created by several long benches. He stopped in front of a pot filled with elderflowers, rose petals, and oak moss.

He scooped out a large handful and held the mixture to his nose. "Sweet. Rich. A woman's scent, no doubt. One of your more profitable recipes?"

"Aye. It will sell well at the spring fair." Clare planted her hands on her hips and tapped one toe as Gareth moved on to another bowl.

"I like this one," he said as he held another handful of dried ingredients to his nose. "Clean and fresh. It smells of the sea."

Clare crossed her arms under her breasts. "'Tis a mixture of spices and mint that is much favored by the wealthy men of London."

Gareth nodded and dropped the mix back into the bowl. He wandered down the row of tables to where several sprays of dried flowers were set out. "And these?"

"Violets, roses, and orris root. I blend them with beeswax to create a scented balm. Twice a year I ship quantities of it to the South. 'Tis quite popular."

Gareth glanced toward the door at the far end of the shed. "What is in the adjoining workroom?"

"That is the place where I create my scented oils. It is where I work with fresh flowers and herbs instead of the dried ones. My lord, I believe you are attempting to distract me."

"Do you find my interest in your work unusual?" Gareth strode toward the connecting door.

"Under the circumstances, I do, sir."

Gareth opened the door and went through into the next workroom. "You cannot blame me for being curious. Now that I have given up the business of hunting cutthroats, my fortunes are in your hands, madam." He halted just inside the room. "It smells like all the flowers on the earth are collected in here."

Clare scowled and hurried after him. "I told you, that workroom is full of fresh petals and other ingredients."

Gareth walked over to a huge covered urn and lifted the lid. He took a deep whiff of the contents. "Hell's teeth. 'Tis enough to make a man light-headed."

"Oil of roses," Clare explained.

"And this?" Gareth lifted another lid.

"'Tis an oil mixture composed of fresh lavender, cloves, and a great many other ingredients. My lord, forgive me if I doubt the extent of your interest in my creations. We both know that you are attempting to avoid a discussion."

"An argument." Gareth took a deep breath of the lavender and clove oil.

"I beg your pardon?"

"I am attempting to avoid an argument." He put the lid back on the urn and surveyed three large pots that stood on a table. "What's in these vessels?"

"Honey, beeswax, and vinegar." Clare hung on to her fraying temper with sheer willpower. "I mix various flowers and herbs into them to create different lotions and creams. My lord, I do not wish to argue with you, but—"

"Excellent." Gareth removed the lid from the honey jar. "I am not fond of arguments." He touched a large, heavy press made of wood and iron. "What is this mechanical device?"

"I use it to extract oil from cinnamon and roses. It is of Arab design."

"Where did you get it?"

"It was my father's. He discovered it on his last journey to Spain. It was packed in one of the chests full of books and other items that he sent to me shortly before he died."

Gareth poked experimentally at one of the iron screws. His expression was one of absorbed curiosity. "Fascinating."

"Unfortunately, it is broken at the moment. I have not been able to repair it."

"Mayhap I can do something about it. I have studied a number of the translated Arab works that describe mechanical devices."

"Have you?" Clare was suddenly intrigued. This was a side of Gareth that she had not seen until now.

"Aye." Gareth jiggled one of the hinges on the press.

"Mayhap you would care to examine my father's workrooms. They are on the other side of the courtyard. I have kept them locked since he left Desire a year ago. They are full of many of the items he discovered on his various journeys."

"I would very much like to see your father's workrooms."

"Aye. Well, then, I shall give you the keys. Mayhap you would also enjoy studying the book he wrote. I have it in my study chamber."

"He wrote a book?" Gareth sounded impressed.

"It is a collection of recipes and treatises that he translated from the Arabic. Unfortunately, my father was not a skilled scribe. It is a rather difficult volume to read."

"I shall look forward to the task."

Clare scowled in exasperation. She suddenly realized that Gareth had successfully deflected her from the topic at hand. "At the moment, however, I intend to have a discussion concerning the nature of our association."

"As a man who has made his living by knowing when to fight and when to keep his sword in its scabbard, I can tell you that you do not want such a discussion. Not now, at any rate."

"Is that so?" she challenged.

"Sometimes 'tis better not to confront a problem directly."

"Such discretion astounds me, sir. I would have thought you would prefer open battle."

"Nay, I have had too many battles in my time."

"You must excuse me if I am somewhat dubious of that statement, my lord."

" 'Tis true." Gareth looked up from the press. "I would far rather inhale the vapors of your perfumes than do battle with you."

"This is one battle you cannot avoid, sir. We are going to settle this matter between us. And we are going to do it now."

"So be it. If it is a battle you want, you shall have one."

Clare eyed him uneasily. "My lord, let us be clear on this matter of who gives the commands on Desire."

"Aye." Gareth wandered over to another urn and peered inside. "The first thing you must come to terms with, madam, is that I am not in your employ. You have not hired my services or my sword. I am your husband."

"I am hardly likely to forget that. I am attempting to adjust to the business of being a proper wife, but you are making things exceedingly difficult."

"You are not making it any easier on either of us by treating me as if I were little more than a hired guard."

"By Saint Hermione's girdle, I do not treat you as if you were a hired guard." Clare was outraged. "I have attempted to show you the respect due a husband. It seems to me that I have given ground at every point."

"Is that how you see the situation? You believe you have been forced to give ground?"

"Aye, that is exactly how it looks to me."

Gareth propped himself against a table and folded his arms across his chest. "What of me? Haven't I made similar compromises? Do you think it simple for me to adjust to this business of being a husband?"

"I fail to see what great difficulties you have had to encounter."

"Shall I list them for you?" Gareth held up his hand and ticked up his complaints on his fingers. "You have made it clear since the moment I arrived that I was not what you ordered."

"You were unexpected," Clare muttered.

Gareth ignored that. He held up another finger. "You announced in front of the entire household that you did not intend to be a proper wife."

"I agreed to share a bedchamber with you."

"You refused to consummate the marriage on our wedding night."

Clare was incensed. "I told you this morning that I regretted that decision. It was wrong of me to refuse to do my duty last night." She took a deep breath. "I stand ready to do it tonight."

He slanted her a derisive glance. "Your duty? You'll forgive me if I fail to get overly enthusiastic about making love to a woman who feels that she is being forced to fulfill her responsibilities in the bedchamber."

Clare had had enough. She stalked down the aisle and came to a halt directly in front of him. "Is that why you refused to consummate our marriage this morning when I gave you the opportunity? You lost your enthusiasm for the task?"

Gareth narrowed his eyes. "Do you blame me?"

Clare's temper flared out of control. "If you no longer have any enthusiasm for the business, we are presented with a difficult problem, are we not?"

"What problem would that be?"

"I have it on good authority that, unlike a woman, a man cannot perform his husbandly obligations unless he is able to work up some degree of enthusiasm for the business."

"Who told you that?"

"Prioress Margaret," Clare shot back triumphantly.

"Ah." Gareth nodded sagely.

"Do you dispute her statement?" Clare demanded.

Gareth shrugged. "Nay. She has the right of it."

"What are we to do, sir, if you fail to regain your enthusiasm? Mayhap we will be forced to annul the marriage."

Gareth went dangerously still. "So that is your plan. You think to end this union of ours before it is even begun."

Clare looked into his eyes and saw the smoke from the fires of the nether regions. But she was too caught up in the flames of her own anger to rein in her wayward tongue.

"An annulment will certainly become a necessity if you are unable to work up sufficient *enthusiasm* for your husbandly tasks."

"The good prioress neglected to tell you one important fact about a man's enthusiasm, madam."

"And what would that be, my lord?"

"Sometimes the oddest things will arouse it." Gareth smiled slowly. "On occasion, for example, a good argument will do the trick."

Too late Clare read the brilliant warning in his eyes. She stepped back quickly, but not quickly enough.

Gareth scooped her up into his arms, took three long strides across the workroom, and dropped Clare squarely into a huge bin full of fresh blossoms and herbs.

Clare shrieked as she sank into the fragrant mass. Rose petals and lavender leaves wafted into the air. The intense scent of fresh flowers engulfed her.

Before she could catch her breath, Gareth plunged into the bin. His mouth covered hers as his weight crushed her into the mountain of soft, fragrant petals.

12

Clare was overwhelmed by the feel of Gareth's body sprawled on top of her. His hands tangled roughly in her hair. His mouth was fierce and hot and urgent on hers. His scent made her head whirl even more than the fragrance of the massed petals in which she lay half buried.

She forgot all about the argument, the insults, and the outrage that had gripped her a moment earlier. Memories of the way Gareth had touched her last night flooded back, only to be swamped beneath the new excitement. A thrilling elation swept through her, driving all else before it. She wanted to know those glorious sensations again.

Gareth tore his mouth from hers. "I congratulate you, madam. I know of no one else who can provoke me the way that you do. Now you must suffer the consequences."

Clare searched his eyes. "Are you truly angry with me?"

"I am not certain how I feel at the moment." Gareth's voice was rough and dark and dangerous. "I only know that when we have finished this, there will be no more talk of an annulment."

She shivered. "I never asked for an annulment. I only brought up the subject because you implied that you might not be able to do your duty in the marriage bed."

"You will discover soon enough that I intend to fulfill my responsibilities." Gareth bent his head and took her lips once more. His tongue invaded her mouth.

Clare's fingers clenched in his hair as she responded to the deep kiss. He was attempting to intimidate her, she thought, mayhap even frighten her a bit. But it was impossible. She craved his touch, and the obvious passion in him set her own clamoring feelings ablaze.

Clare felt his leg sink between her thighs. He drew his knee upward, opening her to his touch. He caught hold of the skirts of her overtunic and the gown beneath it and pushed both all the way to her waist.

Clare shuddered and tightened her hands in his hair. She arched herself against his probing fingers.

"You are as wet as roses after rain." Gareth sounded awed. He stroked her the way he had last night, stroked her until she was trembling and desperate.

Clare clutched at him, her voice breaking on a soft, demanding little cry. She wrapped her leg around his, seeking more of him.

"Why in the name of all the saints did we waste last night?" Gareth whispered, his voice hoarse and strained. "I was a fool." He eased one finger gently into her.

Clare moaned. Her body tightened around him. She gulped air. "It was my fault. I was confused. I thought I wanted to wait."

"You were confused and I was an idiot. What a pair." Gareth dropped a string of heated kisses down her throat to her shoulder. He probed her with a second finger.

"Oh." Clare gasped. "*Oh.*"

"So tight. A sweet, unopened bud."

"Does that diminish your enthusiasm, my lord?" she asked anxiously.

He groaned and lowered his head to kiss the curve of her breast. "Nay, madam, it does not."

She smiled, vastly relieved. "I am glad."

"I seriously doubt that the combined forces of both heaven and hell could diminish my enthusiasm at this moment."

Clare could feel him stretching her, making her grow soft and even more damp than she already was. She was shaking with her need now. The magical tension that she had first experienced last night was twisting her insides again. Anticipation made her restless and impatient.

"Hurry." She nipped at his ear. "Please, hurry."

Gareth raised his head and looked down at her. His eyes were as mysterious as the mist that sometimes shrouded Desire. "I have married a tyrant."

"You must forgive me, my lord. I told you, I am accustomed to being in charge around here."

"When it comes to this, your wish is my command." Gareth loosened his own clothing, freeing his erect manhood.

Clare caught a glimpse of his aroused body as he centered himself between her legs. In spite of her spiraling excitement, she experienced a brief tremor of uncertainty. "Mayhap we should try to diminish some of your enthusiasm before we proceed further."

"It is far too late to do anything to diminish my enthusiasm."

"I did not mean to offend you. 'Tis not your fault that you are not the right size." She hugged him tightly and kissed his throat. "I'm sure we'll manage somehow."

"Aye. We will."

"I am very enthusiastic myself now, Gareth."

"I can tell." He covered her mouth with his own and began to push himself into her.

Clare, expecting a sensation similar to that which she experienced when he slid his fingers into her, was startled by the blunt, hard feel of him.

He pressed harder and she was more than startled. She was stunned. "*Gareth.*"

"Trust me."

"Wait, we must discuss this matter further," Clare squeaked.

"It was your earlier discussion of the matter that got us this far."

"Aye, but—"

"Trust me, Clare," he whispered.

She braced herself and clung to him as if preparing to descend into the Pit. "I am ready," she said bravely.

"It is not going to be all that bad, you know." He thrust deeper. Sweat broke out on his brow. "At least, I do not think it will be too difficult."

Clare squeezed her eyes shut. "Tell me when it's over."

He gave an odd, half-strangled exclamation. "Aye, I'll try to remember to do that."

Clare felt him tense and draw in his breath as if readying himself for a dangerous feat of arms. He surged all the way into her, sheathing himself to the hilt with one powerful motion.

The shock of his entry stole Clare's voice and breath. When she recovered, she clawed at Gareth's broad shoulders. She was furious at finding herself robbed of the thrilling pleasure she had expected.

"Joanna had the right of it. This part of marriage is, indeed, a great nuisance."

"Hold yourself still for a moment." Gareth sounded as shaken as she was. "Be *still*, I said. Stop wriggling."

Clare opened her eyes and scowled up at him. "I thought it would feel the way it did last night."

"It will." Gareth was clearly fighting for his self-control. "Eventually."

"By Saint Hermione's little toe, you have tricked me, Hellhound."

"Nay, 'tis just that I have no experience with virgins."

"I knew you were too big," she grumbled. "I knew it right from the first moment I saw you."

Gareth rained soft, persuasive kisses across her nose and cheeks. "Forgive me Clare. I did not want to hurt you."

The apology mollified her somewhat. "In truth, I am not in any great pain. At least not any longer. But I am very glad the business is finished."

"Clare—"

"You may cease now. Surely this marriage is properly consummated. You no longer need fear that I will have it annulled."

"For the last time, do not move," Gareth bit out each word very carefully and distinctly.

"I was merely attempting to find a more comfortable position."

"I will see to your comfort."

"You will remove yourself?"

"Not just yet."

She was disappointed. "Does that mean you have not yet finished doing your duty?"

"Aye." He began to glide slowly and cautiously back out of her.

"I can certainly understand now why it is difficult for a man to work up sufficient enthusiasm for this sort of thing night after night," Clare muttered.

"It helps if one's wife does not chatter continuously during the effort."

"Oh." Clare was chagrined. "My apologies," she said stiffly. "I did not mean to interfere with your concentration. I was merely trying to—"

"Hell's teeth, that is enough." Gareth sealed her mouth with his own. Simultaneously he pushed himself slowly back into her, filling her to the limit.

Clare moaned, but not with pain.

Gareth withdrew almost completely and repeated the process.

Again and again.

Each stroke was carefully measured and delivered with excruciating control. The rigid lines of Gareth's face and the tensed muscles of his body told their own story. He was a war-horse straining at the reins, all leashed power and trembling readiness.

Clare held her breath and closed her eyes. But after a moment or two she realized the slow strokes of his body within her were not unpleasant.

She could feel the sweat on Gareth's back. It dampened his tunic. Yet despite the obvious effort he was exerting, his enthusiasm showed no sign of fading.

Her eyes flew open when he lifted her legs up over his shoulders. Before she could protest the new position, he moved his hand downward between their bodies and touched her.

Without any warning, the coiling tension seized her once more.

"*Gareth.*"

"I told you to trust me."

He took the small, swollen nubbin between thumb and forefinger and plucked gently.

Clare screamed. The sound was muffled by Gareth's mouth. She dug her fingers into him and gave herself up to the wondrous ripples of pleasure that washed through her.

She was dimly aware of Gareth's ragged shout of satisfaction. It mingled with her own breathless cries as they both sank deeper into the sea of fragrant flower petals.

A long while later Gareth opened his eyes. He stretched luxuriously, unable to recall ever having felt so good in his life.

He squinted at a rose petal that was perched on top of his nose. He blew it off and watched as it fluttered into the air. He was practically buried in scented blossoms.

He smiled.

The heady fragrance of the heaped flowers was threaded through with another earthy smell, one that gave him intense satisfaction. He had made Clare his wife in every sense of the word. There would be no more talk of an annulment.

The mountain of flowers stirred and shifted. He turned his head and watched as Clare sat up. She fussed with her clothing and shook petals from her hair.

When she realized that he was watching her, she smiled shyly down at him. She didn't say a word.

"You may speak now. I did not intent to silence you forever." Gareth reached out to remove a yellow petal from her sleeve.

Clare grinned. "I do not know what to say."

"Neither do I." Gareth wrapped his hand around the back of her head and brought her mouth down to his for a lingering kiss.

Clare leaned closer. Her hair, smelling of fresh herbs, drifted over his face. Her fingers flattened on his chest and slowly worked their way down his body. Gareth felt himself throb gently in response.

"I believe your enthusiasm has been reawakened, my lord."

"I believe you are right." Gareth wrapped his fist in her soft hair. He pulled her closer.

A sudden pounding on the workroom door made Clare flinch. She straightened and sat up again quickly.

"My lord, are you in there?" Ulrich called loudly. "The blacksmith is here."

"Damn it to the Pit." Gareth sat up reluctantly. "I'd better get out there or by supper everyone in the hall will know what we were doing in here."

Clare frowned. "Surely you don't think they will guess that we—"

"Aye."

She turned a lovely shade of pink. "By Saint Hermione's thumb. Is that all anyone can talk about lately?"

"You must face the fact that the details of our marriage will always be of great interest to everyone on this manor."

"I do wish our people would find something else to talk about."

"It is doubtful that they will as long as we provide such interesting entertainment." Gareth climbed out of the flower bin.

He realized that Clare had referred to the inhabitants of Desire as *our people*. It was a good sign.

"My lord?" Ulrich shouted again. "Are you in there?"

"Aye," Gareth called. "I'll be out in a moment." He turned back to assist Clare out of the pile of flowers.

She was a rare sight. He gazed at her, momentarily enthralled. Dripping in soft, fragrant petals, she looked like a creature of magic rising from a woodland bed.

Then he saw the small red stain on her undertunic. He reached out to touch it. His jaw tightened.

"Did I hurt you very badly?"

"Nay." Clare wiped at the petals that clung to her skirts. "Off with you. You have business to attend to. I must straighten my clothing."

Gareth could not tear his eyes from her glowing face. *She was his now.* She belonged to him as she had belonged to no other man, not even Raymond de Coleville, her pattern of chivalry.

Clare might have loved de Coleville—mayhap she still did—but she had not given herself to him. She had kept herself for her lord and husband, the Hellhound of Wyckmere.

I know well how to protect what I have taken by my own hand, Gareth thought with a fierce rush of determination. *And I will protect you, lady of Desire.*

"In time you will forget him, Clare," he said aloud.

She gave him a blank look. "Forget who?"

Ulrich struck the door three more times in quick succession. "Shall I send the blacksmith home and tell him to return later, my lord?"

"Nay, I am on my way." Gareth turned away from the sight of Clare covered in flowers. He went to the door, opened it, and stepped out into the bright sunlight.

"Well, Ulrich? Where is our blacksmith?" Gareth closed the door firmly so that his friend would not see Clare.

"In the stables." Ulrich's gaze was amused. "You spent a great deal of time in the workrooms. I did not realize you were so interested in the mysteries of perfumes."

Gareth started across the courtyard. "You know me, Ulrich, I am always interested to learn how a thing works."

Ulrich fell into step beside him. "Aye, you are certainly one to delve deeply into the most intimate details."

"I have certain responsibilities as the lord of this manor."

"Aye." Ulrich gave him a sage look.

"Only a fool would fail to acquaint himself closely with the inner workings of the source of his future income."

"No one has ever called you a fool, my lord." Ulrich reflected briefly. "Bastard, Hellhound, Devil's Spawn, Opener of the Window of Hell, mayhap, but never a fool."

Several people turned to watch as the two men crossed the courtyard. Gareth frowned when he saw a number of onlookers hastily avert their heads. He had a deep suspicion that they were concealing grins.

That suspicion was given more weight when Gareth noticed that John Blacksmith was gazing at him in openmouthed astonishment.

"Is something wrong, Blacksmith?" Gareth asked with a dangerous politeness. He had the distinct impression that the man was on the verge of bursting into laughter.

"Nay, my lord." John shut his mouth and wiped it on the back of his dirty sleeve. "The sunlight is very bright today. Blinds the eyes."

"I doubt that the sun is any brighter than the fires of your forge."

"Ah, true, my lord. Very true. Ye'd think I'd be accustomed to the brightness, wouldn't ye?" John looked helplessly at Ulrich.

Ulrich merely smiled and said nothing. One of the men-at-arms who was standing nearby turned swiftly away from the scene and rushed into the stables.

Gareth shrugged and let the matter rest. From long experience he knew it was useless for him to attempt to comprehend whatever it was that the blacksmith and everyone else found so amusing.

"Very well, let's get to work, Blacksmith," Gareth said. "I brought no armorer with me when I came to Desire. I can employ one from Seabern if necessary, but I am told that you are uncommonly skilled with hammer and anvil."

John flushed a deep red at the compliment. "Aye, my lord."

"Do you think that you can handle the work of mending my men's equipment as well as keeping the horses properly shod?"

John drew himself up and squared his shoulders proudly. "Aye, my lord. I believe I can handle the task. I've done a fair bit of delicate work for my lady and the prioress. I've even fashioned some keys and locks."

"Excellent." Gareth clapped him on the back and led the way into the stables. "I'll show you what needs to be done. And when we've finished in the stables, I have an interesting mechanical device to show you."

"What mechanical device would that be, my lord?"

"An Arab machine designed for extracting oil from roses and cinnamon and such. It is broken at the moment, but I believe I can repair it. I will need your help."

Twenty minutes later the muffled chuckles and hastily swallowed grins still had not entirely subsided.

Gareth left the blacksmith to his work and walked over to where Ulrich stood leaning against a stable post.

"Do you think," Gareth said in a very low voice, "that you could possibly explain the jest that everyone appears to find so very entertaining this afternoon?"

Ulrich's eyes gleamed with laughter. "I can explain it, but you very likely will not find it amusing."

"That is understood," Gareth muttered. "Nevertheless, I grow curious about the cause of such extended merriment. Just tell me why in the name of the devil every man in the vicinity is struggling not to collapse with laughter."

Ulrich cleared his throat. "I believe it has to do with the rose petals that are tangled in your hair and clinging to the back of your tunic, my lord."

Gareth groaned. "Hell's teeth." He ran his fingers through his hair. Crimson petals fluttered to the stable floor.

"You have the look of a man who has been tumbling about in my lady's flower bin," Ulrich said. "Unless you accidentally fell into it, and I will admit that you are prone to accidents lately, there is little doubt about what you were doing in the perfume workrooms."

Gareth planted his fists on his hips and swept the grinning crowd with a thoughtful look. The smiles vanished instantly from every face.

Satisfied, Gareth threw back his head and roared with laughter.

Three mornings later, Clare took her customary walk along the cliffs into the village. To her great astonishment and secret delight, it was not Joanna who accompanied her, but Gareth.

He'd hailed her from the courtyard as she came down the steps.

"I believe I'll join you, madam." Gareth had left to Ulrich the supervision of the stonemasons who had arrived to start work on the new wall. He had walked over to where Clare stood waiting. "I want to take another look at the cliffs above the two small coves."

The whole day had suddenly seemed brighter to Clare. "Aye, my lord. You are most welcome to walk with me. I am taking some herbal cream to the recluse."

As she and Gareth made their way along the cliffs, it struck her that the salt-laced air had never been more invigorating and the scents of morning had never seemed fresher.

It occurred to her that she had been battling an unfamiliar and unsettling mix of emotions since the moment Gareth had set foot on Desire. The sensations had been as powerful as an alchemist's brew. And just as unpredictable.

But she had finally comprehended the meaning of the volatile mixture three days ago when Gareth had consummated the marriage in her flower bin.

As she watched him walk out of the workroom that day, leaving her drenched in the scent of roses and his own male essence, she had finally acknowledged the truth.

She was falling in love with the Hellhound.

The past two nights had been adventures into the uncharted lands of a passion she had not even dreamed existed. Gareth seemed to take enormous pleasure from bringing her to the peak of physical sensation. He was never satisfied until she shivered and cried out in his arms. He never let her rest until she was exhausted from his lovemaking.

"Have you made all the arrangements to get your perfumes and sweet pots over to Seabern?" Gareth asked absently as he paused along the clifftop.

"Aye. My perfumes will be taken across to Seabern by boat on the first day of the fair." Clare shaded her eyes with her hand and watched Gareth study the foaming water at the base of the cliffs. "Joanna and I shall go with them."

"My men can help." Gareth paced along the top of the cliffs for a few steps and paused again to look down. He frowned. "We have a couple of tents that you may use if you wish."

"Wonderful." Clare hesitated. "What are you looking at?"

"Ulrich suggested that this might be one of the two places along the cliffs other than the harbor where a small boat could be brought ashore. He was right."

"Does that concern you?" Clare walked over to the edge of the cliffs and looked down. The tide was out. Two small caves in the side of the cliffs near the shoreline were visible.

"Not unduly. 'Tis obvious that no large force could be landed here."

Clare frowned. "No hostile force of armed men has ever landed on Desire."

"In my experience 'tis better to be prepared for any eventuality."

"You are a cautious man."

"I am when I have something very valuable to protect."

She gave him a quick sidelong glance and wondered whether he referred to her or his new lands. His lands, no doubt, she thought. Lands, after all, were the lure that had brought him to Desire in the first place.

Gareth did not appear to notice her speculative look. He was studying the landscape spread out before him with an expression of intense satisfaction that was overlaid by an equally fierce watchfulness.

He was not yet accustomed to the notion of having a place of his own in the world, Clare realized. Gareth still looked as though he expected someone to attempt to take Desire from him. Only a fool would dare try, she thought wryly. The Hellhound was on guard.

He looked dangerous even now when he was merely accompanying his wife into the village. His midnight-dark hair was wild and windblown by the sea breeze. His profile was as unyielding as the harsh cliffs below.

Clare stifled a small, wistful sigh. Gareth was concerned with the protection of Desire, of course. She had no doubt that he intended to protect her, too, but that was because she was part of the arrangement.

She was falling in love, but she did not dare to hope that Gareth was suffering the same fate; not yet, at any rate.

His knowledge of lovemaking indicated that he had experienced passion before in his life. During the past three days Clare had learned that he knew well how to control the powerful forces unleashed by physical desire.

She had also learned that he was not above using his own controlled passion to gain the response he wanted from her.

He was a man accustomed to command, Clare reminded herself. It was probably quite natural for him to take command in bed. As for herself, she was still too new at the business to seize the upper hand.

But she was nothing if not a fast learner, she thought optimistically.

Clare searched for a neutral topic. "William and Dallan appear to be doing well in their new program of physical exercise."

"Aye. Boys usually do, if they are properly encouraged. Dallan is still grumbling, Ulrich says, but he shows up on time for practice. At least the minstrel has demonstrated the good sense not to sing any more of his ballads about cuckolded lords."

"Aye, his ballads have become quite tame of late, have they not? One might even say they are rather dull."

"Do you think so?" Gareth looked thoughtful.

Clare hid a smile. "All those sweet little songs about the pretty roses opening their petals to receive the morning dew have begun to bore me. I find they lack the excitement of his earlier ballads."

"Excitement?"

"Aye, there is no danger, no fear of discovery, no thrilling action, no spice in Dallan's new poems."

"Madam, are you teasing me?"

"Mayhap."

"Be warned, I have frequently been told that I do not respond well to jests."

"Nonsense. I have heard you laugh, my lord. I would think you could learn to find amusement in Dallan's more adventurous songs about illicit love and cuckolded lords."

Gareth came to a halt. He grasped her chin and looked down at her with gleaming eyes. "Understand me well, Clare. I will never laugh at the notion of my wife lying in the arms of another man. I am far more likely to exact the devil's own payment for such a betrayal."

"As if I would even think of betraying you," she retorted. "I am a woman of honor, sir."

"Aye," Gareth said softly. "You are. And I am grateful for it."

She warmed beneath his gaze. He trusted her, she thought. It was a good start.

"While we are on the subject," she said gruffly, "I want to make it clear that I would not take a husband's betrayal any better than you would take that of a wife."

He smiled his rare smile. "You do not care for the thought of me in another woman's bed?"

"Nay, my lord, I do not." She felt flustered but determined. "I have my pride, too, sir."

"Pride. Is that why you object to the notion of me bedding another woman? Because it would wound your pride?"

Clare glowered at him. She was certainly not going to confess her love at this point. The Hellhound would take full advantage of such an admission. It would leave her even more vulnerable to him than she already was.

"What other reason could there be except pride, my lord?" she asked innocently. "In that regard I am no different than yourself. Surely it is pride that makes you feel so strongly about the matter of being cuckolded?"

"Aye." Gareth's eyes narrowed a little as he watched her. "A man's pride is a serious business."

"So is a woman's."

"Well, then, young Dallan must continue to sing of roses in the rain and other such dull matters." Gareth bent his head and brushed his mouth lightly across Clare's.

"Gareth—"

"Come. It grows late and I have many things to see to today." He grabbed her hand and swept her along the clifftops toward the village.

Ten minutes later Clare and Gareth reached the convent wall that marked the heart of the village. A cart piled high with thatching reeds clattered past. The thatcher nodded politely at Clare and Gareth. A shepherd did the same as he drove a flock down the center of the street.

Everyone turned to look as the lord and lady of Desire walked hand in hand through the small community.

Clare knew that most of the stares were for Gareth. She herself was too familiar a sight to draw such curious gazes. But Gareth was still new, a strange and largely unknown quantity to the people of the manor. They were only too well aware that their fate was in his hands.

"I must deliver the herbal cream to Beatrice," Clare said as she and Gareth reached the recluse's cell. "I'll only be a moment."

Gareth stopped and glanced at the window of the cell. "The curtain is drawn. Mayhap she is still asleep."

"Not likely." Clare chuckled. "Beatrice is always up and about very early. She usually opens her curtain first thing so as not to miss any news."

Clare went to the window. It was unlocked and ajar, as though Beatrice had recently been peering out into the street. "Beatrice?"

There was no response.

"Beatrice?" Clare hesitated and then reached through the narrow opening to push the heavy wool curtain aside. "Are you ill? Do you need help?"

Only silence came from the darkened interior. Clare gazed into the small front chamber of the little house. At first she could see nothing at all. The curtain on the other window was also drawn shut, leaving the chamber drenched in shadow.

Then Clare's eyes adjusted to the gloom. The first thing she noticed was Beatrice's slippered feet on the floor.

"*Beatrice.*" Clare gripped the stone sill and tried to get a better look at the prone figure inside.

Gareth frowned. He walked closer to the window. "What's wrong?"

"I do not know." Clare looked at him. "She is lying on the floor. She's not moving. Gareth, I think she may be badly hurt."

Gareth studied the interior of the anchorite's cell. "The door is locked. I can see the key hanging on the wall."

"How will we get inside?" Clare asked.

"Send someone for John Blacksmith. Be quick about it, Clare."

Clare did not need further urging.

A short while later the blacksmith jammed a forge tool between the stone wall and the crack of the recluse's door. Then he and Gareth put their shoulders to the heavy wood.

The door popped off its hinges on the third attempt.

Gareth went first into the small cell. He took one look at the body on the floor and shook his head.

"She is dead. And not from any natural cause."

13

"*Murdered.*" Clare stared at Gareth in shocked disbelief.

"I do not believe it." Margaret, who had been summoned immediately, looked stunned. "'Tis not possible. We have never had a murder here in the convent during the fifteen years I have been in charge."

Clare shook her head slowly. "There has not been a murder anywhere on Desire in my lifetime."

"This was most definitely murder." Gareth looked down at the open, sightless eyes of the recluse. He had seen enough of violent death in his time to recognize it.

"Are you certain?" Margaret frowned. "Mayhap she fell ill in the middle of the night, attempted to call for assistance and did not make it to the door."

Gareth crouched beside the body. He touched one of the dead woman's fingers and found it limp. The stiffness that followed death had already passed. "She died during the night, but not from illness." He studied the folds of Beatrice's head covering. "Was she accustomed to sleeping in her wimple?"

"I do not know," Margaret said. "It would appear so. Mayhap it was an act of piety."

"More like simple vanity," Clare said quietly. "Beatrice was very concerned about the sagging line of her chin. She did not want anyone to see it."

"She loved to gossip and she was overly fond of Clare's perfumes and herbal creams," Margaret said. "Small failings, when all is said and done. Would that we all limited our sins to such minor transgressions."

Gareth raised one eyebrow. "Aye."

"She is in her night robe," Clare said thoughtfully. "Yet she is wearing her shoes as well as her wimple."

Margaret peered anxiously at Gareth. "Are you absolutely certain this is not the result of some grave illness, my lord?"

"It was murder." Gareth pointed to the wimple. The fine linen had been crushed and badly wrinkled in the region around Beatrice's throat. "Do you see those marks?"

Margaret leaned closer. "Aye."

Gareth started to lift the hem of the wimple.

Margaret put out a hand as though to stop him. "What are you doing, my lord?"

"I want to see her neck." Gareth peeled back the white linen.

The dark, ugly bruises on Beatrice's throat were obvious for all to see.

"Saint Hermione defend her," Clare whispered.

"God rest her soul," Margaret breathed.

Clare looked at Gareth. "You have seen such marks before?"

"Aye." Gareth lowered the wimple. "The recluse was strangled."

"But that is not possible." Clare's gaze went to the heavy wooden door that Gareth and John had recently forced. "Her door was locked from the inside. And the windows are too narrow for a man to pass through."

Gareth glanced toward the doorway. Through the opening he could see that a cluster of curious onlookers had gathered. Several of the nuns and novices as well as a number of villagers stood just outside, trying to look into the cell.

"Instruct everyone to be off about their own business," Gareth said to Margaret. "I do not want them trampling about out there in front of the cell any more than they already have."

Margaret eyed him consideringly. "Aye, my lord."

She went to the door and dispatched the small crowd.

Clare met Gareth's eyes. "The day before our wedding, Beatrice insisted that she had seen Brother Bartholomew. She claimed that she saw him enter the convent grounds. She said he walked straight through the locked gates."

"Brother Bartholomew?" Gareth recalled the conversation between

Beatrice and Clare that he had overheard. "Ah, yes. The ghost. You never did tell me what that was all about."

"It is merely an old legend, my lord," Margaret said brusquely. "Brother Bartholomew was a wandering monk. He came to Desire many years ago to preach to the villagers and the members of this house. 'Tis said that while he was on the isle he seduced a young nun and persuaded her to run off with him."

"They fled during a storm," Clare explained. "Both were drowned when their boat overturned in the high seas."

"This occurred while you were in charge of this convent, madam?" Gareth asked.

"Most definitely not." Margaret was heartily offended. "I would never have tolerated such nonsense. Nay, the tale is from long before my time."

"And long before mine, also," Clare said. "The legend has it that Brother Bartholomew returns on certain nights seeking his beloved. Whenever he is seen on the convent grounds, disaster is said to follow."

Gareth got to his feet. "I can promise you that your recluse was not killed by a ghost. A flesh-and-blood man left those marks on her throat."

He walked to the door and looked out at the trampled grass. "Hell's teeth, I wish I had thought to keep the curious away. Now it will be impossible to see if there are any strange bootmarks in front of the cell."

"My lord." Clare's voice was quiet and thoughtful. "There is something strange here."

"Aye. Murder is always strange."

"I refer to an unusual odor."

Gareth swung around and fixed her with a sharp gaze. "I have great respect for your sense of smell, madam. What odor do you detect?"

"Mint."

"Mint?" Gareth stepped closer to the body. He drew a deep breath, trying to taste the air. "Aye. Very faint."

Margaret's brow wrinkled in confusion. "What is so odd about the scent of mint? Mayhap the recluse recently used some to prepare a meal."

Clare's nose twitched. "Nay, the scent is on her night robe."

Gareth went back down on one knee beside the body. "You're right. 'Tis on the hem of her gown." He glanced at the green stains on the bottom of the recluse's soft leather slippers. "And on her shoes."

Clare wrapped her arms around her waist. "There is a large patch of mint in the convent gardens. Do you think that Beatrice went outside last night?"

"She never left her cell," Margaret said quickly. "Never in all the years I knew her. Do not forget, she was an anchorite. She wanted to be enclosed.

Indeed, she once told me that she had a great dislike of being in the outside world."

"Aye, but if she really thought that she had seen the ghost of Brother Bartholomew," Clare said, "mayhap she would have been curious enough to leave her cell in order to follow him."

"Clare, surely you do not believe in that old legend," Margaret said.

"Nay, but Beatrice did."

"My lady wife has a point." Gareth looked at Clare. "Mayhap Beatrice did see someone last night, someone she took to be the ghost. And mayhap she went outside to see what he was doing."

Margaret shook her head. "It makes no sense. If she had seen someone she took to be a ghost, surely she would have been alarmed. She would have stayed in here behind a locked door."

"Who knows?" Clare said. "Beatrice was a very curious person. And she knew that no one believed that she had actually seen the ghost of Brother Bartholomew. Mayhap she sought proof of her story. And was murdered for it."

"But there is no one on this isle who had any reason to kill Beatrice," Margaret said.

Gareth kept his gaze on Clare's troubled face. "Let us have a look at that patch of mint."

Clare nodded. "It is planted near the library." She turned and led the way out of the cell.

Margaret set off after her.

Gareth took one last look at the murdered recluse. Then he followed Clare and the prioress down a garden path to a large square plot of dark-green mint located next to a stone wall. The signs of trampled greenery were evident immediately. The odor of crushed mint was strong.

"Someone stood here recently," Gareth said. He walked around the plot, examining it from all sides. Then he glanced up at the window in the wall. "The library is on the other side of this wall?"

"Aye," Margaret said quietly.

"I would like to look inside, if you have no objection, madam."

"Of course not, but I do not see what good it will do."

The heavy keys on Margaret's girdle rattled and clashed as she selected one.

"Another locked door," Clare murmured as Margaret approached the library door and inserted the key.

"Aye," Gareth said. "One would almost think that the murderer really was a ghost."

Clare frowned. "Surely you do not believe that?"

"Nay," Gareth said. "But it would appear that someone wishes us to believe it."

Margaret breathed an audible sigh of relief as she opened the library door and took a quick look around inside. "All is well in here. For a moment there I feared that we had been robbed."

"And that the recluse had been killed because she saw the thieves?" Gareth nodded. "A reasonable assumption."

He walked into the library. Clare followed at his heels. Together they examined the shelves full of heavy books. Many of the richly bound volumes were prudently chained to the wall.

Gareth was impressed. "You have a great many fine books, Prioress."

"Aye. And I'm pleased to say that we have never had a theft from our library during my time here as prioress," Margaret said proudly. "But one can never be too careful with things as valuable as books."

"My lord," Clare called from the last row of library shelves. "There is a volume open on one of the desks."

"Impossible." Margaret hurried down the aisle, clearly alarmed. "All of the books are properly stored after use. I have given strict orders to that effect."

Gareth walked down the aisle to where Clare stood beside an open volume. He glanced down at the beautifully decorated page filled with exquisitely wrought words. The elaborate design that framed the first letter on the page was done in gleaming gold, brilliant red, and rich blue.

"It is a treatise on herbs," Clare explained. "I have consulted it several times myself."

"I cannot believe that any of the members of this house would leave it open on the desk like this," Margaret said. "It is far too valuable to be treated in such a careless fashion."

Gareth glanced toward the window that overlooked the mint patch. The heavy green glass allowed sunlight to filter into the chamber. "I wonder if the murderer was about to steal this book when he realized there was someone outside watching him."

"Do you think he killed poor Beatrice and then fled?" Clare asked.

"Mayhap." Gareth considered the matter for a moment. "But before he ran off, he went to the trouble of carrying the recluse's body back to her cell."

"How could he have locked her inside?" Clare asked. "The key to her door is still hanging on the inside wall of her house. And the murderer did not return to the library for the book he wanted so badly."

"He might have feared discovery," Margaret suggested.

"Aye, or the book was not what he sought, after all." Gareth studied the open volume. "If any of this is true, and we cannot be certain of it, we are left with a very interesting problem."

"You mean we must find a murderer?" Clare asked.

"Aye," Gareth said. "One who can read."

That night Gareth waited, as he always did, until Clare clutched at him, pleaded with him, lifted herself against him, nipped at his shoulder with her small, sharp teeth. Then he entered her with a sense of exultant satisfaction.

He eased himself past the initial restriction of her small, moist sheath and then drove deep. She closed around him, tight and hot and welcoming. He fought the nightly battle to restrain himself until she shivered and cried out in his arms.

"*Gareth.*"

He surged fully into her one last time, shuddered heavily, and finally surrendered to the crashing waves of his own release.

When he eventually rolled off of her and onto his back, the sheets were damp and the air inside the enclosed bed was heavy with the scent of spent passion.

He used his bare foot to part the curtains. Moonlight poured through the window and spilled across the bed.

Clare lay silent and unmoving for a long while. Gareth thought she had fallen asleep. He was surprised when she spoke from the circle of his arm.

"You make love to me as if you feared that, unless you exhaust me with passion, I might run off during the night," she said quietly. "Do all husbands treat their wives in such a fashion?"

Gareth went very still. "You have a complaint to make about my lovemaking?"

"I am not complaining, and well you know it." Clare propped herself on her elbow and looked down at him. Her eyes searched his face in the pale light. "There are times when I do not understand you, Gareth."

"What is there to understand?" He threaded his fingers through her hair. "I am a newly wedded man indulging himself in the pleasures of the marriage bed. There is nothing strange or unusual about that."

"I think there is more to it. What is it you fear, my lord?"

"Not you, madam." He gave her a slow smile.

"I'm not so certain of that."

Gareth dragged her mouth down to his and kissed her thoroughly. He did not release her until her lips were parted and she had softened against him.

"The only thing I fear from you, madam," he said when he was satisfied that he had successfully distracted her, "is that you will drive me mad with desire."

"You tease me, my lord."

"Do I?" He kissed her throat.

"Aye, I have noticed that you often do that when you wish to avoid a serious discussion."

"Is that what you are doing just now? Having a serious discussion?" He cupped her breast in the palm of his hand and ran his thumb lightly over her nipple. It peaked at his touch. "I had not noticed."

"You noticed. You simply chose to pretend that you did not."

"I would rather make love to you."

"You see?" Clare sat up abruptly and curled her legs under her. She propped her elbows on her knees and rested her chin on her hand. "That is exactly what I mean. Every time I try to talk to you about our marriage, you make love to me."

"Is that such a terrible sin to lay at a husband's feet?" He stroked her thigh to her knee. By the saints, her skin was soft. "If you wish to have a serious conversation, let us at least have it about an interesting subject."

"What subject would that be?" she asked suspiciously.

"Let us talk of passion, wife."

"You wish to talk of passion, my lord? Very well, we shall have such a discussion. Only this time, I shall take charge of the conversation."

"Will you?"

"Aye." She reached out and wrapped her fingers tentatively but quite determinedly around his shaft. She tugged experimentally.

"Ah." Gareth sucked in his breath. "This promises to be a most interesting conversation." It was the first time she had initiated such intimacy. It had a stunning effect on his senses.

"I trust you will find it so." She leaned over him, cupping him carefully. Her hair brushed his thigh. "There is certainly a great deal to this topic. Indeed, it appears to be broadening by the second."

Gareth folded his arms behind his head and called on all his formidable powers of self-mastery. "I would not want you to grow bored with the subject."

"Nay, sir, I am not likely to do that."

Without any warning she lowered her head and kissed his stirring manhood.

"Hell's *teeth*." Gareth was so startled by the boldness of her action that he sat bolt upright.

"Do I make you anxious, my lord? Is this subject not to your liking?"

He fell back on his elbows. "What in the name of the saints do you think you're doing?"

"Exploring the topic as thoroughly as possible. I am an excellent scholar, you know." Her small tongue touched him again, warm, moist, tantalizing. "Do you have any objection, my lord?"

Gareth groaned and collapsed back against the pillows. "Nay, madam. I trust that you will cover every detail."

"I shall endeavor to be very thorough."

So much for awkward talk of their relationship as husband and wife, Gareth thought with satisfaction. This was a much safer subject.

It was not until later, when Gareth believed that Clare had finally fallen asleep, that he allowed himself to contemplate her gentle, much too perceptive challenge.

What is it you fear, my lord?

Even had he been willing to admit to such a weakness, he could not have given her an answer. He did not have one.

On the face of it, he now possessed everything he had fought for all of his life. He had lands, a wife, a home of his own. But something was still missing. He did not understand what it was, but he sensed that Clare held the key.

In some way that he could not explain, Gareth knew that he had to bind her to him with every means at his command.

"She predicted death, you know," Clare said into the shadows.

Gareth turned on his side and cradled her against him. "Aren't you ever going to fall asleep tonight?"

"I trust so." Clare yawned. "I need my rest. We shall all be very busy at the fair."

"Who predicted death? The recluse?"

"Aye. But then, she frequently predicted gloom and disaster. This time, unfortunately, she was right." Clare shifted against him, entwining her leg with his. "How will you go about finding the murderer?"

"I shall do what I am most skilled at. I shall set a few snares."

"What do you mean?"

"It appears that the murderer did not have an opportunity to steal whatever it was he sought in the library. He may try again. When he does, we shall be ready for him."

"How?"

Gareth shrugged. "I shall post guards around the convent every night and instruct them to remain out of sight in the shadows. They will be in a position to see if anyone attempts to climb the wall or get through the gates."

"A brilliant plan, my lord."

Gareth was amused by the note of genuine admiration in her voice. Some people were easier to please than others, he reflected. They expected so little that they were overwhelmed by any sign of competency. "Thank you."

"You are certain that the murderer is a man?"

Gareth remembered the grim bruises on the recluse's throat. "Aye. Mayhap a very strong woman could have killed her. But I think a woman would have had to drag the body back to the cell. Beatrice was carried."

"Aye. There were no signs of her being dragged across the flower beds."

"Or along the graveled paths. The pebbles were undisturbed."

"You are a keen observer, my lord."

"You mean for a thick-skulled, overly muscled knight?"

"Hush." She covered his mouth with her fingertips. "I never actually called you that."

"I beg your pardon. My mistake. I do not know how I came by that impression."

"No more of your teasing, sir. I have had quite enough."

"Aye, madam."

Clare fell silent for a few seconds and then she sighed. "It is so difficult to imagine anyone killing a harmless old woman like Beatrice."

Gareth thought back on his years spent hunting violent men. "Unfortunately, 'tis only too easy to imagine someone committing murder. The real question is why."

"To steal a book?"

"Books are valuable, 'tis true, but only to scholars. I do not believe there are many such who would actually kill for one. And even if a man were determined to lay hands on a book, you must admit that Desire is a very distant, out-of-the-way place to travel merely to steal one."

"Many scholars have braved the perils of the roads all the way to Spain and Italy just to get hold of certain books. In a sense my father died because of his thirst for the treasures stored up in the Arab treatises he hunted."

"I had not thought of it in that fashion, but you're right. Sir Humphrey risked his life to seek out books. Mayhap someone else is prepared to do the same."

"It is at times such as this," Nicholas of Seabern said mournfully, "that I comprehend the true extent of all that I lost when I failed to win the hand of the lady of Desire. I trust you appreciate your good fortune, Hellhound."

Gareth followed his gaze to where Clare stood outside a yellow-and-white-striped tent. She was haggling with a merchant. From the few words that reached him, it was obvious that his wife was driving a hard bargain. She appeared to be enjoying herself immensely.

"Aye," Gareth said. He felt a rush of pleasure at the sight of her. She was as vibrant and warm as the spring day. Her eyes were bright with excitement and her hands moved gracefully through the air as she emphasized a point. A few strands of her hair had escaped her yellow net. "I am not one to take fortune for granted."

"She'll make you a nice profit on this one sale alone." Nicholas took a large swallow from his mug of spiced wine. "And there are two more days of good bargaining ahead. You'll be richer than that fat London merchant before the fair is over."

Gareth knew that the merchant in question had come all the way from London to purchase the perfumes of Desire. He was a short, stout man of middle years. His shrewd eyes gleamed with the delight he took in bargaining with an opponent of equal skill. He was dressed in a finely embroidered wool tunic. His cap and mantle were trimmed with fur and velvet and he wore costly rings on his plump fingers.

Nearby Joanna stood outside a green and white tent. She was hard at work dealing with two other merchants. She was selling quantities of exquisitely embroidered sweet bags and scented pillows. She appeared to be enjoying herself as much as Clare was.

Ulrich and one of Gareth's men-at-arms lounged idly between the two tents. They munched hot pies as they kept watch on the tables laden with the wares of Desire. Pickpockets and petty thieves were as much a part of a busy fair as the peddlers, merchants, jugglers, and acrobats.

Gareth rested his hand on the hilt of the Window of Hell and surveyed the array of colorful tents and peddlers' stalls that had been set up in front of Seabern Keep.

The fair had attracted not only the inhabitants of Seabern and Desire but a number of other people from miles around. Pennants flapped in the breeze. Musicians strolled through the crowds with lutes and drums. Tradesmen sold food, spiced wine, and ale. It was a busy, energetic scene and, Gareth knew, a lucrative one for all concerned.

"Do not bemoan your loss to me," he said to Nicholas. "Seabern will see a healthy profit from this fair. Everyone here is making money and spending it."

"Aye." Nicholas grinned. "I should look on the bright side of the matter. You could say that I get to enjoy some of the benefit of your lady's talents without having to put up with her sharp tongue and clever wit."

"I'm pleased that you do not intend to hold my good fortune against me."

"Nay." Nicholas took another swallow of the wine and assumed a philosophical expression. "And I'm pleased you do not feel the need to run me through with the Window of Hell."

"I have been entirely convinced that there is no great need to kill you, Nicholas."

"I told you so." Nicholas clapped him on the back. "So the lady was a virgin, after all, eh? I'll confess it crossed my mind that Raymond de Coleville might have had her, but I'm not surprised he failed to seduce her, too. Clare's got the pride of a queen."

"Aye."

"And blood made from ice water, if you ask me."

"I did not ask your opinion."

Nicholas ignored that. "She'll be grateful when you leave, you know. She has no use for a husband."

"Mayhap she will discover one."

Nicholas hooted with laughter, nearly choking on his spiced wine. "God's eyes, man, but that's an excellent jest. Didn't think you had a sense of mirth. Well, then, as we're neighbors and we both owe allegiance to Thurston of Landry, I say we may as well be friends."

"An interesting thought."

"No offense, but your lady would have made my life a hell on earth." Nicholas shook his head. "'Tis all that education they gave her when she was young. Ruins women, you know. She actually demanded to wed a man who could read. Can you credit it?"

"Astonishing."

"Of what use is such a skill to a knight with a good strong sword arm, I ask?"

"You do not know how to read?" Gareth asked casually.

"Nay." Nicholas belched. "Never saw the point of it. I can hire all the scribes and clerics I need to deal with my accounts and such. Reading is a waste of time and energy for a man."

He could remove one suspect from the list of possible murderers, Gareth thought wryly. Nicholas of Seabern was no doubt quite capable of killing anyone who got in his way, but it was unlikely that he would have gone to the trouble of strangling the recluse for the sake of a book that he could not even read.

"My lord." Clare lifted a hand to summon him over to the green and white tent. "Will you come here a moment, please?"

"You must excuse me," Gareth said to Nicholas. "My lady wants me."

"Aye," Nicholas said grimly. "And likely this is only the start of it. Mark my words. 'Twill get worse as the years go by. She's in the habit of giving commands. You'll spend your days running hither and yon at her whim."

"Do you think so?"

"Aye. I can see it now. She'll summon you and dispatch you and set you to hopping about like a damned servant."

"A man must pay a price for everything." Gareth strolled toward Clare. She fixed him with a seemingly benign smile when he joined her and the merchant. Her eyes, however, glittered with bright warning. "My lord, I would like you to meet Edward Kingsgate, a very clever merchant who sells my perfumes to his customers in London."

"My lord." Kingsgate doffed his velvet cap and swept Gareth a deep bow. "I am honored, sir."

"Merchant." Gareth looked at Clare for further guidance.

Clare's smile sharpened. "My friend Kingsgate, here, has just struck a very good bargain for himself, one that leaves me only the very smallest of profits."

"Nay, my lady," Kingsgate protested, "you have had much the better of the bargain. Indeed, I shall be left with only a few pennies once I have paid my expenses for this journey."

Clare drummed her fingers on the table. "Kingsgate wishes to drive the price down still further on the grounds that he fears robbers on the road back to London."

"I shall be obliged to hire armed guards," Kingsgate explained smoothly. "You know how the roads are, my lord. Extremely dangerous, to say the least. And I shall be carrying a very valuable cargo. I must protect it."

Gareth finally understood what was going on. "You need not concern yourself with the added cost of hiring armed men to guard the shipment. I will send three of my best men to escort you and the goods to London."

The merchant blinked rapidly as he assimilated that information. "Your own men, sir?"

"Aye." Gareth rested his hand on the smoky crystal pommel of the Window of Hell. Kingsgate's gaze followed the movement. "I assure you, they are well trained and experienced in dealing with cutthroats and thieves."

"Ah. I do not doubt it. Your reputation assures me of the truth of that statement," Kingsgate murmured.

"There, you see?" Clare said quickly. "You will be spared the added cost of hiring your own guards. At the same time, you will have the security of knowing that your goods and, indeed, your very life are protected by men in the employ of the famous Hellhound. What more could a man ask as a guarantee of safety?"

Kingsgate cleared his throat. "As you say, madam, what more could a man ask? Very well, then, if you will supply the guards, we have a bargain."

"Excellent." Clare's eyes shone with satisfaction. "I shall look forward to doing business again with you in the fall, Kingsgate."

"Aye, madam. Good day, my lord." Kingsgate swept Clare and Gareth another deep bow and trotted off with a pleased expression.

"Thank you, my lord," Clare murmured. "You handled that very well."

"I try to make myself useful, madam."

She gave him a sharp look. Then her eyes softened. "I vow, we make a good team, sir."

"I am glad you are pleased."

Gareth was about to ask her if he could fetch her something to eat while she was between customers when he spotted William running toward the tent.

The boy was panting with exertion. He looked relieved to see both Gareth and Ulrich. He waved his hand frantically to get their attention.

"My lord, sir," William gasped as he came to a halt. "One of you must come with me. Dallan is in the midst of a terrible fight with a pickpocket. The thief has a dagger and he will likely stab Dallan."

Gareth glanced at Ulrich. "I'll see what this is about. Stay here and keep an eye on our fortunes."

"Aye, my lord." Ulrich grinned. "Try not to have any accidents with the pickpocket's dagger. You have been known to be somewhat clumsy of late."

14

Gareth saw immediately that Dallan was hopelessly overmatched.

The pickpocket was skinny and wiry and not much older than the minstrel. The rigors of his profession, however, had not only toughened him, they had endowed him with basic dagger fighting skills and absolutely no sense of chivalry. He did not appear to mind in the least that his opponent was unarmed.

Although he was at a serious disadvantage, Dallan had somehow managed to corner the thief behind a large brewer's tent. There was blood on Dallan's arm, but most of it appeared to be spewing from his nose, not a dagger cut. Gareth was grateful for that much. He did not relish the thought of explaining to Clare how her precious minstrel had gotten himself nicked.

It was obvious that Dallan was compensating for his lack of skill with sheer, unswerving determination. He faced the pickpocket fearlessly, as aggressive as a young hound with its first boar.

The pickpocket, accustomed to a more stealthy approach to such matters, seemed genuinely confused by his opponent's relentless assault. Nor did he like the attention the fight was receiving.

Several of the brewer's customers had ambled around the corner of the tent to watch the brawl. Loud cheers and shouts of encouragement filled the air as the two young males circled each other. For once Dallan was not twitching.

The pickpocket's eyes darted nervously left and right. He was clearly searching for an opportunity to bolt past Dallan and escape into the crowd.

Gareth swept the ring of onlookers with a single glance, seeking the source of Dallan's newfound boldness.

He spotted her at once. She was a pretty girl with blond curls, blue eyes, and a jaunty green cap. Her expression of rapt excitement and her glowing cheeks told its own story. Dallan had found himself a maiden in need of rescue.

"Halt, both of you."

Gareth strode into the middle of the fight and seized each young man by the scruff of the neck. He gave them both a brief, rough shake. Then he held them apart until they came to their senses long enough to comprehend that an outsider had interfered in the battle.

"This brawl is ended," Gareth said.

"He started it." Dallan wiped his bleeding nose with his sleeve. "He tried to steal Alison's purse."

"I did not. He lies." The pickpocket glowered at Dallan. His dagger had miraculously disappeared into the voluminous folds of his shabby clothes.

Gareth reasoned that Alison was the name of the girl hovering nearby. He glanced at her. "Do you still have your purse?"

Alison looked first startled and then decidedly uneasy at finding herself addressed by the lord of Desire. She flushed a deep pink. "Aye, m'lord. 'Tis safe enough." She patted the small leather pouch that hung from her girdle. Her eyes kindled with feminine admiration as she gazed at her champion. "Thanks to Dallan."

"Bah, I never laid a hand on her purse." The primitive fury of battle faded from the pickpocket's gaze. Wariness took its place. He measured Gareth with a quick, assessing glance, obviously recognizing him. As a professional thief, he would have learned early to mark men of rank in the crowd so as to avoid costly miscalculations. An unfortunate choice of victims could lead to a bad end for his kind. "I'm innocent, m'lord. I swear it on me mother's grave."

"He's a rogue and a thief," Dallan declared.

"Mayhap," Gareth said quietly. "But 'tis as important for a man to know when to end a battle as it is for him to know when to begin one. You've saved Alison's purse. One chivalrous act a day is enough for any man." He looked at the pickpocket. "Off with you. And take care that my squire-in-training is not obliged to deal with you a second time."

The pickpocket stared. "Squire-in-training? By my oath, I didn't know he was yer man, m'lord."

"You do now," Gareth said.

"'Twas an honest mistake," the pickpocket whined. "Could 'ave 'appened to anyone."

"Begone."

The pickpocket needed no further urging. He whirled around and melted into the crowd.

Disappointed with the tame outcome of the event, the onlookers drifted back to the ale tent to refill their mugs.

Dallan looked at the blood on his sleeve and then raised dumbfounded eyes to Gareth's face. "Did you mean that, my lord? I'm going to be your squire?"

"I'd be pleased to have such a brave man in my service." Gareth held out his hands. "Will you swear fealty to me, Dallan of Desire? Think well before you give your oath on this. I demand absolute and unswerving loyalty from those who serve me."

"Dallan of Desire." Dallan repeated the words as though they were a magical incantation. He put his hands in Gareth's, fell to his knees, and bowed his head. "My lord, from this day forward, I vow, I am your man."

"'Tis done, then." Gareth glanced at Alison and William, who were watching the small ceremony with awed expressions on their faces. "You two are my witnesses. Henceforth this man shall be known as Dallan of Desire and he is in my service. He has the right to my protection and in return he has vowed allegiance to me."

"Aye, my lord," William whispered excitedly. "I cannot wait to tell Mother and Lady Clare."

Alison gazed upon Dallan as though he had recently been transformed from a brave minstrel into a hero from a legend. "You serve the Hellhound of Wyckmere," she breathed, clearly entranced by his improved status in life.

Gareth resisted the urge to grin as Dallan staggered to his feet. "Go and wash the blood off, Squire-in-training. You will frighten the ladies."

"Aye, my lord." Dallan straightened his thin shoulders.

"I'll help you get cleaned up," William volunteered eagerly.

"I'll fetch a cloth," Alison said.

Gareth watched as Dallan was led off by his admirers. There was a new swagger to the minstrel's step and masculine pride in the set of his chin.

It was astounding how a man's view of himself and the world altered once he knew he belonged somewhere, Gareth thought.

"Alone at last." Gareth lowered himself down onto the large square of brightly striped cloth that Clare had spread out on the grass. He leaned back on his elbow and gazed out over the busy grounds of the fair. "Thought I'd never get rid of Dallan. The lad's been at my heels all afternoon."

"I'm surprised at how eagerly he entered your service." Clare handed Gareth one of the hot pies stuffed with minced meat and nuts that she had just purchased from a nearby stall. "I would never have thought he'd have been so enthusiastic about becoming your personal squire."

"Squire-in-training," Gareth muttered.

"Is there a difference?"

"Aye. Young Dallan has a long way to go before he qualifies as a fully trained squire. He does not yet know one end of a lance from the other."

"I vow, he has certainly undergone a great change today."

"Becoming an instant hero will do that to a man."

Clare smiled. "It was very generous of you to make him into a hero, my lord."

"No one can make a man heroic. He has to do it for himself. Dallan has courage." Gareth took a large bite out of his pie. "I hate to have to tell you this, madam, but you've lost one of your admirers. I fear he has chosen to devote himself to another lady."

"I saw her. A younger woman. And a blue-eyed blond at that." Clare munched her pie enthusiastically. After a morning's hectic bargaining, she was half starved. "How can I compete?"

"Useless. You must resign yourself to the boredom of being wed to a husband who cannot compose a ballad or sing a single note."

Clare grinned. Gareth looked anything but boring sprawled in the sunshine. He lounged at his ease, graceful and dangerous in the manner of a fierce beast of prey.

She had not had much time to talk to him since they had arrived early this morning to set up the tents and prepare for the day's business. But she had been aware of him checking on her and Joanna from time to time. One or two of his men had always been nearby to make certain petty thieves did not make off with the goods.

"You and Sir Ulrich have been a good influence on Dallan and young William, my lord," Clare said quietly. "I'll admit that at first Joanna and I were uneasy about some of your decisions regarding their welfare."

His eyes gleamed with complacency. "Just as you were uneasy about the business of taking a husband."

"Aye." Clare finished the last of her pie and wrapped her arms around her updrawn knees. "But things seem to be working out well enough."

"Naturally they're working out." Gareth lifted one shoulder in a dismissing movement as he popped the last of the pie into his mouth. "Why shouldn't they? I fail to see what is so difficult about marriage. It all seems very simple and straightforward to me."

"Does it, indeed, my lord?" Clare batted her lashes with mocking admiration.

"Aye." Gareth brushed crumbs from his hands. " 'Tis merely a matter of a man taking command of a household and setting down a few rules. Once everyone knows the rules, matters proceed at an orderly pace and all is harmonious."

Clare picked up the pouch she had used to carry the cloth and the hot pies and hefted it in a threatening fashion. "A matter of a *man* taking command of a household, did you say, sir?"

Gareth held up a placating hand. "Not just any man, of course. One who can read."

She hurled the pouch lightly at his head. Gareth flopped onto his back as though mortally wounded.

"There are some husbands who would take offense at this kind of thing," he said in an injured tone.

"But not you, my lord. You are no ordinary husband."

No ordinary man at all, Clare thought. *You are the man I love.*

"An ordinary husband would no doubt bore you, madam."

"Aye." Clare closed her eyes and took a deep breath. It felt good to be sharing the afternoon with Gareth.

The scents of the fair sorted themselves out for her sensitive nose. She could detect the savory smells from the food booths, the earthy odors of sheep and goats, the fresh essence of the grass on which she had spread the cloth.

Most of all she was aware of the indefinable rightness of the scent of the man beside her.

Gareth waited for the space of a couple of heartbeats, as if he had anticipated more of a reaction from her. When it was not forthcoming, he picked up the leather pouch that she had tossed at him. "There is something left in this bag."

"Aye."

"Another morsel, mayhap?" He opened the leather flap and peered inside. "I could eat a second pie."

"Nay, my lord. No pies." Clare took a deep breath and schooled herself to speak very casually. " 'Tis a gift for you."

"A gift?" Gareth's head came up with unexpected swiftness. All trace of his easygoing manner had vanished. "For me?"

"Aye, my lord." She rested her chin on her knees and studied him.

Gareth stared at her, a very odd expression in his eyes. It was the first time Clare had ever seen him bemused.

"Thank you," he finally said.

"Do not thank me until you have seen it. Mayhap you will not care for it."

Gareth reached into the bag and took out an elegantly fashioned, tightly stoppered flask. He examined it with a look of intense pleasure. "Perfume? For me?"

Clare blushed. "'Tis a special recipe that I created for you and you alone, sir. I hope you will like it."

Gareth carefully removed the stopper and bent his head to inhale the fragrance.

"Wait."

Gareth looked up with an inquiring expression.

"My lord, I very nearly forgot to inquire if you are made ill by mugwort or mint or cloves or some other ingredient."

Gareth shook his head. "Nay. Why do you ask?"

Clare relaxed. "Never mind. 'Tis merely that I knew someone once who had a most violent reaction to mugwort."

"I find mugwort quite pleasant." Gareth took a deep, savoring breath. "This mixture is very, very fine, madam."

"Do you really like it?"

"Aye." He inhaled again. "It smells of many things that I have always enjoyed, the fresh air of dawn and the tang of the sea. I shall keep it in my clothing chest."

"I'm glad you like it." Clare smiled slightly. "Not every man cares for pleasant-smelling tunics and linen."

"Due to the nature of my previous career, I was obliged to smell a great many odors that I would willingly forget," Gareth said. "This perfume will replace them in my mind."

Clare tilted her head. "What sorts of odors were you forced to endure while you hunted outlaws?"

Gareth studied the exquisitely made perfume flask. "When I think on my past I recall the foul smells of burned cottages, dead men, and crying women. Whenever I smelled such odors, I knew I had arrived too late. All that was left was to begin the hunt for the men who had created the stench."

Clare chilled. "How terrible for you, Gareth. No wonder you were eager for a hall of your own."

"I shall think of you whenever I inhale the scent of this perfume," Gareth said quietly.

"And of Desire, my lord, your new home."

"Aye. I shall most certainly think of Desire." His eyes pinned hers. "Was there a special reason for this gift?"

"Nay, my lord," Clare said lightly. "Merely the usual."

"The usual? And what would that be?"

"As a token of my respect, of course."

"Respect?"

"Aye. What other reason would a wife have for giving her husband a gift?"

"A good question, madam."

"Dallan, help Ranulf fold the tent."

Dallan jerked as if he had been stung. "Aye, my lord."

Gareth frowned as he watched the minstrel hurry to assist Ranulf in packing the yellow-and-white-striped tent.

Something was wrong.

Gareth had noted the change in Dallan shortly after noon on this, the last day of the fair. Gone was the minstrel's jaunty swagger and his enthusiasm for his position as squire-in-training. They had magically disappeared in the space of a few short hours. Melancholia and an anxious demeanor had taken their place.

Dallan seemed suddenly preoccupied with matters that weighed down his very soul. He jumped whenever someone spoke to him. He continued to carry out the orders Gareth gave him, but the eagerness which had characterized his behavior since he had sworn fealty to his new lord had vanished.

Gareth thought he understood the nature of the problem. He was less certain of what to do about it. He was no expert at dealing with lovesickness.

He waited until the boats had been loaded for the return trip to the Isle of Desire before he called Dallan aside.

"Dallan."

"Aye, my lord?" Dallan wiped his hands on his tunic in a nervous gesture. "Did I do something wrong?"

"Nay. Walk with me for a moment. I wish to speak to you."

"Aye, my lord." Dallan shot Gareth a quick, uneasy glance as he obediently fell into step beside him.

Gareth clasped his hands behind his back and tried to think of the best way to approach this delicate subject. "You have sung many songs of love, minstrel, but mayhap you have not learned much about the matter."

"I beg your pardon, my lord?"

Gareth cleared his throat. "A man's first taste of passion is as unsettling as his first taste of war. Both are powerful in their own fashion and both have a way of temporarily distorting his view of himself and the world around him."

Dallan looked politely blank.

Gareth sighed and tried again. "I know that you believe you have fallen in love with your pretty Alison. It no doubt saddens you to part from her."

Dallan frowned. "I shall miss her."

"Aye. That is understandable. However—"

"But I do not love her."

Gareth glanced at him speculatively. "You don't?"

"Nay. We had a pleasant time together, but I have told her that I cannot love any woman yet. I must make my way in the world before I can think on such matters."

"Ah." Gareth was vastly relieved. "A very wise statement from a man of your years. I'm impressed with your common sense. I have seen men twice your age make fools of themselves over a woman. 'Tis not a pretty sight."

Dallan gave him a quizzical look. "Was that all you wanted to say to me, my lord?"

"Aye. Run along and help pack the tents."

"Aye, my lord."

Gareth watched Dallan hurry back to join the others. He wondered if he had misinterpreted Dallan's mood. It was possible that the young man suffered from severely unbalanced humors. The disease could prove lethal. Gareth had once known a man who was so severely afflicted with unbalanced humors that he had committed suicide.

Gareth determined to keep a close eye on his new squire-in-training.

Three days later Clare sat at her desk and nibbled at the end of her quill pen. She pondered her latest perfume recipe. It was difficult to properly describe the exact steps required for combining various substances to achieve the desired results of her more complex concoctions.

She studied what she had just written:

*Put a quantity of water into a pan and put the pan into the fire.
When the pan is red hot and the water boiling softly, take a fair
quantity of your best rose leaves and put them in the pan.*

The phrase *fair quantity* did not seem very exact. Abbess Helen had advised her to be very specific when she was writing recipes.

Clare scratched out "fair quantity" and inserted the words "two handfuls."

A single, peremptory knock was all the warning she got before the door opened and Gareth strode into the room. He had the book her father had written open in his hands. He was frowning intently over a passage.

"Clare, do we have any sulfur?"

"Aye, my lord. My father kept a quantity of it in the storerooms along with some other ingredients. The Arabic treatises make frequent reference to recipes that use sulfur. He often expressed his desire to experiment with it. Personally, I have never bothered with the stuff. I do not care for the smell."

"Excellent, excellent. I must see if I can find it." Gareth scowled over whatever it was that he was reading for another moment. "The charcoal will not be a problem. 'Tis easy enough to make."

"Have you found an intriguing recipe?"

"In this volume your father describes some very unusual recipes from the East."

"Recipes that use sulfur?"

"Aye. I shall investigate them later." He closed the heavy volume and tucked it under his arm. "What are you doing?"

"I am working on my own book."

"Ah, yes. Your book of perfume recipes." Gareth surveyed the volumes on the shelves of her study chamber. "Your library is almost as large as the convent's."

"I am very proud of it. Many of the books were collected by my father, of course, but I have acquired one or two on my own. I am especially pleased with the one that was written by Abbess Helen of Ainsley. 'Tis a most learned work on herbs which I consult frequently."

"Abbess Helen of Ainsley?" Gareth repeated in a strangely neutral voice.

"Aye." Clare smiled proudly. "She has been kind enough to enter into a correspondence with me."

"You exchange letters with an abbess?"

"Quite regularly. I find her advice on the properties of herbs invaluable. As it happens, she will be arriving soon for a visit."

"She will?" Gareth looked startled.

Clare nodded happily. "I am very excited. Prioress Margaret sent word this morning. She tells me I can expect Abbess Helen any day now. You will have an opportunity to meet her, my lord."

"That should prove interesting."

"Aye. She will no doubt stay with us here at the hall. That is what she did the last time she came to visit. 'Tis a great honor for us."

"I see." Gareth lowered himself onto the window seat. "Well, that is neither here nor there. At the moment I wish to talk to you about Dallan."

"What about him?" Clare frowned. "I thought he was proving to be very satisfactory in his new position as a squire-in-training. If he is having difficulties or not giving good service, I pray you will be patient with him. He needs time, my lord."

"He performs his duties with right goodwill. That is not the problem. I am concerned about his growing melancholia."

"I know what you mean." Clare put down her pen. "It is very

worrisome. 'Tis almost as bad now as it was when he first arrived on Desire. For a time he improved markedly. But since the fair he seems to have grown very anxious again."

"What do you know of young Dallan's history?"

Clare regarded him thoughtfully. "Very little. He is a bastard, as you know. He claims to have been raised in the home of a man of rank. As you and I have discussed, I suspect he was not well treated."

"That's all you know of him?"

Clare reflected on the question. "Aye, I believe so. He never speaks of his past."

"Or of the man who raised him?"

"Nay. I have the impression that he would prefer to forget both."

"Mayhap he cannot forget, although he tries."

"Aye. Some things cannot be conveniently forgotten."

"True. But a man who cannot forget must learn to deal with the devils that plague him."

"Give him time, my lord. He has only been with us for a short while."

"'Tis the suddenness with which this new fit of melancholia has come upon him that concerns me. He was content and cheerful during the fair until the last day. I thought at first that he was suffering from lovesickness."

Clare smiled. "Young Alison?"

"Aye. I spoke to him of the matter, but he claims he is not afflicted with the illness." Gareth grimaced. "Thanks be to the saints for that. I have not the least notion of how to cure such a disease quickly and I have never known a doctor who could treat it successfully."

"I believe you once told me that you, personally, have not suffered from it for many years," Clare murmured dryly.

"Nay." Gareth shrugged. "Lovesickness is for poets and fools."

"Of course."

"A man in my position cannot afford to indulge himself in such an illness."

"Why not, pray? What harm can it do?"

"What harm?" Gareth scowled. "The harm is obvious. 'Tis a most dangerous fever. It destroys sound judgment and common sense."

"Of course. I do not know what I was thinking of to even ask such a foolish question. Well, then, about Dallan. What do you suggest?"

Gareth considered. "It would no doubt be best to give him something to think about that will take his mind off whatever it is that is plaguing him."

"An excellent plan, my lord. I have noticed that men have a great skill for ignoring certain pressing problems in favor of amusing themselves with other matters."

Gareth cocked a brow. "Have I said something to annoy you, madam?"

"Not at all," Clare assured him very smoothly. "What do you believe would successfully distract Dallan from whatever it is that is unbalancing his humors and inducing melancholy?"

Gareth glanced down at the book he was holding. "Mayhap I shall ask him to assist me in my experiments with sulfur and charcoal."

"I believe he will find that very interesting." Clare was briefly intrigued herself. "Let me know when you are ready to demonstrate the results of your work, my lord. I would enjoy witnessing them even though I do not much care for the odor of sulfur."

"I shall send word when I'm ready with the experiment." Gareth rose from the window seat, kissed her lightly on the mouth, and went toward the door.

Clare watched him leave. She experienced a twinge of melancholy herself as she reflected on their conversation. *Lovesickness is for poets and fools.*

She was neither a poet nor a fool, but she was very much afraid that she was suffering from lovesickness.

She did not enjoy suffering alone.

It was not as if Gareth were completely free of the softer emotions, she told herself. There were some encouraging signs. For example, he always smelled of the new fragrance she had given to him.

And there was no doubting the forcefulness of his passion, she thought. He made no secret of his desire for her and he seemed pleased that she responded so completely to his lovemaking. In truth, he demanded a response from her.

She knew he respected her knowledge, skill, and cleverness in the matter of perfumes, but that was not saying much. Even Nicholas had possessed sufficient wit to appreciate her talent for making money.

What gave her the greatest hope was that, just as he had a moment ago, Gareth had begun consulting her more and more frequently of late before making a decision.

Their marriage was beginning to work just as she had anticipated when she had composed her recipe for a husband. She and Gareth were learning to share their duties and responsibilities. They were learning to trust each other.

In many ways she had gotten exactly what she had wanted in a husband, even if he was somewhat larger than she had specified.

But it was not enough.

She wanted love.

And as far as Gareth was concerned, love was for poets and fools.

Two days later Clare was again at her desk when a great thunderclap resounded across the courtyard.

Startled, she leaped to her feet and went to the window. She frowned when she realized that there was not a single storm cloud in sight.

Confused, she glanced down into the courtyard. A shout went up. A maid screamed. The stonemasons stopped work on the new wall. Men spilled from the stables in alarm. A horse whinnied and plunged in fright. Several chickens cackled madly as they darted across the yard.

And then great, billowing clouds of smoke poured from the windows of her father's workroom. Even as Clare watched, the door burst open and two figures reeled out into the sunlight. Gareth and Dallan were covered in gray ash.

Clare whirled and raced out of the chamber. She ran to the tower stairs and flew down them.

"*Gareth*. My lord, are you all right?" she shouted as she dashed out onto the hall steps. She stared at the ash-covered figures. The acrid scent of sulfur assailed her nostrils.

Dallan smiled weakly. He looked dazed but unhurt.

Gareth's teeth flashed in a triumphant grin through his gray mask. "*It worked.*"

"In the name of Saint Hermione's night robe," Clare gasped as Gareth ran to her and caught her up. "What worked?"

"One of your father's sulfur recipes." Gareth swung her around in a circle. His laughter rang out across the yard. "It worked, Clare. It really worked."

"I can see that. But of what possible use is this sulfur mix?"

"I have no notion yet. The important thing is that the recipe worked."

Clare looked up at his smudged, grinning features and smiled with sudden and complete understanding. Gareth was euphoric with the thrill of discovery. She had experienced the sensation many times herself, albeit in a less spectacular fashion.

"Aye, my lord. Your recipe most certainly worked. Mayhap you have a career in alchemy ahead of you."

"It is certainly a far more interesting business than my former occupation of hunting outlaws."

Clare closed her eyes to shut out the distraction caused by the clash and clang of stonemasons' tools and the shouts of laborers. Outside her workrooms, construction of the new stone wall around the hall was proceeding apace. It created an unceasing din during the day.

It was only in the evening, after the men from Seabern had departed for the day, that a blessed silence descended. Clare hoped the project would be finished soon.

She reached into the pot on the bench in front of her, scooped out a handful of the new mix of dried herbs and flowers, and held it to her nose. The hint of mugwort reminded her of Raymond de Coleville, for some reason. Mugwort had made his eyes water uncontrollably and caused him to sneeze and gasp for air.

She recalled the day that she had surprised him with a pomander that had contained mugwort along with other spices and flowers. It was the only time that she had ever seen Raymond lose his temper.

"God's blood, get that perfume away from me," he had raged. "It must contain mugwort. What are you trying to do? Kill me?"

Clare had been horrified. She'd had no way of knowing that he could not tolerate the mugwort. She had apologized profusely and disposed of the pomander. Raymond had quickly returned to his normal charming self and that had been the end of the matter.

Clare frowned and wondered why the memory had flickered through her mind today. She had not thought much about Raymond de Coleville since the day Gareth had arrived on the Isle of Desire.

In truth, it was difficult to think of any other man except her husband these days. Gareth was too large, too overwhelming, too *interesting* to allow space for others in her mind. He made other men, especially the pale memories of a man who had lied to her, seem very small and quite ordinary.

"Clare?" Joanna appeared at the open door of the workroom. She peered into the shadows. "Are you in here?"

"Aye, Joanna." Clare dropped the handful of dried materials back into the bowl. "Is something amiss?"

"Nay, I merely came to show you my latest embroidery design. I think it will do very nicely for the larger pillows." Joanna shook out a large square of fabric decorated with a rough drawing of a knight kneeling before a lady. The couple appeared to be seated in a leafy bower.

"It's wonderful, Joanna. Romantic scenes such as that always sell very well. What's that creature in the background?"

"A unicorn." Joanna refolded the fabric with an air of satisfaction. "The ladies of London are very fond of unicorns. Well, then, if you approve, I shall set the village women and the nuns to work on the new pillow scenes immediately."

"Excellent."

"We should have a large number ready to fill with your dried herbs and flowers by midsummer."

"At least this shipment will likely reach its destination. Lord Gareth will see to that." Clare added two handfuls of rose petals to the mixture in the pot.

"Aye. The Hellhound has his uses, I'll grant you that much." Joanna gave Clare a speculative look. "I wonder if he'll stay with us through the winter."

"What?" Clare whirled around. "Of course he'll stay with us. This is his home now. Why would he leave?"

Joanna tut-tutted. "Men always leave once they've seen to the business of protecting their lands and getting an heir. Now that you are wed, Desire is safe from Nicholas or some other encroaching lord."

"Aye, but what of the robbers who are a constant threat to our shipments?" Clare felt stunned. A strange tightness gripped her chest.

"I expect it will be no problem for Lord Gareth to arrange for some of his men-at-arms to remain here on Desire to handle the shipments." Joanna sighed. "I suppose Sir Ulrich will accompany Lord Gareth when he leaves. A pity. William is quite fond of him. I do believe this new exercise program is having a beneficial effect on my son, just as Lord Gareth predicted."

"Young William is not the only one who has grown fond of Sir Ulrich, is he?" Clare asked gently.

Joanna blushed. "Is it so obvious?"

"Aye. And he seems equally fond of you."

Joanna studied the pot of herbs and flowers. "He says he loves me."

Lucky Joanna, Clare thought. That was a great deal more than Gareth had ever said to her. "I am happy for you, Joanna."

"He kissed me last night." Joanna shot her a quick glance. "For the first time I understood that lovemaking might be as pleasant for a woman as it is for a man."

"Aye. But I suspect it is only thus with the right man."

Joanna sat down heavily on a stool and folded her hands in her lap. "It will be very lonely around here after they leave, will it not?"

"Lord Gareth has said nothing to me of leaving."

"Men rarely discuss their plans with women. You know that. Did your brother ever bother to inform you of his intentions until he had one foot out the door?"

"Nay, but Lord Gareth is different. He discusses important matters with me."

"Your husband is still at the stage where it amuses him to indulge a new wife. That will soon change," Joanna said sadly. "It always does."

Clare's stomach tightened. She could not bear the thought of Gareth leaving, not now when they were just beginning to get to know each other, to understand each other. To *talk* to each other.

Not now when she had begun to hope that she could make him fall in love with her.

"I shall see about this." Clare started toward the door.

"Where are you going?"

"To find my husband. I wish to speak to him."

Joanna frowned. "He is busy at the moment."

"Doing what?"

"Supervising the repairs of the windmill, I believe. One of the sails is being replaced."

"This won't take but a moment."

Clare went through the door. The windmill stood on the far side of the courtyard. Its sails were still. Several men, including Gareth and Ulrich, were gathered around the mill. From the serious expressions on their faces, one would have thought they stood around an open grave.

She wondered briefly if men assumed such airs of concern when faced with broken mechanical devices merely to impress each other or if they were genuinely alarmed by the challenge of repairing the items.

"My lord." She halted a few paces away from the crowd of males. "I wish to speak to you."

Gareth reluctantly dragged his attention away from the torn sailcloth and glanced at her. "Later, madam. As you can see, I am occupied just now."

"This is very important." Clare was aware that every man in the small crowd was listening with keen interest. "It will not take but a moment."

Gareth's brow rose in reaction to her peremptory tone. "Very well, if it is that important." He nodded at Ulrich. "Continue with the work. I shall return soon."

"Aye, my lord." Ulrich turned back to the flapping sailcloth with an ill-concealed smile.

Gareth strode over to where Clare stood. He looked down at her, his broad shoulders blocking her view of the mill. "Well, then, Clare? What is it that is so urgent that it could not wait?"

Clare suddenly felt ridiculous. But she had to ask the question. "I merely wished to know if you intend to leave Desire in the near future?"

"Leave?"

"Aye." She glowered at him. "There are some who feel that once you've secured your lands and got me with child, you'll be off. I wanted to know if that was your intention."

Gareth stared at her. "Are you with child?"

"Uh, no." Clare cleared her throat. "At least I do not believe that to be the case. Gareth, that is not the issue. I am asking if you plan to leave the isle."

Gareth's mouth tightened grimly. "Hell's teeth, this is not the time to discuss such matters. I'm trying to get that damned windmill fixed."

"Is the mill more important than your future plans, sir?"

He raked his fingers through his hair. "What in the name of the devil made you seek me out to ask me this now?"

"Never mind, my lord. Just answer my question. Are you planning to leave anytime soon?"

"Do you want me gone, then?"

"Nay, my lord." Clare looked at the broad expanse of his chest. "In truth, I find you extremely useful to have around and am not anxious to see you leave."

"Useful?"

"Aye, sir. Useful."

"How am I useful?"

"Well, you did an excellent job of repairing the machine I use for pressing oil from roses and cinnamon." Clare summoned a bright little smile. "It works perfectly now."

"Thank you," Gareth said through set teeth. "I am glad that I was able to give satisfactory service."

Clare realized he was angry. Her own temper flared. "I just want to know your plans so that I can make my own arrangements. Does that seem too much to ask?"

He regarded her with a cool, shuttered gaze. "I have no intention of leaving Desire unless I am summoned by my father. I am Thurston of Landry's vassal and as such, I owe him a set number of days of service each year should he demand such. You know that as well as I do."

Clare scowled. "I am not an idiot. I fully comprehend that, my lord. I wasn't talking about the duty that you owe to Lord Thurston. I was referring to your personal plans."

"At the moment, my personal plans involve getting that damned mill repaired as soon as possible. After that I intend to check on the stonemasons' progress. When I have finished that task, I shall return to my workroom to continue my experiments. Does that answer your question?"

"You definitely do not plan to leave Desire?"

"Nay."

"I have your oath on it?"

"Aye."

Relief poured through Clare. She tried not to let it show. "Very well. That is all I wished to know."

Gareth braced his hands on his hips. "If you are satisfied, madam, may I return to the task of repairing the windmill sail?"

"Of course. My apologies for disturbing your labors." Clare started to turn away.

"Clare."

"Aye?" She paused.

Gareth surveyed her thoughtfully. "I am told that you do not charge the villagers for the use of the mill."

"That is correct. I'm aware that many lords do charge their people for grinding their flour, but I feel there is no need to do so. The villagers supply the hall with all the flour we need, so it is an even trade as far as I am concerned."

"I see."

She eyed him uneasily. "I trust you do not intend to start charging our people for milling their flour, my lord?"

"Nay, madam. You are the one with a head for business in this family. If you believe the present arrangement to be fair, who am I to argue with you?"

"A head for business, aye. That is what I have always been told." She gave him a wry look. "It would appear that we both have our uses, sir."

Gareth's eyes gleamed. "A man could not ask for a more useful wife than you, madam. Now, pray excuse me. 'Tis past time I got back to my tasks." He returned and stalked back to the crowd that hovered around the mill.

Clare gazed wistfully after him for a brief moment. *Useful.*

She had always been useful, she reflected. She had been useful to her mother, who had borne the burden of managing the manor while her lord traipsed about the continent in search of knowledge.

She had been useful to her absentminded, scholarly father, who preferred his studies in Paris and Spain to the responsibilities of being a husband and a father and the lord of Desire.

She had been useful to her brother, who had hungered for the excitement and glory of the tournaments more than he had hungered for the lands he was to inherit.

She had been useful to Raymond de Coleville, who had wished to amuse himself with a bit of dalliance while he studied with her father.

Nicholas of Seabern had thought that she would make him a useful bride, one who could plump up his pockets.

She was useful to Thurston of Landry, who valued the income from Desire.

And now it appeared that the Hellhound found her useful, too.

It was not a cheerful thought, but Clare feared that there were worse fates than being useful.

Fates such as falling in love with a man who did not see love as particularly useful, for example.

That afternoon, Clare finally found time to climb the tower stairs to her study chamber. She hurried around the corner at the top of the staircase and ran headlong into Dallan.

"Ooph." Clare put out a hand to steady herself as she staggered back a step.

"Lady Clare. I beg your pardon." Something that was more than surprise, something that might have been fear, flashed in Dallan's eyes.

She grinned ruefully. "What are you doing up here, Dallan? I thought you were assisting Lord Gareth in his experiments."

"Forgive me, my lady." He glanced nervously down the hall and then looked at her. "I did not hear you on the stairs."

"I am on my way to my study chamber."

"Oh." Dallan wiped his palms on his tunic. "Are you all right?"

"Do not concern yourself. You did no great harm." Clare frowned. "Is anything amiss, Dallan?"

"Nay, madam."

"Are you quite certain? You seem to have grown increasingly downcast since the spring fair. Are you sure that you are not pining for your pretty Alison?"

"Alison?" Dallan looked briefly confused. "Nay, my lady. I am not pining."

"You're certain?"

"Aye, madam. Quite certain."

"Is there something else preying on your mind, mayhap?"

"Nay, madam." Dallan hesitated and then squared his shoulders. There was a sad, almost desperate light in his eyes. "Lady Clare, I have never thanked you for your great kindness to me. I wish to do so now."

Clare smiled. "It is I who should thank you, Dallan. You have brightened our lives here on Desire with your fine music and poems. And I know that Lord Gareth is very pleased to have your assistance in his workroom."

"My lord is a very clever man," Dallan whispered. "As are you, my lady. It has been an honor to serve you."

"Why, thank you, Dallan."

"Pray excuse me, madam," Dallan said softly. "I must go now. His lordship will be waiting for me."

"Off with you, then. I shall see you at supper."

"Farewell, my lady. And thank you again for all your kindness to me. I do not deserve it."

"Nonsense, of course you deserve it." Clare went on down the hall to her study chamber.

She opened the door and made to step inside. Something made her hesitate. She turned and glanced back. Dallan was watching her with an intensely melancholic look in his eyes. She smiled reassuringly once more. Then she stepped into the chamber and closed the door behind herself.

She went to her desk, sat down, and propped her chin on her hands. She reflected for a long time on the manner in which Dallan had thanked her for her kindness.

"It was the strangest thing, Gareth," Clare said that evening when they were alone in their bedchamber. "'Twas as though he were bidding me farewell."

"Who said farewell?" Gareth did not look up from the heavy volume he was studying.

Clare's father had done a fine job of translating Arabic into Latin, he reflected, but Sir Humphrey had not been a skilled scribe. It required painstaking effort to puzzle out the words of the essay on the elements that Gareth was attempting to comprehend.

Although the day had been warm, it had turned cooler than usual that evening. There was a brisk fire on the hearth of the bedchamber. Outside a wind was beginning to howl, promising a storm before dawn.

"Dallan. My lord, are you listening to me?"

"Of course I'm listening to you. I always listen to you when you speak, madam. Did I not leave off repairing the mill today just to listen to you?" Gareth frowned over a clumsily lettered word. He could not make out if it was *vapor* or *viper*. It had to be *vapor*, he decided. *Viper* did not make sense in the context. *Intense heat causes the liquid to boil and give off a vapor which becomes, itself liquid . . .*

"So you always listen to me, do you?" Clare gave a small, ladylike sniff that indicated strong disbelief. "What did I just say?"

Gareth concentrated on the complex discussion of the properties of fire, earth, water, and air. "You said something about Dallan bidding you farewell."

"He *seemed* to be bidding me farewell. It was as if he were planning to leave Desire."

"I told you, I have no plans to leave the isle."

"Not you, my lord. Dallan. There, you see? I knew you weren't listening to me."

Gareth gave up trying to read the translated Arab treatise. He stretched his legs out toward the fire, leaned back in his chair, and looked at Clare.

The sight of her sitting there with a book resting on her lap, her intelligent face screwed into an expression of intense concern, made him momentarily forget about the essay on elements.

My wife, he thought with a sense of wonder. He still could not quite believe that she was his.

The flames highlighted the lustrous darkness of her hair and rendered her skin the color of rich cream. She watched him with her serious, gemlike eyes. He contemplated how he could make her glow with passion and his body started to harden. It always did when he thought of holding Clare naked in his arms.

"What seems to be the problem?" Gareth asked.

"I fear that some dreadful concern is still plaguing Dallan. He is more anxious than ever. His melancholia is not improving."

"Aye." Gareth gazed into the fire. "A strange lad. Ulrich is worried about him, also. Apparently young William came across Dallan just as he was leaving one of the garderobes this afternoon. Dallan had tears in his eyes."

"He was crying? But why?"

"William told Ulrich that he asked Dallan that very question. Dallan told him it was none of his business."

"This is terrible. Dallan will not talk about whatever it is that concerns him," Clare said. "What do you suggest we do, my lord?"

"There is nothing we can do except keep an eye on Dallan. Ulrich will see to that."

"Keep an eye on him?" Clare's eyes widened. "Why is that necessary? Are you afraid he will do himself some harm?"

"'Tis possible. Melancholia is a strange and sometimes dangerous condition."

"This is a most alarming thought, my lord."

"Do not concern yourself tonight. As I said, Ulrich will keep an eye on the lad." Gareth went back to his book. "Clare, do we have any mercury?"

"Aye, my lord," she said absently. "My father kept some about somewhere. Have you had any more ideas concerning who might have killed Beatrice?"

"Nay."

"Do you still believe that the motive involved the theft of a book?"

Gareth gazed down at the alchemic recipe he was studying. He thought of the powerful explosion he had produced with the sulfur and charcoal mixture. "Lately I have begun to realize that there are many great secrets concealed in these ancient treatises that your father translated."

"That is no doubt true, but the books in the convent library are not of Eastern origin. They are primarily English herbals and Church histories. Surely none of them contain any secrets worth murder."

"But what if the thief did not know what he would find there?" Gareth touched the edge of the unevenly cut parchment pages of the book he held. "What if he believed he would find something of great value in one of them?"

"What sort of secret would that be?"

"Mayhap the elixir that will produce gold from base metals."

"Oh, that. Alchemists have searched for such a recipe for years," Clare scoffed. "My father always claimed that it did not exist."

The knock on the bedchamber door came shortly before dawn. It brought Gareth out of a dark, disturbing dream that involved blood and an open book.

In the dream he had been attempting to read the alchemic recipe that had been written in the book. But blood had flowed across the page before he could make out the words.

When the knock sounded, Gareth came awake as he always did, swiftly and completely. With the force of long habit he reached down over the side of the bed. His hand closed around the hilt of the Window of Hell.

"What is it?" Clare asked in a sleepy voice. "Is something wrong?"

"Someone is at the door." Gareth pushed aside the bed curtain and padded across the floor, sword in hand.

"Who's there?"

"Ulrich, my lord."

Gareth opened the door. Ulrich stood in the hall, a candle in his hand. He was fully dressed. He glanced at Gareth, who was naked except for the sword. "I am sorry to disturb you."

"What's wrong?"

"The minstrel has left the hall, as you said he might do."

"Dallan?" Clare stuck her head out between the heavy bed curtains. "Did you say he left?"

Gareth ignored her. "Did he leave empty-handed?"

"I do not know. The door of Lady Clare's study chamber is ajar, however."

"So. The lad was bent on betrayal after all," Gareth said quietly.

"I warned you he might well prove to be dangerous," Ulrich said quietly.

"Aye." He had been prepared for this, Gareth thought, even expected it after contemplating the minstrel's strange behavior during the past few days. Nevertheless, Dallan's actions saddened him in some manner that he could not fully explain. It was the sadness one felt when a friend proves untrustworthy, he decided.

Gareth had convinced himself that he and Dallan had forged a common bond based on the burden of their mutual illegitimacy and on their interest in conducting experiments. Clearly he had been wrong.

"You said if anything such as this occurred, you wanted to handle it yourself." Ulrich did not look toward the bed.

"Aye. I'll get dressed. Have one of the horses readied."

"I'll come with you," Clare said.

"A storm struck a short while ago, my lord." Ulrich politely kept his gaze fixed on Gareth. " 'Tis miserable out there."

"I'll go alone," Gareth said.

"Nay, my lord." Clare thrust aside the curtain. Her night robe hiked up above her knees as she slid her legs over the edge of the high bed. "I shall come with you."

Gareth glanced over his shoulder and scowled. "Get back into bed at once, madam." He turned back to Ulrich. "See to the horse. I'll be down in a moment."

"Aye, my lord." Ulrich took a quick step back into the corridor.

Gareth shut the door. He crossed the room in three swift strides and grabbed his clothing out of a chest.

"Gareth, I want to come with you." Clare rose from the bed and hurried to the chest that contained her tunics and gowns. "You must wait for me."

"Nay. I will handle this matter." Gareth finished dressing and fastened his belt low on his hips. He picked up his sword and scabbard and went toward the door.

Clare struggled to pull her gown over her head. "Why do you suppose Dallan is sneaking off like this?"

"Mayhap because he has found the book he came here to steal," Gareth said from the open door.

"What?" Clare yanked the gown downward. She stared at Gareth with troubled eyes. "I cannot believe that he would do such a thing."

"Then mayhap he is running away because he does not wish to be questioned in the murder of Beatrice the recluse," Gareth said.

He closed the door very firmly on Clare's horrified expression.

The horse was waiting in the courtyard. The howling wind and the crackle of lightning made the gelding restless. The beast pranced and danced on the stones until Gareth vaulted into the saddle. Once the gelding felt the firm hands on the reins, he settled down.

"Open the gate," Gareth ordered.

"Aye, my lord." Ranulf raced toward the gatehouse.

Ulrich looked up at Gareth. "Are you certain you don't want company?"

"I will deal with the minstrel. How long ago did he leave the hall?"

"Not above half an hour ago. I ordered his bedchamber checked every half hour, as you commanded. When the guard found it empty, he reported immediately to me and I came directly to you."

"I assume he did not leave by way of the gate or he would have been seen by the guards."

"Aye. 'Twill be interesting to discover just how he got out of the courtyard without being spotted."

"We'll see to that matter after I apprehend him." Gareth gave the signal to the gelding. The big animal surged toward the open gate.

The gray light of a stormy dawn broke across the isle as Gareth galloped down the road toward the village. His destination was the harbor. The only way off Desire was by boat. The only vessels available were moored at the village quay.

The gelding thundered down the road, past the fields and the scattered cottages. In the early light Gareth could see the rows of flowers bending before the wind.

The convent gatehouse was still locked when Gareth rode past. There was no one up and about yet in the street or the market square.

When Gareth reached the harbor he spotted the lone figure on the quay at once. Dallan's cloak whipped wildly about his thin frame as he struggled with the lines of a small boat. The vessel lurched and heaved on the storm-tossed water of the harbor. A large leather pouch lay on the stone wall of the quay.

"Hold, minstrel." Gareth pitched his voice above the howling wind. "As your liege lord, I command you to stop."

Dallan whirled around, a frightened expression on his face. "Nay, let me go, my lord, I beg you. I have to go. He'll kill her if I do not give him the book."

Gareth swung down from the gelding, wrapped the reins once around a post, and strode toward the quay. "Do as I command, Dallan of Desire, or else learn here and now how I deal with thieves and murderers."

"*Nay.*" Dallan's eyes widened in terror. He grabbed the leather pouch and leaped over the quay into the shallow, bobbing boat.

He landed off center. The boat tipped precariously on its side.

Dallan screamed and dropped the leather pouch into the bottom of the boat. He flailed wildly in an attempt to regain his balance.

The boat bobbed once more. Dallan toppled into the churning water.

Gareth broke into a run. Hoofbeats sounded on the road just as he reached the edge of the quay. He glanced back over his shoulder and saw Clare riding toward him on her palfrey. The hood of her cloak had been blown back by the wind. Her hair lashed her face.

"Gareth, what are you going to do?" she called.

"I'm going to pluck your pet minstrel from the sea and then I shall teach him the price of betrayal."

"My lord, you must not hurt him. I'm certain there is an explanation for his behavior."

"Aye," Gareth muttered. "I vow that there is. And I intend to hear it before I hang him."

"Nay, you cannot hang him," Clare shouted.

"Why not? 'Tis the way in which I generally deal with thieves."

Dallan screamed again. Gareth looked down and saw the boy floundering helplessly in the roiling water. It was obvious that Dallan could not swim.

Gareth unfastened the long length of his leather belt. He looped the end twice around his wrist and then he leaned down over the side of the stone quay. "Catch hold of my belt, Dallan."

"'Tis better if I drown."

"Mayhap, but you are not going to drown. I have other plans for you, vassal. *Take hold of the belt.*"

Dallan reached for the belt.

16

The ominous silence in the firelit chamber made Clare uneasy. She knew that Dallan was beyond uneasy. He was terrified. They both sat very still on their stools and waited for Gareth to speak.

Clare gave Dallan a small smile of encouragement. Dallan did not return the smile.

Gareth did nothing to ease the oppressive atmosphere. Clare had begun to suspect that he was deliberately allowing it to deepen. He lounged in a chair in front of the fire and gazed into the flames with a dark, brooding expression that boded ill. His elbows rested on the carved oak arms of the chair.

He finally spoke, startling Clare.

"What is the name of this other master whom you serve, Dallan of Desire?"

Dallan flinched. Clare saw his mouth open and close nervously. His hands squeezed together in his lap. "My lord, I beg you, do not ask me for his name. To speak it will bring disaster down upon this isle."

"He is such a powerful lord, then?" Gareth's voice was very soft.

"Aye."

"A great knight?"

"Aye."

"You once told me that he went on Crusade."

"Aye."

"You fear him more than you fear me?"

Dallan looked down at his hands. "You will do no more than hang me, my lord. My master can do much worse."

"What is worse than being hung, minstrel?"

Dallan's eyes flickered to Clare. He licked his lips. "He has promised to kill my lady if I betray him."

A terrible stillness settled over Gareth. "He actually said those words? He specifically threatened to kill Lady Clare?"

Dallan shivered, although he was now warm and dry. "He vowed that he would kill all those for whom I had any affection. And then he promised to destroy me in a most hideous manner. No offense, my lord, but I would rather hang than die by magic."

Clare stared at him. "Magic?"

Dallan pressed his lips together as if fearing that he had said too much.

"Magic." Gareth repeated the word curiously, as though tasting it. "This lord whom you fear is a great magician, then?"

Dallan looked down at his clenched hands. "Aye. He is a master of the dark arts. He can walk through locked doors. He can make objects disappear. He knows the secrets of the ancients."

Gareth's brows rose. "This great magician who can walk through locked doors and make things disappear must send a boy of sixteen to steal a book from a lady? Why did he not simply materialize in my wife's study chamber and select the volume himself? Then he could have whisked himself away before anyone was the wiser."

"My lord, I do not pretend to know his reasoning," Dallan said desperately. "He never confides his plans to me or anyone else. 'Tis not his way. He keeps his own counsel."

"What, precisely, did he tell you to do while you were here?" Gareth asked.

"He bid me come here to Desire and enter the household as a minstrel. He said I was to become familiar with the hall and those who live here. He told me to be ready for a signal from him."

Clare frowned. "He knew I would be glad of a minstrel?"

"Aye. My master—" Dallan broke off and cast a quick, uncomfortable look at Gareth. "I mean, my former master said—"

"What did he say?" Clare prodded gently.

Dallan sniffed back a few tears. "He said my foolish poetry would likely please you, my lady. He said you would welcome me because you had a great fondness for romantic nonsense."

"He was right about one thing," Clare said. "You are welcome here, Dallan."

"He *was* welcome," Gareth corrected quietly. "Until he betrayed this house and me."

"I had to do it," Dallan whispered. "I had to take the book. He commanded me to do so."

Gareth's gaze sharpened. "When did he issue this command?"

"He appeared on the last day of the spring fair. He sought me out in the crowd and described the book that he wanted. He said that if I did not bring it to him within a sennight, he would destroy this hall and all those within."

"The spring fair?" Gareth's eyes narrowed. "He was in Seabern?"

"Aye." Dallan sniffed again. "He materialized there in the guise of a peddler."

"So that was why your mood changed so drastically on the last day of the fair," Clare said.

"I had begun to believe that he had forgotten about me," Dallan whispered. "In truth, during the past two months, I made myself believe that he no longer had any use for me, that mayhap I was free."

"Was that why you swore fealty to me, Dallan of Desire?" Gareth asked. "Because you thought the magician had freed you of your oath to him?"

"He never asked for my oath, as you did, my lord." Dallan gazed forlornly at the floor. "To him I was never more than a servant. One does not ask a servant to swear a squire's oath."

Clare looked at the volume lying on the desk. "How did you know which of my father's books your magician wanted you to steal?"

"He described it to me when he sought me out at the fair." Dallan raised his eyes to the book on the desk. "He said it would be a large volume containing many strange recipes scripted in a poor hand. He said it would no doubt be among the items that Sir Humphrey had sent home just before he died."

"You knew that I have been studying just such a volume lately because you had assisted me with some of my experiments," Gareth said.

"Aye, my lord."

Gareth's mouth twisted briefly. "I thought you had a rare talent for experiments. 'Tis because you assisted your magician from time to time, I'll wager."

"Aye." Dallan swallowed heavily. "He taught me the things I needed to know in order to aid him in his studies. My lord, I must know, are you going to hang me tonight?"

"Why do you ask?"

"I do not wish to die unshriven. I realize I have no right to ask for any kindness, but I will be very grateful if you will summon a priest before you hang me."

"By Saint Hermione's merciful heart, Lord Gareth is not going to hang anyone tonight," Clare said quickly. "Are you, my lord?"

Gareth said nothing. He continued to gaze reflectively into the flames.

Dallan bit his lip and looked down at his shaking fingers. "I pray that you will someday be able to forgive me, Lady Clare."

Clare scowled at Gareth and then turned back to Dallan. "Do not pay my lord any heed. He is in a foul mood. He is not going to hang you, Dallan."

Dallan looked at her as if she were mad.

"My lord, will you kindly tell Dallan that you are not going to hang him?" Clare snapped impatiently.

"I am still contemplating the matter," Gareth murmured.

"Sir, you know very well that you are not going to hang your own squire-in-training." Clare smiled at Dallan. "I understand that you took the book because you wanted to protect me, Dallan. Lord Gareth understands that, too."

Dallan appeared unconvinced of Gareth's understanding. "My lord, I know you believe that what I did was an act of betrayal. I wish with all my heart that I could have continued to serve you as your squire-in-training. But you yourself once told me that a man must do whatever was necessary to protect those who depend upon him. I had to protect Lady Clare."

"A man cannot serve two masters, Dallan of Desire."

"Nay, my lord. I know that. But when I gave you my oath, I truly believed that I was free to serve you. I was nothing to the magician, you see. Just a boy he had bought for a few coins. After I had been here on Desire for a time, it was easy to believe that he had either forgotten about me or no longer needed me. I told myself that he would not come for me."

Gareth's eyes were the color of pale gray smoke. "I want the magician's name, Dallan."

Dallan's expression was that of a hunted hare. "I swear, I dare not reveal it. To do so would put all of you, especially Lady Clare, in grave danger."

"Lady Clare is already in jeopardy," Gareth said. "The only way I can protect her, this hall, and those within it is to gain as much information about your master as possible."

"But he is no ordinary knight, my lord. He is a magician," Dallan wailed.

"Hell's teeth. He's an alchemist, from the sound of it. An ordinary man who has mastered a few Eastern tricks. Nothing more. *I want his name.*"

Clare touched Dallan's hand. "Give us the magician's name, Dallan. 'Tis for the best. Lord Gareth will resolve the problem. He is very good at such things."

Dallan's eyes shifted anxiously back and forth between Gareth's hard, unyielding face and Clare's reassuring smile. "Forgive me. I know that you are a great knight, my lord, but even you cannot defend against the magician's magic arts."

"Nonsense," Clare said. "Lord Gareth is perfectly capable of dealing with a mere magician."

Gareth's unreadable gaze rested fleetingly on her face. "Thank you for your confidence, madam."

Clare felt herself grow warm at his wry tone. "I have no doubt about your ability to protect this hall, my lord."

"Now, if I just had a similar degree of confidence from my squire-in-training," Gareth said deliberately, "I would be well on my way to accomplishing my task."

Dallan's face brightened for a second and then crumpled back into an expression of despair. "I am no longer your squire-in-training, my lord. We both know that."

"You say you have never sworn an oath of fealty to this magician?"

"Nay, my lord."

"But you have sworn fealty to me in front of witnesses."

"Aye."

"Did I not accept your oath and give you my own in return?"

"Aye."

"What did I promise you in exchange for your honest service, Dallan of Desire?"

"Your protection, my lord."

"I have never foresworn myself, minstrel. My oath is the only thing that I have ever been able to call my own. I do not give it easily. And once I have given it, I honor it."

"I understand, my lord." Dallan tightened his hands. "But I no longer have the right to claim your protection."

"You do if you have not foresworn yourself," Gareth said softly.

Dallan's head came up swiftly. "But I have done so. At least, you believe that I have."

"What I believe," Gareth said thoughtfully, "is that you fear this alchemist so much that you did as he commanded."

"Aye."

"But I also believe that you obeyed him because you wished to protect Lady Clare."

" 'Tis the truth," Dallan whispered. "I swear it."

"Then you did not betray me," Gareth said. "Your actions were misguided and foolish, but you are not foresworn. You are still my squire-in-training and I am your liege lord."

Dallan closed his eyes and took a deep, shaky breath. "You are most generous, my lord. I do not deserve your kindness."

"The name, Dallan." Gareth's hand closed into a fist on the arm of the chair. "I want the magician's name."

"Lucretius, my lord." Dallan held himself very still. He squeezed his eyes shut, as if he expected to be struck with a bolt of lightning on the spot. When nothing happened, he lifted his lashes warily. His voice firmed. "His name is Lucretius de Valemont."

"Lucretius de Valemont." Gareth repeated softly. "I have never heard of him."

"Nor have I," Clare said.

Dallan rested his head in his hands. "God save us, I fear he will murder us all."

"How did Dallan get out of the courtyard without being spotted by the guard?" Ulrich's bald head gleamed as he studied the parchment map spread out on the desk.

"He waited until the guard had gone past on his rounds." Gareth traced the shoreline with his finger, searching for the two places where a small boat could be landed. "Then he raised a ladder behind the stables. When he reached the top of the curtain wall, he lowered himself to the ground with a rope."

"Clever for a minstrel, is he not?"

"Aye." Gareth glanced out the window at the new day. The storm had passed, but there was a heavy quality in the air. "If someone can get out that easily, someone else can get inside just as easily. Add an extra guard here at the hall, Ulrich."

"I'll have to pull one of the guards away from the convent to do that."

"I do not believe the convent is in danger now. The alchemist knows the book is here in the hall." Gareth found the indentations in the shoreline. "I also want a watch kept at these locations as well as at the village harbor. Check the small cliff caves after every tide."

"We're going to be spread very thin around the isle, my lord. The three men you sent to guard the perfumes that London merchant purchased have not yet returned. We are still short-handed."

"You and I will take a watch. My squire-in-training will also take one."

Ulrich looked up with a curious glint in his eye. "You're going to trust Dallan with guard duty?"

"Dallan is my man. He's frightened of his former master, but he does not serve him. He serves me."

Ulrich hesitated and then nodded. "Very well. You have always been a good judge of men. We'll let him take a watch near the convent."

"I will stay here in the hall," Gareth said. "You take the harbor with two of the men."

"Aye, my lord. Do you believe this Lucretius de Valemont will attempt to bring armed men onto Desire?"

"I do not know. He must realize how difficult it would be to bring an armed company ashore without being seen."

"At this point he has no way of knowing that you are aware of him or his intentions."

"He will soon reason it out." Gareth studied the map. "I have a feeling that when Dallan does not bring him the book, he will come here to look for it. He has already stepped foot on our isle on one previous occasion."

Ulrich looked up with an inquiring frown. "When was that?"

"The night he came to search the convent library."

"You believe it was he who murdered the recluse?"

"Aye."

"Ah, yes. Our mysterious ghost who walks through locked gates," Ulrich said thoughtfully.

"More likely a man in a monk's cowl who knows how to pick a lock. I suspect he came and went in a small boat that he brought ashore at one of these two locations." Gareth stabbed a finger at the small coves drawn on the map.

Ulrich smiled without any of his usual amusement. "If the magician returns a second time, we'll have him."

"Aye. He's only a man, despite what Dallan believes."

"Where is young Dallan?"

"Clare took him out to the kitchens to feed him. He's suddenly starving now that he has recovered from his adventures and no longer fears he will be hung."

Ulrich frowned in thought. "I would like more information about this magician."

"As would I. But Dallan's fear of him is such that he finds it difficult to speak of him. Clare says the minstrel will become more talkative once he is fed."

"You have assigned your lady to question the boy?"

"It was Clare's idea," Gareth admitted.

.   .   .   .

"He's a magician?" Joanna's mouth fell open in astonishment. "Are you certain?"

"That's what Dallan claims." Clare looked at Dallan. "Is that not so?"

"Aye, my lady." Dallan sat at the trestle table in the kitchen. He had a large slice of leftover roast chicken in front of him which he was devouring with the air of a man who had not eaten in weeks. William sat across from him, nibbling on a bit of cheese.

"Sir Ulrich says there is no such thing as magic," William said. "He says Lucretius de Valemont is likely an alchemist, not a real magician."

"Lucretius de Valemont can walk through locked doors," Dallan insisted.

"Is that true?" William asked, intrigued.

"I have seen him enter a locked chamber without using a key," Dallan said around a mouthful of chicken. "I have also seen him make objects appear and disappear. I know that Lord Gareth does not believe me, but 'tis true."

"I'll wager he is not a great knight like Lord Gareth and Sir Ulrich," William said confidently.

Dallan stopped chewing. His eyes were troubled. "I told you, Lucretius de Valemont went on Crusade. He is a fierce knight, although he says only a fool uses a sword when he can use magic."

William took another bite of his cheese. "Is he as large and strong as Lord Gareth and Sir Ulrich?"

"Nay." Dallan looked more cheerful for a moment. "He is not as large as my lord." His face fell again. "But he is very skilled with a sword. And he is extremely clever. He says big men are easy to defeat because they always rely on their muscles instead of their wits."

"The magician has obviously not met Lord Gareth, has he?" Clare sat down on the bench beside William and looked across at Dallan.

"Nay." Dallan appeared to relax slightly at that thought. "Lord Gareth is very clever, too, is he not? Mayhap he is even more clever than the magician."

"I expect he is." Clare helped herself to a slice of hot bread. "Is the magician married?"

"Nay. Women find him handsome. Indeed, they are much taken with him. I have often seen them vie for his attention. But he says he has little use for females."

Joanna set out a portion of custard. Her eyes met Clare's. "Does he prefer the company of men, then?" she asked very casually.

Dallan shrugged. "Nay."

"Young boys, mayhap?" Joanna suggested quietly.

Clare held her breath as she realized the implications of Joanna's question.

But Dallan merely seemed confused by the remark. He shook his head and helped himself to the custard. "Nay. In truth, the magician does not care for anyone. He is devoted to his studies of the black arts. But I have seen him be most courteous to ladies when he wants something from them."

Clare did not move. "What do you mean?"

"He gives them romantic gifts when he wishes to lure them into doing some service for him."

"What sort of gifts?" Clare asked.

"A single blood-red rose. Sometimes he composes poetry for them, even though he thinks it foolish." Dallan grimaced. "The ladies are much impressed by such gifts. They do not know that he feels nothing for them."

"A single blood-red rose." Clare drummed her fingers lightly on the table. "Tell me, Dallan, does the magician perfume his clothing or use a scented soap?"

"Nay. He does not care for perfumes and scents. He says they are for women, but in truth, I believe he does not like them because some of them make him sneeze."

Clare exchanged a glance with Joanna. "What color hair does the magician have?"

"He is fair." Dallan looked at her. "Why do you ask?"

"With golden brown eyes?"

"Aye." Dallan frowned. "How did you know?"

Clare met Joanna's uneasy gaze. "'Twas a guess based on some of the other things you have said of him."

William was visibly impressed. "But how did you guess the color of his eyes, Lady Clare?"

"I believe we know this magician, William."

"We have made his acquaintance?" William stared at her.

"Aye."

"But that is impossible," William said.

"Dear God," Joanna whispered. She met Clare's gaze with dawning horror. "Surely you do not believe—"

"Aye, I do." Clare's mouth tightened. "Think on it, Joanna. He is in the habit of giving ladies a single blood-red rose. He composes poetry for them. He is a courteous knight who studies the secrets of the Arabic texts. He is medium-sized and scoffs at large men who rely on their strength. And he does not care for perfume because some recipes make him sneeze."

"And," Gareth said quietly from the doorway, "he knows a great deal about this isle and this hall. Enough to send Dallan here with clear instructions on how to ingratiate himself into this household."

"My lord." Dallan leaped to his feet. "I did not hear you come in."

William scowled. "I don't understand. Who is this magician?"

Clare looked at Gareth, whose gray eyes matched the color of the sky behind him. He watched her intently, waiting for her answer.

"We knew him as Raymond de Coleville," Clare said.

"By the saints," Joanna whispered. "Your handsome Raymond?"

"Aye." Clare did not take her gaze off Gareth's grim face. "Well, that's a relief, is it not?"

"Why is it a relief?" Dallan asked.

"Because I know both Sir Raymond and Lord Gareth very well." Clare rose to her feet and gazed at the expectant faces surrounding her. She smiled calmly. "And I can assure you that the magician is no match for our Hellhound."

Gareth stood at the window of Clare's study chamber and gazed out over the sea. There was an unpleasant gray mist pooling above the steel-colored waves. It had the look of a dense fog that could quickly shroud the isle.

"He was your ideal knight, the pattern of chivalry on which you based your recipe for a husband," Gareth said without any inflection in his voice.

"'Tis true, I used Raymond de Coleville as a model." Clare sat very straight in her chair and clasped her hands on top of her desk. "A woman needs a basic recipe to work from, after all."

"Does she?"

Clare sighed. "I have not made the acquaintance of many knights, my lord. The few I have known were not very impressive. They tended to resemble Sir Nicholas or my brother. My father was a knight and I held him in great affection, but I certainly did not want a husband who shirked his responsibilities as he did."

"And then the magician appeared here on your isle and cast his spells on you."

Clare wrinkled her nose. "I do not think I'd put it quite like that."

"There is one thing that I would like to know," Gareth said.

"Aye, my lord?"

"Do you still love him?"

Clare froze. "Nay. I do not love Raymond de Coleville or Lucretius, or whatever he calls himself."

Gareth turned to face her. His jaw was rigid. "Are you certain? Because I shall very likely have to kill him, Clare."

She shuddered. "I'd rather you did not kill anyone."

"So would I. But this magician is a murderer."

"Beatrice?"

"It must have been he who strangled her."

"Aye, I suppose it was, although 'tis impossible to think of Raymond as a murderer."

"You must also face the possibility that he killed your father."

"My *father*." Clare was stunned. "But my father was killed by thieves in Spain."

"What did your father have that was worth his life?" Gareth asked softly. "Think about it, Clare."

"His book of translated alchemic recipes," she whispered. "The same thing that the magician seeks."

"Aye. We know the magician has killed once for the book. Mayhap he has killed twice."

Clare closed her eyes in pain. "'Tis hard to comprehend. I am very sorry that we here on Desire are proving to be such a great nuisance, my lord. I know you had hoped for a quiet, peaceful life."

"Nothing comes without a price. Not even a quiet, peaceful existence. I am willing to pay the cost for what I want."

Clare opened her eyes and searched his face. "Aye. I know that. I only pray that one day you find what you seek."

"So do I." Gareth lowered his lashes, veiling his gaze. "You are certain that you do not love the magician?"

"I am very certain, my lord. In truth, I knew a long time ago that I could not ever love him."

"How did you—" Gareth broke off as if to search for the words he wanted. "What convinced you that you were not in love with him? How do you know that you are not still in love with him?"

"There are two reasons. The first one you will likely not comprehend."

"What is it?"

Clare shrugged. "He never smelled *right* to me."

Gareth blinked. "I beg your pardon? Did he fail to bathe regularly?"

"Oh, no. He was most fastidious in his personal habits." Clare smiled faintly. "But he just did not smell right to me, if you see what I mean."

"Nay, I do not see what you mean, but who am I to argue?" Gareth paused briefly. "And your second reason for being so certain that you do not love him?"

Clare took a deep breath. "I cannot possibly be in love with the magician, my lord, because I am in love with you."

"Me?" Gareth stared at her.

"Aye. You do smell right. I knew that the first day when you plucked me off the convent wall and set me down in front of you. I believe I fell in love with you at that very moment."

17

Gareth stared at the soft smile that played around Clare's lips and felt his blood turn to ice.

"Do not jest with me." He crossed the chamber in a few swift strides, circled the desk, and reached for Clare with both hands. "Not about this."

"My lord, what are you doing?" Clare's smile vanished in a heartbeat. She struggled to escape from the chair.

Gareth caught hold of her arms and hauled her upright. He lifted her straight off her feet so that she was eye-to-eye with him.

"I have warned you that I do not find amusement in the clever japes and sly words that cause others to laugh."

"By Saint Hermione's thumb, I was not jesting, my lord." Clare braced her hands on his shoulders and glowered at him. "Put me down at once. This is precisely the sort of overbearing behavior that I find so objectionable in large males."

He ignored the command. "Say that again."

"I said, this is precisely the sort of overbearing behavior—"

"Not that nonsense." He looked straight into her eyes. "The other."

"The other nonsense?" She repeated weakly.

"Hell's fire, madam, I am in no mood for this."

Clare's wistful smile flitted again about the curve of her mouth. "I love you."

"Because I *smell* good?"

"Not always *good*," she temporized. "But you have always smelled right."

"Right? *Right?*"

"I know that probably sounds rather odd to you, sir, but I am a person who judges many things by scent."

"Including men?"

Clare turned pink. "I knew you would think my explanation sounded frivolous."

"'Twas more than frivolous. A bold lie, more like. When I plucked you off that wall and sat you in front of me, I had just finished a hard four-day ride. I had not bathed in all that time, except to wash face and hands. I stank of horse and sweat and road dust."

"Aye. But there was something else, too. Something that I recognized."

"I did not smell like a lover."

She searched his face. "What does a lover smell like, my lord?"

"I know not. Roses, lavender, and cloves, I suspect. Certainly not horse and sweat and dust."

"Mayhap you are right about the odor of other lovers, my lord. I do not know." Clare framed his face gently between her palms. "I only know your scent. I recognized it that first day, although I did not know that it was the fragrance of a lover. I only knew that it was right."

"What is my scent, then?"

"'Tis the scent of the storm upon the wind, the scent of the sea at dawn. 'Tis a fierce, exciting perfume that dazzles my senses and makes my blood sing."

"Clare." He eased her slowly down the length of his body until her toes touched the floor. "*Clare.*" He crushed her mouth beneath his own.

Very likely it was passion that had made her believe she loved him, Gareth thought. She was still new to the force of it. Or mayhap it was her natural inclination to shelter the homeless.

Or mayhap—

Aye, mayhap she truly did love him.

He was afraid to let himself believe the latter, but he was not above taking whatever he could get.

She wound her arms around his neck and opened her mouth beneath his. Gareth felt her fingers in his hair. He shuddered with his need.

The desperate hunger welled up in him, as it always did when he held her in his arms. Along with it came an equally powerful need to protect her. He had to keep her safe. Clare was the most important thing in his world.

He tightened his grasp on her. The urgency within him was not purely sexual in nature. It was far more potent. Gareth knew that he had to hold on to Clare with greater strength and determination than he had ever used to grip his sword.

The Window of Hell, after all, was merely an instrument of death.

Clare was life.

"Damned fog," Ranulf muttered. "'Tis so thick now we will not be able to see the signal torches if they are lit by the guards who are keeping watch along the cliffs."

"Aye." Gareth wrapped both hands around the old watchtower railing and gazed out into the fog-shrouded night. "On the other hand, 'tis so thick that no sane man would attempt to row a boat from Seabern to Desire tonight. He would surely lose his way in this soup."

"No sane man," Ranulf agreed. "But mayhap a magician would make the attempt."

Gareth glanced at him. "Don't tell me that you have begun to believe my squire-in-training's wild tales. We are not laying in wait for a magician, Ranulf. Merely a very clever man who will stop at nothing to get what he wants."

"As you say, my lord."

"Do you fear that we cannot deal with Lucretius de Valemont?"

"Nay." The glowing embers of the nearby brazier lit Ranulf's set face. "As my lady says, you are more than a match for any magician, my lord."

"Thank you, Ranulf."

"But I cannot help thinking that it would have been more convenient for all of us if we were not short the men who have not yet returned from London."

"'Tis the fact that we are short those men that makes me believe the magician will try his luck soon," Gareth said.

Ranulf frowned. "You think he knows we are undermanned?"

"Aye."

Ranulf's eyes widened. "Do you believe he is so powerful he can use the dark arts to learn such information, then?"

"Nay." Gareth smiled faintly. "He no doubt learned it in the usual manner. By simple observation. The magician was at the Seabern fair. He would have had no difficulty learning of our plans to send an armed escort back to London with the merchant. It would have been a simple matter to deduce our remaining strength."

"Of course." Ranulf visibly relaxed. "Forgive me, my lord. Mayhap I have been paying too much attention to Dallan's stories. To hear him tell it, the magician can appear and disappear at will."

Footsteps on the wooden tower stairs made Gareth turn his head. Clare emerged from the opening, two steaming mugs in her hands. The hood of her green mantle was drawn up against the chill. The brazier's light played on her quiet, composed face.

"I thought you might appreciate something warm to drink," she said.

"My thanks." Gareth's fingers brushed Clare's as he took one of the mugs from her. He met her eyes and warmed himself in the gentle fire he saw there.

"Thank you, my lady." Ranulf took the other mug. "You certainly know how to ease the rigors of guard duty."

Clare went to the railing and looked out into the black mist. " 'Twill be dawn in a couple of hours, but even when the sun rises it will be impossible to see anything through this fog. How will you be able to see a signal torch?"

"We won't." Gareth sipped the hot pottage. "If anything happens, a messenger will be sent back here with the news."

"Aye, that makes sense," Clare said. "I did not think of such a simple thing."

" 'Tis not your responsibility to think about such matters," Gareth said. "Leave the simple things to me. I am well equipped to deal with them."

Ranulf choked on a swallow of pottage. Gareth looked at him with cool disapproval. The young guard quickly composed his face into a serious expression.

Clare did not appear to notice the byplay. She hugged herself and rubbed her hands up and down her arms. "Does it seem to you that there is something rather unpleasant about the smell of the fog?"

"Nay." Gareth rested his hand on the hilt of the Window of Hell. "It smells as all fog smells. Of dampness and the night."

Clare sniffed experimentally. "I think there is another odor embedded in it."

"What odor is that, my lady?" Ranulf asked.

"I do not recognize it," Clare said. "But I do not much care for it."

Hoofbeats sounded in the distance. The light of a torch glowed in the swirling fog.

"Open the gate," a familiar voice shouted from the road. "I have news."

Ranulf leaned over the railing and peered intently down at the man on the horse who had appeared out of the fog. " 'Tis Malden Comstock, my lord."

"Open the gate," Gareth ordered. He looked down as the horseman trotted through the gate and into the torchlit courtyard. "What news, Malden?"

"My lord, a boat carrying five armed men came ashore at the harbor under cover of fog. We killed two, but the others have retreated to a boathouse."

"So the magician did find a way through the mist," Ranulf muttered. "Mayhap he really does comprehend the black arts."

Gareth ignored him. "Why have the other three not been captured, Malden?"

"They are skilled bowmen, sir. Thus far they have managed to keep our men pinned down. Sir Ulrich has ordered us to wait until they use up all of their arrows. He says we'll have them soon enough."

"Aye. From the sound of things, we will. I'll be right down." Gareth turned to Ranulf. "I'm going to the harbor. You stay here in the tower."

"Aye, my lord." Ranulf looked disappointed, but he did not argue. "Do you believe that one of the men Sir Ulrich and the others have trapped is the magician?"

"I don't know yet. When one is dealing with an alchemist, nothing is for certain."

Clare stirred in the shadows. "My lord, please have a care. I do not like this."

Gareth took a step toward her. He captured her chin in his hand. "'Twill all be over by dawn." He kissed her quickly. "Go back into the hall and bar the door. Do not come out for any reason until I return. Do you comprehend me?"

She touched his cheek with gentle fingers. "Aye, my lord."

There was so much he suddenly wanted to say, but this was not the time or the place. Gareth looked into Clare's eyes for a few seconds. "Later. We will talk later." He released her chin and headed for the tower stairs.

The horse that he had ordered to be kept saddled and ready was waiting for him in the courtyard. William held the beast's head.

"Can I go with you, my lord?"

"Nay." Gareth vaulted onto the horse's back and took up the reins. "You will stay here with Clare and your mother and the servants. You are to guard the inside of the hall while Ranulf keeps watch outside. Is that understood?"

William straightened his shoulders. "Aye, my lord."

Gareth swung the horse's head around and set off at a gallop into the fog. Malden Comstock raised his torch and wheeled his own mount to follow.

One of the servants closed the gate solidly behind them.

Ulrich had just completed his task when Gareth and Malden Comstock reached the harbor. Flickering torches cast a hellish glow over the bodies of the two dead intruders. Three others stood in sullen silence, their hands bound behind them.

A cluster of villagers had emerged from their cottages to watch the excitement.

Gareth dismounted and tossed the reins of his horse to Malden. "Well done, Ulrich."

"This is the lot," Ulrich said. "They were not much trouble."

Gareth looked at the three surviving bowmen. "Which of you is Lucretius de Valemont?"

The captives stared at him. One shook his head.

Gareth contemplated the men thoughtfully. "There are many ways to die. Not all of them are swift. Give me the answers I seek."

One of the bowmen, a barrel-chested man of middle years, peered at him. "Your men call you the Hellhound of Wyckmere. Do they speak the truth?"

"Aye," Gareth said.

"'Tis said your oath is as strong as your sword."

"Aye."

"If we speak the truth, will you give us your word that our ends will be quick?"

"Aye." He had never tortured a man in his entire career as a hunter of cutthroats and thieves, Gareth thought. But there was no need for these three to know that.

The bowman considered for a short time. "The thing is, m'lord, we don't know any Lucretius de Valemont. And that's the truth. I swear it."

"Who hired you?"

The man shrugged. "A masterless knight who called himself Sir Raymond. He paid us well to come ashore in a boat tonight. He said he knew how to get us through the fog."

"Why did he want you to come here to Desire?"

"Said we'd find easy pickings here in the village. But I swear he said nothing about the isle being defended by the Hellhound's men."

"How did he guide you through the mist?"

The bowman exchanged uneasy glances. The spokesman looked at Gareth. "Sir Raymond came with us. He gave us directions after he consulted some magical device that he kept hidden in his cloak."

"Magic." One of the bowmen spat on the ground in disgust. "Told ye we should never have taken up with his kind. I never liked this business, even if that damned renegade knight did promise us enough loot from the convent to sink a ship."

The third man glowered at him. "Ye were eager enough to talk Brock and Dagget and the rest of us into it. We'd be set for life, ye said. Instead, we're all going to hang, thanks to ye."

Gareth rested his hand on the hilt of his sword, effectively silencing the argument. "Where is this Sir Raymond?"

"Like Brock told ye, we don't know, m'lord," one of the men said.

The spokesman stirred uneasily. "He got out of our boat a few yards offshore. He climbed into a smaller boat that we had brought along to carry the booty. Said he'd meet up with us later at the convent gate. Then he up and disappeared in the fog."

Gareth stilled. "And you five continued on into the harbor?"

"Aye. Not like we had any choice in the matter. We could not return to Seabern in this fog without Sir Raymond and his damned magical device." The bowman gave a fatalistic shrug. "Your men were waiting for us on the quay and that was the end of the thing."

"Me ma always said I'd finish me life at the end of a rope," one of the other bowmen remarked.

Ulrich looked at Gareth. "These three may well be lying, my lord."

"Aye." Gareth scanned the faces of the bowmen. He saw nothing in their eyes but stupidity and dumb resignation. He looked at the two dead bodies on the quay. "Fetch Dallan."

"Aye, my lord. He joined us earlier." Ulrich turned to the men gathered nearby. "Dallan, come here, lad. We need your help."

There was no response.

"He's not here, sir," one of the men-at-arms said. He looked around in confusion. "Mayhap he was injured by one of the bowmen's arrows."

"I'll check with the villagers," Malden said. He went over to the small cluster of curious onlookers.

When he returned a moment later, his eyes were grave.

"Well?" Gareth asked.

"Dallan seems to have vanished, my lord."

Ulrich looked thoughtful. "I warned you the lad might well prove dangerous, my lord. Mayhap he has lied to you all along."

Clare poked at the glowing coals in the brazier that warmed the chamber where she sat with Joanna and William. "Does it seem especially cold to you tonight, Joanna?"

"Summer will soon be here." Joanna studied her embroidery by the light of the lamp.

William stood at the window, his eyes on the torchlit courtyard. "I wonder if they have flushed out the magician yet. Do you suppose that one of the bowmen they have run to ground at the harbor really is Lucretius de Valemont?"

Clare frowned. "Sir Raymond never said anything about being a bowman. 'Tis not the sort of skill a knight learns."

Joanna glanced at her. "Very true. Knights do not train with such weapons. Bows are for common men-at-arms."

William continued to stare out the window. "Lord Gareth says such thinking is foolish. He says a man who wishes to survive must become adept with a variety of weapons, including the bow. Dallan and I have been practicing archery skills with Ranulf and the others."

"You have?" Joanna looked startled. "I did not know of this. I do not believe that archery is a beneficial form of exercise."

Clare hastened to change the subject. "Mayhap one of the men who was killed at the harbor was Lucretius de Valemont."

"Not likely," William said, "Dallan would have recognized him and sent word back with Malden Comstock."

"Hmm. You have a point," Clare said. "The magician must be one of the men trapped inside the house."

"Aye." William nodded with satisfaction. "Sir Ulrich and the others will no doubt have captured them by the time Lord Gareth arrives."

"I pray it will all be over quickly," Clare whispered.

"Of course it will." Joanna set another stitch. "Lord Gareth and Sir Ulrich will see to the matter."

"I don't know. It almost seems too simple." Clare crossed her arms beneath her breasts. She could not shake off the chill she had been feeling all evening.

Joanna looked up sharply. "Why do you say that?"

"I suppose because after all the turmoil he has caused, I cannot believe Raymond—I mean, Lucretius—will be stopped so easily."

William made a fist on the windowsill. "Sir Ulrich says the magician likely killed Sir Humphrey."

Clare shivered. "All because of an alchemic recipe book. Raymond or Lucretius, or whatever his name is, must be mad."

Joanna stabbed her needle into the fabric. "I never did trust that man."

Clare exchanged a small, wry look with William. Neither of them reminded Joanna that she had once praised Raymond de Coleville to the skies.

Clare walked over to the window. Together she and William looked out into the night and waited for the glow of a torch to appear on the road.

"I wish we knew what was going on at the harbor," William said.

Clare stirred after a while. She peered at the shadowed watchtower. "Does it seem to you that the tower torch is burning low, William?"

William shifted his glance toward the tower. "Aye. Mayhap Ranulf does not have a spare torch. Shall I go and see if he needs a fresh one?"

"Nay, I'll go downstairs to the hall and find Eadgar. He can send one of the servants across to the tower with a fresh torch."

Clare turned toward the door, grateful for something to do.

"Will you ask Eadgar to bring us something to eat?" William said with a hopeful look. "I vow, I am starved."

Clare smiled. "Very well." She made to open the door.

"*Lady Clare,* come quickly." William's voice was sharp with fear.

Clare whirled around. She saw that William had both hands planted on the windowsill. He was staring down at the courtyard.

"What is it?" she asked. "What's wrong?"

"Come see. There are men in the courtyard. *But the gate is still closed.*"

"By Saint Hermione's needle." Clare hurried across the chamber. "What are you talking about? Is Lord Gareth back?"

" 'Tis not Lord Gareth and his men. These are strangers." William turned a shocked face toward her. "They were not there a moment ago. You and I both saw that the courtyard was empty. And no one has opened the gate. This is truly magic."

Joanna dropped her embroidery. Her face was stark with terror. "The magician."

Clare reached the window and stared down at the torchlit courtyard. She could hardly believe what she saw. Half a dozen men armed with swords and dressed in black hooded cloaks strode toward the front steps of the hall.

Several of the men had the edges of their cloaks pushed back over their shoulders. Torchlight glinted on their mail.

The leader of the group held a familiar figure in front of him, a dagger at his throat.

" 'Tis Dallan," William whispered. "He's captured Dallan."

"Dear God." Joanna's voice cracked.

The man who held Dallan signaled to one of the others. A cloaked figure went up the steps and pounded on the front door of the hall with the hilt of his sword.

"Open in the name of the Grand Master of the Order of the Star Stone. Open or die."

Clare gripped the window ledge with shaking fingers. She leaned out. "Who goes there?"

The man who held Dallan at dagger point looked up at the open window. He threw back his hood and smiled.

Clare found herself gazing down at the man she had once known as Raymond de Coleville.

"Good evening to you, Lady Clare," Lucretius's polished voice and flashing grin were as charming as ever.

Clare stared down at him, unwilling for an instant to believe that he was actually there inside the wall.

But she could not deny the truth.

The fiery light of the torches cast an evil glow on Lucretius's handsome, falcon-sharp features. He was slender and graceful, just as she remembered, a devastatingly attractive man with long, tapered fingers. His black cloak swirled around him like the ebony wings of a great bird of prey.

"How did you get inside the wall?" Clare demanded.

"What a foolish question. I am a magician." Lucretius's smile was brilliant. "Open your hall, madam. I want the book that this foolish boy failed to bring to me."

"Don't do it, Lady Clare," Dallan shouted. "Don't let him inside." He broke off, choking, as Lucretius squeezed his arm around his throat.

Clare watched Lucretius's face carefully. "If you are indeed a great magician, sir, why do you not simply materialize inside my hall and take the book?"

Lucretius continued to smile. "Materializing and dematerializing are hard work, madam, even for a magician as accomplished as myself. I would prefer to do this in the simplest manner."

"Are you mad?"

"You will bring me your father's recipe book, or I shall kill your minstrel here and now." The dagger in Lucretius's hand glinted. "And then I shall enter your hall and kill your people one by one in front of your eyes until you choose to bring me the book."

"Let him kill me, Lady Clare," Dallan pleaded. "I beg you, let him kill me. You must not open the hall to him."

Lucretius's smile was cold. "I congratulate you, Clare. I did not believe that you could win young Dallan to your service so easily, but obviously he is now devoted to you. I thought the boy had enough wit to know better than to turn against me, but apparently he does not."

"Don't give him the book," Dallan cried. "I don't care if he kills me."

Lucretius did not take his eyes off Clare. "You do not know your lady very well, boy. She is too softhearted. She will never allow you to die for the sake of a mere book. Is that not right Clare? No book is worth the death of one you care about, is it?"

"Nay," Clare said quickly. "I will bring you the book if you will promise to release Dallan."

"You may have your minstrel back as soon as I have Sir Humphrey's book. The clumsy boy was never of much use, anyway."

"Very well, I shall drop the book down to you from this window," Clare said.

"Nay, madam. You will bring it to me. I want you as well as the book."

"Me? Why do you want me?"

"I am a prudent man. I desire a more useful hostage than Dallan to ensure my escape. You are going to accompany me until I am safely off Desire."

"But why?" Clare asked desperately.

"Something tells me that the Hellhound will bargain more seriously for your life than he will for the boy's. You are vastly more important to Sir Gareth, are you not? After all, you are the source of the wealth of this isle."

"I will bring you the book." Clare whirled away from the window and ran to the door.

"Clare, you must not open the hall door," Joanna said. "You will risk all our lives."

William's eyes were huge. "Maybe he truly is a magician. If that is so, we are doomed."

"That is ridiculous. He is no magician. There is no such thing as true magic. Lord Gareth had the right of it. Lucretius is merely a clever alchemist." Clare opened the door and raced down the hall to her study chamber.

Joanna and William followed.

"William, bring me a large pouch that has a flap," Clare said.

"Aye." William took off in the other direction.

Clare dashed into the study chamber and grabbed the heavy leather-bound book off the shelf. She unlocked the clasp and reached for a nearby urn of dried flowers.

Joanna stared at her. "What are you doing?"

"This mixture contains a large amount of mugwort." Clare sprinkled several handfuls of the dried concoction inside the heavy covers of the book. "The magician does not care for mugwort. It makes him sneeze uncontrollably."

William appeared in the door. "Here's the pouch, Clare."

"Give it to me." Clare took the bag from him. She emptied the remaining contents of the urn into the pouch. Then she closed the flap and slung the leather bag over her shoulder. She picked up the book in both hands. "Lucretius will want to see the book before it goes into the pouch in order to be certain that he had not been tricked."

"Clare, please do not do this, I beg you," Joanna whispered. " 'Tis much too dangerous."

Clare looked at her. "I shall go out alone. Close the door and bar it behind me the instant I have stepped onto the steps. Do not open it until Lucretius and his men have gone."

"But what about you?" Joanna wailed.

"Lord Gareth will soon realize what has happened. He will return to retake the hall. And then he will come for me." Clare smiled wistfully. "The magician is right. I do have a certain value to the Hellhound. These lands would not be nearly so profitable without me."

She went quickly past Joanna and William. Her soft boots made no sound on the stone floor of the corridor as she raced toward the tower stairs.

Downstairs in the main hall she found Eadgar and the servants huddled near the hearth. Their faces were stark with fear.

"Unbar the door, Eadgar," Clare said.

"But my lady—"

"Please do as I say."

"Aye, my lady." Eadgar bowed his head and went to the door.

Eunice and Agnes wrung their hands.

Eadgar raised the heavy iron bar that secured the front door.

Clare stepped out into the night. "Close the door, Eadgar. Hurry."

The door swung shut behind her. She heard the bar drop back into place.

She had never felt so alone in her life.

"You have the book?" Lucretius asked.

"Aye." Clare held it up so that he could see the volume. "And a pouch to carry it." She raised the flap of the pouch and dropped the book inside. It settled amid the mugwort mixture. "Now release Dallan."

"Come to me, Clare," Lucretius commanded.

"Nay," Dallan pleaded.

Clare started down the steps.

At that instant a hail of fiery arrows arced down into the courtyard. The black-cloaked knights yelled in warning and confusion.

"What in the name of the devil?" Lucretius's cloak swung wide as he turned around to see what was happening.

Gareth and his men appeared on the roof of Clare's workrooms. Three of them held bows.

"Gareth," Clare whispered.

"Damned Hellhound," Lucretius muttered. He thrust Dallan out of his way. "Take them, men," he shouted. "They are no match for the Knights of the Star Stone. *Take them now*, I command you."

Swords drawn, the cloaked knights started warily toward the workrooms.

Before they had gone more than three paces, the fire arrows that had landed nearby in the courtyard exploded in a series of thunderclaps.

"What magic is this?" one of the men yelled.

Thick smoke, denser than any fog, billowed aloft into the torchlit night, obscuring the scene.

A man screamed.

Dallan ran up the steps to Clare's side. He stared in wonder. "'Tis Lord Gareth's sulfur and charcoal recipe, my lady. We told you that it worked."

"Aye," Clare said. "So you did. You did not mention that you had discovered a use for it."

Another round of thunder shook the yard. Panic set in among the cloaked knights. Screams echoed above the din of exploding arrows.

"'Tis the damned Hellhound who is the true magician," one knight shouted. "Run for your lives."

More smoke rolled across the courtyard. Lucretius suddenly appeared from the thick of it. He lurched toward the hall steps, his hand reaching out to grasp Clare.

"Do not dare to touch her." Dallan caught Clare's hand and yanked her out of Lucretius's reach.

"Aye, heed him well, magician." Gareth's voice was a dark, disembodied command that could have issued from the mouth of hell itself. "Do not dare to put your hands on my wife."

In the glow of the torchlight, Clare saw the clouds of smoke swirl and part. Gareth came toward the steps, striding through the hellish mist as though he were the hellhound men called him.

Lucretius stared at him. "What strange alchemy is this? What secrets have you learned from the book, bastard? *What have you wrought here?*"

Gareth's teeth flashed in a smile that would have done credit to the devil. "What's the matter, magician? Did you think you were the only knight who knew how to read?"

All would have been well if William had not rushed out onto the hall steps at that point. Joanna was right behind him.

"William, come back here," Joanna screamed.

"Clare, Clare, are you all right?" William shouted.

Before Gareth could intervene, the boy careened straight into Lucretius.

The magician proved immediately how he had gotten at least a portion of his formidable reputation. He grabbed William with a deft movement.

"One shield is as good as another." With one hand Lucretius dragged his struggling victim back against himself. He unsheathed his sword with his free hand. "Stay back, Hellhound."

Joanna cried out and collapsed in a dead faint in the doorway. No one paid any attention. Out of the corner of his eye, Gareth saw Clare impulsively start forward toward Lucretius.

"Do as he says," Gareth said. "Stay back."

Clare halted and stared at him with a desperate expression. "Gareth—"

Gareth looked at Lucretius. "The best you can hope for at this juncture is to escape the isle with the damned book, Lucretius."

Lucretius smiled grimly. "'Tis all I ever wanted in the first place. Dallan, you stupid little cur, toss the pouch to me."

Dallan looked at Gareth.

"Do it," Gareth said.

Dallan picked up the leather pouch and tossed it toward Lucretius, who managed to grab it without releasing William.

Lucretius slung the long strap over his opposite shoulder so that the pouch hung crosswise across his body. "There. I have everything I need. Now all I must do is vanish."

"Through the hidden door in the old curtain wall that one of the stonemasons built for you?" Gareth asked softly.

"So you reasoned that out, did you?" Lucretius chuckled. "The man owed me a favor. His life, to be precise. Constructing the secret entrance in your wall was the price I put on his continued existence."

"Very clever, magician. But you had best hurry. My men have almost subdued the last of your knights. You have only the smoke and fog to cover your retreat."

Lucretius assessed the situation with a single glance at the smoke-shrouded courtyard. It was impossible to see much of what was happening, but it was clear that the clash of swords was lessening rapidly. Ulrich's voice could be heard above the din, demanding that the invaders yield.

Lucretius looked at Clare. "I would rather have a more certain shield. Come here, Clare. I shall exchange young William for you."

"No," Gareth said. "You do not need her. You have my word that I will not stop you from leaving this courtyard."

"Forgive me if I do not trust the depth of your feelings for this boy," Lucretius said. "But I know that you will most certainly think carefully before you risk your lady's neck. Clare is, after all, the most valuable member of your household, is she not? Without her, the flowers of Desire are worthless. Clare, come here at once."

"Clare, no," Gareth said roughly. He felt his stomach clench with fear.

"'Tis for the best, my lord," Clare said. "Trust me."

She went calmly down the steps.

Lucretius did not hesitate. He released William, grabbed Clare, and crooked his arm around her throat.

Then he retreated swiftly into the haze that filled the courtyard.

"Damn your soul to hell, magician." Rage lanced through Gareth, hot and fierce. He moved to follow Lucretius and Clare.

"My lord, wait." William caught hold of Gareth's arm.

"Go back inside the hall." The damned magician was already disappearing into the smoke, Gareth realized.

"But there is something I must tell you before you go after the magician," William hissed softly. "Clare put mugwort inside the pouch. Sir Lucretius will soon begin to sneeze uncontrollably. His eyes will water and he will be rendered helpless."

Gareth looked down at William. "Are you certain?"

"Aye, my lord. He has a terrible reaction to mugwort. I saw what happened when Clare once gave him a pomander that was filled with it. He accused her of trying to poison him."

"Go back inside the hall and wait until Sir Ulrich tells you to open the door."

"Aye, my lord." William hesitated. "You will fetch Clare back, will you not?"

"Aye." He looked at Dallan. "Come with me, Squire."

Dallan turned a stark face to him. "He will kill her, my lord."

"Nay. We will rescue her. It is the magician who will not survive this night."

He strode toward the gate and called to one of the men-at-arms to open it.

Ulrich hailed him through the smoke. "We have the magician's knights, my lord."

"Lock them up until I return."

"But where are you going?"

"To hunt a magician."

Once outside the gate, Gareth discovered that an eerie silence now gripped the isle. The chill of dawn had caused the fog to thicken measurably.

The gray mist glowed with the pale light of morning. Unfortunately, that pearly luminescence only served to veil the landscape more completely. Attempting to see through the fog was akin to peering into the smoked crystal stone in the pommel of his sword, Gareth thought. There was light there, but it fooled the eye and obscured the depths.

"What are we going to do?" Dallan asked in a whisper.

"I believe he will head for the first of the small coves. He will seek the small boat that he hid there."

Dallan glanced at Gareth, startled. "You found a boat in one of the caves?"

"Aye. I gave orders that the caves were to be searched every few hours. One of the men discovered a vessel concealed there a short while ago."

"The magician's boat?"

"No doubt. The bowmen were merely a distraction. He never intended to meet up with them or to leave by way of the harbor." Gareth glanced around, searching for familiar landmarks in the fog. Through the mist he spotted the shape of one of the outbuildings. "That way. Henceforth, say nothing. Walk as silently as you can."

Dallan nodded.

Gareth led the way across the mist-shrouded field. When the outbuilding faded into the fog, he used the sound of the waves as a guide.

He and Dallan had not gone more than twenty paces when they heard the first great sneeze. It came from up ahead and off to the left.

Dallan looked at Gareth, his eyes widening with realization.

Gareth smiled. *My sweet, clever Clare. You have snared the magician for me. Now all I have to do is wait for the right moment to kill him.*

The second sneeze was accompanied by a raging curse.

"Goddamn this isle and all your obnoxious perfumes, Clare. There must be a field of mugwort nearby."

"Release me, sir," Clare commanded. "You do not need me any longer."

"Hush. Do not speak again. That damned Hellhound is no doubt following us." Lucretius broke off to sneeze.

Gareth used the sound to guide himself closer to his quarry. He motioned Dallan to stay behind him.

They were very near the edge of the cliffs now. Gareth could hear the echo of the waves in the cove. He heard Clare cry out softly as she stumbled over some object.

"The boat is hidden in the cave down below," Lucretius muttered. "You will go down the cliff path ahead of me. There is no place to run, so don't even think of doing so. Go. I will be right behind you—"

The magician's words were cut off by a swift series of loud, convulsive sneezes. He swore again, violently. And sneezed again.

The sound of a brief scuffle ensued.

"Nay," Clare said. "I'll not go with you."

"Come back here, you stupid wench. I will kill you with my magic if you do not return to me." Another sneezing fit overcame Lucretius. "What is this?" he gasped. "What have you done to me? Damn you, 'tis the book."

Something heavy fell to earth. Gareth knew that it was the leather pouch Lucretius had slung across his body. The magician had thrown it down onto the ground in rage.

"*You have tried to poison me,*" Lucretius screamed. "I'll kill you for this, just as I killed your father."

"Leave," Clare cried. "Flee while you still can, magician. If my husband finds you, he will surely destroy you."

Gareth saw the flash of Clare's gown in the fog. A new fear seized him. He realized that Clare could not see any more clearly than he could. If she chanced to lose her bearings, she might fall into the sea.

"Clare, this way," he shouted. *"Do not run toward the cliffs. Run to me."*

Footsteps thudded softly in the moist ground. Clare appeared out of the mist. She ran blindly toward the sound of his voice. Then she saw him.

"Gareth."

"Stay with Dallan." Gareth raised his sword and went past her.

He nearly stumbled over the leather pouch that was lying on the ground. The book had fallen out. Dried flowers were scattered about. The familiar scent of mugwort was strong.

Another loud sneeze made Gareth whirl to the left. Lucretius stood in the swirling gray mist. His black cloak was thrown back behind his shoulders, revealing his mail hauberk.

"So you think that you are a more clever magician than I, Hellhound?" Gareth did not answer. He paced toward Lucretius.

"Stay back." Lucretius held his sword ready for battle with one hand. With his other, he reached into the folds of his cape and withdrew an object the size of a cup. "I can throw the contents of this vial farther than you can reach with a sword, Hellhound."

Gareth glanced at the large vial. It was filled with a green-tinged potion that he did not recognize. "Do you think I fear whatever you have in that jar?"

"You would do well to fear it." Lucretius's smile was savage. "'Tis a corrosive elixir that burns whatever it touches, including skin and eyes, Hellhound."

"He's right, my lord." Dallan took a step forward. He stared at the vial in Lucretius's hand. "'Tis a mixture that he concocted when he tried to create gold from base metals. It burns like fire."

Lucretius laughed softly. "Listen to the boy, Hellhound. Or risk your eyes. What good is a blind hound?"

"Gareth, I believe that he speaks the truth," Clare said. "Do not get close to him."

"He does speak the truth," Dallan insisted. "Have a care, my lord."

Clare did not take her eyes off Lucretius. "Why did you kill the recluse?"

Lucretius shrugged. "The foolish old woman saw me. She believed me to be the ghost of Brother Bartholomew come to search for his lost Sister Maud. But for some reason she felt she had to prove the point."

"She followed you to the convent library and you killed her," Clare whispered.

"I wanted to see if you had stored your father's books in the convent library before I went to the trouble of trying to find it in your hall. It would have been so much simpler if you had handed it over to the nuns, Clare."

"They were not interested in it," Clare said. "So I kept it."

"Idiots." Lucretius glanced at the book lying near the pouch. "The greatest secrets of the ancients are in that volume. Your father found them in the Arabic treatises that he translated. Mayhap the very secret of immortality is in there."

"Do you intend to leave the isle without your precious book, magician?" Gareth prodded the volume with the toe of his boot.

"It appears that I shall be forced to leave it behind today, but you may be certain that I shall return for it." Lucretius smiled his cold, dazzling smile once more. "And you will never know when or where I shall next appear. The knowledge will no doubt keep you awake at night, eh, Hellhound?"

"I stopped you this time, did I not? I can do it again, if need be."

"Bah! You were fortunate this time, that is all. Next time, things will be different."

"Leave, then, if that is your intent. Take your foul elixir and get off this isle."

"As you wish, Hellhound. But first I will leave you something by which you shall always remember me." Lucretius hurled the vial, straight at Gareth's face.

"No," Dallan yelled. He leaped to intercept the vial, reaching for it with his bare hands.

"Dallan," Clare shouted.

Gareth did not even think about his reaction. It was instantaneous, the sort of quick, physical response that had saved his life on countless occasions.

With one hand he grabbed Dallan and yanked him out of the way. With the other he brought his sword up in a swift, short arc. He caught the vial on the flat of the blade.

Gareth used the momentum of the swing to propel the small jar off to the side. It struck a rock and shattered. There was a soft hissing sound.

"Dear God," Clare breathed. "It is eating away at the rock."

"You have the devil's own luck, Hellhound." Lucretius raced toward the cliff path. "But it cannot last forever."

"There is no boat waiting for you down in the cove, magician," Gareth said softly. "My men discovered it a short while ago."

"Nay, that cannot be." Lucretius's cloak whipped around him as he halted at the top of the cliff path. "You *lie.* I discovered those caves. No one knows about the cliff caves."

Gareth smiled. "You do not know much about young boys. They are insatiably curious. William found the caves long ago."

"Damn you, Hellhound." Lucretius lunged toward him, sword raised.

Gareth met the rush easily. Steel clashed against steel. Lucretius leaped back out of reach, feinted, and closed once more.

The magician was good, Gareth conceded privately as the two men circled each other. He was both fast and clever. Lucretius might make a show of disdaining the fighting arts in favor of magic, but it was obvious he had a talent for swordplay.

Conscious of the sheer drop at the edge of the cliff, Gareth maneuvered to ensure that it was Lucretius's back that was to the sea, not his own. Out of the corner of his eye he saw Clare drag Dallan out of harm's way.

Lucretius attempted another rushing charge. Gareth sidestepped it.

The magician swung around and this time Gareth found himself in the position he had wished to avoid. His back was to the cliffs.

Lucretius closed again, sword glinting dully in the gray light. Gareth felt the ground give way beneath his left boot heel. The edge of the cliff began to crumble beneath him. The waves below were very loud.

With all of his strength, he dove forward, headfirst, in an attempt to dive beneath the thrust of Lucretius's steel.

Lucretius was already committed to the blow. His face contorted with rage as Gareth slid in low, just beneath the blade, hit the ground with his shoulder, and rolled.

"Die, Hellhound." Lucretius swung around as Gareth surged to his feet. "*Die*, damn you."

Gareth saw the opening and moved in, sword ready. Lucretius could not get his own blade up swiftly enough to effectively parry the blow.

But even as Gareth went in for the kill, Lucretius screamed and dropped his sword. He flailed wildly as the ground gave way beneath his feet.

"No," Lucretius yelled. "No, it cannot happen like this. *I'm a magician.*"

Gareth caught himself and stepped swiftly back from the disintegrating cliff edge.

Lucretius pitched backward into the gray nothingness that waited for him. His scream rent the air for endless seconds and then it abruptly ceased.

In the great silence that followed, Gareth met Clare's eyes.

"Gareth." She ran toward him and threw herself into his arms, hugging him fiercely. "You are safe."

"Aye." Gareth looked over the top of her head at Dallan, who was staring at the place where Lucretius had last been seen.

"Do you think he is truly dead, my lord?" Dallan asked in a strange voice.

"Aye. You and I shall go down to the cove together. Be assured that we will find his body lying on the rocks. He was only a man, after all."

"A terrible man," Clare said distinctly from the circle of Gareth's arm. "Not at all a good recipe for a husband."

Clare had still not recovered from the shock of the day's events by the time she and Gareth retired to their bedchamber that evening.

On the surface, all had returned to normal. Ranulf had been found, alive but unconscious, in the watchtower. He had soon recovered from the blow to his head, but Clare suspected his pride would take longer to heal.

Lucretius's body had been retrieved from the cove. The four black-cloaked knights that had survived the conflict and the three hapless bowmen were securely locked up in a storage cellar beneath the hall.

Joanna had recovered from her faint, hugged William until he pleaded with her to cease, and then thrown herself straight into Ulrich's arms.

The village was abuzz with excitement as neighbor retold the tale to neighbor. With each telling, the exploits of the Hellhound grew more impressive. Clare knew that her people were taking a great deal of pride in the fact that their lord had proven himself more powerful than any magician.

There had been much merriment and jubilation among Gareth's men at supper. Cook had produced an elaborate array of dishes to celebrate the events. The servants had talked and jested with the men-at-arms.

Dallan had contributed to the air of celebration by singing a thrilling ballad narrating the rescue of Desire. He had composed it in less than two hours and everyone was extremely admiring of his talents.

Clare had managed to maintain a reasonably serene facade as the courtyard was cleaned and all was set to rights. But it was only a facade. She had not been able to eat a thing at the evening meal.

"Are you all right, Clare?" Gareth asked quietly. He stood in front of the hearth fire and stripped off his tunic and boots.

"Aye. Just a little cold." She clenched her hands around the edge of the quilt and watched Gareth as he undressed.

Gareth coiled his leather belt around his fist. "You've been acting oddly this evening."

"Well, it has been a rather odd day, my lord."

He cocked a brow as he set the coiled belt down on top of a carved chest. "I understand."

"Do you, Gareth?"

"Aye. You are not accustomed to violence here on Desire."

"That is very true."

"Well, calm yourself, madam." Gareth yawned. "'Tis very unlikely that we'll be confronted with a similar situation anytime soon. The hall is safe. Desire is safe. Our people are safe."

"Thanks to you, my lord."

His broad shoulder moved in a massive shrug as he crossed the room to the bed. "The magician was nothing more than a well-dressed thief. I am good at dealing with thieves, madam. I've had a fair amount of practice, if you will recall."

His careless attitude to the devastating events of the day was too much. Clare sat straight up in bed. She clutched the quilt to her throat with shaking fingers. "By Saint Hermione's eyes, how can you be so casual about this, my lord?"

He stopped, clearly surprised by her burst of anger. Then concern furrowed his brow. "Clare? Are you well? Do you need a warm drink to help you sleep? You've been through a great deal today."

"I most certainly have been through a great deal." Clare scrambled to her feet and stood squarely in the middle of the bed. She braced her fists on her hips and glowered at him. *You very nearly got yourself killed today, Hellhound.*"

He regarded her with a quizzical expression. "There was very little likelihood of that."

"There was every likelihood of it. I witnessed that last battle with the magician. It could just as easily have been you who went over the cliff."

Gareth yawned again. "But I didn't."

"Don't you dare treat this matter so lightly, my lord. What would I have done if it had been your body we brought up from the cove?"

"Clare—"

Tears of anguish and rage filled her eyes. "I could not have borne it, damn you."

"Clare, all is well, I swear it. Calm yourself, madam."

"Do not treat me as though I were an anxious mare. I almost lost you today."

Gareth gave her a slight smile. "I have no doubt but that you could have replaced me easily enough, madam. There are no lack of homeless knights in England. Mayhap you would have found one who came closer to meeting your specifications than I do."

"Do not jest with me, sir. I am in no mood for it. I told you that I love you. Can you not comprehend what that means?"

"I believe so," Gareth said slowly.

"Bah, you have no notion whatsoever of love, do you? If you had been killed today, my heart would have been broken forever. Does that mean nothing to you?"

"It means everything to me," Gareth said simply.

"Oh, *Gareth*." Clare hurled herself straight into his arms. "You are the only man I have ever known who makes me feel something more than merely useful."

Gareth wrapped his arms around her. "You have the same effect on me, madam. I begin to believe that I belong here on Desire."

"You do. This is your home, Gareth. You must never forget that for a single moment. You must not take any more foolish risks."

"Ease your mind, wife. We are both safe and I intend to keep us so."

"I was so terrified that I would lose you," she mumbled against his shoulder.

He tangled his hands in her hair. "How do you think I felt when I returned to the hall and found you standing on the steps conversing with Lucretius de Valemont?"

Clare choked back a sob. "I was not conversing with him. We were bargaining. I am very good at bargaining."

"Aye, so you are." Gareth gently stroked the nape of her neck with his thumb and forefinger. "That was a very clever trick you played on the magician."

"I knew the mugwort would cause him to sneeze most violently. I had hoped that his reaction would give Dallan a chance to escape."

"Instead it provided you with your chance." Gareth paused meaningfully. "A chance which you would not have needed if you had stayed safely inside the hall as I commanded."

"I had to do something. He threatened Dallan's life."

"So you went to the rescue." Gareth groaned in resignation. "I suppose there is no point berating you for your foolishness."

"I had no choice."

Gareth captured her face between his palms. "We will not argue the point. 'Tis over and done. You are safe now and that is all that matters."

She smiled and blinked back the last of her tears. "Oh, Gareth." She wound her arms around his neck and pressed close.

He gave a deep, husky exclamation, picked her up, and settled her onto the herb-scented sheets. There was enough light from the banked fire for Clare to see the brilliant intensity of his eyes. The heat in those crystal depths warmed her as nothing else had been able to do all day.

"Ah, my sweet Clare." Gareth sprawled heavily on top of her, crushing her into the bedding. "You are not the only one who got a sound scare today. Do not ever do that to me again."

"Nay, my lord." Clare pulled his mouth down to hers and kissed him with a frantic need that she did not bother to disguise.

His response overwhelmed her, as it always did.

•   •   •   •

A long while later Clare shifted languidly alongside Gareth. Neither of them had bothered to draw the curtains around the bed yet. The embers of the fire cast a warm light onto the rumpled sheets.

Clare snuggled deeper into her husband's warmth and breathed in the scent of his relaxed, satiated body. Just as she closed her eyes, a drowsy thought flitted through her brain.

"Gareth?"

"Hmm?" Gareth's voice was little more than a rumbling purr in the shadows.

"I almost forgot. Eadgar wants to know how long we shall be obliged to feed the prisoners. He says he will need to acquire provisions if they are to be housed in the storage rooms for any length of time."

"He need only bother with them for another day or so at the most. They'll all be gone soon."

"Good. He'll be grateful to learn that." Clare patted away a tiny yawn and nestled closer. "'Tis a problem for him, you know. We are not accustomed to dealing with prisoners here on Desire."

"Uh-huh." Gareth sounded as though he were already half asleep.

Clare gazed thoughtfully into the glowing coals on the hearth. "Where do you suppose such men will go now that their master is dead?"

"Huh?"

"I was wondering what will become of those four knights who served Sir Lucretius. And those three bowmen you took captive. Poor men. It must be very hard not to have a home or good lord to serve."

"Finding a new home is not going to be a problem for them, Clare."

She turned her head on the pillow. "Why not?"

"Because I'm going to have them all hung, that's why not."

"*What?*" Clare shot bolt upright. "You cannot do that, Gareth."

He opened one eye and looked at her as though she had gone mad. "'Tis the usual procedure for dealing with men of that sort."

"Impossible. Absolutely impossible. You are not going to hang seven men here on Desire, my lord. By Saint Hermione's ring, it is out of the question." Clare's imagination conjured up a vision of seven bodies dangling from gibbets. "I absolutely forbid it."

Gareth opened his other eye and studied her with a blank look. "You forbid it?"

"Aye, I most certainly do. There has never been a hanging here on Desire. My father never found it necessary to hang anyone. I do not intend to change that custom."

"Clare," Gareth said with an ominous patience, "those men downstairs in the cellar are masterless men. Thieves. Renegade knights. They are likely murderers and worse."

"They killed no one here."

"By purest chance."

"They were led by an evil man who is now dead."

"Aye, and if I turn them loose, they'll soon find themselves another such master to serve. That is their nature."

Clare stared at him, shaken by the implacable expression on his face. "My lord, I cannot abide the thought of so many terrible deaths taking place on this isle. You cannot do it."

Gareth hesitated. "I suppose I could have them sent to Seabern. Sir Nicholas will likely not mind seeing to the matter."

Clare pounded the bedding with clenched fists. "That is not the point. The point is, I do not want them all to hang."

Gareth made an obvious bid for his patience. "We agreed that we each had our responsibilities as lord and lady of this manor."

"Aye, but—"

"You must allow me to carry out my duties, madam."

"Surely you do not need to hang them. There are alternatives."

"What alternatives?"

"You can banish them," she suggested swiftly. "Make them swear to abjure the territory. They would not dare to return."

"Clare—"

"They fear you, sir. They believe you to be more powerful than Lucretius de Valemont."

"Mayhap they would not be of much concern to us in the future," Gareth conceded, "but declaring them outlaws and sending them away only serves to make them someone else's problem."

"Gareth, I will not have seven bodies twisting in the breeze of Desire, and that is final."

"Nay, madam. In this matter, my decision is final."

"We shall see about that." Clare swept up the quilt and wrapped it around herself. She slid off the edge of the bed.

"Where the devil do you think you are going, wife?"

"I am going to sleep in the wardrobe until you grant me the boon I have asked of you, my lord."

Wearing the quilt like an overlong cloak, Clare spun on her heel and stalked across the bedchamber into the wardrobe.

19

"By the devil, they are all so young," Gareth muttered. "Not a one of them is above nineteen years." He surveyed the faces of Lucretius's four surviving knights as they were led into the hall for questioning. "Why did that damned magician have to choose boys to carry out his plans?"

"They are not boys, they are men." Ulrich shrugged. "And you know the answer to your question as well as I do."

"Aye." Gareth braced his elbow on the arm of the heavy oak chair and rested his chin on the heel of his hand. He never relished this aspect of the business. "Young men of that age are easier to control and more easily impressed than are their elders. They do not question commands. Or a magician's tricks."

"De Valemont no doubt used a combination of terror and promises of knighthood and a fortune to lure them into his service. 'Tis an old and much-proven technique for recruiting young men."

"My lady wife wishes me to show mercy." Gareth gazed moodily at the prisoners. "She has bid me set them free."

"So I have heard. Indeed, my lord, the entire hall is aware of Lady Clare's, ah, request."

"I knew she would not be able to keep the matter private."

"I believe the rumors started when a serving maid found Lady Clare asleep in the wardrobe this morning."

Gareth tapped his forefinger against his set jaw and said nothing.

Ulrich politely cleared his throat. "Mayhap your gentle lady feels sorry for these men because they are not much older than Dallan. I'm surprised she feels equally charitable toward the would-be thieves we caught at the harbor, however. There is no denying they are a seasoned lot."

"She would have me banish them all and bid them good fortune in their next endeavors."

"Women are inclined to be softhearted, especially those who have not had much experience with violence."

"She says she does not want Abbess Helen to arrive on our fair isle to find seven corpses twisting in the scented breezes."

"Something tells me our lady abbess has seen worse in her time," Ulrich murmured.

"True. In any event, if we get on with the matter, we can be rid of the corpses before the abbess arrives." Gareth watched the four knights come to a halt in front of his chair.

They were not only young, they were scared and trying hard to conceal the fear behind masks of stoic defiance. Gareth nodded once to the guards, who stepped back a pace. Then he looked straight at the eldest of the young men.

"You. What is your name?"

"Sir Robert."

"Where is your hall?"

Robert hesitated and then shrugged. "I do not have a hall now that Lord Lucretius is dead."

"You have no family?"

"Nay, my lord."

"Your parents?"

Robert looked puzzled by the line of questioning. "I never knew my father. My mother died at my birth."

Gareth glanced at the next young knight. "And you? What is your name? Where is your family's hall?"

"My name is John." There was a slight tremor in John's voice. He took a deep breath and managed to control it. "I was the magician's sworn man. Now that he is dead, I do not have a hall."

"I believe I see a pattern here," Ulrich said softly.

"Aye." Gareth looked at the remaining two knights. "Do either of you have families? A hall?"

Both shook their heads.

"If it pleases you, my lord." Robert took a single step forward.

Gareth glanced at him. "What is it?"

"None of us has any relatives or friends who will ransom us. All that we possess was given to us by the magician. Our armor and our swords are the only things of value that we own." Robert's mouth was a tight, grim line. His eyes held fierce pride as well as fear. "And you have already stripped them from us. You may as well get on with the hanging."

"In good time, Sir Robert, in good time. Death always comes soon enough for most." Gareth motioned for the guards to take the knights back to their makeshift prison.

Ulrich clasped his hands behind his back and waited until the hall was empty once more. Then he looked at Gareth. "Do you wish to question the bowmen we caught at the harbor, my lord?"

"Nay. There is nothing new to be learned from them. They are typical of their kind. Freebooters who hired themselves out to the magician on the promise of easy plunder."

"Masterless men."

"Aye." Gareth got to his feet. "Men without villages or families."

"Such men are always dangerous. Best to hang them quickly and be done with it."

"Aye." Gareth walked to a nearby table where he had spread out an assortment of items that he and Dallan had discovered in Lucretius de Valemont's cloak. "Have you seen this yet, Ulrich?"

"Nay." Ulrich crossed to the table. He looked down at the handful of tiny slivers of metal floating in a bowl of water. "What are they?"

"Dallan tells me that de Valemont called them his iron fish. Watch." Gareth dipped a finger into the water and spun the small iron slivers in a circle. When the water settled, so did the iron fish. "Notice that they are pointing in the same direction in which they pointed before I disturbed the water."

Ulrich frowned. "What of it?"

"They are pointing north, my friend. Always north. It is the mysterious device the magician used to guide his hired thieves to the isle in the fog. He would have used it again to make his escape."

"Iron fish?"

"I heard of such a few years ago," Gareth said. "I read about them again in Sir Humphrey's book. But this is the first time I have actually seen a device that uses them. Amazing, is it not?"

"Aye." Ulrich stabbed a finger into the water and ruffled the surface of the liquid. He watched, fascinated, as the slivers realigned themselves. "Most interesting."

"Sir Humphrey's book says that the invention comes from China. As does the recipe for the sulfur and charcoal powder that we used to route de Valemont's men."

"What of these other objects?" Ulrich picked up a round, polished sphere.

"A mirror. Dallan says de Valemont used it to signal messages to his men on occasion." Gareth picked up a ring of oddly shaped keys. "He used these to open locks of all kinds."

"Ah. So that is how he got through the convent gates and into the library."

"Aye." Gareth dropped the keys back onto the table. "And how he managed to relock the recluse's cell after he had carried her body back into it."

"This is all quite interesting, sir, and knowing you, I'm sure you will be occupied for days playing with the magician's bag of tricks. But what am I to do about our prisoners in the meantime? Shall I see that they are dispatched immediately?"

"Nay. Hold off awhile longer. I may think of some more questions to ask them."

Gareth was aware of Ulrich's amused gaze resting on him as he walked out of the hall. As usual, he did not comprehend the jest.

The fog that had shrouded the isle for the past two days had finally cleared. The courtyard was humming with activity.

William and Dallan dashed to and fro, carrying out Eadgar's instructions and assisting the servants. As he went down the steps, Gareth saw two of his men-at-arms come through the open gate. They were laden with armfuls of fresh flowers. The sight of his hardened warriors buried in blossoms made him grin briefly.

His amusement faded as he crossed the courtyard to Clare's workrooms.

He could have forced her to return to the bed last night, of course. He was a lot bigger and a lot stronger than she was. It would have been a simple matter to fetch her out of the wardrobe. But he had been too annoyed to do so. He had told himself that a night spent on the hard floor, wrapped in a quilt, would teach her a lesson.

It was unfortunate that the serving maid had entered the wardrobe chamber earlier than usual. Clare had still been sound asleep.

Gareth had been awake, however. To his disgust, he had slept little during the night. Three times he had wandered into the wardrobe to adjust the quilt over Clare's shoulders.

It was one thing to let her sleep on the hard stone floor. It was another to let her take a chill. He had no intention of allowing her to risk her health while she did battle with him. He had a duty as a husband to see to it that she did not become ill through her foolish actions.

This morning she was astonishingly calm about the open warfare which she had more or less declared. She acted as if she had already won and was merely waiting for him to concede defeat.

Gareth wondered if she realized that he had never surrendered to anyone in his entire life.

He reached the first of the long series of workrooms and stepped into the open doorway. The scent of flowers, vanilla, and mint hit him like a soft pillow in the face.

"Clare?"

"In here, my lord," Clare called from the adjoining chamber.

Gareth walked through the mixing room into the drying room. He saw her standing at one of the wide tables. Something inside him twisted with yearning.

He had come close to losing her yesterday. The last thing he wished to do today was argue with her. He sighed. He knew better than to show weakness.

Clare held a handful of dried flowers to her nose. Her eyes were closed as she concentrated on the fragrance. Sunlight streamed through the window behind her, creating a golden halo around her graceful figure.

She was the most wonderful thing in his life, Gareth thought. She had given him a home.

He shook off the strange blend of emotions that he did not fully comprehend and went toward her.

"What are you doing?" he asked, more for something to say than any real curiosity.

"I'm mixing a special pomander for the abbess." Clare opened her eyes. "A very complex recipe that will be hers alone. Do you think she will appreciate it?"

"I'm certain she will." Gareth hesitated. "The household is in an uproar."

"She will be here any day now. Mayhap even this afternoon."

"Uh, Clare, I know you're very excited about this visit."

"I certainly am. Abbess Helen has been most gracious to me in her letters. I am eager to repay her kindness."

"Mayhap I should tell you—"

"Have you freed the prisoners, my lord?"

"Nay."

"I know you'll do the right thing before the day is out."

"Hell's teeth, woman, hanging them is the right thing."

"Not in this case. Have you taken a close look at Lucretius's knights? They are not much older than Dallan."

"Well, what about those professional thieves Ulrich captured at the harbor?" Gareth retorted. "They cannot be excused by reason of youth. One of them is forty, if he's a day. He's made a lifetime career out of robbing people."

"Aye, but if we are going to free the others, we may as well free him. I do not want even one corpse hanging above my beautiful flowers."

"Clare, you're a woman and you have led a rather sheltered life here on Desire. If you—" Gareth broke off as voices rose outside.

"Lady Clare, Lady Clare, your guests have arrived," a servant called. "Lady Joanna said to tell you to come quickly."

"Abbess Helen is here." Clare opened her fingers and let the dried flowers drop back into the bowl.

"Clare, wait." Gareth reached for her as she sailed past him. He missed.

Clare rushed out through the door into the courtyard. "Joanna? Where is the abbess? Mayhap she will stop first at the convent to meet with the prioress. By Saint Hermione's girdle, we are not ready. I wanted all to be in perfect order when she got here."

Gareth walked slowly out of the drying shed and found Ulrich standing nearby. Together they surveyed the busy scene.

"The abbess is here?" Gareth asked.

"Aye. She came over from Seabern with an escort a short while ago. One of the men just rode up from the village with the news."

"An escort?" Gareth raised an inquiring brow.

"It seems that Thurston of Landry and three of his knights just happened to be traveling in the same direction as the abbess. They offered to provide protection for her and her retainers. The entire crowd should be here any minute."

"Just what I needed," Gareth said.

A screech of dismay rose above the commotion in the courtyard. Gareth glanced at Clare, who was gesticulating wildly with her hands.

"What do you mean, Thurston of Landry is on his way here?" Clare yelled at Joanna. "'Tis impossible. He cannot be here."

"Calm yourself, Clare," Joanna said. "We shall manage."

Clare scowled furiously. "How dare Lord Thurston do this to me? Has he no consideration? I am entertaining an abbess tonight; I cannot be bothered with a stupid baron."

"We shall manage," Joanna said soothingly.

"Nay, 'tis simply not possible. He has ruined everything. How am I to deal with my father-in-law when I am trying to entertain a great abbess?"

"An excellent question under the circumstances," Gareth observed to Ulrich.

"You're smiling, my lord. You know it makes me uneasy when you smile." Ulrich hesitated. "What about the prisoners?"

"You had better hold them in the cellar for another day or so. There is too much chaos around here as it is. Hanging a bunch of thieves would no doubt create even more of an uproar."

"Aye," Ulrich said. "It should prove to be an interesting evening."

Shouts from the watchtower and a cloud of dust heralded the arrival of the company and a host of retainers.

"They're here," someone yelled. "The abbess and Thurston of Landry are at the gates."

Clare stalked over to Gareth. "This is really too much. The least your father could have done was send word that he intended to pay a visit."

"I suspect he made his decision on the spur of the moment when he learned that the abbess was on her way to Desire."

"But why would he do that? It makes no sense." Clare broke off as the riders clattered through the gates.

There was a general air of confusion as servants rushed to take the horses' heads.

"Come along, Clare. We must greet our guests." Gareth took her arm and started forward.

"That lady on the palfrey is the abbess." Clare's disgruntled expression gave way to renewed enthusiasm. "She appears to be in excellent health."

"She generally is."

"What do you mean?"

"Never mind." Gareth watched as Thurston dismounted and gallantly went to assist the abbess. The pair turned to meet their host and hostess.

"My Lady Abbess." Clare rushed forward to kiss the ring of the tall, handsome woman in the Benedictine habit. "Welcome to Desire. We are honored."

"'Tis good to see you again, Lady Clare." Abbess Helen smiled. "It is always a great pleasure to visit with you. I continue to enjoy our correspondence more than I can say."

"You are too kind." Clare turned with obvious reluctance to Thurston. "My lord, you honor us with your presence."

The frost in her voice appeared to amuse Thurston. "I have been looking forward to meeting you again after all these years, Lady Clare."

"What a pity you did not send word so that we could have prepared a proper reception," Clare muttered.

Thurston kissed her hand with the easy grace he always displayed around women. "My apologies. It was a sudden decision on my part. Allow me to tell you that I am pleased to learn that my son met your requirements in a husband."

"Aye, well, I was not quite certain that he would do, at first, but as it happens he is very well suited to the position."

"I had hoped that would be the case."

Gareth watched with satisfaction as Clare impatiently withdrew her hand from his father's grasp. Few women were immune to Thurston of Landry's charm. Clare appeared utterly oblivious to it.

Clare's brows drew together in a sharp frown. "My lord, I do not wish to be rude, but I must warn you, if you have come to summon Lord Gareth away from Desire for some purpose, you are wasting your time."

"I am?"

"Aye, you cannot have him. He is needed here at home. You sent him to me and I must insist upon being allowed to keep him. There is a great deal to be done around here. This isle has not had a proper lord for years."

"I see." Thurston gave Gareth an amused sidelong glance.

"If you wish this manor to remain profitable . . ." Clare paused meaningfully, "mayhap even increase its profits, then you will have to let Sir Gareth remain with us."

A smile edged Thurston's mouth. "I assure you, madam, I certainly do not wish to interfere in any way with increasing profits."

"Well, that settles that, then." Clare looked relieved. "I suppose we can find room for you and your men."

"Thank you. That is very kind of you, madam."

Gareth recalled something Nicholas of Seabern had said to him at the spring fair. *She'll be grateful when you leave. She has no use for a husband.*

Nicholas was wrong, Gareth thought. Clare wanted him to stay here on Desire. And not just because she found him useful. She loved him. A joyous elation shot through him.

Clare turned eagerly back to Abbess Helen. "My lady, you will no doubt wish to refresh yourself after your long journey. Your chambers are prepared."

"Thank you." Abbess Helen's voice was low and husky. It resonated with quiet power.

Clare glowered at Gareth. "You have not welcomed our Lady Abbess properly, my lord."

"Very true." Gareth took the abbess's proffered hand and looked down into the gray eyes that were reflections of his own. "Welcome to Desire, Mother."

Clare stormed up and down the length of her chamber while Eunice attempted to dress her.

"His *mother*. I cannot believe it, Joanna. Abbess Helen is his lady mother. This is so embarrassing. How could he do this to me?"

"I suspect Lord Gareth did not want you to know of his relationship to the abbess just yet." Joanna watched as Eunice darted in close to Clare and dropped a saffron-yellow gown over her head.

"Whyever not?" Clare struggled to get her face free of the folds of the gown. It settled into place. Eunice seized the opportunity. She grabbed the laces and set to work.

"Mayhap because he knew that you held her in such high esteem. He no doubt preferred to win your affections on his own merits."

Clare stared at her. "I had not thought of that. Do you think that was the case?"

"It is a possibility." Joanna rose from the stool and went to the door. "Do not concern yourself about the evening meal. All is in readiness." She paused, one hand on the knob. "Oh, by the way, Dallan has composed several more verses of his new ballad for the occasion."

Clare smiled in spite of her mood. "More verses featuring the brave, bold, daring Lord Gareth?"

"I believe so. He is eager to perform his poem for the company."

Eunice yanked on Clare's hair with just enough force to make her stand still. Grumbling, Clare allowed her aging servant to tuck her tresses into a gold-threaded net.

"Has Sir Ulrich given any indication of when the prisoners will be set free?" Clare asked.

Joanna sighed. "Nay, he has not. Do not expect Lord Gareth to release those men, Clare. You know very well 'tis not the way such matters are handled. The entire lot deserves to hang, if you ask me."

"Aye, and that's a fact," Eunice muttered.

"When I think of what might have become of you and William," Joanna said, "I feel quite faint all over again." She went out the door and closed it softly behind her.

"Lady Joanna is right." Eunice adjusted the orange and blue girdle around Clare's hips. "Lord Gareth has a reputation for dealing firmly with outlaws and thieves. He'll not show mercy to this vile lot. Nor should he, if ye ask me."

"No one asked you, Eunice."

"Ye think he'll do it for ye, don't ye, my lady? Ye believe he cares enough for ye to grant ye this great boon." Eunice gave her a pitying look as she anchored the glittering net in place with a circlet of silver. "I warn ye, 'tis too much to expect of any man, especially the Hellhound."

"Mayhap I can persuade his father to reason with him."

"That's a good one, that is." Eunice cackled loudly. "Thurston of Landry will more likely offer to help his son construct the gibbets."

"Then mayhap Abbess Helen can have some influence," Clare suggested hopefully.

"Nay, madam. 'Twill do no good. This is none of her affair and she'll likely agree with the men that hanging's the proper answer to the problem."

Clare closed her eyes in brief, silent prayer. She seemed to be the only one on the isle who felt that hanging seven men above the flowers of Desire was wrong.

Could no one else see that there had been enough violence already? Could none of them comprehend that the magician's men were just homeless young boys who had taken service with the only knight who had offered it?

And as for the poor bowmen, they were simply unfortunate, masterless men who had been driven to their careers because they had no other way to make their living.

She pictured the horrific scene of seven men hanging over a bed of roses and her stomach recoiled.

A short while later Clare ushered Abbess Helen into the study chamber.

"This is such an exciting event for me, my Lady Abbess. I do so enjoy your rare visits. But I cannot tell you how mortified I am that I did not know you were my husband's mother. I vow he never mentioned the fact to me."

"My son is a rather unusual man, much inclined to keep his own counsel." Helen glided gracefully over to the bookshelves. Her habit was as magnificently cut and sewn as the most costly of gowns. Her wimple was exquisitely draped to form a perfect frame for her elegant face and crystal eyes. "He does not reveal much of himself to others."

Clare grimaced. "Aye, that is certainly true."

Helen smiled. "I would have you know that I am well pleased with this match, Clare."

"So am I." Clare went to stand by the window. "You know better than most, madam, that I did not particularly wish to marry."

"Aye. But we both knew that you had a duty to do so. You had no choice in the matter."

"You chose your son for me, did you not? It was all your idea, wasn't it?"

"Aye. I wrote to Lord Thurston and suggested that it would be a good match."

"I am honored that you felt I would be a suitable wife for your son," Clare whispered.

"You are the only woman I have ever met who could give Gareth what he seeks most."

Clare glanced at her. "What is that?"

"A home of his own."

"Oh."

Helen gave her a speculative look. "I have heard that he has learned to laugh."

"Your son possesses an odd notion of amusement, madam, but he definitely does possess it."

"You have fallen in love with him, have you not?"

"Aye."

"Have you told him?"

"Aye."

"What did he say?"

Clare shrugged. "Nothing. He seemed content with the knowledge."

"But he did not tell you that he loves you, too?"

"Nay."

Helen sighed. "As I said, my son has never been the sort to reveal his feelings to others. I do not know if he will ever be able to do so. You must learn to look beneath the surface if you would know him well."

"I believe I know him very well, madam. But there are some things that must be put into words." She swung around to face Helen. "You may as well know that Gareth and I are involved in what some might term a quarrel."

Helen looked amused. "So I am told. 'Twill be interesting to witness the outcome. My son has never had much practice at losing battles."

"Your mother is as beautiful as ever." Thurston contemplated the magician's toys that Gareth had spread out on the chamber table.

"Uh-huh." Gareth frowned intently over a page in Sir Humphrey's book. "What do you make of this reference to a machine that is powered by the same mechanism that causes a water clock to function?"

"I have no notion." Thurston glanced down at the page without much interest. "It was all her idea, you know."

"What was?"

"Marrying you off to Lady Clare."

"I assumed as much when I learned that Mother and Clare had formed a long-standing correspondence."

"You seem satisfied with the marriage."

"Aye." Gareth turned the page.

"She appears quite determined to keep you tied close to home and hearth."

"Aye."

"The, uh, rumors of her loss of virginity at the hands of Sir Nicholas were unfortunate."

"Not that it is any of your affair, sir, but the rumors proved unfounded."

"Ah. I see. 'Twas not the lady's reputation that concerned me, you know."

"I know what concerned you, sir." Gareth bent closer to study a small drawing. "You feared that I would feel obliged to kill Sir Nicholas and thus deprive you of his services."

"Aye. I'm glad it did not come to that. Nicholas may not be every woman's dream of a chivalrous knight, but he is a good man with a sword and loyal into the bargain. Such men are all too rare."

"Aye."

"I have heard other rumors," Thurston continued.

"Have you?"

"I am informed that you and your lady are locked in a quarrel concerning the hanging of those men you captured when you retook your hall."

"She would have me set them free. Clare is very softhearted. She is unaccustomed to violence. And its aftermath."

"Women." Thurston sighed. "They simply do not understand such matters."

Gareth met his father's amused gaze. "On that we agree, sir."

And thus did open the Window of Hell

And into it the wicked magician fell.

Henceforth let all evildoers bewareth

the strength and the fury of the mighty Sir Gareth.

Gareth winced. He leaned toward Clare, who, along with everyone else in the crowded hall, was busily cheering the final verses of Dallan's newest song.

"Bewareth Sir Gareth?" he repeated dryly.

"I think it has a nice ring to it." Clare smiled proudly at Dallan, who was flushed with the joys of success. "The only thing wrong with the song as far as I am concerned is the second to the last verse. I do not like the part about the seven men being hung."

Abbess Helen took a bite of an almond-stuffed fig. "What ending would you prefer, Clare?"

Clare slid Gareth a glance that spoke volumes. "I believe that mighty Sir Gareth should show mercy to the men he captured. Tell me, madam, doesn't the Church encourage that sort of thing?"

"It rather depends on the situation," Helen murmured. "The Church can be remarkably practical about such matters. Furthermore, it teaches the need for justice."

"Aye, but—"

"*Enough.*" Gareth struck the table a resounding blow that set the mugs to rattling.

Every head in the hall turned instantly toward the head table.

Clare jumped. Her spoon clattered back into the bowl in front of her. "Gareth, really, this is neither the time nor the place—"

"I disagree." Gareth rose ominously to his feet. "It is most definitely the time and the place, lady wife. We are going to settle this matter here tonight. I will have no more of this unceasing scolding, madam."

Clare glowered up at him. Gareth never appeared small or even medium-sized at the best of times, but towering over her like this he looked absolutely huge. "I am not scolding you, my lord. I never scold."

"On the contrary, you have made yourself a thorn in my side over this matter and I will not tolerate it any longer."

Clare barely restrained herself from throwing the remains of her pottage at him. She glanced quickly at the faces of her guests and was horrified to see that Lord Thurston and Lady Helen appeared to be greatly amused.

"My lord, you are embarrassing me in front of this company," Clare said through her teeth. "Kindly sit down and behave yourself."

Gareth folded his arms across his broad chest. "Not until we have done with this idiocy. Everyone in this hall knows that freeing those seven men is a ludicrous notion. Give me a single sound reason for doing it."

Clare was rapidly losing her temper. "It would be an act of mercy and compassion."

"This is not sufficient reason."

"It would be just the sort of gracious gesture that would do proper honor to the birthday of Saint Hermione."

"Madam, until I came to this isle, I had never even heard of Saint Hermione. I am certainly not going to release those men on her account. Give me another reason."

"To celebrate the visit of your parents?" she tried desperately.

"Nay, that is not sufficient reason."

Clare could not stand it anymore. She leaped to her feet. "I ask a favor of you, sir. I vow, Hellhound, if you have the smallest spark of affection in your heart for me, you will show mercy toward those men."

Gareth's eyes were unreadable. "The smallest spark of affection, did you say?"

"Aye," she flung back, goaded beyond endurance. "If you returned even a portion of the love that I have for you, my lord, you would have no difficulty granting me this boon."

As soon as the words were out of her mouth, Clare wanted to disappear in a puff of smoke. She could not believe she had been such a fool.

Not a single person moved. Even the servants were frozen in place.

"Let me make certain that I comprehend this, madam," Gareth said slowly. "What you are saying is that if I loved you, I would free those seven men?"

Fool, fool, fool. Clare wondered if she would ever live down this humiliation. But there was no going back. She lifted her chin and looked straight into the smoky depths of Gareth's eyes.

"Aye, my lord. That is exactly what I am saying."

"So be it."

Clare's mouth opened and closed. She gazed at him, uncomprehending. "I beg your pardon, my lord?"

Gareth started to smile. "I said, so be it. Those men in the cellar shall be escorted off Desire in the morning. They shall be banished from the isle and the vicinity of Seabern."

Clare could not believe her ears. "You are actually going to do it? You'll free them? For my sake?"

"As proof of my love for you."

"Oh, *Gareth.*" Clare threw herself into his arms. "You do have a wondrous way of making a grand and gracious gesture. Thank you, my lord."

Gareth caught her close and started to laugh. The great, roaring sound filled the hall and bounced off the ceiling. The guests grinned at one another.

"You really do love me?" Clare's voice was muffled against Gareth's broad chest.

Gareth stopped laughing. He looked down at her, his crystal eyes suddenly so clear that Clare could see all the way to his soul. The truth blazed there in the depths.

"How could I not love you, Clare? You hold my heart and my future in your hands."

The hall broke into wild, thundering applause as the Hellhound bent his head to kiss his lady wife.

Out of the corner of her eye Clare saw Helen lean slightly toward Thurston. The abbess whispered something. Thurston nodded and smiled with satisfaction.

Lost in the wonder of the moment, Clare felt happiness rise within her. It flooded her senses, a unique, intoxicating scent that she recognized at once as the perfume of love.

About the Author

Amanda Quick, who also writes as Jayne Ann Krentz, is a best-selling, award-winning author of contemporary and historical romances. There are nearly twenty million copies of her books in print. She feels that the romance novel is a vital and compelling element in the world of woman's fiction. It is a skill that romancing action historical romance. In particular defines the very word "romance."

Amanda Quick makes her home in the Northwest with her husband, Frank.